The Feud of Oakfield Creek

Josiah Royce

LITERATURE HOUSE / GREGG PRESS
Upper Saddle River, N. J.

Republished in 1970 by
LITERATURE HOUSE
an imprint of The Gregg Press
121 Pleasant Avenue
Upper Saddle River, N. J. 07458

Standard Book Number–8398-1770-3
Library of Congress Card–71-104560

Printed in United States of America

THE

FEUD OF OAKFIELD CREEK

A NOVEL OF CALIFORNIA LIFE

BY

JOSIAH ROYCE

BOSTON AND NEW YORK
HOUGHTON, MIFFLIN AND COMPANY
The Riverside Press, Cambridge
1887

The Riverside Press, Cambridge:
Electrotyped and Printed by H. O. Houghton & Co.

To

MY HONORED COLLEAGUE AND FRIEND,

WILLIAM JAMES,

I DEDICATE THIS BOOK.

CONTENTS.

BOOK I.

BOOK II.

BOOK III.

THE FEUD OF OAKFIELD CREEK.

BOOK I. — ELLEN ESCOTT.

CHAPTER I.

THE LADY OF THE HILLSIDE.

TOM ELDON was the son of one of California's wealthiest and oldest citizens, the well-known millionaire, Alonzo Eldon. But a few years since Tom lived on the old Dover estate, near East Oakland. This estate was his wife's property, which she had inherited from her former husband, Peter Dover. Both Tom Eldon and his wife were still young. Tom was thirty-five. Margaret Eldon was five or six years younger. Her first marriage had been made by her mother's ambition. It had been followed, after only a year, by the sudden death of the aged Peter Dover. Margaret, left free and rich, had been wooed by Tom Eldon, whom she had at first regarded with amusement, and afterwards had very mildly loved. They were married in 1878. They had one child, born the next year. In the autumn of 1882, when this tale begins, their friends knew that their lives had long been darkened by one very gloomy shadow. Exactly how it had affected their relations, nobody could be sure. But obviously, as the years went by, it did not bring them any closer together.

Jealousy is a familiar cause for such griefs. But their jealousy, if it still existed, had had a curious beginning. Nobody was apt to call Tom Eldon, since his marriage, a man of careless life. Nor even before his marriage had the world at large ever thought ill of his morals or of his heart. Only one great mistake he had made. It was no greater mistake than many other men make. Yet fate had chosen to punish his fault almost beyond belief.

His fault was his unhappy relation, during the very year before his marriage, to Ellen Escott, the daughter of Alf Escott, an odd old literary man, half Bohemian, half professor, whom you may have heard mentioned occasionally by San Franciscans. Escott had formerly been a close friend of his contemporary, Alonzo Eldon, Tom's father. But the two old men had quarreled, and Alf Escott, largely through the great Alonzo's influence, had finally been driven from the professorship which he had held in the Sunset College. Tom Eldon, who had once been Alf Escott's pupil in the Sunset College itself, had somehow taken Escott's side in the quarrel. After Escott, driven from his professorship, began once more to earn his living in his old way, as a newspaper writer in San Francisco, Tom Eldon had remained his warm personal friend, and was constantly in his house. Alf Escott was a high-spirited and warm-hearted man, and he loved Tom Eldon as a son, while Tom seemed to find in this friendship compensation for the loss of the great Alonzo's favor. So things had gone on for some years before Tom's marriage was thought of. Escott, who for many reasons had become a very unpopular man since his quarrel with Alonzo Eldon, had now lived a very quiet life. Save for his work as a newspaper writer on general, not on local, topics, he had little intercourse with his fellow-men. Tom used to talk with Escott about literature and about the world in general, and no doubt found very pleasing the flattery and the affection that the old professor showed him from day to day. Tom himself was a very gentle and mild-mannered youth. His mother had been the daughter of a Spanish heiress of old California days, and although Tom Eldon was but one fourth Spanish in blood, he had inherited enough of the Californian temperament to be indolent, clever, charming, promising, soft-voiced, and ineffective. Alf Escott had been fairly in love with him from the time of their first acquaintance.

Alf Escott's daughter Ellen, meanwhile, had been her father's favorite child. She showed her father's strength of will, though not his rugged independence. She could love as he did, but she could not quarrel as he had so often done. Like her father, she was unsuspicious, careless of the world's opinion, devoted to her friends, naturally cheerful, and fond of new things. Doubtless she came to love Tom Eldon quite unconsciously, and from the very simplicity and innocence of her heart. When he offered her his hand one day, she was overwhelmed with joyous terror. She was sure that she had never thought of such a thing. She was also sure that she had never been happy before. As for Alf Escott, he hailed the engagement as the fulfillment of all his hopes. This was late in the autumn of 1877. Many people, on hearing of this engagement (which for the rest was kept as private as possible), regarded the Escotts as very clever. To abuse the great Alonzo in public, to quarrel with him so fearlessly and bitterly, and then to capture his son and heir in this fashion,—who would have thought Alf Escott so worldly-wise? What would Alonzo say? Would he disinherit Tom? But Tom, as it chanced, had inherited from an uncle a little fortune in his own right. In any case the Escotts had gained a great triumph!

As a fact, however, Alf Escott and his daughter were quite innocent of any such thoughts. Tom seemed to them their most faithful friend, who had long been almost a member of their family. They had loved him so devotedly, and their love seemed to them so natural, that they never thought how it might appear to the world when they thus won the heir of so prominent a man. Moreover, Alf Escott was at heart still devoted to his old friend Alonzo. It was the tragedy of Escott's life that, prone as he was to quarrel, quarreling could never affect his fidelity. He might seem an uncompromising enemy, but if he had once loved you, he could never change his secret heart towards you. Amidst all his bitterness he would yearn to be reconciled. These men of strong inner life, too proud to show forbearance, too loyal to forget an old love, live very sad lives, and cannot be blamed if they eagerly hail a prospect of escape from any of their conflicts. Such a prospect Tom's union with Ellen seemed to hold out to Escott. In fact, shortly after the betrothal of Tom and Ellen, the two fathers met once more, and agreed to bury the past. The meeting, to be sure, was rather a cold and formal one. They were both old Californians, and they dreaded to appear to each other in any wise unmanly. Bitter words had more than once passed between them. Cruel wrong had been done. Neither was ready to admit his fault. Both longed for forgetfulness. And in this interview they seemed to have made a beginning.

The reconciliation proved to be very transient; for only a few months passed ere Escott accidentally discovered that Tom had all along been playing them false. Not Ellen, but Peter Dover's widow, had been from the first Tom's true beloved. And just before Tom offered his hand to Ellen, Mrs. Dover had either rejected him, or else had first accepted and then jilted him. Escott never cared to learn which. It was enough that the Escotts, by reason of their retirement from the world, and of their indifference to nearly all the people in it save Tom, had never heard before of

Tom's friendship for the beautiful Mrs. Dover. As for her, she had lived, since her husband's death, on the great Dover estate beyond the bay. Her mother was with her most of the time. Mrs. Dover was regarded as a brilliant woman, but she was very independent and exclusive in her life. San Francisco saw her seldom, although she was well acquainted with prominent families. Escott knew nothing of her, though her former husband, Peter Dover, had been well known to him. Tom had never mentioned her to Escott. And now, as suddenly appeared, Tom had been a suitor for her hand. Only when his suit had somehow failed had he offered himself to Ellen Escott, simply out of spite, it appeared, or else because he knew that Ellen was always to be had by him for the asking.

Escott, as it chanced, found out these facts all of a sudden, and in such a way as to make them appear to him in the worst possible light. His rage at this treachery knew no bounds. The old feud of the Escotts and the Eldons opened afresh, and became far more bitter than before. The engagement between Tom and Ellen was summarily broken off.

Then, however, followed in quick succession the events that ended in the darkening of Tom Eldon's married life. When his relation to the Escotts had been finally broken off, he returned to his former love. How well or ill Margaret Dover understood at that time what had passed between Tom Eldon and the Escotts, nobody among her friends learned. The engagement between Tom Eldon and Ellen had never been made fairly public. Margaret must surely have been ignorant of the extent of Tom's treachery. At any rate, he managed after some time to win her favor once more, to explain his relation to Ellen Escott in some plausible way, and finally to marry Margaret in the autumn of 1878.

Tom Eldon acted through all this with what he thought a clear conscience. There were reasons why he had never seen his conduct in the light in which the Escotts saw it. There were reasons why he fancied that he had acted very considerately towards all concerned. He now saw no necessity for explaining everything to the beautiful Margaret Dover, at least before their marriage. He doubted not that their happiness would be as unclouded as their new home beyond the bay was charming. To think of the Escotts gave him pain. As they were obscure people, and nowadays hated publicity, he knew that they would do nothing to molest him. In his heart he was conscious of having treated them very generously! If they had broken with him, was that his fault? Moreover, his father seemed to have sided with Tom in this latest dispute, a thing which put the young man's conscience yet more at rest. Tom's new life thus began very joyously.

The storm came, however, a few months later, with that singular tragedy of Ellen Escott's death. Death, which hides so many things, here managed to reveal everything in the worst possible light.

Out of Tom's blunders, Ellen's death made a scandal. Out of what he had called a pardonable weakness, this tragedy somehow managed to bring to light the vilest treason. Fate was very unjust to Tom! It not only fully explained to Margaret everything that was unpleasant in the past, but it convinced her of even more than the truth. The great shadow fell on their married life, and endured. They were in this shadow when our story opens.

To reach the old Dover estate, you drive along the East Oakland side of Lake Merritt for perhaps a mile. Then you follow a road that leads towards the higher hills. You pass two or three groves of the dark eucalyptus-trees, some large grain-fields, and a number of country houses. Dover's former dwelling rises at last, in the midst of a jungle of shade-trees, on the slope of a high hill. On one side of the house runs a little ravine, full of dwarf oaks and low shrubbery. There is just room for a garden between the house and the edge of the ravine. On the other side there extends the long and evenly slanting hillside itself, where a large orchard has already attained an almost respectable age. The estate has its own water-works, with abundant supplies for lawn and gardens. Of the house you cannot say much, save that it might easily be far worse. It is very large, of course; it has gable ends and very gently sloping roofs. It is commonplace, roomy, comfortable, and free from useless display. Dover, indeed, had in his day a certain love of show; but he lived in his house, and wanted only his old man's comfort there. Display and art, which to his mind meant the same thing, he had therefore banished to a certain spot on his front lawn, where he had reared a twenty-thousand-dollar fountain. The design of this was original. A vast and benevolent-looking bronze angel, on a high and dangerous perch, that bore the motto, "Peace, Good-Will to Men," was engaged in pouring from a big goblet a flood of water down upon a few naked babies, and upon a mass of turtles, dragons, lizards, and snakes, all of which were artistically disposed about the base. They of course spouted, feebly and thankfully, in return, while, in the narrow tank of the fountain, real live fishes restlessly wandered amid the foam, seeking an exit from their noisy metallic prison. Dover was a pious man, and had believed this fountain to be an accurate symbol of the dealings of divine providence.

Elsewhere about the place there was little to catch the eye of a novelty-hunter; and there were many things of a restful and homely sort: fine old oak-trees, gnarled and twisted by unnumbered summers of brisk sea-wind; pleasant nooks in the shrubbery; plain and simple lawns, diversified with but very few attempts at ornamental gardening. The new occupants had made but insignificant changes in the grounds.

Margaret Eldon, Tom's wife, was passionately fond of her own little garden-plot, on the west side of the house, towards the ravine and just under her chamber-window. There she worked awhile, early in the morning, or just after sundown, whenever the season permitted. She was proudest of her roses; they grew luxuriantly, and she sometimes simply overwhelmed her numerous friends with gifts from her treasury.

Margaret's other open-air recreation was riding. She had a beautiful little bay mare for her own use. She enjoyed best the long stretches to the southwards, towards the San Leandro region. She generally rode quite alone, and was as fearless and graceful in her flight as a sparrow-hawk. At home she read a good deal, but never played music, or even dabbled in fine art. Her garden was her only artistic activity. She was, however, in her way, quite an entertainer. Her circle of friends was carefully chosen; her talk was vivacious, fairly well informed, and even, according to some of the very youngest of her friends, at times profound. She had an uncommonly well-skilled practical sense, and some knowledge of business. She had a longing, and not a very secret one, to be thought, moreover, generally intelligent. She loved to fix her dark-brown eyes on any learned man whom she might have enticed to the house, and to fascinate him with her modest and rapturous delight in the subject of his specialty. She was not precisely insincere in all this, for the first sight of a learned man, particularly if he chanced to be a little noted, always made her heart beat with a warm enthusiasm.

Learning was something so far above commonplace life, so pure and so religiously cold! To be learned, she thought, ought to be much the same thing as to be saintly. Unhappily, the concrete cases of men of learning, when she saw them, usually disappointed her, though her melting brown eyes and her pale, gently admiring face never revealed the fact to them.

But among more ordinary human beings also she knew how to be a favorite. She had traveled quite enough to impose upon her purely provincial young California friends, and still she remained quite enough of a Californian to fascinate Eastern visitors. Her wealth and that of her husband were ample; her position was excellent; her life, despite one terrible event, for which none but malicious gossips, obscure ignoramuses, and interested personal enemies had ever blamed her, was above reproach; and her beauty still showed no sign of fading. Margaret was tall and slim, and very light and graceful in movement. Her voice was low and very musical, and had a curious and somehow very pleasant monotony about it. A part of every winter she used to pass in town with her mother, and for a short time in the summer she was often somewhere on the southern sea-coast; but for the most part her own house was the scene of her triumphs and of her kindly social activity.

Some of her friends misjudged her in a very singular way. They missed in her, they said, any real depth of feeling or of sympathy. She was, they asserted, with all her pretenses, hard and cold. They even doubted whether she had ever loved anything but her roses. This misjudgment was one of those tributes which sentimentality is accustomed to pay to self-possession. The friends of this type observed that Margaret managed her husband with perfect and graceful ease. He feared her, — that was plain; and he certainly seemed to love her. But these critics declared — and in this one respect, perchance, correctly — that if she was fond of him she was at any rate hardly a devoted wife. Close friends and more distant gossips united in conjecturally explaining their relations, to some extent at least, by the terrible incident of some three years and a half since, — an incident which everybody had agreed to leave forevermore unmentioned in her presence as well as in general company, but which nobody could forget. Margaret Eldon's spirit was too high and strong to let her show to any friend, after the first shock was past, the least sign of her feelings. Only her mother knew, if any third person did, her present relations to her husband.

Her child, a boy, had been born a few months after the tragedy of Ellen Escott's death. The mother was no doubt fond of him; but these same critical friends of Margaret's, who saw how little time she devoted to him, wondered if she really gave him a true mother's love. She mentioned him but seldom to the friends; she was not a boastful mother, and at home seemed to them to be not over-anxious for his baby affection. Visitors at the house hardly ever had occasion even to learn of his existence. These dear and misjudging friends thought her a very cold mother. Though they had some apparent reason for their view, they were not quite just in this.

One morning in the autumn of 1882, Margaret Eldon awoke early. She was alone; Tom was passing his time of late very much in the city. Last evening she had received a note saying that he would come home about noon, and that he was very anxious for her advice about something important. She was glad of this. She knew that her advice was always influential with Tom; she had a pleasant sense of power in giving it; and as for the "important" topic itself, she had nowadays only enough mild curiosity about what Tom might call important to look forward to the interview with amusement. She expected nothing startling. It was now nearly three years since she had been startled, and she felt almost above such a weakness.

She passed her hour before breakfast, as usual, with her roses. The September sun was but an hour above the horizon when she sat down to the morning meal. She loved these early hours whenever she was alone. They gave her a long day, which she usually knew how to make amusing. After breakfast she spent a good while in the nursery. It was in fact her custom of late not to see her child until after he had been washed and dressed and fed. Afterwards she took a little walk in the oak-grove with the nurse and child.

One who had seen her for a while this morning would have been less disposed to call her a cold-hearted mother, for she was plainly trying hard to amuse him. The boy, who was named Alonzo, after his grandfather, regarded her with longing and fascination as a beautiful playfellow, who was never enough with him, but who, according to his way of thinking, was very good so often as she came. His nurse was very fond of him, considering that she was, comparatively speaking, a new-comer, who had spent but three months at the house thus far, and who was certain to quarrel with the mistress and be dismissed before another three months had passed. But the boy, notwithstanding the nurse's affection, was a lonesome child. He seldom saw other children; he was somewhat ill-tempered; his constitution, naturally sturdy, had suffered a little from a too frequent change of nurses, and from a constant change of the plans for his welfare. Moreover, he was longing to know about hundreds of things that nobody told him, and he had not even quite attained full skill in the childish accomplishment of asking questions. With his mother, therefore, he was restless, hiding much of his delight in her presence beneath a certain anxious care to keep her attention fixed upon him, and to be sure that she should not leave him. This morning, as they walked, he once gathered from the roots of an oak-tree, close down by the creek, a clump of moss to bring to her. Moss was his favorite among things that grow. When she complained that he had got his feet wet in doing this, he made her sit down on a rock, and then nestled close beside her, and patted her arm and her cheek very nervously with his little muddy hands. She smiled, but forbade any more such caresses, and begged nurse to take him at once to wash his hands. At this he cried and showed temper, while she frowned, looked unhappy, and wandered off to the front lawn.

Erelong he was pursuing her again, frantic with his eagerness not to lose the one hour of the morning that she was always willing to devote to him. He begged of her a story, but when she began one he interrupted her, and demanded another. She knew this other very ill, as it chanced, and so his attention soon wandered. At length he stopped her, displeased, no doubt, at her hesitating manner; then he looked sullen, and began to tear leaves from one of the plants. To forbid this meant to excite more temper, and thereafter poor Margaret began to think that if her boy had no love for her, and could take no joy of her efforts to please him, it must be hardly worth while to spend even so much time with him.

Then she grew anxious about his health, and began to question the nurse. He was pale; had he slept well? She wondered if that room was the best for him, after all, — the room that they had last fixed upon for the nursery. They were always changing nurseries in this house, having so many possible places to choose from up-stairs. Margaret, who was very conservative in all her other habits, could find no rest as to this matter.

Nothing, after all, seemed quite to suit his needs. The nurse, in reply, attributed all his pallor to his illness of some two weeks since. He had never recovered, she said, and it was all owing to that doctor. Margaret did not wish to recur to the old quarrel of nurse and doctor, so she went on inquiring as to the child's diet. The nurse mentioned that yesterday, just after lunch, he had stolen unobserved into the pantry, and had devoured two or three bunches of grapes. Margaret wondered why she had not been told of all this before, and spoke severely to little Alonzo about his misdeeds. Grapes were very bad for him, she said. They might kill him. He did not hang his head in the least, but took the opportunity to tell her gleefully how, as he stole the grapes, the cat got into the pantry too; how he gave her a chicken-bone, and then tried to get her to share his grapes. Puss declined them, whereupon he threw her violently out of the dining-room window, receiving several scratches, of which he seemed very proud.

Margaret was in despair. Could the boy never be taught to let mischief alone? It was mean, she told him, to be a little thief, and to be so cruel to the cat. She should not love him if he acted so. She was going to leave him now, just to punish him. He should not see her again until evening; nurse must take him away. He screamed in despair, threw himself on the ground, fought, and shouted that he hated his nurse, his mother, everybody, everything, and that he wished God had made some other little boy instead of him. The nurse at last carried him away, and Margaret, vexed and nervous, retired to the house.

She passed a short time after this in good resolutions. She must ask the doctor more about little Alonzo's health. She mistrusted the nurse; she must get a new one. She mistrusted the nursery; she must change it. And then she must pass more time with him. The morning hours, the quite early ones before breakfast, ought to be the best for being in the boy's company. She had loved them dearly when he was but a little baby. But of late she had left him wholly to the nurse at that time, her chief reason being that he always quarreled about the temperature of his bath, and was uniformly cross at his breakfast. Scenes of that sort always made her nervous, because, when he was cross in the morning, he screamed hard, held his breath until his face turned purple, stiffened himself till he grew rigid, fought everybody, and was generally intolerable. The morning, however, she liked to have as peaceful as possible, else the whole day would be ruined. She always felt innocent, almost pious, in the early morning. She could not bear to be made wretched and ill-tempered at just the one most saintly hour. Hence she had fallen into the habit of not seeing the boy until after breakfast. The rose-garden was the gentlest and most friendly companion. But now, after all, she asked herself whether this was quite right. She would try to sacrifice more for the boy. She felt that he was growing up ill-tempered, peevish, and unhealthy. She owed him more care. Next Sunday she would really make the experiment of staying all day with him. There would be no company then. It would really be a good fashion of spending Sunday.

In the midst of this reverie she was suddenly disturbed once more by the boy himself. His face was now radiant with laughter. He was carrying a little pasteboard box. His eyes were full of love and resolution. He ran up to her, holding out the box. "Oh, mamma," he cried, "I brought you my green box. You may cuddle it and rattle it for to make it sound pretty. I love you." Trembling with his new anxiety and delight, he put the box into her hand. It contained a few black beads, and was one of his most cherished treasures. He had managed to slip away from his nurse, and was bringing this as his peace-offering. Margaret was quite overcome; but though she kissed him rapturously, little Alonzo had no intention of staying in the forbidden room. He knew that the nurse was in hot pursuit now, and he instinctively wished to avoid another collision. He dashed out of the front door, crying that he must go and look for his cat. The nurse passed through in a passion of apology and chagrin, and pursued him out-of-doors.

Margaret sat still for a while, full of affection and of her new resolutions. These latter now seemed to her so simple and clear that, after she had fixed upon Monday as the time to have her next consultation about Alonzo with the doctor, and upon Sunday as the day to spend wholly in the child's company, she saw no further use in reflecting upon the matter, and soon completely forgot it. Hers was, after all, a happy, resigned temperament, which quickly recovered from all ordinary shocks.

Her next occupations were more steadily and uninterruptedly amusing. She looked over the morning's mail, ran through the current number of a magazine, wrote a letter or two, and then, about eleven o'clock, went up-stairs to dress for her ride. The ride itself was much as usual. She was dressed for lunch by the time Tom arrived.

The pale, graceful, and dark-eyed Tom was plainly rather abstracted and anxious. During lunch-time he did not introduce his important topic, and she, who disdained curiosity, had no questions to ask about it. After lunch she went back to the parlor, and sat by the window, looking off over the lawn. Beyond it, and between the great shade-trees, she could catch glimpses of the town, of San Antonio Creek, and of the bay, with the San Mateo hills beyond it. Tom followed her after a few moments, and seated himself opposite to her. He still seemed very thoughtful and somewhat anxious. He joined his hands nervously over his crossed knees, as was his wont when ill at ease, and then he sat looking hard at his feet. There was a little time of silence.

CHAPTER II.

THE SETTLERS AT OAKFIELD CREEK.

"I DON'T quite like Alonzo's condition," Margaret said at last. "He seems nervous. He's not quite well. I wish that I had stayed longer at Monterey. He was doing very well there."

"Do you think it serious?" said Tom. "He was very merry with me before lunch. I thought he seemed in fine spirits."

"No, it's never serious. Only he's discontented. He quarrels even with me — much more with nurse. He's lonesome here, I suppose."

Tom suggested bringing him oftener into company with some of the neighbors' children, but Margaret had objections to make. There were very few of them whom she wanted him to know, and they were hard to get at. It was all the consequence of living in this lonesome place, she declared. If it had n't grown so dear to her, she would be anxious to change once for all, and go over to San Francisco. For the rest, she was sure that that would be more convenient for Tom, who was getting, she said with a smile, to be more of a truant nowadays than ever. But the older the child grew, the more she felt that it was cruel to bring him up here all alone in the country, where he would never find playmates, nor be contented. He was seldom ill, but she confessed that she worried about him a good deal. In fact, it sometimes came over her that he would be grown up before long, and she found it a sad, yes, sometimes a painful thought, she said (with a faint tinge of bitterness in her voice), that he would then always be leaving her, and betaking himself to the city, where one could never know what he did, nor what acquaintances he had, nor what attachments he formed. All mothers, she added, knew beforehand that they must lose their sons some day. It was, however, the special dread of the mother who lived in the country that her boy would be lost by wandering off to some strange city. One who lived in a city had more chance to keep her boy contented near by his home, where she could have some faint idea of his surroundings.

Tom was always much interested in everything she said, and he was really pleased to-day to find her in so serious a mood. If her mocking humor had been upon her, he would have felt great trouble in approaching his present theme. Besides, for her to be troubled, and to tell him so, meant to invite his sympathy, a thing which she very seldom did. Her voice to-day was, moreover, even softer and gentler than usual. She always spoke in her low, musical tone, with the shortest pauses, and a certain pleasant monotony of accent.

"How melancholy you are to-day!" he said. "What shall I do, then, to cheer you? Shall I send for the doctor, for you to consult him about little Alonzo?"

"No, not that to-day. I've set that visit in my

mind for Monday. There 's no pressing need, of course. I only want general advice." Margaret said this with the pleasantly prim manner of the country lady who announces her fixed arrangements. "I 've set that for such a day," was one of Margaret's commonest expressions. She delighted to predetermine her simple life down to all the smallest details, and it was in vain that you sought to suggest any unnecessary change in the predicted order of her doings. She would in fact have been very unhappy in the city, where there would have been so many more accidents to deal with in her experience. She went on, after a little pause: —

"I suppose I seem to brood a good deal. I do it whenever I 'm much alone for a while. I 'm glad we 're going to have a full house again at the end of next week. By the way, did you know that mother had come back from Santa Cruz? She wrote me last night. I got the letter this morning. She does n't want me to come to her now, though, because she has yet to run over to San Rafael until Monday."

"I called to see her last night," said Tom. "I hoped to find her returned, and I was n't disappointed."

"Dear me, why did n't you tell me at once that you had seen her, you cold-blooded man? Is she looking in better health?"

"Yes, indeed. She is n't so pale. The recent reports have been well founded. She walks more easily, and looks every way better."

"I 'm so glad. She has said as much in all her letters, yet I did n't quite believe her. But tell me, Tom; what can there have been between mother and you, that you should be looking her up so carefully before even I myself knew just when she was to return? I did n't expect her to be there until Monday, or else I should have gone over last night to greet her. Have you taken to making secret appointments to conspire with mother about something or other?"

"Odd conspirators mother and I should make, Margaret, should n't we? No, to tell the truth, I had only hoped to find her. I knew no more than you. But I was glad of my good luck. Perhaps you 'd call what passed between us a conspiracy, after all. If so, then I nevertheless mean to make you a fellow-conspirator. I was waiting until you should be ready to hear me out before I mentioned the fact of my visit. It seemed to me the easiest way to begin."

"Really, Tom, you must be at some most deadly plot. You, indeed, calling on mother in this way, and then waiting until I should be ready to hear you out before you would even mention that you had seen her! The easiest way to begin, to be sure! Come, now, no more airs. Begin at once."

"Have I then succeeded in making you actually curious?" said Tom, a little playfully, taking all possible advantage of his success so far.

"If you don't at once go on, I 'll never hear another word from you about the matter, whatever it is," answered Margaret, with half-assumed indignation. "Don't you suppose mother will tell me, if you don't? What do I care for your little mysteries, any way?"

Tom grew serious again at once. "Well," he replied, "I suppose you'll forgive my hesitation when you know the topic. It concerns some old friends of mine, not of yours, and you must also forgive me for bringing it up at all. Yet you'll agree that I had to. To begin very bluntly, I've just heard fresh and sad news about — Alf Escott." Tom hesitated. The word had been hard to bring out. He looked down again very hard, so as not to catch her eye. Her frank gaze had been very pleasantly fixed upon him as he began his remark, but now she turned paler than was her wont, and her eyes wandered once more to the window, while her face wore a pained and puzzled expression. There was another pause.

"And you carried this news to — mother?" she said at length.

"Yes, and surely that shows you that I must have good reason to bring it also to you. I won't pretend to talk of the thing otherwise than plainly. Surely you know that I would be the last to plague you with it save for cause. But you also know that I have wronged him as deeply — as — as — I have wronged you." Tom's voice hesitated and he seemed a little choked. It was years since she had heard this tone from him, and, much as she hated whatever had any touch of a scene about it, she pitied him a little now; for, after all, from the first days of their married life he had been very sparing of the emotional in her presence. Then he went on again, after a moment, and once more firmly: —

"His new misfortune is of a very crushing sort, at his age and in his circumstances. He was living until three days since in the second story of a house, corner of S—— and P—— streets, over a plumber's shop. But the other night the whole block of houses there burned down, in true San Francisco style, and he lost everything. His family barely escaped with their lives. I understand that he had some dramatic manuscripts still in his possession, and that he regarded them as worth something from a pecuniary point of view. I suppose he was right. He also had some ready money that he had drawn from a bank a day or two before, intending to make some new disposition of it, — I can't say what. At all events the money constituted all his savings, and he lost it. The manuscripts were also destroyed. At present only his family is left to him, save, to be sure, one piece of property that I'll soon mention. His family consists of his wife and his daughter Emily (both in poor health), and a son, who, I regret to say, although an innocent and well-meaning young man of about twenty-four or twenty-five, is a notorious good-for-nothing, almost a case of arrested development, so to speak, when you consider whose son he is. Escott himself is infirm, and is in constantly failing health. All that, you see, makes his prospects poor enough. But he has all his old rugged independence. He will accept no direct help, though he die for the lack of it. How long he may yet be able to work I can't tell. He has for a good while lived by writing for the papers, for one or two of the dailies occasionally, and also for the 'Warrior.' His failing health may end all this at any time. Meanwhile, the climate of San Francisco is very bad for him. He ought to be living in the country."

Tom paused a little, and looked up at Margaret to judge the effect of his words. She had grown more interested as he went on. Her look was very kindly, he fancied. Plainly she nourished no such bitterness in her heart as would make her unable to consider the case. Tom already in secret began to cherish a little more warmly the distant hope that he had had in mind since he began his new undertaking. Meanwhile, he must keep himself to the business directly before him.

"But what," she said, "can you then have in your thought to do for the old man? Your account of his 'rugged independence' puts him quite beyond our aid, does n't it? Yet, to be sure, it seems as if we must find some way."

"No, not quite beyond our aid," Tom said. "There remains one thing to consider. More than two years ago, when father's suits about the Oakfield Creek property were just beginning, Escott chanced to receive quite a sum as a legacy from some Eastern relative. I think it must have been some ten or twelve thousand dollars. You know enough of his disposition to understand what he thereupon did. He heard of the Oakfield

Creek suits. Certain of his friends, in particular certain people who were members of Reverend Mr. Rawley's church, to which his wife belongs, were involved. Escott espoused enthusiastically the settlers' side in the controversy, against my father ; he wrote a series of articles for one of the papers about the matter, and then, quite counter to the advice of his friends, he bought up several of the claims at the highest possible figure, and from some of the poorest of the claimants. They were people who had been especially dear to members of his wife's family. Since then he has been in his way a leader in the settlers' opposition to father. His whole property, at this very moment, consists of his interest in those claims. If they were clear titles, he would own a home, and something more. As things stand, he probably owns nothing."

"That is an unpleasant reflection, surely. Are you interested in the Oakfield Creek property, yourself, Tom?" Margaret's really quick sympathy was now strongly aroused.

"Slightly, very slightly. I've always favored a compromise. The case of the settlers, taken in and for itself, has always seemed to me to have a good deal of common sense in its favor, whatever you may say about the law. I think father himself would have so regarded it, if it had n't been for the way the opposition came to grow up in the first place. That's the fashion with father. Everything depends on how such a matter is brought before him. He's liberality itself at one time, while at another, in case he 's once aroused, he may be as merciless as an old-fashioned conqueror. I 'm afraid Escott's opposition has not tended to weaken his feeling in the matter. Coming as that did, it seemed to father peculiarly unbearable. I 'm responsible for that also, I suppose." Tom sighed, and looked down once more.

"Tell me," said Margaret, speaking very deliberately now, with the thoughtful pride of a woman who finds herself unexpectedly appealed to by a man concerning a matter of business. "Has your father ever shown any signs of admitting that the settlers are right?"

"He used to admit almost as much, very often. If they alone were concerned, he said, he could actually give up the whole thing. But they were n't. Yet even as it was, even with all the other interests to consider that would be affected, he would be willing to yield the settlers a great deal, if they would only show some disposition to compromise. So he used to speak. But later — you know how things are with father. He grew very bitter. I seldom have heard a word from him about compromise since Escott went into the struggle. It 's now all a part of the old-time feud."

"I can't see how it all is," said Margaret, reflectively. "Men are so strange. You call us women mere creatures of feeling. But dear me, the thing seems easy enough to me. Perhaps it 's all my womanly stupidity, but if the poor people have their rights, and you know it, why do you want to turn them out of house and home, just for a mere matter of pride? I think men are the least rational beings on earth. Women would n't have such troubles with settlers, I know."

"It 's a mixed-up business, of course," responded Tom. "Perhaps if you knew better what one of these perennial fights is, you would n't be so hard on us. Yet I don't quite justify father. I know how roughly he has been pressed from some sides, and I appreciate more or less his position and feelings. But I wish he could be persuaded to yield, if only ever so little. And now, at any rate, you 'll see what I have in mind about poor Escott. And if you see, you 'll forgive me for plaguing you by the mention of his name to-day. Won't you, Margaret?"

"Why, certainly," she responded, very simply and kindly. In mind she wondered, meanwhile, that he had understood her so ill. Of course Escott's name must pain her. But did he think her a raw girl, to go off into a pet whenever a painful thing had to be mentioned? She flattered herself that she was at least a woman of experience, and of some sense, both of the inevitable and of the demands of humanity. And he spoke, too, as if she must cherish some kind of vague resentment at the thought of the Escott family. That idea of his was, indeed, in a certain way exasperating, because it showed that he must still be a very vain fellow, who had not been in the least cured by his long sojourn in the cool shades of her disfavor. Resentment towards the poor

Escotts! What could be further from her thoughts? Was not their great wrong her daily regret? Had she ever forgotten that wrong, or indulged any feeling so absurd and degrading as jealousy? But at all events, Tom was now plainly anxious to do his duty on this one occasion. However vain he was, however obviously selfish his purposes were, she liked his hesitating and humble demeanor, his fear of her anger, his apparently straightforward appeal to her on a matter that involved some considerations of pure business, and his whole assumed tone of earnestness and submission. She felt flattered, and even to some extent appeased, although she was not for a moment deceived about him. It was long since they had been so close together in conversation as this. She experienced a certain pleasurable excitement, which, however, in no wise disturbed her calm of manner, or the long cultivated repose of her general feelings towards him. It was amusing, all the while, that, in trying to appease her, he was playing what he obviously regarded as a deep game, although his absurd fear lest the very name of Escott should somehow anger her revealed his shallow vanity, and his real object in so ostentatiously doing his duty. She was willing to let him go on, of course, and she was cordially disposed to help him in his plans for Escott's good. But as for being actually won over by these devices, — the thought of it was comical! And this man had, among men, a great reputation as a diplomatist, and even as an out-and-out intriguer! She went on, after a moment's pause: —

"What you have in mind, is to hit upon some plan whereby Escott shall get an undisputed right to his claim at Oakfield Creek."

"Yes," he replied, "and you see how delicate an undertaking it is. There might be no insurmountable obstacle, I fancy, to prevent my persuading father, if I wished, to let me buy his own claim as against Escott, and make Escott a present of it. If father objected to that plan, as looking too much like a general surrender from our side, I know friends of Escott who would be overjoyed to buy up father's rights in their own name, and settle for the land with Escott later. That would avoid any appearance of an offer of compromise from father, since these persons would have no connection with the family. In fact, of course, there would be no difficulty about giving Escott a dozen farms outright, if he 'd take 'em. But all that 's out of the question. Escott is a confirmed romancer. What he wants, in this matter, is to sink or swim with his fellow-claimants. The business, in his eyes, is one of eternal justice. No doubt his original enmity to — myself, and, in consequence, to father (with whom, as you know, he was once fully reconciled)," — Tom's voice was faltering a little again, — "caused him to look into the matter at all. But having once begun, he feels bound to continue the struggle to the end. So then, what does he demand? He demands that father shall give up the fight, and come to terms with the Oakfield Creek claimants. He demands that now, as much as ever he did. And when he 's approached concerning this, his one last piece of property, he says that he knows it 's his property ; and intends to have it on the same terms as any other Oakfield Creek claimant. There he stands, and he won't budge."

" And what, then, do you still hope to do for him ? "

" There 's just the point I 'm coming to, though I fear it 's a very long story. I 'm heartily weary of these conflicts ; above all, of the Oakfield Creek conflict. Father will yet wear his life away in such things, without ever getting time to do his proper work. His life has been a long and hard one. By way of a well-earned reward, he 's been promising himself leisure to spend his last years in endowing and getting into running order one or two great public trusts, such as shall remain to perpetuate his name here in the State, and to do lasting good. You know that wish of his as well as I do. It 's a noble wish, and he 's just the man to carry it out. Most of our pioneer millionaires have cherished such desires, and several have tried to accomplish something of the sort. Father is the best fitted of all, I fancy, to do work of the kind without crudity and without vacillation. He has magnificent plans. I want to see them mature during his lifetime. Nobody could really carry them out for him if he died. Well, as I say, with all his obstinate persistence in fighting to the last for whatever he regards as his rights, he not only has made himself many enemies, who still try to injure his name, but he has kept himself in the thick of the struggle, rendering it hopeless that he will ever find his longed-for leisure. I want him to get out of this hurly-burly. And I 'm very anxious about that, I assure you." Tom was warming to his subject more and more. His pale and usually so impassive face was growing all the time fuller of life and earnestness. His eyes were sparkling with animation.

"And now," he went on, "as to the Oakfield Creek matter itself. It 's to be throughout regretted. Here 's the case, in as brief a statement as I can make. The thing is sadly mixed. Father long ago bought a title to the *sobrante*, or surplus land, surrounding an ill-defined Spanish grant. The original grant was confirmed, as well as the grant of the sobrante, but the survey long remained in dispute, and, pending that, father, of course, had no perfectly clear title, although his right to the sobrante itself, when it should be surveyed, was admitted, and he awaited only the survey to find where his property was. The thing dragged on from year to year, and the property, lying as it does in one of those rather inaccessible valleys between Mount Diablo and the Contra Costa hills, remained, owing to the clouded titles, almost worthless. Then father, some ten years ago, conceived his plan (there are many rival plans afoot among our capitalists, you know) to run the long-talked-of narrow-gauge road through the hills into the Mount Diablo region. That would bring the land near to market. But to persuade others to invest capital in his scheme, father took yet another step. He got the holders of the opposing claims to subscribe to shares of the proposed railway company, and to do so upon this agreement: Neither side should yield its land claims to the other, until the survey case should have been decided by the courts. Both should cooperate, however, in getting the railway started, and above all in getting the land into the hands of settlers. For, as father insisted, both parties had, to a certain extent, undisputed claims, and so had interests in common, and both could take stock in the proposed railway, and steps to develop the property in question, without giving up an iota of their respective claims to the portion of the land which was still actually in dispute. Thus delay in developing the property would be avoided. Do you follow me, Margaret?"

"Of course; your statement is clear enough for even poor me."

"Well, forgive me if it 's stupid. Father owned a great deal of other land over there, and this matter was only one among many kindred enterprises. But such, at all events, was the agreement on which the projected railway was to be begun. In fact, what with hard times and long fights, no rail of it has ever yet been laid beyond the hills. I 've no doubt some other company will step in very soon and capture the prize. But, at all events, the other part of the plan went on for a time more successfully. Father and his rivals both began to attract settlers to their land. The soil is fertile, the railway is sure to come some day, the climate is excellent. The only trouble at the outset was that the tract in dispute between father and the others was just the best part of the land thereabouts. It was, namely, the long strip that borders Oakfield Creek, on both sides, for miles. Of course, when you talked to a settler about the region he always said: 'I 'm in for that bottom-land there, and I won't look at any other.' Now, however, as you see, neither father, as owner of the sobrante, nor the other party to the controversy, could give a settler a clear title within the borders of that tract. And neither of the litigant parties was ready to compromise in advance of the decision of the Supreme Court at Washington, which was as slow as usual in getting to the case of this particular Spanish grant survey. But father was equal, so he thought, to this perplexity. He got the other side to join with him in an advertisement to settlers, and, of course, in an agreement upon which this advertisement could be based. The advertisement opened the disputed land, for settlement, to all comers who in good faith should take up and improve small tracts along Oakfield Creek. Whenever the title should be clearly in the hands of one or the other of the principal disputants, it was declared, according to the terms of the advertisement, that the land should then be offered by the successful litigant to the actual settlers, and at very low rates. The rates, it was agreed, should not be raised meanwhile on account of any increase in the value of the land through improvements made by the occupants themselves. Both father and his opponents signed this document. A goodly number of settlers, in all perhaps sixty or eighty families, very soon availed themselves of the joint offer. A good many more followed later. They could get a home, you see, without having to think of paying for it until the United States Supreme Court should be done with that survey case. That seemed an eternity to look forward to. They trusted implicitly in the zeal and skill of the wealthy litigants to keep the end a good way off. Whenever the end should come, they were promised the easiest of terms. Meanwhile, father and his opponents both gained a certain direct advantage from the presence of these settlers; for, first, in advance of the railway, a stage and transportation company was set up. That, of course, was in itself a very little thing. But, as a result, the undisputed property of both parties became more salable; while the railway, in view of the increasing population, looked daily more feasible, and more and more outside capital was promised for the enterprise. If it had n't been for the sudden and stubborn financial troubles that began in 1875, with the failure of the Bank of California, I 'm sure that the railway would have been begun and finished within a very short time. Meanwhile, father began improvements in that region on land to which he had a clear title. He planted thousands of eucalyptus-trees, started an irrigation company, and was full of great plans.

"But now, as you see, misunderstandings came instead of further progress. The hard times made everybody unwilling to invest in the proposed enterprises over there, and the excitements of the new constitution period did n't better the prospects of such speculative undertakings. The occupants of the disputed lands began to get discontented with their homes, which did n't prove so profitable, in the absence of a railway, as they had expected. Father was erelong equally discontented with the whole venture. He often loses interest in past undertakings that don't prove successful. This one, you see, had cost him a comparatively moderate sum, after all, but it had proved tedious and unproductive. I 'm afraid he even sometimes half forgot about his old dreams concerning that region. At last the survey suit was decided, and in his favor. The disputed Oakfield Creek property was his. To be sure, he had already disposed of part of his interest in it to a new Land and Improvement Company, and that fact tied his hands a little about the decision of the later disputes. However, he still was substantially in control of the whole thing. But here the settlers interposed. They had been disappointed, they said. Some of them had invested more money in improving the land than the outcome had warranted. All of them had waited patiently for a railroad that never came. It seemed just to them, therefore, that, whatever should be done with the still untouched portions of the tract, the original occupants should get their land at rates still lower than those originally agreed upon. The inducement had been cheap land plus a railway. The railway was still in the cave of dreams. Meanwhile, they said, these original settlers, by their presence and hard labor, had much increased the value of all the surrounding real estate. It was just, therefore, that they should get at least the equivalent of their original inducements. And that, they said, would mean cheaper rates still than the original ones.

"I think they were wrong in this notion. But father had a counter-claim to make. He had invested something in the land himself. His own improvements, he said, had vastly assisted these occupants; while the tracts of undisputed land that he had sold out and out to other settlers, and the improvements that these purchasing settlers had made, formed, he asserted, yet another source of increased value, such as had not been named in the original inducements to the occupants of the disputed tracts. He gave other reasons that I won't go into. And he said, too, that if others had been disappointed, he had been far more so. The long and short of it was that he saw, on the whole, good cause for raising the old demand, instead of lowering it. He had given more than he had promised, he said, not less. He ought to be compensated.

"I think he put forward this statement at the outset in a rather tentative way, to offset the unreasonable demands of the occupants. But perhaps he stated the thing too strongly. He often does. The settlers flared up, some of them, and attacked him in the papers. Then father also grew angry. He and the Land and Improvement Company (the latter was, of course, largely under his control) joined in an assertion that the settlers must justly pay far more for their land than had at first been asked. The price was on the average just about quintupled. So the battle began. The longer it continued the worse it grew. Father at last felt himself so injured that he provisionally sold some of the occupied land to 'jumpers,' whom he promised to protect, and suits were begun to put these in possession. The occupants, meanwhile, of course, have no actual title, but they claim the letter of the original agreement. They say that they have frequently tendered father the sum agreed upon. Father's lawyers, I 'm sorry to say, lay stress on the legal worthlessness of the form of the document upon which the settlers' claims are founded. This document, namely, is in form only an agreement between father and his old opponents, who now, of course, have vanished from the field. I fear very much that the claimants have legally nothing to stand upon. The title is vested in father; a binding and valid agreement to sell at a fixed figure was, legally speaking, never made at all, I fancy, and the claimants will probably have to pay father's price or go. In the course of the controversy he was once so much wrought up that he said he would never settle with the old claimants at any price. They had betrayed him, he declared, and he would eject them, if it cost him half a million. Those were the words of passion. Father is not so bad as that. Only I have feared that he may indeed fight the settlers hard, and that they may have to pay him a very large sum. For the money he does n't care now, I believe, at all. But the abuse and the hot blood have made him anxious to fight for victory."

"Your account is n't flattering to father, Tom, is it? It 's as I said before: a woman simply can't understand such passions. Sixty or eighty families, you said, Tom. And many more since, — think of that! Families, you must remember! It 's a great word, that. Ah, what shall we do with father, Tom, if he goes on in this way?"

"Perhaps I'm unjust to him. I grant I was not thinking just now of defending him to you, so much as of letting you understand the other side. You 've known father too long, Margaret, you 've been first his dread and then his idol too successfully, to need me to defend him. All his weaknesses you know, — as you know all mine too, I 'm afraid." Tom sighed once more, and tried timidly to catch her eye, but this time he failed. "Well, for good or for ill this struggle 's gone on. Escott's interference, I said, made things worse. You may wonder what, after all, he really bought from the settlers whose claims he took up. He bought, of course, these settlers' improvements; and then he bought what all of them out there regard, of course, as most sacred property, the claim in equity upon father for a delivery of the title to the tracts, on a proper tender of the sum mentioned in the old advertisement. Escott has lived on one of the tracts twice or thrice since he purchased the claim, though always for short periods. Part of the land he has lent, without rent, to poor families. At other times he has employed two men to take care of some of it for him. He now has, of course, no means to pay these. He, who in the city has long been almost forgotten, is a great character when he goes out to Oakfield Creek. The settlers actually revere him, and hang on his words as if he were inspired."

"But what is going to happen, then, Tom? Are the suits never to end? Is the agony a thing for all time?"

"I ought to have said that the settlers, as a last defense, have in their despair undertaken to raise again the old issues, by contesting the validity of father's title itself. They have pleaded informality in the survey, fraud on the part of surveyors, collusion between father and his old opponents to defraud the settlers, and I don't know what else, in addition to their own supposed equity, based upon that original notice of invitation. The ejectment suits are being contested on all these questions in the United States courts; and the trial will be finished and the decision reached, I fancy, in from six to twelve months. I've little doubt but the thing will go against the settlers. Appeal would, I believe, be useless to them. But I have great fear of trouble, very serious trouble, to follow."

"What? Do you fear anything like a pitched battle?"

"Precisely so. The settlers may take to using their shot-guns. Such things have happened often enough before, you know."

"But Escott, himself, — surely the professor would n't take to a shot-gun."

"Why not? The man is reckless, and a genuine hero to boot. If his friends were in any sort of danger, he would cross all the seas and lands, if need be, to stand beside them. I never knew a more faithful nature."

"Indeed?" Margaret was the least bit malicious in tone; but she went on at once: "But did he ever get into trouble of just that sort?"

"Oh, never into a brawl, to be sure. He once fought the Indians in Washoe, you know, but he 's not the man ordinary fellows would be apt to want to fight. Once or twice, in the old days, I think he sent a challenge to somebody or other. And, if report is correct, the case was settled each time without delay, by an ample apology from the other side. I doubt if anybody ever challenged him. He 's not the man to give needless offense. He 's the gentlest of natures when he is n't aroused."

"You seem to have a singular admiration for Escott, Tom, which I am *very* glad to observe, let me say. But that," she went on hastily, "is neither here nor there. I still want to know what we are to do for him."

"Ah, how long I am about it! Well, father is

just of late in a gentler mood. He has his more peaceable times, also, as you know. He has mentioned the pending suits with even a sort of regret in his tone. He heartily wishes, no doubt, that he had n't been forced by his high spirits into a place where he appears as oppressor of the poor. And a really magnanimous action he 's always glad to do, if he can but see the chance. And so, this has occurred to me. Can't we" — here Tom allowed himself a slightly more confidential tone — "*can't* we persuade him to take advantage of Escott's misfortune, and to admit to Escott, out and out, that the settlers are more than half right, and then to propose himself that Escott shall accept, and shall persuade the others to accept, a reasonable compromise? Bold this plan of mine looks, — impossible to one who does n't know father. But consider, Margaret: father has at heart the greatest admiration for Escott's indomitable pluck, and he has never recovered from his feeling that many years since — you remember it well — he did to Escott, as he did to you, a terrible injury. Then there 's father's friendship of long ago, in early days, with Escott. They were together, you know, in Washoe. They once fought the Indians together. All that 's in father's mind. He never forgets anything of the sort. It has been the sense of the hopelessness of repairing that injury, or of renewing in any way the old friendship, with Escott so stern and repellent, that has made father all the more bitter. A proud man can never live quiet under such a sense. And, as

I said, it's Escott's presence in this fight that has rendered father seemingly so irreconcilable towards the settlers. Take Escott out, and father would compromise. Keep Escott in, and father 's unutterably miserable. Now here 's our chance. Perhaps we can take Escott out, not by any ordinary course of conduct, but by proposing to father a finely magnanimous act in an attractive way. We can say, 'Here 's your old friend, and also your old foe, a man whom you 're conscious of having deeply injured. Here he is at your feet, helpless. He has no valid legal rights, as against you. He has nothing that will be good enough to pass muster in the courts. He is old; he is despised or forgotten in the city; he is infirm. But in one way he still offends you. He leads the settlers' company out there at Oakfield Creek. Now, surely,' we can say to father, 'you in no sense confess weakness by going to this man now, just at this very crisis of his misfortunes, and holding out your hand. You need n't offer him charity. Just say that you 're willing now to stand up and talk to him like a man, and that you want to grant to him and his friends their righteous, yes, even their barely plausible demands, precisely as if nothing had happened to make hard feeling.' That 's what we can say to father, Margaret. And I believe the very novelty of the idea, if he 's only rightly approached, will charm him. I know father; he likes to do good, but he wants it to look picturesque. And this thing may be made to look so, may n't it?" Tom paused, a little breathless.

Had he not spoken well? To be sure, there was something lacking about his eloquence, yet might it not move her just a little?

Margaret was smiling very approvingly, but she looked provokingly at her finger-tips. "Bravo, Tom!" she said, with a soft laugh. "If you were a youth again I might almost be fool enough to say, 'Why don't you speak for yourself, John?' But, alas! we 're very old people now, and I 'm afraid I can't encourage this boyishness in you." She changed her manner suddenly again, as she spoke the last of these words, and she grew sober and mildly forbidding once more, so that he felt a little chilled while she went on, in her usual tone of cheerful resignation: "But seriously now, Tom, to come back to real life; why am I so important for all this undertaking? I approve it heartily, though I beg you to see that there 's nothing heroic, no, nor even anything 'picturesque,' about your proposed action, or your father's. The matter is one of the simplest possible sort. It 's just plain duty. You have both of you wronged a man bitterly, and he has a just claim, meanwhile, to a bit of land which you men have somehow been trying to get away from him for years past. You don't need his land the least in the world. You 've no business with it, so long as he stands ready to pay somehow what was originally agreed upon. Now, at last, however, as he 's very weak, and poor, and old, it happens to occur to you that it 's a little mean to keep on kicking him while he lies there helpless, so you (you and your father together, I mean, of course) are to offer him your manly regrets and a kindly present of his indisputable rights. That 's a very pretty idea. I like it. I want to help you carry it out, of course. Why not? But now what can I do? Tell me, and I 'll sit up all night for a week planning my part of the job."

Tom sighed, a little despairingly. That was a withering manner of hers, when she chose to adopt it. He knew it of old. Yet he, too, was learned in resignation, and he showed no further sign of vexation as he went on: "Well, there again I 'm slow in making myself clear. Whatever this thing really is, picturesque or not, it 's got to seem picturesque to father. And ever since you chose to make a conquest of him (as you do of whomsoever you please to assail, Margaret), there 's been nobody your equal for controlling him. I 've long been puzzling, you must know, to see what I could do for Escott. I 'm a wretch, no doubt, but it is n't to-day or yesterday that my knowledge of that fact may be said to have begun. It 's only now that I 've seen my way clear to help him. And so I most humbly come to you, Margaret, for help, and you must n't quite disdain me, or I shall become a lost soul altogether."

"No, Tom," she said, smiling, "you must n't make me responsible for so grave a thing as that. I 'm at your service, of course, in any good cause. And so, how and when am I to display the picturesque sight to father's awe-struck gaze? I 'm delighted to be such a show-woman, of course.

Think of me: 'Here, dear father, behold this portrayal of an unexampled deed of virtue. See this lovely picture: the good Samaritan disdaining even to pick a certain man's pocket of the last penny the thieves accidentally left him. Noble spectacle! Observe, and do likewise!' How impressive I shall be saying all this! How a woman loves to exert her powers for a great end!" She laughed merrily. "But, seriously, Tom, please don't look disconsolate. I won't bite, if I do snarl so. You 're very good, I don't doubt. It 's my proudest delight to praise you when you 've done a noble action, and, of course, as far as in you lies, you 're doubtless planning one now. I never did a noble action myself, and have n't the least idea how it may feel; but it 's a woman's commonplace duty to help in these minor affairs. Men have a monopoly of the really noble deeds. I 'm overjoyed at this chance to be a spectator of even the least approach to one of them. When shall we have father over here to try the new game on him?"

"Whenever you will, Margaret."

"Sunday?"

"Why not?"

"Alas! Sunday I had set as the day to do, not a noble action, but a decent one. I was going to spend all day in baby's company."

"If his health seems to you to need"—

"Oh, nonsense! His health 's not perfect; but as if my staying with him of a Sunday would better it! No, I was only about to begin acquiring a few stray bits of information about the poor boy's character and habits. He and I have a sort of bowing acquaintance at present. I'm afraid he may cut me dead, by accident, before long, if I don't beware."

"How you malign yourself!"

"No, Tom. You mean how I spare myself! But, of course, to-morrow is the time for father. The sooner the better. Noble actions fly fast. We must spread our nets at once. Yet what part had dear mother to play in this great moral show of yours, Tom? Her first appearance can't be until later, you know."

"Oh, I went to her for first advice and encouragement. She was less cruel than you are, Margaret, towards my feeble efforts to do right."

"Cruelty is my only virtue. All the others are dear mother's. For what would you do without a little cruelty, you spoiled child?" Margaret smiled, certainly in the most cruel possible fashion. "But what then did dear mother counsel?"

"Much what I have done so far, and what you approve for the future. But there is still another aspect of the case. We need, of course, a person through whom we can deal with Escott. The old man himself is, I grant, a trifle hard for us to approach. And if the first approach to Escott were to be a wrong one, well, then, there 'd only be a little more lightning than ever, I suppose."

"You speak of him as if he were a fiery dragon, poor man. I saw, however, all the time, that you had some such person in mind as might serve for a go-between. How otherwise should you know so much about Escott's condition and prospects, if you had n't a go-between already? Who, then, is the Moses that may thus go up into burning mountains?"

"A man whom I have only recently learned to know at all well, — a friend of Williamson's; one William Harold by name. He 's a man about my age."

"Harold? Oh, yes. I used to hear of him already years ago. He married Annie Thornton, and she died some four or five years since. Then he went abroad. Have I heard him mentioned since he came back? I should say so, indeed! A poet, is n't he, or else a naturalist, or an amateur musician, or something of the sort, or perhaps all of them at once? And a confirmed woman-hater, too! Lives alone; keeps an owl, three parrots, seven cats, and a big inlaid chess-board, with great ivory chess-men; smokes all day long; lives in general in a mystical cloud of contemplation; is esteemed a sage, in fact is one; has charming blue-gray eyes, much old china, numerous books on the black art, and an altar with three candles burning before his wife's picture. Is n't all that true? Oh, I know of him very well, you may believe! Louise Parkhurst tells me everything that 's going, you know."

"Louise is n't precisely a historian, Margaret, but she 's a good chronicler, in her way. If all that is n't precisely so, it 's better than the truth, as an account of Harold. Yes, barring a certain inaccuracy in all your facts, he 's much that sort of man."

"But, see here, now, Tom. My inspirations are instantaneous. I 'm to conduct the picturesque moral show for father's reformation. That 's solemn business. And you, personally, can't detract much from the solemnity, try as you will. What 's needed to give diversity, and to keep us all from yawning our heads off, is another member of the stock company of this dime museum, a second assistant showman and scene-shifter, a person, too, of some cleverness and originality. I take it, Harold 's deeply interested in Escott, is n't he?"

"He has Escott staying with him since the fire. All our negotiations are, of course, so far a profound secret from the old man himself."

"Bravo! Perfect! Fetch Harold over here at *once*, Sunday. *That 's* my inspiration. He and I can arrange it to bring father round straightway. He 'll represent Escott, I 'll represent eternal justice. I feel in my bones the sense that he 's just the man. Father 'll have no chance. You, of course, being in such delicate matters notoriously stupid, though very well meaning, poor boy, shall sit by and look on benevolently at the success of your heroic and self-sacrificing schemes. That 's the plan. Can you do it, Tom?"

"Why not? Whatever you will." Her mood fascinated as well as baffled him; but he had every wish to please her. "Perhaps," he went on, "I can't get Harold so soon. I 'll try, though. He really is very much interested in Escott's case.

He was formerly one of Escott's faithful band of disciples, I think, when we all were young. We knew little of each other, however. That was natural, too, being the fashion of Escott's friendships." Tom sighed yet once more, but felt when he did so what a foolish blunder he was committing all the while, as, for that matter, she had just shown him. Why must he be so melancholy in her presence? That wearied her. Yet how could he ever predict what she would take seriously, and what not? He had felt this old ground so dangerous to tread. And she — she merely laughed in his face, now that her first mood of soberness was past.

"As for me," she said, with the merriest of voices, "you see I 'm so much lost in pride at the thought of enticing the unattainable, the icy, the profound Harold into our humble dwelling, that I 'm near forgetting the noble task itself. But when he 's once here we 'll work it out. Now, however, what were you going to do to-day to secure father for Sunday?" Margaret's face wore just now her most beautiful expression.

"I was going back to the city before dinner, and coming out with father Sunday morning. Of him I feel sure, notwithstanding, or perhaps I should say because, he 's no idea what awaits him."

"Excellent! Then hear your orders. You are to invite Harold to come over with you Sunday morning, on this special business of consulting with father and me about the whole affair. He's to come, of course, for Escott's sake. Tell him it's absolutely imperative for the success of the whole enterprise, because, of course, we must act quickly, before father has had time to get used to the new situation, or to get up some new prejudice about it. And mind you, you 're to bring over Harold yourself in person, early, and in time for lunch. But you 're to see that father himself does *not* get here until after lunch. Have him come early in the afternoon, say at three o'clock. Tell father we 'll dine late. against the usual Sunday custom, for his sake, and that we have some other sort of little fandango running earlier in the day. You need n't say what. The purpose of all this is to give time for me to take Harold into my plots, and to arrange matters with him. Then, when father comes, the show will proceed, — trained elephants, conjurers, and all the rest that may be called moral and picturesque. The effect, as you may leave me to determine, will be all that any one could desire. Both Harold and father are, of course, to stay here all night. Lest as lone lorn woman I should feel too unprotected in the company of so many of you men, I may take it upon myself to have other company also at dinner. But I 'm not sure yet. At any rate, we 're to have the great conversion take place before dinner, if possible."

"Well," said Tom submissively, "if this is what I have to arrange for, I must go back to town forthwith, that no time may be lost. I must order up the carriage, I suppose."

A few minutes later Tom reverently and sedately took his leave, feeling, as had happened before after certain of his interviews with Margaret, that his ears must have been somehow softly boxed, he could hardly tell when or by whom. Margaret was just now fairly radiant. She even let him kiss her hand as he left. It seemed to him long since he had seen just such a look in her face. He grew once more hopeful.

CHAPTER III.

BOSCOWITZ AND ESCOTT.

In those days there flourished for a little time in San Francisco a weekly journal called the "Warrior." Its proprietor was a decidedly noteworthy person, named Louis Boscowitz. It is hard to be sure of his precise nationality, and, if report be true, he had very little. People say, namely, that he was born in London, and that his mother was English, while his father, according to the same story, was a political refugee from somewhere in Austria. Louis himself passed his early years in London. Later he lived in New York, where he studied American politics, and had some training in newspaper work. Then he wandered for years from city to city, until he found himself in San Francisco. Here he was at first an antiquarian bookseller. If you have ever dealt with him, you will remember his monstrous prices, and his other curious methods of business. Then he joined local politics to his bookselling; and at length he was clever enough to think of publishing the "Warrior." Erelong his paper had made him both prosperous and famous.

Probably Boscowitz had some Jewish blood in his veins. But his English mother was surely no Jewess, and Boscowitz himself never admitted that he had any relationship with the race. In person he was short, spare, active, with strong but ugly features, a sallow complexion, and very keen little black eyes. His dress, at least during the days of his prosperity, was always showy. It is a little hard to say just how he managed to be so influential as he was in his dealings with other men. At first sight you would have set him down as a person of no importance. But if he talked with you, you soon saw him to be both a very clever and a very malicious fellow, with a remarkable skill in judging character. He had seen much of the world. To a certain extent he could adapt his manners to his company. On all occasions he carefully studied the men about him. He never forgot their weaknesses, nor failed to record their misdeeds in his excellent memory. He joined caution with an easy show of recklessness. He was especially skillful in appearing to be extremely frank at the very moment when he was best keeping his secrets, and best developing his own little plots. He was always an unsafe man to deal with. As a foe he was a very dangerous person indeed.

But much more interesting than Boscowitz's person was his journal. He wrote very little for it. He was a man of no literary education, and his English was whatever it chanced to be. This he well knew. His success came from his skill in choosing clever writers. He concealed the individuality of some of these even from the regular employés of his own office, so that all but the wise among his readers took him to be the author of many of his best columns. And he was actually responsible for the spirit of nearly every editorial article. It was the wording that he left to others. His choice of assistants was for his purposes indeed admirable. More than once I have heard San Franciscans remark about him: "When Boscowitz talks in that paper of his, it makes no difference whether you believe what he says or not; somehow you 've got to read the 'Warrior,' whatever he puts into it." This feeling that you must read the "Warrior" was wide-spread, and it was what had made Boscowitz's fortune.

The "Warrior" was a journal of literature, society, and politics. Unlike some of its rivals, it represented to a certain extent the cause and the interests of the foreign population of San Francisco; but it managed, meanwhile, to be pleasing to Americans, and to find special favor among the wealthy classes. In politics it pretended to be independent. It had a fondness, meanwhile, for bold political schemes, and more than once, during its brief career, it led a forlorn hope through an election campaign. Such heroism always brings to such journals numerous readers. Yet to one person the "Warrior" remained true through all its changes of side and of principle; and that person was the famous pioneer millionaire, Alonzo Eldon, a man who, though himself no professional politician, had very great commercial interests at stake, such as political changes might easily affect. The "Warrior" was always a stout supporter of Eldon. It praised him personally, and defended him against all assailants. It even seemed to be at times the great man's semi-official organ. It had private information in advance about some of his immense industrial undertakings. It foresaw and sought to counteract public opposition to his plans, and to the numerous corporations that he represented. It was in every way highly serviceable to Eldon. In return, Eldon, of course, helped to give the "Warrior" its due share of support and of influence.

Yet, after all, not so much for these causes as for its literary and social qualities was the "Warrior" a triumph. It appealed most skillfully to the varied and not very highly organized tastes of a certain public in San Francisco. It was a singular and most diabolical combination, this paper, of cleverness, wisdom, and taste, with immorality of many sorts, political and social, and even, on occasion, with positive indecency. It always pretended to great frankness and sincerity of judgment, and thus its brief editorials gained their marvelous success in catching and holding the reader's attention. Personalities the "Warrior" never feared, but still never carried to wearisome length. Yet to have the "Warrior" for your enemy meant to be exterminated in short order. The paper had a literary department, where an only half-respectable sort of French jokes and novelettes, hastily but effectively translated, stood side by side with actually learned and very sober critical essays, and with ambitious and excellent poems or stories. Gossip, sometimes instructive, sometimes vile, in letters from Eastern or from foreign cities, was also to be found. While you were reading in this department, you never knew whether what was next to meet your eye would be poetical or scandalous, scholarly or nasty, profound or degrading, high tragedy or low jest. Therein lay, in fact, the secret of this journal's literary successes. Its readers had no desire to know such things in advance. They bought their paper because it was literary. If it amused them by a little indecency now and then, so much the better. It lay on their parlor tables, and their children might do what they liked with it. For themselves, they found, in following this waywardness of their paper, a delightful sense of personal freedom. And Boscowitz's device for producing the waywardness was simply to employ all sorts of contributors, provided they were ingenious originators, translators, or thieves, and to see that what they brought was well mixed together in the columns. Of himself, Boscowitz could furnish little or nothing. His talent lay in managing other men.

Actual principles, then, political or social, the

"Warrior" had none. It sometimes even coquetted with anarchical notions, though always in a harmlessly jocular way. It was violently partisan during those heroic efforts before described; but, on the whole, it affected political independence with a leaning towards conservatism. Boscowitz had no important early political record to remember; he had never been prominently connected with either of the political parties. He could ignore all their family disputes. Yet he now rendered himself a power in their councils, because his influence with the public was great, and was especially potent, strange to say, with the wealthy classes. For Boscowitz had very cleverly chosen to appear in general, of late years, as the defender of vested interests. His earliest connections had been with foreign communists. But all that part of his life was now forgotten, save as jokes about it might sometimes give zest to his own columns.

The great mischief of this paper's existence lay, after all, less in the positive harm that it did than in that pulpy, disorganized state of the public mind which it tended to render more and more a chronic social disease. People read it simply for its cleverness, and it never guided them. Its readers cared little for the State, much for amusement, and nothing for political principles. Its general flippancy was theirs. The really good things in it were consequently like gold grains dropped into a plum pudding. Many swallowed them, and never noticed them, some few hated them, nobody was helped by them. It was the pudding that the people opened their mouths for, when, Saturday mornings, the newsboys shouted "Warrior," on the streets and in the cars. The pudding, however, only made men dyspeptic; the gold grains made them, if anything, yet more so.

After we have said all this, it may seem strange to add that one of Boscowitz's most useful assistants had been, from the start, Alf Escott, a man who personally abhorred trickery, believed in plain speech, and cultivated the ideal. Yet, if anything was characteristic of Escott, it was his sense of irresponsibility where the conduct of others was concerned, in case these others were men for whom he had no personal respect. He never wrote for anybody what did not seem to himself both true and good. But where his writings were printed, or with whom he might be associating himself, all that troubled him very little. Boscowitz he regarded as once for all a lost soul. The "Warrior" seemed to him the devil's own paper. But if this paper wanted him as one of its contributors, and still did not demand of him the writing of anything that went against his conscience, Escott was not the man to be harassed by the company that he must keep. As for the "Warrior," it indeed needed the devil's help, but it also needed such aid as Escott's. It throve by reason of its entertaining variety; for wickedness, if unvaried, is never entertaining. In fact, about two thirds of the "Warrior," Boscowitz knew, ought by rights to be really good every week. Then the devil's third, so to speak, would appear with all its genuine force and brilliancy by contrast. The great problem, therefore, was to get a sufficient number of excellent things into the paper. The evil things offered themselves without lack. Escott, however, despite his advancing age and his infirmities, was one of the few men who always had something good to say. He had a wide experience of life; he was bright, ready, fearless, no time-server, no flatterer, and no slanderer. When he wrote a sketch, it was fresh and stirring; when he tried argument, one followed him with amusement, if not always with conviction; when he produced a story, it was manly and humane. He always composed for the "Warrior" very hastily; he never polished his work; he was apt to be inaccurate. But he had the charm of a true Bohemian, together with the information of a man who formerly used to be a scholar. He had sadly degenerated in style and in learning during the last ten years. But the readers of the "Warrior" always admired his brief, facile, and often highly exciting contributions. Among the writers of the "Warrior" he thus stood, in many ways, alone. He never signed his true name. He had as many as three assumed signatures. He was equally successful in writing over all of them.

Since the fire that had burned poor Escott out of house and home, Boscowitz had begun to fear that fortune might deprive the "Warrior" of this able contributor. Escott's family had gone for temporary refuge to the house of the Rev. Mr. Rawley, whose wife was Mrs. Escott's sister.

Escott, however, whom the prevailing and aggressive piety of the Rawley household somewhat overawed, was glad to find a welcome for the moment with his young friend, William Harold, whose lodgings were on P—— Street. Harold, as Boscowitz suspected, had some entirely new plan for Escott's future.

William Harold, at just this time, had but recently come back to California, after an absence of rather more than four years, which he had been spending in travel and study. He had been driven away from the State by the great calamity of his life, his young wife's sudden death. He had returned for the sake of finding, amidst the old scenes, some healthy and absorbing occupation. He was a man of independent means, of some literary skill, taste, and ambition, of no fixed calling, of an innocent and sensitive heart, of an indolent disposition, and of a mind too much given to brooding. Ever since the death of his wife he had become absorbed in numerous trifling though intellectual pursuits. He lived lazily and contemplatively. His rooms were now already elaborately furnished, notwithstanding that he had so recently returned. He was a genial and sentimental man of taste, of ideals, and of good temper.

In his secret heart, meanwhile, Harold was a prey to many not altogether healthy fancies. He was by nature a religious man, and, as it happened, he had no religion save his wife's memory. Over this he brooded altogether too much. He feared that an active life would inevitably draw him out of his willing bondage to his now distant but always sacred sorrow. And one of his inner conflicts, at just this time, was especially characteristic of his state. It concerned the question whether and how he ought to revisit the house, on the hillside near Oakland, where he and his wife had passed the two happy years of their married life. Your eyes, in this world, always profane your memories, thought Harold. It would, therefore, be better never to go. But, on the other hand, he had a habit of thinking of his possible visit as a kind of holy pilgrimage, which should arouse afresh all his old enthusiasm in his chosen faith. Daily, for some weeks, he planned out the journey, with fairly childlike precision of detail; and daily he avoided going. His wife's grave was at Lone Mountain, on the city side of the bay. But to visit that, as he often did, was one thing; to see once more the house would be something quite different, and of far deeper meaning. He feared and cherished the plan. For a good while, however, Harold used to climb almost every day some one of the San Francisco hills, and look over towards the familiar Contra Costa range, and even try, with a large field-glass, to search out the house in the oak-grove, on the well-remembered spot. Especially he loved, for some reason, a particular vacant space near the summit of Russian Hill, as his place of observation. Just there, as you stand, you get an exceptionally fine view of the great bay to the north and east; of

Alcatraz Island, which seems to lie almost at your feet; of the dark and rugged peak of Tamalpais, opposite to you, on the north shore, and then of the Contra Costa itself, filling the whole eastern horizon. The great city is beneath you, on the east and southeast; the ferry-boats trace their curved paths on the still water beyond the city; all along the water-front the clusters of masts rise, close by the wharves. In presence of this scene, so familiar to all San Franciscans, Harold, with his glass in hand, used to search out the dark green grove, nestled close by the entrance of a long cañon, a little north of Oakland, and used to try to follow the thread-like line of road that ran up to the grove. The house itself, however, he could never clearly see. Although it had years ago passed out of his ownership, he knew it to be still standing; yet something, perhaps the growth of the large shade-trees directly in front of the place, now hid it altogether, and no effort could bring to his sight even its roof. After a good many trials, made under various conditions of light and shade, Harold gave up this search, and returned to his old problems. Should he go or not, and when?

Of all these fancies Harold told nobody a word, though certain persons were discerning enough to guess a little of their nature. There is a deep satisfaction in being the sole member of a religious sect. You need not propagate the faith, you are relieved from all the rivalry of fellow-worshipers, you enjoy alone the sacred fountains. There is, meanwhile, something in your devotion that the world would heartily despise, but this only shows you that the world is the world. Harold's friends all knew him to be odd and reserved; but, strangely enough, many of them thought him unsentimental. He was too appreciative of all their notions to get the full reputation that his moods deserved; for sentimental people are supposed to be aggressive with their own feelings, and irresponsive to the feelings of others. But Harold, by reason of his liberality of soul, escaped this fault.

To complete our idea of his broodings at this time, we have only to add the fact that he was a great dreamer, and that he had a remnant of superstitious faith in omens. His antipathy to Boscowitz, whom he occasionally met, took the form of a dread, and Boscowitz used to haunt those dreams of Harold's, appearing in all sorts of shapes, but always seeming scornful and malicious. The very night of the fire at Escott's, Harold had been dreaming of trying to visit the old home. But he could never get there, in the dream; for Boscowitz always managed to prevent him. Once Harold seemed to reach the foot of the last ascent, on the way to his house, when, just at the edge of the little grove, he met his dead wife. She looked very sad, and was leading a wounded horse. Boscowitz appeared just behind her. Harold tried in his dream to ask her why they could never meet again at the old home, and also why the meadow-larks in the fields would not sing any more; for it seemed to him that all the birds had lost their voices. But she said nothing, and only looked the sadder. All at once Boscowitz spoke. "Do you see all these new-made graves here on the hillside?" he called out, tauntingly. "Why have you been filling them all of a sudden in this way?" And then Harold seemed to know, in his dream, that by trying to visit his old home he had been somehow the cause of the death of all the men buried here. The new graves seemed to fill the whole hillside; and his wife had vanished. Harold awoke shuddering.

With all his dreaming and his fine notions, Harold was a loyal friend, and in practical matters he did not lack good sense. When he found Escott in the new trouble, he took the old man in, inquired into his circumstances, offered in a very delicate way to relieve his pressing wants, and fell to planning about his future. Harold had had, since his own return, but the barest bowing acquaintance with Tom Eldon, and he knew the Eldon family chiefly by their public reputation. At heart he dreaded them all, as prominent and worldly persons. But now, when he learned the truth about the Oakfield Creek settlers, whose tale he had not previously known, he resolved to approach the Eldons, and to see whether some compromise in Escott's favor might not be possible. Harold felt that he at least, as a disinterested and newly returned stranger, had a right to expect a fair reception from the Eldons. But Alonzo was too great a man to be approached directly, even by Harold: and so Harold appealed to Tom. His first success we have already learned.

Though always so little acquainted with each other, Tom and Harold had long ago stood in a closely similar relation to Escott. While Escott held his professorship in the Sunset College (that once promising but now almost forgotten private institution, founded and ultimately wrecked by a conspiracy of millionaires and clergymen), the old professor used to delight in making disciples of young men. He gloried in them. He influenced them deeply. What he had to offer them was rather his manhood than his scholarship; for Alf Escott, although an omnivorous reader, a good linguist, and a great lover of literature, was not precisely what an older community would have called a scholar. When he talked in private, he spoke as a Californian, simply, fearlessly, often roughly. Learning was in his eyes a secondary affair. With his fellow instructors he used to quarrel, in his frank and warm fashion, almost constantly. They found him very unconventional, not to say unbearable, and he called them pedants. His hope and comfort was in the young men. For these his heart was always open. He criticised them unsparingly; but he was so simple and sincere about it that the best ones seldom took offense. Escott's chief comfort, when the great final quarrel came, was that a chosen few among these youth stood by him. Tom Eldon was one of the faithful, Harold another. It was never Escott's way to force his friends to meet together. His disciples formed no united band. He enjoyed the fidelity of each one separately.

Escott's downfall as professor had a rather curious and characteristic history. Peter Dover, the former husband of the present Mrs. Eldon, had been, during his career, a prominent politician. He was a very pious but also a very pedantic man, benevolent, enterprising, crotchety, and almost useless. He had outlived two or three wives before Margaret was driven by her mother into her brief union with him. When he died, he left a great fortune, but no children. He was in his day a stout, bald, florid, anxious-looking person, who usually kept his gray eyes fixed on his immense watch-chain, while his lips were always nervously twitching. He and Escott had come into public collision on several occasions long before the days when Escott's professorship began. Finally, as report had it, they were reconciled after all their conflicts in a very curious way. For in the midst of one of their public controversies it happened that Escott was living for a time with his family near what is now East Oakland. His daughter Ellen, then but seven, wandered off alone, away from home, one day, among the spring flowers, and never stopped until she reached Dover's great house, more than a mile distant. No one knows what may have been in her mind, but she somehow found old Peter Dover in his garden, and, though she had never seen him before, she proceeded to make friends with him on the spot. Dover was just then a widower. He had always a passion for children, and in their presence his behavior was perfect. He found out who Ellen was, and drove her home himself. By the time they had reached Escott's house, Dover and the little Ellen had sworn eternal friendship. The anxious father, who had long been looking for his little girl, now met his enemy at the door of the house ; and the two, so report had it, shook hands then and there, and were reconciled for all subsequent time. This result was, after all, not so strange for a man of Alf Escott's heart; and the childless Dover's weakest point was in this love for children. The two men had nothing in common, and never became intimate, yet they never again quarreled.

But the outcome of this child-made reconciliation was disastrous for Escott. Years later, when Escott's hold on the professorship at the Sunset College was already growing weak, by reason of his plain speech and his obstinacy, it chanced that Peter Dover fell under the displeasure of the public prints, and began to be abused for supposed malfeasance in an office of trust that he had held. The accusation was in fact unjust. Yet not only the press, but also Alonzo Eldon, took part against Dover. But as for Escott, — loyalty to a man threatened with injustice was his first thought. Disapproval of Alonzo Eldon's course joined itself to this hatred of injustice. Yet Alonzo was a great benefactor of the Sunset College. He was, moreover, one of Escott's oldest and most admired friends. The two had already frequently differed, but this time what passed between them was far more bitter than ever before. Escott took Dover's side, and took it so warmly as to make himself impossible in the Sunset College. Stormy scenes followed. The newspapers fell upon the erring professor, who had thus boldly ventured beyond his class-room. The body of the students in the college also took the Eldon side, and gleefully burned their honored professor in effigy. Escott was accused of the basest ingratitude, and was finally driven in disgrace from his chair, amid all sorts of unfounded accusations, and so he fled into the welcome obscurity of the city of San Francisco. Everything was said meanwhile that could render his life a burden to him; all his motives were misjudged; and the public fury went so far in the condemnation of Escott that poor Peter Dover's supposed misdeeds were almost forgotten. It was through this controversy that Tom Eldon had firmly stood by Escott, and had meanwhile withstood his own father.

After such outbursts of public fury, the people of San Francisco and thereabouts always feel benevolent and forgiving. They soon let Escott fall almost out of mind. But they turned back quite apologetically to Peter Dover, of whom the papers began to speak well forthwith. He was very properly acquitted on all the charges of malfeasance. The public desire for vengeance had been sufficiently gratified by Escott's downfall. People began to praise Dover. Had it not been for that pestilent Escott, some of the more discerning ones said, there would have been no trouble at all! Just then Peter Dover, who had been married but a year to Margaret, suddenly died of apoplexy; and, to end the affair, everybody attended his funeral, which was one of the most magnificent ever known in San Francisco. The Rev. Mr. Chrysostom Hahn preached the sermon, the house was packed to suffocation, the flowers were in masses, and everybody went away convinced that Peter Dover was one of the great characters of American history. Thereafter nobody mentioned him, and all was again tranquil.

Escott, too, was at the funeral of the man for whom he had sacrificed so much. Nobody paid especial attention to the tall, worn, sallow, deeply wrinkled professor, with those large dark eyes, with the strong, prominent features, the stooping shoulders, and the gray hair. Escott was well known, as an old Californian, to many there; but he was now a beaten and disgraced man, who had been convicted of ingratitude towards his old benefactor, Alonzo Eldon, and who had been dropped from his professorship as an unfit guide for the youth of the Sunset College. Nobody addressed him save in the most formal way, and after the funeral Escott walked home through Chinatown, to forget thereby, as he said to somebody, "the perfume of those lying flowers." Thenceforth he never spoke of Peter Dover, however, otherwise than with sincere sympathy and regard.

Naturally, when Escott again found work, he was glad of a chance to refrain from general intercourse with a world for which his temper was so ill adapted. As a writer for the press he thenceforth earned his living, partly indeed by dramatic and musical criticism, but mostly by such impersonal work as he later did for Boscowitz.

His earlier friendship with Harold was interrupted, in part by Harold's marriage, and afterwards by the young man's departure for foreign parts. Others of his "disciples," as he himself loved to call them, forsook him. The affair with Tom Eldon finally left the old man almost alone.

Escott's family, after Ellen's death, consisted of his wife and two children, — a son, named Sam, who had been two years younger than Ellen, and a daughter, Emily, the only child of Escott's second marriage, and herself five years the junior of Sam. Escott's second wife, still living, was a devoted and homely little person, with no will of her own, with boundless affection for her household, and with a remarkably able and energetic sister, Mrs. Rawley, the pastor's wife. Mrs. Rawley and Escott had for each other's powers a certain admiration; but their relations towards each other's interests were those of a well-armed and watchful non-interference. Both of Escott's surviving children were a disappointment to him. They repeated some of their father's traits, but with a disappointing one-sidedness. Sam had his father's energy, and even something of Escott's imagination, but lacked the father's coolness and self-command, as well as his intellect. Most people even called Sam silly. He was an innocent and straightforward boy, who loved a very active life. He hated, however, the restraints of business. He had no wits for professional life. He longed for the days when men used to be soldiers and kill one another for a living. Emily, on the other hand, lacked both her father's intellect and his imagination. She had only his loyalty and his cheerfulness. Escott, however, looked in vain, in this household of his, for a trace of what Ellen had been to him. She, he said to himself, had been in a very true sense his only child.

CHAPTER IV.

THE STORY OF A LOST LOVE.

DURING the days just after the fire, Escott and Harold spent much time in talking over the past. Escott's health and circumstances plainly forbade, just at the moment, any work. His family were safe for the time at the Rawleys' house. Escott had no thought of giving up, worn and weak though he was, after this latest calamity. He spoke of the future with perfect cheerfulness. He had no thought of accepting any but the most transient aid from anybody. He made only a few jocular complaints of his new luck. And yet this recent reverse had been one of his worst. Manuscripts very valuable to him, the summary, in a sense, of his whole life's work, had been lost in the fire. His health had suffered sadly of late years, and was apt soon to be wholly ruined, unless he could find some much easier mode of life. To replace his literary losses was simply impossible. His ambitions had vanished in smoke.

Under these circumstances, it was natural that such a man as Escott should amuse himself for a few days by lounging on Harold's comfortable sofas, in drinking a little of Harold's wine, in smoking Harold's cigars, and in talking over old times. A thorough-going defeat may give you a good opportunity to rest, and, to Escott's mind, a man was worse than a fool who would not nerve himself for future work by using such a chance.

In their talks, when cheerful or indifferent topics had been exhausted, it was natural that they should come to more serious ones. Harold had long been curious to learn the particulars about Ellen Escott's death, which had occurred during his own absence from the State. He found his opportunity to ask Escott about this matter on Saturday afternoon, the day before the visit which Harold had now been privately invited to make, on Escott's behalf, to the hillside house of Tom Eldon. Harold felt that he must learn beforehand all that was possible about the past relations of the Escotts and Eldons. He felt, meanwhile, somewhat guilty in hiding from Escott the fact of his little negotiation. But for the moment this fact must needs be hidden. Escott was quite unsuspicious. The old man was in a mood to-day, as it chanced, for the freest talk, and he went over the tale in full, beginning with the affair of Peter Dover, and going on to the quarrel with Alonzo

Eldon, the close friendship between Tom and himself, and the betrothal of Tom and Ellen. Escott told much of his story while he reclined on one of Harold's sofas. But ever and anon, if he grew excited, he would rise and walk about while he spoke. Then he would seat himself once more in a chair, and look closely into Harold's face with his great dark eyes, as if searching narrowly for the listener's sympathy.

Ill health had by this time left of Alf Escott only the shadow of his former strength. He was now not only spare, but shrunken. The skin of his face was like wrinkled parchment. His movements were infirm and often awkward. But his voice and his eyes still showed what he used to be. You could see, too, the old strength in his features. His voice itself was very musical. In his early youth, before he first became a professor, and long before he thought of coming to California, he had studied for the stage. He had never wholly lost the natural grace of countenance and expression that must once have made him a fascinating youth. Through all the marks of age and illness, you could find the former charm showing itself. The latter part of his long story ran somewhat as follows: —

"And now," said he, pausing for a moment in his tale, — "and now I come to the miserable little incident that began the end. So contemptible that incident seems, in all its surroundings, that it shames me to think of it; yet it was serious enough in its meaning. One day in May (this was in 1878) I was with Boscowitz. In those times he still kept his second-hand bookstore, well up town, on E—— Street. The 'Warrior' was published at a God-forsaken little office down town; but most of the writing was done in the back-office of Boscowitz's book concern. It was a damp, dingy place, that back-office. It had been leaking at every shower all through the previous rainy season. It was still clammy and miserable, although Boscowitz's shop was neat and even pretentious in the front part. But all the rear alcoves, shelves, and store-rooms were full of dust and rotten old books. Boscowitz was a curious sort of business man in those days. He hung on to his stock like a puppy to a root. He used to lose a hundred customers for the sake of cheating one, and you would often say that he carried on his business for the purely æsthetic pleasure of making would-be purchasers ferocious, and hearing 'em swear at his prices. He was as overbearing as he is now, but withal he was as keen as a razor, for he already had made his shop a perfect bureau of information for his own use. Small politicians assembled in his back-room, played cards, drank his whiskey, and were prepared to follow his leadership. By certain pretenses of knowing where rare books could be got at, and how to stock libraries for rich numskulls, Boscowitz also kept himself on good terms with a better sort of people, whom he could cheat without offense, and bleed without first having to bully them. For them his front shelves were stocked. He even had, near his front window, a well-lighted alcove, fitted up as a sort of reading-room, where well-to-do customers were invited to sit and examine books, or to read a few of the current magazines. By this double-ended sort of establishment, rich noodles in front, impecunious scoundrels in the rear, Boscowitz really accomplished his purpose of being up in every sort of gossip, and having relations with all kinds of people. The success of the 'Warrior' has since sent him into other fields of industry, and the rats have long ere this eaten the rotten books that filled the most of his shop. But at that time he was still confined to this method. And, as the 'Warrior' was quite a new thing, people in general had n't yet quite fathomed his designs.

"As I said, I had been that morning working on manuscript for Boscowitz, in the rear of his shop, — for, of course, my end was the scoundrels' end of the place, — when he himself was called to the front for a little time. When he came back he was looking very jolly and triumphant. 'I ve just had a talk with two very excellent ladies,' he said, — 'good customers they are, and yet better game.' I 've got half a dozen personals out of 'em, without their knowing it.' And he chuckled heartily.

"Perhaps you are n't really acquainted with Boscowitz. If you are n't, you won't easily understand what followed between us. That fellow is the strangest compound of brutality and sensibility that I ever saw. He is a keen judge of men's characters and feelings, and yet he has nothing of what you 'd commonly call sympathy or consideration for anybody, save once in a while and by caprice. He really understands the people that he meets as readily as if he were a most delicate and tender-minded person; and yet he misuses most of these people as if he were a perfect brute. I am, indeed, an exception in this respect. We are n't exactly affectionate, but, to be sure, he has always been honest and frank enough to me, and I 've really little personal antipathy to him, despite all his meanness. But most of the world he regards merely as his tools, and he studies them as cleverly as he maltreats them cruelly. He has a very strange voice, harsh like a crow's, and generally, though not always, he speaks with a violent tone of self-assertion. His accent, you know, is not exactly foreign, though you 'd see somehow at once that he 's no pure American. His good side, as shown to me, consists in his plain-spoken fidelity to one whom he regards as a useful assistant in his undertakings. I have found him even generous, and at times seemingly very thoughtful for my comfort, although I know that also to be mere caprice on his part.

"'Well, who are the ladies?' I said, without looking up from my work. 'Oh, persons that I think you know about,' Boscowitz replied, with a rather unpleasant good humor in his air. 'I can't say,' he went on, 'whether I dare name 'em to you or not. I think you 'll not love 'em overmuch.' 'What excellent ladies are these that I know and don't like?' I responded, — 'and plainly they must be noted ladies, too,' I added. 'I 'm not so great a man as to despise noted acquaintances,' I went on, ironically; 'and I 'm good-hearted enough to be generally very fond of such ladies as ever take a second look at me. Perhaps, though,' I continued, 'they may be wives or relatives of some of my old colleagues at the Sunset College. Those, I think, I could indeed well spare.' Boscowitz laughed. 'Worse 'n that,' he said. His laugh was harsh and a little mean, for he had chosen for the moment to show me no consideration, just as I, for my part, had no sort of consideration for him when, in reply, I told him he might be hanged for his mysterious airs, and that if he had anything to say he might speak up. There were never any manners lost yet between me and Boscowitz, my boy; and we 've consequently always known where to find each other. So the old fellow stopped his laugh, but he kept a sort of sneer on his face while he replied, 'They are the widow Dover and her mother.' I was simply puzzled, and I asked him, in a tone of the sincerest amazement, why in thunder the widow Dover and her mother should be anything to me, as friends or as enemies. 'You 're a good gossip,' I said, 'old man, but you 've blundered this time.' I wondered, of course, whether my ancient defense of old Peter Dover could be in his mind, somehow. That, thought I, would be the funniest gossip yet. But no, it was n't that. He only looked at me sharply a second, and then turned away. I minded my business, of course, and had no more to say. I was writing, and I clean forgot the affair. But perhaps an hour later, the back-office being then quite empty of all but us two, Boscowitz came again, seated himself on a tall pivot chair beside me, and fell to nursing his knee, and to looking at me with his sharp, keen little eyes. You know, Harold, his ugly sallow face, with its mixture of cunning, greed, and intelligence. Yet, as you also know, Boscowitz manages with all this to look somehow like a very able man, and he can be as civil as you could wish when he pleases. He has a genius for influencing men, after all, or so rough a customer as he is would never have been so successful. But, as I was saying, he looked at me keenly a minute, and then began: 'Escott, I admire your good sense.' 'Thank you,' said I. 'Is that all?' 'No,' said he. 'I want to tell you what I remarked about you, the other day, to some of the boys.' 'Go on,' I said, 'only be sure you tell me something that I don't know already.' 'No,' said Boscowitz, 'that I sha'n't. I'll only tell you an honest man's opinion of you. Some of the boys were laughing at you for becoming just now what they called a little worldly-minded, after being so lofty and soaring a fellow heretofore. And I said to them that you could be lofty for yourself and sensible for your children, and that I admired a man the more who looked out for his own flesh and blood, even if he was indifferent to himself.' 'See here, Boscowitz,' I replied, 'if you're wanting to borrow money of me, it 's no use, for I 'm dead broke; but if you 're trying to flatter me for any other reason, hold off. I'm as soaring in mind for my children as I choose to be, and that 's my own business any way. And as for myself, I crawl round and shift for my living as I may, and ask no fine speeches from any man, and you know it. So what are you driving at, after all?' 'Well,' he said, 'I was curious, just because we are such old friends now, to find out from you what is your real opinion of your future son-in-law, Tom Eldon. I know him, and he puzzles me, and I thought you might understand his past life better than I do.' 'My opinion of him,' I said, 'is that he is to be, as you say, my son-in-law, and long has been as good as my son, in any case. And that 's all I have to say about his past life or his present either.' 'So you mean,' Boscowitz answered, 'that his past life seems to you to call for no comments.' By this time I was fighting mad, and I asked Boscowitz, with the aid of whatever good word came to me handle first, what he might have to do between Tom Eldon and me any way. 'Nothing,' he said, 'only indeed you 're a more practical man than I used to think, and I congratulate you.' I considered a minute over what he had just been saying, and then kept on with my strong language, while I assured him that if he wanted to use my own failings for his personal-column he could use me and be blessed. But as a plain matter of fact, I said, if anybody from this time henceforth ever again hinted that a recent engagement between Tom Eldon and a certain person (who should be nameless in that back-office of his until it should be a deal cleaner place than now) was an engagement for the sake of money, then the person who so hinted would be *not* a practical man, but a blessed liar. That, I said, might be the end of this conversation, and I hoped he would so regard it. Boscowitz never flinched. 'If you were any other man,' he said, 'than the poet and the fine-feeling person that, for all your bad language, I know you to be, I should n't wonder at you; and if I were anybody but your friend, I should n't inquire about your affairs. But now tell me one thing more: did you really mean it this morning when you said that to hear the widow Dover's name did n't in the least displease you? I ask again, because we want to know each other in this office, and there never yet has been any concealment between us.'

"Boscowitz was so blunt and so persistent with his insolence that I could n't for the life of me kick him, as I wanted to. 'I don't know anything about the widow Dover,' I said, 'except that God made her and Dover married her. Are you satisfied now?' 'No, I'm not,' said Boscowitz, 'and surely you 'll see that I 'm your real friend when I go on to declare before God himself' (Boscowitz always likes this sort of talk) 'that no private interest of mine, save the warmest friendship for you, makes me anxious to have you understand about this matter. You speak of Tom Eldon as in effect your son for years. Don't you know, then, that meanwhile his attentions to the widow Dover have caused much gossip? Don't you know that they 've been engaged to be married two or three times, and have broken it off as many, to the great amusement of the young club-men, Tom's friends? Don't you know that last time, as people say, she jilted him without any sort of quarrel, for pure fun, and that just afterwards, when his heart was supposed to be broken, his engagement with your daughter was heard of? Most people think it only his device to spite the widow, and in consequence people think that it puts your family in a very practical light. All that,' he went on, 'I know either at first hand or otherwise, but well enough to suit me. I did n't think it a very serious thing, of course. I laughed at it, as everybody did. I supposed you knew it. I thought, like all the boys, that you yourself wanted the present engagement for the sake of Tom Eldon's money. I did n't blame you. It surprised me a little that you should be the man to do it, but I 've defended you. I thought, meanwhile, that you were fair game, of course, and that 's why I mentioned those two women, and laughed as I did it. As it is, I beg your pardon.' I suppose that all this while Boscowitz must have been seeing something odd in my face, and must have gathered therefrom that all this stupid gossip had decidedly more meaning for me than for him. He closed in quite a considerate tone. For my part, I saw in *his* face that what he was telling me was perfectly sincere, and must be well founded. But I looked out of the window a little, and then called him a liar outright, with further additions, and left the shop. He looked after me with a really friendly concern, and now did n't answer me by so much as a laugh or a word.

"Of course, when I got outside I perceived that nothing was very clear in my mind, and that I had behaved like a fool. I wandered about, however, rather aimlessly, for an hour or more. Then I went back, pretended that I had been out to take my lunch, and said to Boscowitz that I hoped he would n't remember my last words. He was in the best of humors, and held out his hand. I took it, and thereupon assured him that I wanted a clear understanding with him then and there. Whoever Tom Eldon had been engaged to before he became engaged to my daughter was, I observed, none of my business, nor Boscowitz's either. Tom, I went on, might have courted all the widows that had ever been made by political squabbles, or, for that matter, by vigilance committees. I cared nothing for the whole army of rich widows since Jezebel. Meanwhile, whoever said that my daughter was engaged to Tom Eldon for his money was a liar, with embellishments and qualifications as aforesaid, and ought to be shot. 'And now, Boscowitz,' I added, 'if you ever mention my daughter's name again in this rat-hole of yours, I 'll wring your infernal neck, and use your old hide to mend the leaks in your miserable ceiling there.' So with this we were at peace again, and no more was said about the thing before I left the place for the day. I worked very long and hard, and tried to keep my mind quiet.

"If you 've seen how sentimental I was about Tom, Harold, you 'll understand my mood as I set out towards home. What could I do? Should I go to Tom and demand explanation? That idea was the only sensible one, of course, but it frightened me inexpressibly. What could I say to Ellen, or how meet her? Had you been near by, Harold, I should have run over the bay to you. But, alas! you were not to be thought of. You had left the country months before. I thought of our old friend Williamson, and at length I determined to go to him.

"His lodgings were n't far away, but the walk seemed to be a long one. The day was cold, and I was suffering with neuralgic pains. I seemed, also, to be a little blind, and once on the way I found myself almost under a horse's feet. I remember that I stopped and quarreled with the driver two or three minutes, and we said all sorts of disagreeable things. May be he thought I was drunk. At last I got to Williamson's lodgings, and climbed the stairs to his room. He ought by rights to have been at home by that time of day, but he was n't. I felt, somehow, very blank and very angry at not finding him there. Despite all my neuralgic pains, I stood about for a long time in the hall and at the head of the stairs, in the cold draughts. I got up a long talk with the negro janitor about politics and religion. He said, I remember, that he thought everybody might be saved, except Alonzo Eldon, who had just frozen all the boys out on a big operation in mining stocks. The negro janitor had been nipped with the rest, for of course he speculated, and hence his present theological views. He did n't see any use for hell, he said, if Alonzo stayed out of it. We also talked about neuralgia and kindred disorders, and I recall the old fellow's tone of whining vanity as he described to me his own tremendous sufferings with rheumatism. Finally, I grew too impatient, and wandered off. But on the street, near the door, I met Williamson. He looked surprised at my woe-begone appearance, for by this time I was pretty well exhausted with my twinges; and when he had got me up-stairs once more, he made me lie on his sofa, stirred up his fire, and gave me hot whiskey and water. I was as sulky as you please, for it riled me all the more to be treated like a baby; so, as soon as I could, I began with my business. Williamson is a neat little fellow, I 've always thought, — just a trifle ineffective, but always well-meaning, and at heart as good and true as pure gold. His face showed immense concern, for he saw at once what this bit of news, coming so suddenly, must mean to me, who had made of Tom a very idol. Of course, I said, anybody must admit that Tom had a right to pay court to the new love as soon as he was free of the old one, even if he had been engaged to the widow fifty times. I did n't deny that. What offended me was, of course, only the boy's concealment, his failure to deal frankly with us, and the shock to my own foolish and sentimental notions about him. But then, to be sure, I added, that what made it worse was Boscowitz's tone, which plainly showed how he regarded the thing as meaning more still than the facts on their face would seem to indicate. Thus, you see, I tried to state my case as calmly as possible, without any exaggeration. I did n't even do it justice.

"Williamson's first answer to me was to inquire, in a very quiet and reasonable way, why, after all, then, I still seemed to want Tom, who was now a man of full thirty years, to have had no previous affairs of the heart, in order to be a good suitor for my daughter. And why could n't a young man, by rights, keep his little affairs to himself, if he chose? Why was that a lack of frankness? Even the most sentimental woman, he said, could easily make up her mind to being her husband's second, or, for that matter, his twenty-second love, if only she could be sure that this time he was a true lover. That was an every-day affair. Why should I be more exacting than a woman?

"'Williamson,' I replied, 'you know better than to put me off this way. This thing's different. If Boscowitz is right, Tom, after a long, and, as it seems, not perfectly admirable affair with the widow Dover, all of which he absolutely concealed from me, was jilted. Forthwith, mark you, — not after a little decent waiting, but at once, — he turned to us, who, because of my last long illness, were at the moment almost dependent on him, — dependent on him, do you hear? — there 's one point of the sting, — and whom he thought good game, and he claimed my daughter in as off-hand a way as if she was his lawful inheritance. This he does to spite the widow, and he does it so openly that, though we remain perfectly ignorant and duped, people like Boscowitz stand by and laugh at us for eating such humble pie so meekly. Boscowitz thinks it perfectly plain, under such circumstances, that we must find Tom's money good enough to comfort us for being the mere instruments of his spite against Mrs. Dover. Now, think, Williamson,' I said, 'this happens not in case of an ordinary suitor, but in case of Tom, who has almost lived in my house, and whom I thought of as my own son long before I dreamed of him as Ellen's lover. I have worshiped Tom, you know,' I said, 'and to have him treat me so is altogether too much. My question to you is, what is the truth in Boscowitz's yarn?'

"Williamson listened to me very quietly till I was done, and then, indeed, he made no more attempt to argue with me on preliminaries. He knew Tom as a club friend of his, he said. At the club the supposed affair — 'mind you,' Williamson said, 'the supposed affair' — between Tom and Mrs. Dover had been occasionally talked about for the last two or three years, perhaps more. Not as if there had been any scandal,— quite the contrary; but she was both a wealthy widow, and a beautiful woman, well known in her own little society, a favorite in a select circle of prominent people, and, on the whole, a person of mark, in a good sense. She was herself not at all fond of notoriety, Williamson declared, but her family and her position inevitably made her a somewhat distinguished lady. Now, Tom had been a caller at her house for a long time, and within these two or three years people had constantly supposed him a suitor; but Mrs. Dover, if she was n't precisely a flirt, was, at least, fond of admiration, and quite able to keep a suitor at a distance. As for engagements, therefore, made, broken off, and begun again, Williamson was n't sure how much truth there was in the story of them; but none had ever been actually announced. Gossip had probably created them out of blue air. Of course, Boscowitz would speak confidently, because that was his trade, and he represented gossip. Yet Williamson could n't doubt, after all, that Tom, at least, had been in earnest in his suit for Mrs. Dover's hand, and that there had recently been some misunderstanding between him and Mrs. Dover,— very shortly, too, before the date of Tom's engagement with Ellen. So much Williamson was bound to say.

"When Williamson had finished I talked to him like a fool. I asked him why he had n't ever dropped me any hint of all this. I upbraided him for neglecting me so. If I was an outcast, I said, and a poor man, who had even been Tom's dependent for a while, that was no reason why I should be Tom's dupe. My daughter and I, I said, had had one thing to give, so far as Tom was concerned, and that was the charge of our sacred honor, the gift of our perfect trust, of our unbounded love and confidence. What had we ever concealed from Tom? Was it fair, merely because we — that is, my little daughter and I — were a pair of innocent lovers, ignorant of the ways of the world about us, separated from society, lost in our dreams, for Tom to play on us as on a pipe? 'Boscowitz and his public notoriety be hanged!' I said. 'He 's a liar, and always was. What hurts me is not the notoriety that he lied about, but the real wrong that he made known to me. My nearest friend,' I said, 'has betrayed both myself, who am nobody, and the perfect love of my little daughter, which is everything.' I know not what Williamson and I said further. I only know that at last he got a coupé and drove me home, where I, by his urgent advice, determined to say nothing further about the thing that night, to eat my supper alone, as the family were through by this time, and so soon as I had eaten supper to plead neuralgia, and to go to bed alone, forbidding anybody to disturb me until late the next morning. In fact, I was suffering severely from my twinges. But I needed 'em, that time, for company.

"Those are terrible nights, Harold, that we

spend alone, as we all at some time do, face to face with our hopeless blunders. For I now saw, of course, that, whatever part Tom had had in this, I alone was to blame for his power to do us any such wrong. And it was a wrong that, for me, was worse than a far greater wrong would have seemed to some men. My great failure as professor had driven me mad, I perceived, after all. I had said to myself that if the world did n't need me, the world might go hang. And so I had turned my back on the world. I had stubbornly cut myself off from knowing anything about anybody. Save a few young men whom I too seldom saw, men who were n't exactly worldly-minded,—save, then, such friends as you, and Williamson, and Tom Eldon, I had refused to meet a soul. I had passed old friends on the street, because they had spoken against me. I had clean forgotten people who had once been close to me, because I had first learned to hate them. And the pity had been that I had felt so gloriously free and strong in doing this. 'Give me my home and my one or two friends,' I had said, 'and I defy the whole accursed pack of fools wherewith the world is filled.' I had been so proud, too, of the fact that, even while I got my living from the newspapers, I knew and cared nothing any longer for their readers, their gossip, their reporters, or their politics. I had remained a critic clever enough for the papers ; I had known, in a business way, what I needed to know of the persons whom, as artists or as authors, I criticised; I had been a good sketch-writer on topics of a general character; I had read current books; and I had dealt on good terms with the editors of the papers; but whatever did not directly concern me I had utterly ignored. I had rejoiced to be able to sit in a newspaper office for hours, day after day, without having more than strictly business intercourse with the editor-in-chief and a bare acquaintance with most of the force. I had refused to recognize the advances of other people. I had been even rude in order to preserve my isolation. Such, then, had been my defiance of the world's meanness. Thus I had earned my liberty; but thus, too, I had earned my new calamity. Here was my nearest friend, my comrade, the one whom I had fondly called my son after the spirit. With him I had lived almost daily for years; yet I had known nothing of him. Every gossip whom I had most despised had learned more of him than I had. Every fool had seen that I was his dupe; and meanwhile I had been worshiping him. To be sure, this vexation of mine was, indeed, nothing, after all. But Ellen, — to what had not my isolation of her whole life condemned her? She had learned to follow my ways, and despise the world at large. She had gone to school for a time, but had refused to make any friends. She had been hated at school for her shyness and her eccentricity, and had rejoiced in the fact. And this was the life to which I had condemned her: one being alone, beyond the circle of her own family, she had learned to love, and he regarded her as a tool!

" To-morrow, meanwhile, I should have to talk with Ellen — and with Tom. I knew that her love for him was far more innocent and trusting still than mine. I knew that she thought his love as perfect and simple as her own. I knew that he had deceived her, too, as well as me. I knew that this deceit, coming in just this form, must destroy her happiness whenever she learned of it. So tender and single-hearted a love as hers could not bear to be so coarsely wounded. No explanation that he could give would bring back the old days of absolute faith. We had nothing to look forward to but a bitter misunderstanding, and perhaps a final parting. Perhaps, I say, for my mind is always sanguine, and despite my bitterness the feeling would again and again come back that after all a man of sense must n't be so squeamish, that Tom might have a right to his own affairs, that the whole thing might be explained, that I was a fool to worry over a young man's past fancies, and that, in short, my lonesome life must be making me into a brooding old idiot. And at last I found myself bitterly repeating, as I lay there hour after hour, that nothing whatever matters in a world which is made for the worms and for the final darkness."

" But after all, Harold, life is so much wealthier than our miserable comments upon it! When I awoke next morning from a short sleep of two hours or so into which I had at last fallen, all my reflections of the night seemed idle and worthless.

My plain business was to hunt up Tom, and to speak to him simply and frankly, as a father would to his son. I had trusted the boy. I must continue to trust him so long as possible. If there had been any misunderstanding, or any lack of ingenuousness on his part, or any other source of mischief, we must find it out, and if possible make an end of it. Meanwhile, it was useless to condemn him unheard, or to worry Ellen by talking of the matter to her in advance of consulting him. I had plainly been an old dolt to worry so absurdly all day yesterday. Worry was not a man's part. I felt very cool and firm as I rose and dressed, and I was already busy planning how quietly and plainly I should speak to Tom when I should meet him that morning, and how quickly and easily we might be able to settle the whole matter. I ought to tell you that this day was Saturday.

"At breakfast-time I assured the family that my neuralgia had left me, and that I should now go about my business as usual. But fair little Ellen, who had kept her blue eyes on me all through breakfast, followed me into the front entry as I was about to leave, and stopped me. 'Father,' she said, with an agitated air that seemed to me very odd in her, 'what have you had on your mind last night and this morning? Please do tell me, I have been so worried all night.' 'Why, Ellen,' I answered, 'you surely know all about me. I 've been a little ill, of course, and that made me moody.' 'No, father,' she went on, 'that 's bad enough, but it is n't that I 'm so worried about. What *have* I been doing to you that 's wrong?' 'Nothing under heaven, my darling,' I responded. 'And what can have put such a notion into your head?' 'Why, last night,' she said, almost crying as she spoke (and Ellen very seldom shed tears), 'when you came in, you seemed so strange — I don't know — I saw it was something beside your illness. I begged that I might sit beside you while you ate your supper (you looked so mournful trying to eat all alone), or might read to you for a time while you should lie on the sofa and get warm, — you were so cold. But you, father, said out loud, not to me but to yourself, "No, not Ellen! Ellen least of all just now." What is it, father, that made you speak so?' Ellen could only just keep her voice through this speech, while, as for me, I could n't remember, and I cannot now remember in the least having used any such words to her or to myself. I must have come home pretty well dazed with my troubles, you perceive. But now I tried as I could to comfort Ellen, and to reassure her by any fib that I could think of. It was plain she had jumped at once to the conclusion that I was somehow either angry with her, or worried about her affairs. In trying to convince her, however, that what I was troubled about had no connection with her, I indeed soon saw that, taken by surprise as I was, my hesitating manner was in itself a confession. At last I hit on a compromise. 'To be sure,' I said,

'I have a matter or two on my mind that may concern you and all of us. I had, to speak frankly, a little set-to with Boscowitz yesterday, and the consequence of such things may always be vexatious when one is in my position. That is all, I assure you, Ellen. Of course I am a trifle afraid of you whenever my affairs go the least wrong, for you know, Ellen, that you always were my little conscience. But now that those twinges are gone from my nerves, I have recovered all the spirits that I had lost, and feel sure that I can set everything right to-day. I feel perfectly confident, I pledge you.' As I went on with this stupid mixture of lies and truth I grew, indeed, more confident in tone, and felt myself certain of avoiding any premature explanation to Ellen just now. She looked down while I was speaking, but when I finished she gave me one more very searching look with her deep blue eyes, and then dropped them again. She was very disappointed, and even, I thought, a trifle hurt and offended. As for me, I stood somehow hesitating an instant, and not taking advantage of the chance to retreat, while she remained with her eyes still cast down, and her hands nervously joined.

"At length I said, not knowing how else to get away, 'Ellen, won't you bid me good-by?' 'Good-by,' she answered, very coldly and stiffly, and started to walk back into the library. 'Oh, Ellen!' I burst out, all my foolishness and my physical weakness uniting to overcome me. 'Forgive your lying old father. It was indeed about you that I was troubled. And you have done nothing wrong, — nothing. I am not angry with you in the least. Only some things will trouble me when I think of your future. I can't explain just yet, but I do hope that all will be well.' She came back to me at once, for I was not used to speak to her in such a tone, and she looked really anxious at the instant, not about herself, but about me. 'You poor father,' she began, taking my hand, 'you must not leave the house to-day. You look so ill.' 'Yes, I must,' I replied; and now thoroughly frightened at myself for making such a mess of my secret, I hurried off without more than one glance behind. That glance showed me Ellen's troubled face, watching me from the window as I walked to my car.

"First, of course, I rode down to Boscowitz's office, and excused myself for the morning, pleading another engagement. Then I started to hunt up Tom. He lived quite alone, in those days, rather far out on the —— Street cable railway, in a house of his own. As I sat in the car, I found my agitation about the expected meeting singularly and very unpleasantly growing. I have often had the oddest experience, Harold, as to this matter of agitation. All through the long Peter Dover fight, though I was frequently angry and excited, I never once felt the sort of agitation that sometimes fairly takes away your voice when you are about to address one man, or a company. But on dozens of occasions in my life I have been overcome by such an agitation, perhaps in the presence of some very near friend, or when talking about a matter of almost no importance. It 's all a sign of weak nerves and wits, I suppose. Doubtless a screw 's lose somewhere.

"This feeling, then, I know very well. By the time I had reached Tom's door it was very vexatious. I feared lest I should be quite unable to address him in a manly way when the moment should come for our mutual explanation. But I knew by experience that long waiting would only make matters worse. So, as soon as I found myself at his lodgings, I rang his door-bell stoutly, and waited for an answer. The Chinaman who at last responded to the bell stared at me a little sullenly, and said sternly: 'He go way yessaday, he no heah. You cum nex' Tussday. He no heah.' I stood like one thunderstruck. I can hardly tell why, only something about that Chinaman's cheerless face was depressing in itself; and I found myself reflecting in amazement, 'How should Tom have gone without telling me? Has he deserted us? Next Thursday, indeed? And this Saturday? How shall we live?' I spoke again after a moment: 'Has he gone away from the city? He lef' city?' I repeated myself, using more of our customary jargon the second time, you see, as we always do in presence of one of those stolid Chinese faces. 'You cum Tussday. He cum back Tussday. He no heah till Tussday,' reiterated the Chinaman, with unmoved sternness, and I found myself alone on the steps.

I retreated with a feeling of the deepest vexation. Was I to be turned from his door? I angrily asked myself. Then I reflected again. Why had Tom this new servant? for I had never seen the stupid fellow before. Did this change mean anything? And Ellen, — had not her strange manner in the morning also meant more than it had seemed to mean? Had she perhaps not known already of Tom's departure? Was it not conceivable that they had quarreled? I was in a world of mysteries. Above all, this stupid suspense vexed me. You see how imbecile I was with my suspicions about this Chinaman and about Ellen's manner and about Tom's absence, all flung into a heap together in my mind; but at any rate there was no work for me to-day until things should be cleared up. I therefore returned to Boscowitz's shop, gave my ill-health as a reason why I had concluded not to appear at all for my work on this day, and then walked homewards. As the 'Warrior' was published on Saturday, my presence at Boscowitz's desk was in any case little needed. Ellen was looking out of the window, as I came up, just as if she had been there expecting me to return all the while since I left. My wife was of course much surprised to see me, but to her also, as to Boscowitz, I gave my ill-health as sufficient reason, and announced that I would lie on the library sofa, with Ellen for my company, until I should feel better. Ellen followed me without a word, covered me, when I lay down on the sofa, with a long afghan, and then seated herself on a low cricket close beside me, her face turned towards my own. One of her hands held mine very gently, while the other rested on the edge of the sofa. Her eyes now looked very frankly and anxiously into my face, but for a long time she remained quiet, while I hardly dared to glance at her. What should I say? I felt that I ought by rights to tell her nothing, and that I had nevertheless come home for the express purpose of telling her everything. Meanwhile, how much did she herself know already? To blurt things out, as Boscowitz had done, would be simply brutal. Yet perchance she was already beyond the need of any instruction from me.

"'Ellen,' I said at last, 'you knew that Tom had left town, did n't you?' 'Yes, of course,' she answered, looking a trifle frightened. 'What do you mean?' 'Why, then,' I went on, 'have n't you told me before? I did n't know anything about him, and don't know now. I 've just been to see him. His Chinaman met me at the door, and told me he was gone, and would n't be back until Thursday. I was very anxious to find him.' 'Why so, father?' 'That 's my lookout,' I answered. 'Have n't I a right to hunt up Tom? What I asked was why you did n't tell me of his going.' I spoke to her a little harshly, I confess, but that was only a blind to hide my characteristic agitation, which was now once more coming over me with a vengeance. 'Father,' she said, 'why are you angry with Tom? I know now that you aren't angry with me. What has Tom done?' 'Don't ask me,' I responded curtly. The answer was the worst I could have given, of course, unless I wanted to be as brutal as Boscowitz, but for my life I could n't see how to take it back, and so I went on just to cover up my agitation and to fill up time: 'That accursed Chinaman,— I felt as if he must have been put there to drive me off! He looked so mean with his miserable "you cum Tussday." I hated him.' 'But, father,' insisted Ellen, 'Tom did n't tell me that anything was wrong between you and himself. I won't have it. If he has been offending you, he shall suffer for it, be sure. He has to obey me now, at least. How could he have made you feel so, you poor man?' She was overflowing with pity for me, dear girl, for she saw my excitement; but at this point, since the mischief seemed to me once for all done, and I saw that I was too much worked up to control myself or to spare her, I let it all out with a rush, far more brutally, I fear, than Boscowitz himself could have done. You must remember, Harold, my nervousness and weakness. No man in the physical state that I was then in could have behaved very wisely, but I have never forgiven myself since for the cruel way in which I then hurled the whole thing upon her: Boscowitz's sneers, Tom's reported treachery, Mrs. Dover's past triumphs, and all the miserable gossip. It was in vain that, when the words were once out, I began to try to explain to her how the whole thing might still be nonsense, and how, in any case, during the night, I had more than once resolved to accept without serious question whatever account Tom might choose to give, and to let his bygone affairs be bygone. All my mass of words, at first coming in husky and broken tones, afterwards running glibly and even almost calmly, from my tongue (as my excitement wore itself out), she heard without speaking, her face flushed and bitter, her eyes cast down, her hands playing first with mine, then with each other, then fiercely with the edge of the afghan. At length I finished. A long pause followed. I was now feeling very repentant and not a little exhausted, for the night, after all, had been a hard one. I longed to find the right word to undo the mischief I had wrought, but I could say no more. At last she spoke, very slowly and with great difficulty, every fibre of her body tense and rigid, her fingers still fiercely teasing the afghan. 'If — it — were n't — that you seem — somehow—to believe — all this — I should have to hate you — for being able — to say a word of it.' 'Oh, no, Ellen!' I cried. 'I can't believe it. It must n't be true. Oh, if Tom were only here! Where has he gone? You have n't yet told me that.' She had turned from me, and was looking towards the opposite wall. 'Ellen, I repeated, 'won't you tell me where Tom has gone?' She rose, walked very firmly to the library window, and looked out into the street for a while. I was silent, too, and terrified. I began to get up to go to her, feeling all the while what an old wretch I had been to let her know of this in such a way. But she and I had lived so near together in heart and mind for so long! How could I have kept such a secret from her at this moment, however much I had tried? At last she turned to me again. Her face was very calm now, though it was very pale. Her whole body was as tense and as rigidly erect as ever. Her voice was quite firm. 'I don't know in the least where Tom has gone. I think you were asking me about him just now, were n't you?' With this she turned and left the library. I heard her go up-stairs to her own room. There was nothing more to do for the time but to wait and to worry. And so the rest of that day passed, and the night."

CHAPTER V.

A WEARY SUNDAY.

"NEITHER Ellen nor I had any thought of trying the next day to discover where Tom had gone. In fact, Ellen had been right when she said that he had not told her. Exactly what he had said to her by way of explaining his absence, I never found out. At all events, he had not given her any clue to his whereabouts between this and Thursday. He had called on Friday, the day of my interview with Boscowitz, and had taken his leave. He was meaning to go out of town on special business. More of his account of himself was never repeated to me. Whatever it was, it must of course have been a lie. As for me, so soon as I was convinced of Ellen's ignorance, I saw nothing before us but some very tedious waiting until Thursday. There would be no dignity in trying to hunt up Tom in person, even had I the time and health for it. But poor Ellen's wounded spirits seemed to me very piteous. Bitterly I lamented my selfishness, and my nervous agitation, and my inability to bear the burden cheerfully and alone. Surely I had not lightened my load by increasing hers. But there was no help for it now.

"That Sunday was one of the days that we get in May-time, just before the fogs begin, and when our spring is dying. It was as clear as crystal, the air was delightfully warm and gentle, and the dullness in-doors was trebly hateful in such weather. Thus it was that Ellen and I, feeling of course quite alone in the midst of the family, by reason of these our unhappy confidences, both tacitly reached the plan to take a little outing together in the afternoon. You will see at once, Harold, when I take the trouble to mention this, that I am coming to something of a very simple nature. We took our outing — and we met Tom. That is, after all, a very small thing, is n't it? We, or rather I should say Ellen, met him, and he was in company. That is really the whole story of that afternoon. But the manner of it needs, perhaps, a few words more.

"He could not have thought such a meeting in the least a probable contingency, because he knew our habits, and we had taken no such outing as we then took for years, if ever. The Oakland boats, you know, are, at a certain hour Sunday afternoon, not very well filled with people leaving the city, while the crowds returning at that time make the west-bound boats quite lively. Now, since I could not very well walk far, and since we had no special plans, and had started rather late, it was after all not strange that for this one time Ellen and I should find ourselves on an afternoon ferry-boat, bound east, and intending to do no more than perhaps, after crossing the bay, to ride out, and directly back, on one of the local trains. We reached the boat only some three minutes before she left. We seated ourselves at first at the rear end of the cabin deck, just on the south side of the great cabin, and together we looked off towards the San Mateo hills. The bay was as calm as a river. There were only a very few people near us. We knew none of them. We had little to say to each other, but that little was on indifferent matters. Ellen's treatment of me, since the talk of yesterday, had been the gentlest and sweetest possible. She had never returned, save for one moment, and in answer to a question of mine, to the great topic. She spoke, if at all, of pleasant and, if possible, of decidedly amusing things. Her voice was often quite caressing in its playfulness. At moments she had been even vivacious. There was no trace of the bitterness of yesterday anywhere discoverable in her manner. We now spoke of the scenery, queried how much one could really see of Redwood City from where we sat, and wondered about the foreign man-of-war that we passed in the stream. We had reached the end of Goat Island, and were passing along quite near the south shore of it when I, notwithstanding my so warm winter overcoat, which Ellen had carefully made me bring with me, began to feel cold. In those days I had n't suffered so much with my aches and pains as I since have done, or I should never have been sitting out there on deck at all. Ellen had from the first urged me to go in, but I had a spirit of bravado about me in those times, which was even stronger than my love of fresh air itself. Well, I rose at last to get into the cabin, and entered by the southwest door. But Ellen was enjoying the air so much that I begged her to wait outside. I had hardly got in, however, before I saw Ellen rise, walk round by the west end of the cabin to the Goat Island side of the boat, and pass along slowly forwards. She had always loved the island, and also those northern hills on the Contra Costa, about Grizzly Peak, and I knew that she was hunting up her favorite views. Much, however, was I surprised to see her again, a moment later, walking rapidly back again, past the wheel-house on the island side, and then, through the door on that side, entering the cabin close by where I sat. Her veil was down, a change which also much astonished me, and her step was very nervous, even the least trifle unsteady. She looked about an instant, as if not seeing me, and then nestled down, as it were, close beside me, — so quickly and so helplessly did she sink into her seat. 'Why, Ellen,' I said, in a low and rather startled tone, fearing that the passengers at this end of the great cabin, although they were but few, might observe her singular manner, 'what has happened?' She caught her breath and laughed, — a little nervous laugh it was. 'Oh, it's so funny,' she said joyfully. 'I saw Tom.' 'Tom?' I queried in a sort of terror, but still in a low voice. 'Was he alone?' 'No,' she answered, confidentially, and with another laugh, 'he was with ever such a lady, so tall and dark-eyed and stately. I shall never let Tom hear the last of it. It's so funny. Oh, was n't I most running, though, to get away? But they did n't see me. It was magnificent to slip off so.' Her tone was one of fairly childish triumph, and she laughed yet again, but she was trembling all over. I could say nothing. 'Father,' she went on, after a little pause, still with the same gleeful tone of childish excitement, 'if you really don't want me to faint, you must take me down-stairs at once, at the rear end of the boat, down to the lower deck. There won't be anybody much out there at the back. And I must hide. Think only, — they might come in here. What should I do? Take me down quick, or I'll jump overboard.' I had never heard such a strange tone in her voice. I could see her expression through her veil, and it was all a confused mixture of laughter and fright. I arose at once, and together we went out by the door through which I had just entered, and found our way downstairs, where we stood, close behind the great shut folding-doors of the lower-deck passage-way. I think all these odd doings must have aroused some attention, for I remember that two or three persons looked at us very curiously through the glass doors, or over the railing of the cabin deck; but for the most part I was too much absorbed in Ellen and the gloomy thoughts of the moment to care about anything else. She talked almost incessantly, in the same low tone and with the same childish excitement, almost all the while we stood there. She volunteered the assurance that Tom's companion was Mrs. Dover. She had once seen Mrs. Dover, and could never forget her. Mrs. Dover was a great beauty, simply lovely, and today she looked fairer than ever. For the rest, we must not leave the boat, when we should reach the other shore. We must stay where we were. Ellen would not move from the place. We must go back with the boat, and get home as soon as we could. We had had pleasure enough for one day. That was sure.

"I shall never forget the anxiety of those few moments that passed before the boat landed. Ellen's manner seemed to me so strange that I should not have wondered at any instant if she had actually tried to leap overboard. The impossibility of finding any explanation for Tom's conduct, the puzzle what we should do next, and the doubt whether, after all, she had really seen Tom, helped to make the suspense unbearable. I asked her whether she was quite sure that it was really Tom she had seen, and in answer she described to me in full his dress and attitude and Mrs. Dover's appearance. It was wonderful how much she had taken in at a glance. I inwardly resolved to leave nothing undone, both that evening and the next day, to solve our mystery at once. Meanwhile, I could do nothing for Ellen just now but let her talk out her mood. The boat, soon, of course, though I found the time an age, reached her wharf, and, after a moment's waiting, I tried to convince Ellen that the two must now have left for the train. 'They are going to the old house near what used to be San Antonio,' I said, as quietly as I could. The words seemed to act on Ellen's behavior like water upon a lighted candle. Her fire died out at once, she spoke for the time no word, and when we had waited a little longer I found no trouble in persuading her to go up-stairs with me. She touched my arm, however, as we reached the upper deck. 'Let me go,' she said, imperiously; 'I must look for them. They would not see me. You would be seen if you went with me. Wait in the cabin there, just where you were.' She walked quickly forward, stood at the end of the upper deck an instant, then went clear around the great long cabin, and at length returned to me. We had by this time attracted in our lonesomeness the attention of the deck-clerk, who came to collect our return fare. While I paid him, Ellen was still nervously gazing all about, and she stepped once across the cabin to look out of the window at a couple who, like ourselves, were remaining on the boat. At last she seated herself, with a sigh of relief, just as the west-bound passengers began to crowd in from the trains. 'They are not aboard,' she said; 'you must have been right.' Then she relapsed into utter silence. The crowd was large, the cabin soon became both close and noisy. The sun was now rather low, and shone through the windows at our back, lighting the white walls of the big closed engine-room that passes up through the midst of the cabin. After a long time Ellen rose very deliberately, and, walking to the engine-room, gazed through the great plate-glass window at the machinery, standing close beside two little children who were doing the same thing. Her act in leaving me in this crowd, without a word, looked a little odd, and I followed her. After I had reached her, she was still silent for a time. Then she said, 'I 've been feeling just like the children. Is n't it pretty, and gentle, — the engine? Do you think it could kill me?' 'Nonsense,' I answered. 'Come out and look at the water with me.' 'Can't one see the bay from the house near old San Antonio?' she asked. 'Yes,' I said. She silently took a seat just made vacant near us by somebody's leaving, and I found once more a place beside her. The new seat gave us a view of the engine-room, and of one of the paddle-boxes visible through the windows. The waterview was nearly all behind us, mostly out of sight. We remained here without another word until we reached the city wharf, and as silently, in a close and crowded street car, we found our way homewards. Ellen went at once to her room, and locked herself in. At supper she appeared, as gentle and quiet as ever, and she sat by my sofa in the library for a while afterwards.

"At about eight o'clock I rose to go, but she tried to detain me. I had already done too much for her, she said, that day. I was too tired. I must stay. I asked how she could know what I was about to do, since I had not told her. She only smiled very faintly and sadly, and repeated her request. But I was firm. I begged her not to worry, to trust still that all would be well, and to get herself early to bed. Once more she smiled in the same gloomy way, and kissed me good-by. I knew that, at whatever hour I should return, she would be still awake to meet me.

"And in fact I had no intention of being out late. My plan was a simple one: to go to Boscowitz, who seemed to know everything, and to ask him about this latest affair. Of mere personal dignity there need be, in his company, no further thought. Our understanding was once for all complete, and, ferociously as I had forbidden him ever to mention this matter to me again, I had now no wish to insist upon my command. I knew that for his part he would never remind me of it. At all events, I felt that I could trust him to tell me at least as much as he actually knew. For the moment he seemed to me my especially appointed friend in need. Thus can our views change within a few hours!

"One thing, as I ought to say, however, I had never yet appreciated about Boscowitz, and that was his especially close relation just then to Tom himself. This relationship was indeed of the sort that would easily escape me, for it had to do with politics. Those were the busy days just before the great Constitutional Convention; and Tom, immediately after his reconciliation with his father, had returned into active life as his father's general right-hand man. Alonzo, however, was, as usual, in the very thick of the fray. In May of that year, as you have heard, the canvass for the coming election of members to the Convention was going on. Everything was intrigue and confusion. There were parties and rumors of parties without end. I suppose Alonzo must have bought the 'Warrior' for temporary use during that early period of its life. I can't tell how that was, or whether Tom was himself mixed up in any of the darker politics of that stupid year. I don't know, and, of course, I now don't care. At all events, it was n't generally found very convenient at the moment for Eldon to consort openly with Boscowitz about the business between them. They were to act in seeming independence, for greater effect. Alonzo, I fancy, used Tom as go-between, and Tom met Boscowitz in out-of-the-way places and manners. After all, take off the halo with which I used to surround that boy's head, and I suppose you may call him a youngster well fitted by nature for intrigue and for the management of men. His self-possession, his secretiveness, his winning ways, his wide circle of acquaintances, and his disposition to keep his various groups of friends well sundered from one another, make him first and last a capital Jesuit. To me, of course, he never talked politics. Why should he? I hated politics. I kept away from Boscowitz's little group of politicians as well as I could, although they used often to sit in that back part of the bookstore, separated from me by only a thin partition. Into my part of the office they less frequently came. I never listened to their gabble, wherever they were. I never believed that they could do this State of California any good, or any harm either; for I used to think that the whole place was sold to the devil, once for all, — bargain finished, and cash paid down. A 'New Constitution' would help or hurt it, I used to say, about as much as a new hat would alter a lunatic's brains. I was wrong, no doubt, but my part of the 'Warrior' was literary, theatrical, and such like. The politics of all San Francisco I laughed at and ignored. So then this other ignorance about Tom's private relations to Boscowitz was (my tastes and Tom's nature being what they were) simply inevitable. But had I known that Boscowitz's talk with me on Friday was just part of his ordinary effort to find out all about the private life of the men whom he was as thick with as he was with Tom, and had I been aware how carefully he was just then pumping Tom, and spying into Tom's whole life, just for the sake of getting all possible control over the youngster, I should n't have gone to the old fox that night.

"But I did go. And what thereupon happened stands out in my mind as the most ghastly and tragic farce that I ever conceived of. It 's my nature never to have any great trouble that is n't mixed up with all sorts of at once horrible and contemptible absurdities. This whole affair was like the rest. It served me right, to be sure, for going in the dark to Boscowitz, of all God's creatures and the devil's servants, for help about my daughter. Yet what could I have done? Poor Ellen's eyes (that look of a wounded bird in them) were enough to have sent me wandering through all hell for a word or a thought that might comfort her. I have no patience in my make-up; and here we were, with this mystery, this lie of Tom's, on our hearts, and nothing but a long wait until next Thursday for an explanation, even if it should come then. Well, enough; I made my way to Boscowitz's dwelling-place as fast as I could.

"Boscowitz's household is as singular as everything else about the man. He must have married very early in life, but he is long since a widower, with one tall, gaunt, fierce-looking, but very sickly maiden daughter, surely not much more than twenty-five years his junior. She is an odd girl, indeed. She lives a very retired life. She is subject to some heart trouble, I think, and often has long fainting-fits. She has great hungry black eyes, high cheek-bones, a big lower jaw, a sunken chest, and long skinny fingers. Though, of course, most people hate her at first sight, and though she is ferociously shy until you know her well, it still must be said that she is, at the worst, an impressive person. That is shown by the numerous anecdotes people tell about her. There is much dispute whether she is a lunatic or a genius. People tell alarming tales of the big books she has read, and of the long words she can use. Her forte is history, with a certain inclination to literature, especially poetry. She is said to know Spenser's 'Faery Queen' by heart. But she can't add three and five; she does n't know whether the moon is made of green cheese or not; she has n't any true notion of the social conditions about her. Her passions are violent, and quite beyond prediction. She watches the doings of others very slyly, but she understands only a very few of these doings. She is affectionate to a few people, and naturally hates most others. She worries easily, and broods long over things, but then acts impulsively. She is usually impenetrably silent, but when she talks, she talks in a flood. She had known Ellen as a child, long before we were acquainted with Boscowitz himself. She was once, in fact, a special and, of course, an unmatriculated student in the Sunset College, during the time of my professorship there. She used to try to take a few courses in literature. The young men hated her, and wrote squibs about her in their college papers. But she always despised both the men and what they wrote. She used to come to me for advice. Her ignorance about most matters was too dense to be enlightened, but in spots, so to speak, she was actually learned, and even brilliant. Her usual fashion of talk was that of a kitchen-girl who had somehow managed halfway to educate herself. My Ellen, I should say, she had always loved most fondly. My wife could hardly bear her in the house, but somehow we were all well acquainted with her. Bertha is actually a very benevolent girl, and withal, of late years, extremely pious. The Rev. Rawley got hold of her somehow, and, to her father's infinite amusement, made a religious person of her. She and Boscowitz used to quarrel like cat and dog; but they long since agreed to differ, and have thenceforth dwelt peacefully together.

"In those days, before his good fortune came, Boscowitz used to live above his bookstore, in the second story and attic of the house. I knew well what I should have to do on any Sunday night in order to find him. If he was at home at all, he would be, as I fully believed, alone at this hour, for I felt certain that his pious daughter must have gone to church. I had waited for this to be the case, because I wanted to see the man himself, and I instinctively dreaded the daughter's curiosity. But Boscowitz, if at home Sunday evening, would try to be inaccessible. For, whether because he wanted to keep just this time free for special intrigues, or because he simply desired for himself a show of mystery, he was accustomed to be visible at this hour only to his closest followers, or by private appointment. His front door was at the foot of the stairway that led down on one side of his building. But in vain should I ring if I were to go to that door now. Boscowitz, at that time, kept no servant, and would make no answer. I must enter his yard from the rear, by way of the alley, and I must give a certain knock at his back-door, which we who wrote for him all knew. In this way we were privileged to approach him on important business even at this time.

"Well, I took this way, and entered the yard. The leaky back-office that I mentioned before was a one-story addition at the rear of the house. I could just see my way through the yard past this shed-like structure; for the sea-fog had come up at night-fall, and the place was cheerlessly dark, and seemed very solitary. The back entrance to the dwelling itself was reached by going up a long and dangerous stairway to the second story of the main building. Then you came to a little covered porch, and there was the door. It opened into a kitchen. Beyond the kitchen was a hallway, which led to three or four other rooms, and there were front stairways that led up to the attic and down to the first floor. I did n't know how loud I might have to make my signal before I should be heard. It would depend on where Boscowitz might be, in case he was at home at all. But, to my surprise, I had not even to knock. The door opened as I reached the head of the stairs, and there, in the dim light of a very bad lamp, stood the tall figure of Bertha Boscowitz.

"I had made sure, as I said, that she would be at church, and to see her now surprised me not a little. 'Why, Miss Bertha,' I said, 'you 're playing truant this evening. What will the Rev. Rawley say?' You see, we had been on familiar terms for a long time, and Bertha was used to my little pleasantries. She made, however, at first no reply, but retreated a little into the light. I saw at once that she looked both surprised and anxious. 'Where is your father?' I went on. She hesitated, and seemed to look away past me into the darkness, with her great glaring eyes. 'Are you quite alone, Mr. Escott?' she said at last. 'Why not?' I responded. 'Do I usually make a raid with an armed band?' She stood a moment longer, as if dazed. I was used to her absurdities, more or less, and without more ado I entered, and shut the door. 'I think you can't — I doubt if you can see him just now,' she stammered at length, still standing awkwardly there. 'Why?' I said. 'Is he engaged?' 'Somebody 's with him,' she responded. 'Well, but I have a question to ask, that may take me only a moment,' said I. 'And as it is a special personal favor to me, I think I know your father well enough to interrupt him. I want, namely, a word of reply about some important private business of my own.' I hoped that she would take this business to relate to money, and would have no further thoughts concerning it. But she stared at me very curiously as I spoke.

Her forehead has deep lines in it, and when she stares they grow deeper, while her mouth is always a little open. My manner had naturally some signs of my anxiety about it, I suppose. At all events, she lowered her voice, and said very mysteriously, leaning a little forward, 'If it 's 'bout *him*, *he 's* in there now with father. They 're plannin' politics together, if you want to know. I had to stay home to watch out. He did n't want anybody to get wind he was here.' 'He!' I exclaimed with wonder. 'Who?' 'Tom Eldon.' She spoke abruptly, and there was another instant's dead silence. I replied in a somewhat severe tone. 'Miss Boscowitz,' I said, 'what makes you speak so about Mr. Eldon? If he has private business with your father, I will not interrupt them. I don't know why you should speak of the young man, however, in this way as *him*. Is he Prince Bismarck, or the chief of the Nihilists, that he should be called by no other name? You know that I care nothing for politics, and you know that he 's my best friend. Please say, by and by, to them both that I was sorry not to see them, that I would n't for the world have interrupted them, and that I can be trusted to keep a secret, such as the fact of Mr. Eldon's being here. And so, good-evening. It has been a beautiful day to-day, has n't it?' I had opened the door, and was going off in a huff, when she sprang forward, and touched my arm. 'Wait a minute,' she said; 'come back — no — come outside here.' She pushed me gently out on to the dark balcony, and shut the door after us. 'See here,' she said, 'I know all about it.' She caught her breath excitedly, and stopped short. 'All about what?' I answered rather gruffly. 'About Tom Eldon and you,' was her reply. 'Indeed?' said I, a little bitterly. 'That 's nothing. Who does n't know all about Mr. Eldon and me? I seem to be the only ignorant person, except, to be sure' — I interrupted myself, and then, after a moment, during which the sound of her excited breathing became to me so decidedly disagreeable, I went on, 'Well, if you know all about me, and know why I came here, and have anything to tell, why don't you tell it?'

"It was cruel in me, of course, to be so curt, for she was a queer creature, but very good, and was trying her best to do me a favor under grave difficulties. But I could n't help myself. 'My father,' she began at last (she always said 'my father,' never 'father'), 'told me this mornin' — not to tell you — if you — should come here — that Tom Eldon — had come back — to the city.' It was odd to hear her speak so tremblingly of her father, she being a woman almost thirty, and at this very moment engaged in disobeying him. 'Did he?' I responded, ironically. 'And so you did n't tell me, did you?' 'Please, sir,' she said pleadingly, 'don't be angry with me. I said he told me. That means that when he told me I saw there was somethin' wrong. I like your daughter. I used to know, a long time ago, a little about Tom Eldon and Mrs. Dover. I did n't think much about it.

It was n't my way to. But lately I 've been watchin' out, and I 've got awful troubled in my mind. And last night I got anxious about you again. I made my father tell me everythin' he knows. He never talks to me much, but he was good-humored this time, and I made him. I questioned him a long time. I wanted to find out, because I was anxious about your Ellen as soon as I heard my father say what he did about my not tellin' you. I said to myself, Here 's goin' to be an awful quarrel, sure. And my father told me that Tom Eldon was a good deal cut up about this thing just now. He does n't care anythin' much, Tom Eldon does n't, I guess, about your Ellen, only he sort of pitied of her, and liked her a little, and the widow and he had quarreled somehow, I guess, and he was n't happy about his engagement to her, and he broke it off, or she did, — I don't know which. And then he sort of thought he liked your Ellen well enough, and would get away from Mrs. Dover, and so he got engaged to your Ellen. And now, you see, he feels sort of cut up, 'cause he 's found he likes the widow better.' Once started in her speech, Bertha had spoken very rapidly, in a low, excited voice, just above a whisper. I could not quite judge from my knowledge of her whether, after all, she was n't thus excited merely because she had found a piece of gossip, and was amusing herself with the rather rare pleasure of imparting it to some one, especially since that some one was myself, one of the persons most concerned. 'Will you tell me,' I replied, imitating her low tone, but speaking as ill-humoredly, I fear, as ever, 'what good you think it does to my daughter, or to myself, for you to be telling me all this gossip here in the dark? I thank you for your good will. Of course you mean well by me. But what worth can this stuff have? I came here to-night for one thing only. To be sure, you may call that gossip, too, if you will. I came here to find whether your father knew that Mr. Eldon was still in town. Mr. Eldon had told us that he would be out of the city until Thursday next. Our relations are such that I am surprised to have him deceive me. I learned of his being in the city to-day. I thought I had a right to ask your father, who apparently knows everything, what the meaning of this might be. I don't want to hear from you whether Mr. Eldon means to be true to my daughter or to anybody else. He will have to explain that to me, face to face, very soon. As for his feelings, nobody can judge them but himself. Perhaps I am foolish to ask anything at all of your father, Miss Bertha. But I am much worried about my daughter's state of mind. As it is, I can gain no more by waiting to-night. I must go.' 'No, no,' she went on, 'you must n't go yet. What I just told you my father got out of him Friday and this mornin'. You see they 've been mixed up in politics together lately, and my father has an awful way of pumpin' a man.' 'Did Mr. Eldon, then, talk with your father in this way about my daughter?' I said, horrified. 'Oh, you don't know my father,' she replied. 'He always pretends to know everythin' about a man already, and then Tom Eldon had to begin talkin' over this thing, so's to 'xplain the need for keepin' his bein' in town a secret from you till Thursday.' 'But why need he keep it secret?' I asked. 'Oh, you *don't* see at all. Friday he lef' town, because he was feelin' so bad. He'd just had a talk with Mrs. Dover, and it upset him. So my father says, and my father saw him Friday mornin'. Mrs. Dover had come over to town Friday mornin'. Tom Eldon and she met somehow at her mother's house. Afterwards she was with her mother at my father's store. Then my father saw Tom Eldon later. My father met him up-stairs here while you were away from the office, about lunch-time. My father saw how cut up he was, and wormed out of him somehow that he had seen Mrs. Dover. So my father knew what was the matter at once, and told Tom Eldon so. Then Tom Eldon got mad at my father, and the madder he got the more father let on as if he knew everythin', and pumped Tom Eldon for more yet. And at last Tom Eldon said he was goin' to leave town awhile. And my father said to him to go off anyhow on a political trip to Sacramento or somewheres. And Tom Eldon went to your house, and later he went off, that same afternoon. But he an' my father were telegraphin' back and forth about politics. And Tom Eldon did n't go to Sacramento at all, but only to Alameda, I think. And yesterday my father wanted him to come back to have some kind of a confab about politics. Somethin' new had come up. And he came this mornin' and again this evenin'. But after church-time this mornin' he drove from here in a hack to Mrs. Dover's mother's house, for I heard him say so just now. And I think he saw Mrs. Dover there. And I tell you, I just *know* from what my father 's told me, and what Tom Eldon said when he came here, and what I 've long seen in his looks, that he 's jus' dyin' for the love of Mrs. Dover. And I tell you, Mr. Escott, I like your daughter first-rate, and she did me a big favor more 'n once, helpin' me and comfortin' me when I was sick, and always bein' my best friend under God. I want to see her happy. And that 's why I say this. I 've got nothin' against Tom Eldon, to be sure, but lately I 've been watchin' out more and more about this business. And I guess I know what I 'm a-talkin' about to-night. And what I tell you is, that the sooner you get shut o' that Tom Eldon, the better for you and yours.'

"The poor woman was quite breathless now, and I was not much better off. But I persisted: 'Was there no better reason, then, why his coming back should have to be such a secret from us?' 'Oh, *can't* you see?' she said. 'He 's seen the widow again, and they 're like to make up, most. But Tom Eldon, he 's a gentleman, after all, I suppose. And he don't jus' like to go back on you. And he 's taken the fancy to let himself see Mrs. Dover jus' the weest bit more, for the *last* time. And, meanwhile, he feels awful bad. And so he don't want to see you till he has to again. And he 's goin' back to Alameda to-night.' 'Let him go then,' I replied, quite simply.

"I felt that there was really no more to say. The dismal absurdity of gossiping with this creature at the head of Boscowitz's back-stairs was overwhelming me. I wanted to get off into lonesomeness again, anywhere. The farce of our contemptible life was growing, I felt, too hideous. My daughter's love, the most sacred and precious thing in all this great dark world, was here being made the plaything of a miserable intriguer, the object of garrulous pity to his fool of a daughter. I could have broken down and wept over it, had I not all the while been so furiously angry. I wanted to walk back into the house, and kill Eldon on the spot. Was Ellen's sacred name perhaps already the laughing-stock of every street boy? But I had hardly taken the first step down the stairs, when I heard voices in-doors. The two men were evidently just coming out. With a sudden impulse I turned sharp around once more. 'Go, oh, go!' begged the poor woman, in a terrified voice. But I could not think of her now. The black shut door there seemed to me, at the instant, the embodiment of the miserable lies that were blocking my pathway. I wanted to see the light once more. I groped for the latch. 'Who is there?' I heard Boscowitz saying. 'Bertha, where are you?' 'She is *here!*' I shouted, still groping. 'Open the door there, Boscowitz, will you, *at once*, I say.'

"Boscowitz, for this one time in his life, lost

his presence of mind. He must have recognized my voice, but he made no effort to get Tom out of sight, and in his alarm opened the door forthwith. Tom was standing still in the middle of the room. His face scarcely changed as he saw me. He remained just as pale and calm as ever he was wont to be. As for me, I felt, by a curious revulsion, fairly elated and triumphant at this instant. My position was such an absurd and contemptible one, — and yet, even so, I knew that I could not be overcome by it. I could and would face them. And in this feeling itself was my triumph. I was a fool, a silly, wretched, gossiping, deluded old fool, the prey of their lies and of their scorn, the butt of their ridicule, a listener to worthless back-stairs gossip; and yet I was infinitely better than they all, for I had trusted in their honor, and they had despised it. Boscowitz, as I reëntered, bowed to me mechanically, with a natural amazement in his face, and gazed darkly past me at Bertha. Tom merely looked down at the floor.

" 'It 's a good guard you have here, Boscowitz,' I said in a loud and careless tone, — 'your daughter, I mean. But you see I 'm a spy. I 've been gossiping here with her at the back door, in the dark.'

"It was never Boscowitz's way, as you have already discovered, to get angry with me. He laughed a little nervously, however. 'Well,' he began, 'what 's up, then?' 'Oh, nothing,' I rejoined. 'I just called to see Mr. Eldon a moment, as soon as the political conference should be finished. How far have you got, by the way, with the new constitution to-night?' Boscowitz had recovered with a great effort his usual insolent calm. 'It 's well enough,' he responded. 'We 'll break the money-power of this State, always saving and excepting that of good men, like Mr. Eldon and his father. The golden age will soon be dawning. No Chinese, the railroad and the farmers at peace, public benefactors rewarded, workingmen elevated, commercial depression forever ended: that 's the programme for the coming constitutional convention. We 've just drawn it up, if you must know. No other party in the field has yet seen the glorious possibilities of the moment. The old parties are as good as dead. The Fusion movement is a fraud. The Workingmen's party is disposed, at this very moment, to split into fragments. It has long since fallen under the control of unprincipled agitators. The only true party is so far made up of Mr. Eldon's father, Mr. Eldon, and myself. Won't you join us?'

"'Certainly,' I replied. 'Only would you kindly first inform me why you keep your back doorstep so dark? I had to bang like a fool just now, because I could n't find the latch. And your daughter somehow could n't or would n't help me.' 'Damned funny, I declare,' said Boscowitz. 'Would you mind telling us how long you 've been here?' 'Not I,' I responded. 'I came here some time ago to see, as I said, Mr.

Eldon. I knew, of course, that he would be here, for he had told me so. He tells me everything — you understand — *everything*. I wanted a word with him, as I just said, whenever your constitution-making in there should be over for the night. I did n't want to disturb statesmen, of course; so I told Miss Bertha not to alarm you. Meanwhile, the air was pleasant outside, the night is fine, — gloriously clear and bright, you know, — and your back-yard is one of the best of nocturnal landscapes. So Miss Bertha and I stood out there, and talked confidentially of old times at college, until we heard your voices. Then we tried to come back in again. You know the rest.' 'The rest was damned noisy,' replied Boscowitz, curtly. He still did n't show anger, at least towards me. But of course he was puzzled, and was no doubt casting about in his mind to see how he might best use this occurrence for his own ends. Tom never moved a muscle. We were all four silent for a little.

"'Bertha,' said Boscowitz, presently, in a stern tone, 'go to bed at once, won't you?' The great woman, looking in face at the moment even more like an aged baby than was usual with her, and thoroughly dazed with terror and amazement, wandered awkwardly and uneasily across the room, reached the hall door, stared back at us all helplessly for a moment, and then vanished. 'Shut the door there, will you?' shouted Boscowitz after her. She returned. He was evidently disposed to give her the full benefit of his righteous wrath. 'See here,' he said, 'we don't want no women about to-night any more. D'ye understand?' Her lower jaw had fallen, as usual, and the deep lines were more marked than ever on her brow. 'Good-night, Mr. Escott,' she said to me solemnly, fixing her eyes on me reproachfully. 'Good-night,' I answered. 'I do beg your pardon indeed for troubling you so, and I thank you very much.' 'Good-night, Mr. Eldon,' she continued, after a little pause, and with a really pathetic terror in her voice. 'Shut that door there, will you, *quick*, I say!' shouted Boscowitz, before Tom could have replied. The door shut like a steel-trap, and we three were alone. We listened to the tramp of her feet along the hall and up the attic stairs, and presently another door was heard to close.

"'Mr. Escott,' said Boscowitz finally, 'I suppose you know what you 're about. Mr. Eldon's presence to-night in town, and especially here, is, for reasons connected with the politics of the moment, not exactly public property. Of course he told you, as you just said, where to find him. But perhaps he did n't warn you of this. It is to his interest to have certain political intriguers who are passing through town find him not at home, and not elsewhere in the city, for these few days. These are busy times, and the air is full of rumors. I hope you 'll be discreet. Of course you, as Mr. Eldon's closest friend, won't misinterpret his conduct. But I also hope you won't mention having seen him here. I *beg* your pardon, gentlemen, won't you take seats?' In the little kitchen there were just three wooden chairs. The room was a model of cheerlessness. A small round clock ticked with ferocious insolence from the wall. The dark, unpapered, and smoky walls themselves almost quenched the light that fell upon them. The room smelt vilely of brown soap and lamp oil, and was plainly scrubbed frequently and piously.

"I declined at first to sit down, and so did Tom. My business with Mr. Eldon, I said, might be very shortly dispatched, and so far as I could now see there was nothing secret about it. Would Boscowitz permit me to speak my mind plainly and simply, in his own presence? Boscowitz promptly assented. He insisted, however, that we should take chairs, and we yielded. To sit down in the place with Boscowitz seemed an added degradation of the name and the cause that I must now mention. I felt the hateful ticking of the clock more than ever when I had once taken the chair. I noticed now, moreover, that the water was rapidly dripping from the faucet of the sink that stood across the room, just opposite to me. I felt dimly that before long my accursed agitation might come back to me again. I looked hard at the dripping water, and began very firmly.

"'What I came here to ask of Mr. Eldon is, in the first place, simply this, and I want the plainest and directest answer, without any sort of evasion. Has he ever been betrothed to Mrs. Dover, Peter Dover's widow?' There was a brief pause, of which the fiendish clock took exultant possession. Then Tom answered very firmly and musically, just as he always spoke, 'Yes, I have been.' 'How long was this engagement broken off before Mr. Eldon became betrothed to my daughter?' 'Not long,' said Tom. 'Exactly how long?' 'I don't see that I should do any service by answering that question just now.' 'Ah, well! Then why did Mr. Eldon give us no hint of the fact of this betrothal?' 'Because I thought that to dwell on the past could do no good.' 'Yet further, if Mr. Eldon will have patience with me, did he not falsely tell my daughter on Friday last that he meant to be out of town until next Thursday?' 'I did mean to stay out of town until Thursday. I was called back on political business.' 'Was it political business, if I may continue, that brought Mr. Eldon, in company with Mrs. Dover, on to the Oakland boat this afternoon, and that earlier in the day had brought about a social meeting between these two persons at the house of a lady in this city?' Both Boscowitz and Tom started a little, and I turned to look from one to the other. 'I cannot admit,' said Tom, 'that it is exactly right for you, sir, to question me thus here, and about such matters. If I have done amiss, is there not some other time to accuse me? And if I have any explanation to make, I appeal to your own delicacy of feeling to tell you whether I can fittingly make it just now. Nor can I see why Mr. Boscowitz can be interested in the matter. It is something solely between ourselves.' Tom spoke very reasonably. How convincing his words would have sounded to any disinterested person!

"You know, Harold, how at such moments a man's whole case will seem to be slipping away from his grasp, and leaving him helpless. Tom's impenetrable self-control, Boscowitz's unsympathetic face, combined to make me feel how all these trifles, light as air, on which my furious indignation had just been feeding, were thoughts utterly incommunicable at such a time and in this dismal presence. How hasty it was, after all, to talk thus before a third person! But then, how clear the whole case against Tom! And yet how helpless I was to state it just now well enough to drive him from his defenses! And what, then, had I come there for? Was this my satisfaction? One's mind works quickly at such crises. I thought of the gloomy night outside, and all in one instant, with some curious sort of mental fusing, I fancied the long, cold walk home, from Boscowitz's treacherous stairway, across the dark yard to the dismal alley, and then through the weary streets, and past the rows of lights, until I should reach our own house. I conceived myself as coming up to the door. It would be opened for me, just as this hideous door of Boscowitz's own house had been opened when I first came to-night, only behind that door would be — Ellen. I could not image her face. I could think only of her hand taking mine in the dark, of her little form gently touching me as she kissed me, of her soft, quick breathing as she waited for my answer. She would not know for what she was waiting, but only that she was hoping for some word of truth, for some ray of light in all this hateful gloom. And I, what could I tell her, if they all thus scorned and baffled me, and put me off until the morrow, and assured me with this calm and righteous air that I was wrong to question so pointedly at this time and place? What could I tell her save that I was gossiped to and befooled, and sent home beaten and hopeless, more ignorant than ever of what it all meant? It was in vain now that I looked hard at the dripping water. My agitation was overcoming me. It was very hard for me to begin speaking again. But I felt that I must not falter. It was for Ellen that I was fighting.

"Just here, after what must have been, I suppose, if measured by that hideous clock, a very short time, Boscowitz interposed: 'Gentlemen,' he said, 'perhaps you won't mind a word from a plain man, who may dare humbly to call himself a friend of both of you' (it was of course solely to Tom that Boscowitz was really talking). 'I respect,' he continued, 'Mr. Escott's talents very highly, and I esteem his character not less than his talents. And I need not remark, Mr. Eldon, how I stand towards yourself. I know, I am sorry to say, something about this affair, chiefly what Mr. Escott has honored me by telling me. I want to interpose a friendly word, especially since Mr. Escott takes me again into confidence this evening, as he had already done on a previous'—

Beside myself, almost, I interrupted him, striving all the while to appear calm: 'When, sir, have I ever before taken you into my confidence about this matter? I speak as I have done to-night because I am forced to do so. You know, quite apart from any words of mine, all about this thing. Yes, everybody knows. It is the gossip of the clubs, the laughing-stock of all Mr. Eldon's friends. He, here, who has made me and my daughter the tools of his spite against the woman that jilted him, has managed until within two days to keep us as ignorant as babies of what the whole town knows and jokes about.' Tom rose suddenly, and with a pained expression, 'You have no right, sir' — he began. 'Right?' I burst out. 'Hold, Mr. Eldon, you shall not go yet. I am here for plain speech. No mere compromise is possible between us to-night. Sit down again for a little. You, indeed, need not fear any more such words from me as my last were. I shall say nothing further, if I can help it, to offend your feelings. I only want a clear understanding with you about my own business. These things concern not just this moment only; they concern the heart and the whole life of one who is very near and very dear to me, and whom you, too, have sworn, as an honorable man, not to injure, but rather to cherish and protect. I demand of you a present hearing. I must not be put off. Wait, then! I require it of you!' Tom looked at me a little wonderingly, I fancied, and seated himself once more. Boscowitz was silent.

I was now indeed excited enough, but I felt sure that I had myself fully under control. I spoke once more, and now no longer in a loud tone, but, as I trust, with a more quiet precision and earnestness. I said that I would set the case plainly before Tom, that he might understand my feelings. I told him enough of my conversation of Friday, in Boscowitz's back-office, to make plain to him what, on the whole, I had then learned, and what it had meant to me. I mentioned, too, in a few words, the result of my talk with Williamson. I described very briefly the thoughts of Friday night, the effort to find Tom on Saturday, and the discovery made this afternoon on the boat. I said that I appealed to him, as a man of honor and of insight, to appreciate my feelings. That I had just heard anything new from Bertha I tried so far as possible to suppress, although of course it must have been obvious to both of them that she had told me something. But the result of what I had in various fashions learned was, I said, that my daughter and I must not and could not honorably endure this relation a moment longer, unless Tom could offer us some plain and manly explanation, such as should convince us of his fidelity. He might have made us, in the past, his dependents, I said; but in the future he should not make us anything but his frank and open and equal friends, or else we must finally and irrevocably break off all connection with him. There was his alternative. What could he say?

"I was almost ready, as I finished, to thank Boscowitz for having, by his interruption, brought me to such a pitch of excitement that I must now certainly be able to overcome this iron barrier of Tom's reserve, which, in the first part of the conversation, had almost defeated me. I felt that I had spoken well. Now, at least, I should hear the decisive word. Tom's head was bowed. His knees were crossed, and his hands were nervously playing with each other on one of them. He sat for a while longer, speechless. Boscowitz, too, had now nothing to say. His ends could at present best be reached by letting us finish our affair for ourselves, that we might completely expose it to his view. There was an interval of entire silence. Now again my excitement overcame me. I rose, walked about the room, stared at the little clock, at the great stove, at the window, at the dripping water. The suspense was horrible. I noticed, as I walked, that under the little clock there was a very small shelf, on which lay a clock-key. Close beside this key there was a small revolver, but that, oddly enough, I hardly saw. My mind suddenly busied itself feverishly for the moment, with the idea that the little clock had not been wound to-night, that poor Bertha had been sent to bed before she could wind it, and that it was her own kitchen-clock, which her father would forget about, to her great inconvenience, when she should come down again in the morning. I longed to repay her for her goodness by winding it now; but in the midst of these thoughts came, like a burning coal, the other and terrible one into my mind: '*The next word he speaks will end everything.*' I turned once more, and looked at him.

"His eyes were fixed upon mine at last. His face was a little graver and more anxious than before. 'I must frankly tell you, sir,' he began, 'that it is impossible here and to-night for me to explain all these matters to you. To-morrow I will see you at your own house.' On the instant came to me the idea, 'He's in league with Boscowitz to draw everything out of me, to display my inmost heart, and then to give me nothing in return.' 'Here and now?' I almost shouted. 'Ay, here and now it is. An honest man answers at once an honest question. Here and now, indeed! Have *I* not spoken out my whole soul here and now, in Boscowitz's presence? Have I not been forced to this disgrace and agony? Answer me at once, then, fairly, clearly, and as an honorable lover should, or never, never, see my face or my daughter's again.' Tom is as proud as Lucifer, whatever else he is. He rose quietly and silently, and said, 'Gentlemen, I must bid you good-evening. I hope, sir' (turning to me), 'that at some other time you will let me make all clear, as I am sure that I can do. Good-evening.' We stood all three now, very awkwardly, Tom somehow not going at once, Boscowitz hesitating, I myself full of the wildest fancies, my brain whirling. Of a sudden the hall door opened, and there again stood Bertha Boscowitz, pale, haggard, trembling with some strange emotion. She had plainly not yet thought of going to bed. We ourselves had been too busy to hear her come back. She was plainly in the wildest excitement, but every trace of her former terrified manner was gone. She came into the room with a firm, even solemn step, and walked straight up to me. 'Mr. Escott,' she said, with her great eyes fixed upon me, 'you must n't do anything to *him* there' (motioning to Tom); 'it all came over me when I got up-stairs, and remembered the pistol lyin' on the clock-shelf there yonder, and heard your voice talkin' so, that you must be sorely tempted to kill him. And I think it was the Lord that put it into my mind to come down now and say to you that you should n't. It's murder that's in your heart, Mr. Escott. Beware of it.' She paused, and stood there, with her great eyes still fixed upon me, and her face almost insane, I thought, in its excitement. In fact, no such idea had entered my mind as that which she had morbidly fancied to be mine. I was wild enough, to be sure, but this was not the moment for such plans. I don't know what there was about her strange bearing, however, that at just this instant overcame us all three, even her father, with a sort of awe. She turned to Tom, who stood as if dazed. 'You, sir,' she said, 'need n't be denyin' to Mr. Escott, as I believe you must 've been, how false you 've been to him and to his Ellen. I 've watched you long since. I know it all. Don't you deny it. The Lord will judge you.

You 're the lover of the widow Dover. Go back to her. Don't be breakin' the hearts of poor girls like Ellen Escott. You taught her to love you, and now you 've deceived her. The Lord will judge you.' Her voice, sounded, indeed, like a judgment, so solemn it was, through all its excitement. She was plainly in no very sane frame of mind. But the spell was now broken. 'Bertha! Bertha!' said Boscowitz sternly. Tom laid his hand on the door-knob to go. The woman turned, walked a step or two towards the hall door, and fell in a dead faint.

"What followed I cannot easily describe. The shock of the instant, the wonder what it all meant, changed our whole bearing. We succeeded in reviving the poor girl after some minutes, but very slowly and with much trouble, and then we bore her into the front room of the house and laid her on a sofa. Boscowitz seemed much more moved than I should have thought possible for him. He assured us that it was no common fainting-fit. The girl had some trouble with her heart-action. He never had understood what. She would be well for months together, and then on occasion would have these fits time after time. There was danger that she would some time go off in one of them altogether, he supposed. He did n't want any doctor, to be sure. There was a woman across the way whom he always called as nurse in such cases. He would go after her now. Could I wait with his daughter a moment? Mr. Eldon might as well go down with him the front way.

There was no danger at this hour of his being recognized. Tom, meanwhile, seemed greatly agitated. I don't think the boy was used to see sudden attacks of any sort. The solemn accusation, followed by this mishap, had overcome him altogether for the moment. The poor girl still lay in a sort of stupor, as Boscowitz turned to go out. Tom himself looked once more towards me. His voice trembled. 'She is right,' he said. 'I have no explanation to make to you that can or that ought to satisfy you. I am the worst and the lowest of God's creatures. Give my farewell to Ellen, whom I must never see again. If God gives me the manhood, I shall kill myself before another day has passed. Good-by!' With this he was gone.

"As I sat there during Boscowitz's absence, I was of no more possible worth as a guardian for this poor woman than if I had been a corpse. I heard nothing, saw nothing, but only lay back helpless in the great chair by her sofa. The blankest despair was in my heart. All was over, and there was but one thing to be hoped for by any of us. How welcome it would have been if this dying creature could but have been my Ellen, and if I myself could but have been dying there beside her!

"At last I heard a sound. It was the opening of the front door, and Boscowitz's heavy tramp up the stairs. A shuffling step followed him, and then a bent, little old woman entered the room just after him. I rose to my feet as they came up. The woman's face was cheerful, and her voice was hopeful enough as she looked at her patient, and declared that she would 'soon have her feeling all right again.'

"I remember little or nothing further, save a dim sense of streets and lamps, until I found myself at my own door. Ellen met me, as I had expected: only, to my surprise, she had a light burning in my library. When I came in there with her I saw that she had on the table, close beside the chair where she had been sitting, the little ebony box in which, as I well knew, she used to keep the letters Tom had sent her. She had been reading them, poor girl, for comfort in her hours of waiting. I said nothing whatever, for what could I say? until Ellen had gently forced me on to my sofa, and had covered me with all her most careful skill. I was shivering with cold. Then, just as so often before, she seated herself on her cricket beside me. My throat was dry and choking. For a long time I strove in vain to begin. At last I shut my eyes, so as not to see hers; for they, pleading as they were, and full of terror and suspense, would still have forced me into silence had I watched them and struggled for speech through all eternity. 'Ellen,' I now said, 'I have seen him — himself, — and all is over.' How I longed at once to recall the words! But her hand scarcely trembled in mine. She was perfectly still. After a long time I went on: 'Bertha Boscowitz is very ill. I am afraid she will die. You, Ellen, must not die. You must tell me that you will surely live, even now, even after all.' She kissed my forehead gently. 'Father,' she said, 'I am your own child. I will never forsake you, and I will not die. But just now I must be alone. Please don't think any more about me, father.' Then her hand dropped mine, I heard her soft step as she left my side, and then, still without opening my eyes, I heard her pick up the little box from the table, and softly go out of the room."

CHAPTER VI.

A WINTER STORM.

"I NEED not describe to you," continued Escott, after a long pause, "the life that we led in the first short time immediately after that Sunday. Bertha Boscowitz soon recovered as much health as she ever has. Tom found no encouragement from Providence for his expressed design to put himself out of the world, and very soon, probably that very night, gave up the design. His country needed him, you see. At the time of the interview between Boscowitz and Tom that Sunday, the Boscowitz-Eldon political party were, so to speak, manœuvring for position. During that May campaign, the political movements were very complex, all the more so because nobody could in the least foresee what would happen in any constitutional convention. Bodies of that sort are anomalous things, and the condition of all our parties, in those days, was in any case one of terrible disorganization. The workingmen knew best what they were about, but even they were once in danger of splitting for good before the election of delegates; and their relation to the Granger movement was for a little time an unsettled question. The two older parties were at the outset uncertain how best to meet the storm; whether to plunge ahead, or to lie by until all was over. A fusion, or 'non-partisan' movement, was begun, and had great success. Some people accused it from the first of being under the influence of the great corporations, but it had the confidence of the more conservative classes almost everywhere. In this city, before the election, several efforts were made to start new parties. These, I suppose, were meant in most cases merely to influence the conventions of the actual parties in the field. That undertaking is what I mean by manœuvring for position, and when Boscowitz talked that night of the new programme he meant some such scheme. But by whatever trading the result was accomplished, Tom Eldon himself was in the end elected to the Constitutional Convention, and sat in it, ostensibly as a moderate conservative, devoted on the whole to the interests of his class; but he was quite capable of seeing the other side when certain people, who knew him well, pointed out to him privately the advantages that the State, Alonzo, and other great and good things might gain from timely compromises. In short, Tom Eldon sat in that convention as a tool, and was well used. What else could you expect? The boy had shown courage and ability in the old conflict concerning Dover, but he knew nothing of politics, and could not judge for himself about constitution-making. You see, Harold, what a servant my years of friendly training had provided for the State! As an alumnus of a young college here on the coast, Tom gained, of course, much patronizing notice in the convention. As for me, I continued to write for Boscowitz, although I still would none of his politics, and let public affairs as much alone as ever. But, for the rest, our new calamity made me feverishly active. I unearthed old plays, half finished, from the rubbish of my literary efforts of years since, when I tried at home already to produce for the stage. I recast and finished some of these plays. My mind, meanwhile, was painfully alive. I wondered whether I could be renewing my youth, or whether I was on the point of death. My projects were endless, and my powers of accomplishment were better than for years. This blow of fortune's whip had seemed, as it were, to awaken me. I wondered where my wits had been for so long. I had had many literary projects to confide to Tom; but they were none of them equal to my present work. I wondered if the youngster had been putting me to sleep with all his gentleness, his flattery, his indolence, and his treachery. I had awakened at last, at all events. I now had a feeling that I must really finish something worth leaving behind me when I should go. My daughter,

I fancied, would survive me, and I did n't want her to hear anybody say, over my grave, that I had died like a beaten snake. This mood of feverish activity continued, even after Ellen's death, for a long time, slowly wearing itself away, to be sure, and having its occasional breaks. I think it ended on the night of the late fire. Not even the greatest blow of all in those years could take it from me. For her memory, too, I felt that I must work, and I continued long after she had left me.

"Tom had not fulfilled his promise of dying, Harold; why should poor Ellen have fulfilled hers of living? Yet no one shall say that his cruelty alone could have killed her. She was my daughter, and if he did all he could to murder her, and indirectly succeeded, it was not he alone that could have found the way. Her own pride, her own indomitable courage, was her death.

"For a few days after that evening I saw little of her. Some words passed between us, enough to explain further what I had learned; there was a little consultation with Fanny about what was yet to be done, and then there were two or three letters back and forth between Tom and me, — formal letters, that closed forever our intercourse. Then Ellen's little ebony box lay empty on the table, and she herself was once more out of her room, sitting in my library sometimes, much in the old fashion, only very silently; or else busy in the family-room, quietly talking about indifferent things with Sam and Emily. They, by the way, were her greatest comfort. It rejoiced me to see how much they both tried to help her. They stood in a kind of awe of her now, I think. She had looked on the face of a strange sorrow that they could hardly conceive, nearly grown up though they were; and while they are not in the least sentimental, and both of them seem to me very obtuse young people about all matters of the kind, their bearing was just then perfect. For days together Sam, on his way home from the lawyer's office where he was then trying to be an under-clerk, used to take care to get for Ellen the most beautiful flowers that he could find. He would bring them and lay them softly in her lap, and then lumber rapidly and sullenly away. Emily used to amuse Ellen by reading to her, for Ellen always loved Emily's voice. And Emily, I ought to say, hates books herself. For a week or two Ellen was thus the special charge and care of all of us.

"Then of a sudden, one day, she seemed to come to herself. She spoke to me in the morning alone, in my library, just before I left for the office. I must not suppose, she said, that she was brooding. She had not been letting herself brood, she hoped. Bad thoughts would come, but she had been fighting them. What she had really most thought about, meanwhile, was the worthlessness that I had so far in her life let her cultivate, and the absolute necessity that she should now work for her living and for us. She had been planning how she could best learn to teach, and get a position. I must help her to decide, and to accomplish her plans.

"The decision was as firmly held to as it had been silently reached. In vain I begged Ellen to remain content with what she already was to us. She was not to be moved. And of course she now soon found an ally in Mrs. Rawley. The one thing my sister-in-law had never been able to bear in Ellen had been her gentle repose of disposition, which Mrs. Rawley had called her ineffectiveness. Ellen's reserved manners, her freedom from ordinary worry, her natural and quiet optimism, had always offended my good sister inexpressibly. Mrs. Rawley is benevolent, but very wisely, no doubt, she regards discontent as a religious duty. She is continually harassed herself, and she thinks God meant everybody else to be. A peaceful child, full of mere large-eyed confidence in the perfection of God's world, is her special abhorrence. Such a child Ellen had been before sorrow found her. 'Are you, then, what you ought to be?' Mrs. Rawley would say to any such poor innocent. 'Consider your manners, how immature and awkward they are; your mind, how ignorant it is; your heart, how evil it appears in the sight of God! Be up and doing, my child. You 're but a slumbering sinner.' All these exhortations must be, no doubt, sound enough. Applied to Ellen, in the old days, they had merely made me angry, while, for Ellen, I am sorry to say, they had had no meaning. Now, however, she was in one sense awake to them. She and Mrs. Rawley became for the time close companions. Not, to be sure, that Ellen grew to like the Rawleyan theology, nor yet as if my sister spared Ellen's feelings any more than she had ever done. On the contrary, she took pains, in her vigorous way, to let Ellen see just how wrong all the past had been, how kind Heaven was to give her such good discipline so early in life, and how valuable a lesson this ought to be for her in the future. Mrs. Rawley always speaks very rapidly and incisively, but still with a certain large-minded and abstract coldness about even her most emphatic sayings. 'I *don't* want,' she said, 'to pry into your feelings. I would n't for the world say anything to hurt you. But it is my duty to be plain with you, my dear niece. Of course you did n't desire or think of money or of worldly position. I would n't for an instant hint that you did. But let all this warn you how easy it is for our wayward hearts to fix upon objects that, *if* our eyes were only open, and *if* our desires were only quite pure, *would* appear to us to appeal less to our higher natures than to our sordid ambitions. Be warned, I say, *in time.* Doubt your own heart. I know all about young girls. It 's so easy to feel now that you can never recover from these the first sorrows of life, and that the world is henceforth dead to you. Don't trust yourself. You 're *just* as worldly as ever. Erelong, some other object (mind you, I *don't* mean some other lover, I would n't for the *world* hint that; yet I *do* say that I can't tell in the *least* what object it may prove to be) will seem to you just as pure and noble as this one. If it 's a worldly object, be *sure* that, unless God's grace is with you, it will be just as base and ignoble as this one proved. Make up your mind, then, if you ever can get so far in your faith, to be guided by God ; and meanwhile desire nothing else, in any case, so much as an honest and womanly business, by which you can earn your living, and can forget, not your misfortunes, — for those you must always look back to with thankfulness, as a hard lesson and a great deliverance, — but your idle and hollow life that has brought you to these misfortunes. You don't seem yet, my dear, to see your way to accepting God's grace itself ; so you must n't understand me as preaching religion to you now. I never preach, at any time. What I 'm giving you at present is just plain common sense. It seems hard, I know ; yet, as my dear father used to say in his sermons sometimes, "All that glitters is not gold, but all that is gold is always hard." Remember that, my dear, and cheer up. Don't ever wear a long face.' Ellen listened to all this with a seemingly cheerful submissiveness. In fact, she accepted only as much of it as appeared good to her ; but what she wanted from Mrs. Rawley at that instant was painful stimulation. And this truly rational advice gave her precisely the thing. Hers was no quarrelsome temperament. She never rebelled nor protested, though at the same time she cared not a snap of her finger for the good woman's opinion of the past. But what she wanted, in her sorrow and in the first flush of her new resolution, was, not tenderness or sympathy, but precisely the reverse, — something stinging and cheerless. I have always loved, in a similar mood, a cold norther, or a political fight, or a night with the neuralgia. She loved her good aunt's exhortations. Moreover, Mrs. Rawley was really a great help as to more strictly practical advice. She knew what Ellen would have to do to get a position. She had herself many friends in various parts of the State, among the church members of her own little sect, and she at once undertook to use her influence on Ellen's behalf. The great drawback, as she rightly said, would be Ellen's ignorance. That girl knew any amount about such miserable stuff as fiction, essay-literature, ancient history, celebrated poetry, and all the rest that makes people what Mrs. Rawley calls over-educated. What poor Ellen did n't know was the one infallible modern method of teaching children how to multiply and divide, and the one infallible modern fashion of making children learn the boundaries, the capitals, the productions, the animals, and the water-courses of all the States in South America, without either a strain upon their memories or a hindrance to their acquirement of other useful knowledge. These devices were the true sorts of information for a teacher to have. No child wants to hear about mere poetry. No over-educated person can teach a child arithmetic. To succeed as a teacher you must be commonplace, dull, patient, plodding, even, if possible, personally uninteresting; but you must, meanwhile, be well up in the infallible modern tricks as aforesaid, you must be a kind but firm disciplinarian, and you must have your heart devoted solely to that one work. Too much knowledge of the wrong sort, such as literary knowledge, ruins you. Ambition that goes beyond the walls of your schoolroom, and sentimentality that looks for some impossible happiness in the future, are alike fatal. School-teaching is steady work, and God meant every young girl to work for her living. Why otherwise was she born unmarried?

"The actual outcome of all this good advice was that Ellen began to prepare herself to pass a teacher's examination. But she was not content with this. So intensely anxious was she to become useful to us that, meanwhile, she was full of plans for other kinds of pedagogical work, to be resorted to if the regular school-teaching failed. The trouble with a bright woman at such a crisis is not that she has too few resources, but that she has too many. They wear her out by their wealth. Ellen had a variety of tastes; she could draw passably, she could play a trifle, she could even write for the papers, she knew two or three foreign languages well enough to be able to give private lessons in them. Against Mrs. Rawley's advice she tried to develop these other possibilities, even while she aimed for a position as a school-teacher. She toiled day and night. Her mind was intensely strained to keep itself fully awake to the new life, and wholly dead to the old. She knew not herself how hard the work was, or how near she long was to a break-down. All that summer she was thus active, and, at least in mercilessness to herself, she fully satisfied even my sister-in-law's exactions. The tension soon told upon her. She was not a strong girl; she had had no experience in playing such a rough game of life as this, while she had no true knowledge of her own weakness itself. My wife looked on in wonder, and was silent. I feared, and could do nothing. Mrs. Rawley, tireless and merciless, rejoiced to see at least so much of her good advice taken as was taken, and felt no fear of the consequences. The Lord was leading that girl, she said. All must be well.

"Towards the end of August, Tom and Mrs. Dover were married. I knew when Ellen first heard of the approaching wedding, though she gave no sign that any one else could have observed. Fate was not minded to release her even yet. The wedding was a quiet affair, but of course the papers had somewhat to say of it. A few days afterwards, however, a horrible thing occurred to poor Ellen, something all of a piece with the rest of our life, to be sure, — and that means that it was no less ridiculous than horrible. Sam Paddington, whom you must know of as the editor of the 'Spirit of the West Wind,' had just been visiting Japan and China. He came back at this time, and landed from the steamer some days after the wedding. He was full of his bluster. Paddington is a man who never hears or sees anything straight, and just now he was puffing and blowing like a whale, and talking about the glories of his ocean journey, and about the horrors of Chinese barbarism. It chanced that in the midst of his ranting he heard somebody say that Tom was married. He did n't stop to ask to whom. He had been away during our earlier troubles; he had known, before starting on his journey, about the original betrothal of Tom and Ellen; he had been on the ocean at the time of the wedding. So then, he being what he is, and things having come to his knowledge as they did, it is not surprising that just after hearing, in this confused way, of the wedding, he met Ellen, in company with her aunt, in the rooms of the Board of Education, and cordially, in the presence of a number of persons, strangers and acquaintances, greeted Ellen as Mrs. Eldon. He had just heard of the wedding, so he hurriedly explained before anybody could stop him. He had long known Mr. Eldon, to whom he hoped erelong to be able to offer his congratulations, just as now he begged leave to pay his humblest respects to— But the thing need n't be remembered further! I was n't there to see, thank God! I only know that Ellen never flinched at the time, that Mrs. Rawley behaved like a sensible woman, and escaped with her as well as possible, and that, when Ellen reached home that day, she was very ill, and lay in her room all the next day. It was then that we first realized how hard the poor girl had been overworking herself. By one of her spirit, I believe that even the shock of that meeting with Paddington might have been borne as quietly and as proudly as she had borne everything else, had she not already been so worn and weary.

"Well, Harold, all this overwork and excitement could have but one ending, and that came early in October. Ellen fell ill with brain fever. I need not tell you how we all then repented of our conspiracy of carelessness, how we felt guilty of the murder of Ellen, how we watched and waited and hoped, until at last we seemed to have been spared the worst. She recovered, — so we thought, — but very slowly and wearily. It was far into January before she could leave the house. That season was, in its early part, uncommonly cold and unhealthy. Everything was against her. But at last she seemed to conquer her enemy, and rose, never complaining, but plainly no longer quite herself. She had lost hope and courage. Yet, so soon as she could once more go about, she returned, as well as she could, to the old round of ideas. She must work, she must be of service. She must not be a burden. The idea now became almost a mania. It haunted her day and night. Her worst troubles were her dreams, which she at last confided to me. For her habit of talking freely with me returned again after her illness. These dreams retained obvious traces of her fever-delirium. In them she would seem to herself to be always wandering in the night, and through horrible storms, in search of the longed-for work as a teacher. The roads would be heavy with deep clay mire, but she would have to go on through the mire; the hills would be steep, but she would have to climb them. A terrible weariness always oppressed her, but still something ordered her to go on. The something usually spoke to her in her dreams in an audible voice. She often tried to describe to me the voice, but could not well succeed. It was, at all events, like the voice of one in great agony, far off somewhere in the dark; it was a complaining, pleading, and yet irresistibly commanding voice. She never could pause while she heard it. It was a little like a child's voice, never, as you might expect, like her good aunt's. Her aunt appeared in the dreams, oddly enough, only as a kindly comforter. But what made the voice still more fearful to Ellen was the fact that, as she told me, it often seemed to be her own voice thus supernaturally dissevered from herself. Yet she also had another delirious dream-fancy about it. It was not only her own voice, but it was that of all forsaken womankind; of all who, like herself, were struggling in a world where duty is everything and there is no love, — struggling, like herself, to be useful, to get a foothold upon life, to accomplish their bitter tasks. They pleaded with her to press on, to be strong, and to save them. But she could never find them, nor the place whither she seemed to be going. And then, again, they would all seem to be a delusion, and those awful and commanding tones would be only her own voice, helplessly begging and wailing far off there in the dark.

"Tom never actually appeared in these dreams,

she told me, although she was constantly thinking of him as she wandered. But never, as it seemed, did she think of him with the faintest anger, or as if he were unkind. It always appeared to her that he was distant, but still loving; shut off from her somehow, but her protector still. She often found herself, as she wandered, praying to him that the great darkness might not weigh her down and altogether crush her. She used to fancy that, though he could never come and find her, he still somehow helped her a little. She used to weep tears of thankfulness, in the dreams, because even in the darkness, as she knew, he never forgot her, always loved her, and tried to aid her all he could. Her hope was that at some time he might be able merely to speak to her, and then, she felt, that other and terrible voice would stop. That was all she hoped for, and that seemed enough, — not that he should ever come, but that he should just once speak.

"The girl must have been very weak-minded, no doubt, to tell me all this. I was, once more, her only confidant. I rejoiced to have found her again. There is a sad pleasure in remembering those last days of her life at home. She seemed to grow very fond of me once more. I had for a while feared, during her great struggle, that she was becoming very hard and cold. All that was now past. She was often very child-like in my company, and I found myself thinking more of the old days, just before her mother died, or again of that time in her life when she ran about so merrily near the house in San Antonio, and when she once found her way to Dover's great dwelling, and talked to him so beautifully.

"At last, just as her convalescence seemed to be fully established, she rose one morning in what seemed the best of spirits. She sang in snatches, and laughed as she talked with us in the family-room; she was full of jokes and merriment; she assured us that she felt her very strongest once more. Now at last, she said, all would go well with her. Of a sudden, just before my regular time of leaving, she grew silent and restless, walked nervously about the room for a little, gazed out of the window into the yard, and finally went off up to her own chamber. She did not appear to bid me good-by, and I went away wondering at the change in her manner. I never saw her alive again. A couple of hours later, when nobody was in the front part of the house, she managed to slip out of the front door. Some of the neighbors saw her go, and later told us about it. She then had on a dark brown traveling suit. In her hand she carried a satchel. She had taken with her some money that she had long been saving up; it may have amounted to thirty or forty dollars. That was all she took. She bade no one farewell, but went away thus in broad daylight — and vanished.

As for us, of course, after looking for her where she might most naturally have gone, we began our search in the most vigorous way. We notified the police; we were very soon, in our anguish, not even afraid of newspaper publicity. We published descriptions of her; we sent word to all who might have occasion to help us. In fact, she evaded us, in her insane simplicity, by merely taking the least expected direction in her wanderings. From our house she first walked out to San Miguel station, and there took the first train that passed going south. She left it at Mayfield, walked into the mountains, and found refuge for the night in a farm-house. There she appeared, on the whole, despite some oddness, fairly rational and self-possessed. Her story seemed unsatisfactory to the people, but for that night they could not be sure but it all might be somehow true. She had a school promised her, she said, in the mountains near La Honda. She appeared to know the district well, and gave the real names of its trustees. She had set out from Mayfield that afternoon in a carriage, with an aunt of hers, to go up there; but the carriage had broken down on the road. Her aunt had got assistance from some one in getting the broken carriage back to Mayfield, and she herself had ventured to walk to the nearest farm-house for shelter. To-morrow morning her aunt would return, with the repaired vehicle. Then they would go on together. Such was her story. Ellen spoke a little wildly, however, just once, of a certain Peter Dover, a rich old man, she said, who had once in her childhood promised always to help her. She seemed, moreover, a little fearful of conversing too freely. She said to the farmer's wife that she knew herself to be an odd person, with some very singular notions. She was always afraid to talk to strangers, because nobody would quite understand her without first well knowing her. Ellen, meanwhile, appeared strong and unwearied, even after all her long walk. The next morning she rose before dawn, and silently left the house, which had but one story, by way of her own window, leaving four or five dollars to pay for her lodging, and a note to say that her aunt had called for her in the night. Then, of course, the people knew what this all must have meant. But she evaded pursuit by taking a hill-path. She purchased food that day at another farm-house, managed within another twenty-four hours to reach Menlo Park, took the train there for San Jose, under the guidance of some new illusion, and so wandered on, escaping our pursuit by the very readiness with which she at times seemed to court observation. Perhaps the police were to blame for it all. At any rate, it is hard to see how she could have kept out of our sight so long.

Her hallucination, during her wandering, was, despite all variations, always the same as to the main thing. She was looking for a country school which had been promised her, and she had one great patron, a very old and wealthy man, Peter Dover by name, who had also promised her his aid in all her undertakings. To one or two people, young girls in each case, she did indeed hint that there was another patron, whose name she would not tell, and who was even richer and kinder than Peter Dover himself. This patron, however, was a great way off. She would, doubtless, never see him again. Everybody who had much to do with her concluded before long that she was insane. But this conclusion was usually not fully reached until she had already gone away. She always evaded pursuit.

"These wanderings lasted five days. After those first two days, she did less walking, seemed a little less tireless, but was still cheerful, and used for the most part the cars, — stopping at out-of-the-way stations, and inquiring for people whom nobody knew. On the fourth and fifth days the weather was cloudy and threatening. The end of the fifth day found her in Alameda, at a hotel, where she passed the night without being suspected. She had thus gone clear around the bay. She was now very grave and quiet. The people who later described her presence at the hotel all thought her much older than in fact she was. That night there was a great storm, with heavy rain, which lasted all the next day. Ellen left the hotel the next morning, ostensibly to take the cars for the city. At seven o'clock in the evening she appeared, drenched with rain, haggard, wild-looking, and plainly insane, at a house far out beyond the suburbs of East Oakland, and inquired the way to Peter Dover's estate. At the place where she called there chanced at this hour to be one woman alone on the premises. This woman, terrified beyond expression at the sight of the insane girl, still tried her best, as a decent Christian must needs do at such a moment, to keep Ellen from going out again into the storm. Peter Dover was dead, she said, dead for years and years. Ellen wept at this, and begged once more for the direction, and at last went off, raving and sobbing, into the darkness and the storm.

"Why should I add the rest, Harold? You no doubt know already that Mrs. Eldon, Tom's newly married wife, who was still living in the great house that had once been Dover's, was just then alone. Tom, as I told you, was serving his country in Sacramento. He used to return every few days. He was constantly running back and forth. But during that storm he did not return. And Mrs. Eldon, the very next morning, the furious wind having a little abated, found Ellen in the garden, just under her own chamber window — dead.

"The same day I heard of it, and went to bring my Ellen home. Her face was very gentle and peaceful now, with even more than her old childish contentment in it. As I stood in that house there beside her, I saw, for that time, and for that time only, the face of the woman who had destroyed her. We buried Ellen three days later. Only the family were permitted at the funeral. The coroner's inquest lasted a long time afterwards. There were all sorts of pretenses made for lengthening it. Public curiosity was aroused, and so the whole thing was investigated, — her flight, her wanderings, her sayings, her doings, her death. There was gossip, shoulder-shrugging, pity, scorn, the idiot gabble of newspapers and of lying men, the vile sympathy of an accursed world, for us — and for Mrs. Eldon. At last the sacrilege was over, and our Ellen's memory was now once more our own."

With these words Escott's story ended.

CHAPTER VII.

A STRANGER GUEST.

Tom Eldon had appointed to meet Harold Sunday morning, at the Oakland ferry-boat, for the purpose of conducting him on the intended visit. Just before the time for setting out to keep the appointment, Tom Eldon found himself thinking afresh of the unhappy fatality that had always attended his best efforts to be heroic and self-sacrificing. During his career he had done at least a few good deeds, — so he often used to assert to himself; and yet those were the very deeds that had invariably resulted in mischief. Just now, as he reflected, his life had but one very dark shadow in it; and that need n't have been there at all, had he not chosen, on a certain great occasion, to attempt a picturesque and quite uncalled-for act of devotion.

The younger Eldon, in fact, at the moment when we now meet him, had just reached the age at which a man who has disappointed the great expectations of numerous friends feels a little keenly how commonplace an affair life is. In his early youth, Tom had fascinated a great many people besides the susceptible Alf Escott. Nobody had understood him, but everybody had recognized his talents. His mother had died during his childhood. With his father he had never had close acquaintance. He had spent enough of his boyhood away from California to lose close sympathy with his fellows at home. His intercourse with strangers had made him a good converser, an easy dissembler, and a very well informed man. His ambitions had been numerous, and his capacities for a time extraordinary. His father's position, however, had been, of course, a serious handicap to his own ambitions; for Tom had never had his father's tastes, and yet was sure to inherit at least a part of his father's responsibilities. But friends had formerly hoped that he would some day grow up to his duties. Years ago, however, the course of his life carried him yet further away from these duties.

For just as Tom came of age, his father's brother, also a California pioneer, and a man almost equal in energy and ability to the great Alonzo himself, died unexpectedly, leaving a considerable fortune and no children. The two brothers had for years been bitter enemies; but Tom's uncle had loved the boy's gentle ways, and had long admired his cleverness. The result hereof was that Tom found himself suddenly possessed of a modest fortune in his own right, his uncle's whole estate having been bequeathed to him. This first triumph of his boyish diplomacy proved to be the great obstacle in the way of Tom's further career. The inherited wealth was, indeed, not comparable in size to Alonzo's vast fortune; but Tom was now relatively independent of his father. He became thenceforth for a while not only indolent but also erratic. His close friendship with Alf Escott was much more useful to the affectionate professor than to himself. He received, indeed, a great deal of inspiration; but he did nothing with it. His ambitions grew warmer and warmer; but they simply boiled away into idle clouds of vapor. He wondered how soon he should begin to accomplish great things. In fact, he accomplished nothing.

In those days, of course, he used to have numerous love-affairs, — all shallow, for a long time at least, and harmlessly amusing. He sighed, and wrote little poems about them, — poems which he sometimes read to the too appreciative Escott. Then he soon forgot the loves, and sometimes even burned the poems. For the rest, he was a comparatively innocent man. He had few close friends. Many of the young men of his set called him a Jesuit, and were suspicious of his pale face, and of his voice that sounded like the flowing of a streamlet in spring-time. Such men thought him rather affected, accused him of making eyes at people for a living, and damned his self-conceit generally. Tom laughed at all this, in his quiet way, and retained considerable influence over these acquaintances, despite their damning. For once that he offended them, he fascinated them twice. He never joined in their worse dissipations, whether they remained his friends or became his enemies. He regarded himself as a person of rather ideal purity. He accordingly used to feel quite out of place in California.

In the background of his consciousness, through all these days, the image of Margaret Dover might often have been found, had he dared to look for it. People are supposed to love their exact opposites. Yet she was in many ways like him; and for that very reason he admired her. The fact is that we hate nothing so bitterly as the sight of our own faults in other people; but if we have certain virtues that we vaingloriously observe and admire in ourselves, we may even revere them in another, especially if the other is a woman. For, as woman, she excites in us no feeling of rivalry. She only seems to be a slight indication of what we shall become when we get to heaven.

Margaret was with perfect ease so much that Tom would already have loved to be! Many of her qualities were, he saw, but the fulfillment of his own. She was thoughtful, soft-voiced, self-contained, and a perfect manager of other people; she was clever, appreciative, clear-headed, sensible, practical; take her for all in all, she was also, he thought, even something of a genius. But there were in her, besides, plenty of characteristics that not even he could suspect himself of possessing, vain as he was. She was naturally so contented with everything, so certain of what she wanted to do, so full of interest in people of many kinds, so free from all sentimental notions and from all foolish ambitions! Whenever he met her in social life, he felt lifted entirely out of his ordinary self. She did not arouse him to all sorts of wild and frothy schemes, such as came into his head when he talked with Alf Escott. She simply contented him with life and the world. To talk with her, he used to say to himself, was like watching the pole-star. Yet for a long time he did not dare to think of her with any affection. She seemed altogether too nearly perfect for that.

What instinct kept him, during these years, from mentioning her to Alf Escott he could not have told. Doubtless at first it was little more than an unwillingness to excite comments. He did not dare to confess, even to himself, his true feeling towards her. Much less, as secretive man, did he wish to call forth any questions from another. And, in general, as he knew, Escott had obstinately determined, in those years, to think nothing and to hear nothing of the great world beyond the quondam professor's own desk.

There came a time, however, when Tom Eldon began to see another reason for silence. He had consciously become at last an undeclared lover of Margaret Dover. And at Escott's house he saw, meanwhile, the father and the daughter, Ellen, and was not the last person in the group to predict what their relations might become in case he should ever choose. The situation charmed Eldon, and terrified him. He had never meant to be a breaker of hearts, but he could not for his life keep from enjoying the homage that he got at Escott's home. He resolved to be at least a true friend to the family, and to give them no ground for accusing him of any actual betrayal. They might worship him, if they must, and he would amuse himself; and still he would be a faithful helper, and an affectionate son to the old professor, — not to say an ideal friend to the daughter!

Vanity and Benevolence are beautiful comrades. They walk gayly side by side, each charmed with the other, each amusing the other by means of an endless wealth of pious lies. It is not until they come to a very deep stream, and try to ford or to swim it, that they part company. For Benevolence, always being, as the inferior virtue, a little awkward and clumsy in such crises, is apt to get lost somewhere in the floods. Then the other, after long and hard swimming, has to weep in lone some and shivering nakedness on the further bank, fruitlessly calling for the old friend, who has sunk out of sight, perhaps forever.

Such was the actual experience of Tom Eldon. The thing came about, however, so unexpectedly that it simply stunned him. First, before he really knew what he was intending to do, he found himself Margaret's accepted lover. The two agreed to keep the matter a secret from the world for a little time, although their secrecy was an absurd delusion, so far as concerned the gossips. But now, Tom, as he visited Escott from time to time, during a period when Escott was in ill-health, and was accepting some pecuniary aid from him, felt fairly like a traitor. Not a word had yet passed to commit him in that quarter, but he knew, even better than the Escotts, how they looked up to him. He daily made good resolutions. He would be benevolent, affectionate, loyal, — in short, a brother. When they came to know about his betrothal, the news would doubtless vex them at first. But later they would appreciate his delicacy of feeling and his honesty of purpose. He wondered how and when he could best tell them about it. Often he tried to begin. But something prevented him. He saw the Escotts very frequently, and yet he lamented that his efforts to win them over to a gradual understanding of his new position now only made them more distant than they used to be. How could he speak to Escott about the new life, when the whole family had grown so reserved? And then again, did he dare persuade Margaret to let him reveal the secret as yet? On the whole, he thus had to keep silent.

Then came his quarrel with Margaret. For, despite the gossips, there never had been but one quarrel. Its beginning was so slight, he could hardly remember how or when it started. But it was the first struggle of two proud natures, and it was no trifling matter. Tom saw through the whole of it how much more he cared for her than she for him, — how unnecessary he was to her, how endlessly important she had become to him. The discovery, however, only increased both his anguish and his stubbornness. She seemed to him immeasurably unkind. He became very cruel to himself, also, and the whole relation was broken off. His life for the time was as terrible as you please. Then he heard gossiping remarks among his friends, and knew that he was an object of pitying curiosity, and thereafter he felt himself afresh the forlornest and worst deceived lover on God's earth, and contemplated suicide, — and then offered himself to Ellen.

This last was, without exception, he felt, the noblest act of his life. Another man, defeated, despised, scorned, by the fairest of women, might have been crushed. He, — he knew his duty as a man, he perceived that he was necessary to the Escotts, he rose proudly above his horrible misfortunes, he disregarded his anguish, and with still bleeding heart he resolved to devote himself to the happiness of these loving people. It was indeed his crowning act! He could n't help feeling that, try as he would. He looked in vain among his acquaintances for a man who would have been capable of such a deed. He doubted if men of the sort often grew in California. California was too sordid a place for them. There was a deep and secret comfort, therefore, in feeling that he alone served the ideal to this extent, among a race that did naught but bow the knee to Baal. This consciousness nerved him for his trial, made him tender and reverent to Ellen above the custom of ordinary lovers, and before long almost gave him back his peace of mind.

The candid Boscowitz gave, to be sure, in that unlucky conversation with Escott, another interpretation to the matter. He called it spiting the widow. Tom knew, long before Boscowitz spoke thus to Escott, that some such opinion was abroad. But part of his heroism, as we see, lay in being willing to face just such calumnies. The finest deeds are the ones that can most easily be called bad names, — a truth which Satan, whenever he appears among the Sons of God, is doubtless accustomed to demonstrate by what he says against the saints. Just as it 's the highest courage to be called a coward for refusing to fight a duel, so, of course, it must be the deepest devotion to do for pure benevolence what some Boscowitz, or Satan, or other gossip, regards as done for pure spite. Conscience is of course the only test ; and if ever a man's conscience approved him, Tom's now did. He was making Ellen so happy, he was devoting himself to her so fully, he was serving the ideal so simply and purely! Whose praise was he thinking of? She did n't know the facts; and the people who knew misinterpreted them. What was there in all this to tickle his pride? For what was he therefore doing this but the noblest inner joy and peace of the spirit? Tom felt now the real beauty of true goodness. He could appreciate the ardor of the men who by faith had subdued kingdoms, wrought righteousness, stopped the mouths of lions, and all the rest!

He could even understand about their being persecuted, sawn asunder, or what not! They wandered about in sheep-skins and goat-skins; while he, — he, as jilted lover, devoted absolutely to the service of one whom he did not love, could at all events appreciate their feelings!

But the catastrophe, — that was as simple a matter as it was contemptible in all its surroundings and horrible in its results. A man could n't live through such an ordeal as Tom had deliberately chosen for himself without, of course, a little inner strife. And when he met Margaret, by chance, at a moment that somehow forced them both to forget mere pride, how could he avoid falling at her feet, as it were, and confessing all? He did n't confess it plainly, of course; that would have been unmanly. He only hinted, and looked pleadingly into her eyes, and so prepared himself to bear through life the memory of a heart-breaking parting. That too, he felt, he must endure. He somehow even had a painful longing to endure it. It would be part of the sentimental heritage that noble-minded youth passes on to toilsome middle life, and that a busy man once in a while mournfully remembers, over a bottle of wine, or amid the smoke of a cigar! It 's all heart-rending, we know; but it 's inevitable. Only at this price do we serve the ideal! So the heart-breaking parting took place, very simply and properly, of course — just a word or two, a touch of hands, a never-to-be-forgotten last gaze of eye into eye. Then all was over forever. There has seldom been a more tragic scene!

A few days later, however, they met again by accident. There turned out to be a service that Margaret needed done for her. Tom found it out somehow. Surely there was nothing wrong in that! He did the service, and it brought them together yet once more. Her behavior was perfect. She was simple, formal, distant, only barely civil as it were. She understood the calls of duty, without any doubt. She never by a word or a look tempted him. But then, in the course of that little transaction, there came, purely as a matter of business, the Sunday afternoon journey on the boat, mixed up just as it was with that infernal constitution-making and all the rest! And afterwards, the disgraceful and overwhelming interview with Escott in Boscowitz's presence, and the frantic conduct of that wild girl, Bertha, who, by the way, as Tom had observed long ago, was herself dumbly and insanely in love with him! What could he do? What is a man's life worth under such persecution? What wonder that he was again near suicide? What wonder that when it was at last all over, and his good deeds were all flung back into his face, he saw no refuge but his old true love again? If you can't serve the ideal in deserts, are you then forbidden to serve it in palaces? If the angel with the fiery sword drives you from the straight and narrow way, are you not permitted to make a trial of some more flowery path instead, so long as you steadfastly scheme to go heavenwards? Besides, with all this undeserved reproach and slander added, Tom felt that his new duties would be not altogether thornless, even if they were to be rose-embowered.

One more mistake he did indeed make. When he returned to Margaret, to throw himself at her feet, to beg pardon for the past, and to tell her that he had been scorned in his humble efforts to be a saint, he did not dare to tell her everything. He kept back some things that Escott, not to mention Boscowitz and Satan, would most emphatically have insisted upon. But what would you expect? Is a man to scourge himself with a rope and wear hair-cloth, every time he goes near the only beloved lady of his heart? Tom spared himself and the truth a little, as any man once for all must do when he talks with a woman! Tom did not describe all that had happened that night at Boscowitz's. He let Escott's jealousy seem perhaps a trifle too manifest. And he did not make much mention of Ellen. In fact, he thenceforth hated to think of her. She, like the base, — whoever he may have been, — had thrown a pearl away. Tom did not like to price it; modesty forbade; but the act seemed to him an unkind one. So he failed to represent the thing quite justly to Margaret, who, after what he thought long hesitation, yielded to his pleadings, took him back again, and gracefully let herself be loved by him.

But fate was so unmerciful! That he had not told everything to Margaret was visited upon him with a horrible cruelty after their marriage, upon the occurrence of that last and worst catastrophe of all. Margaret would then hear nothing, would believe nothing, would forgive nothing. It was a terror thenceforth to think of the wrath of that proud nature in those first weeks after Ellen's death. Never had a well-meaning man been so misused! And if in time Margaret had been even proud enough to recover herself, to give no sign thereafter to the most familiar friends of what she felt, to treat Tom himself with the most cruel of distant kindness, to humiliate his still loving soul to the dust, her newly adopted manner was only worse than her old wrath. What hope was there now of ever removing this dark shadow, or of ever winning back the old peace? Such had been their life since the birth of their child. For the boy's sake and for form's sake, Margaret was now outwardly, but only outwardly, reconciled. Yet, alas, in what lonesome separation from her and her love had Tom not been forced all the while to live, even until this very day!

The whole thing, of course, had begun by this time to degrade him, as even he himself felt. He was now no longer an ideal nature. He had lost faith. He was without those old noble purposes; he was even a mildly sensuous man. He tried to enjoy the good things of the world in a reasonable fashion, he amused himself as he might, he comforted his lonesomeness as quietly as he was able; while she, — she no longer inquired or cared what he did. She treated him with a cruel and playful show of considerate friendliness; she bestowed upon him no deeper feeling of any sort. She never quarreled with him, and was always endlessly fascinating to him. Yet he had almost given up the hope of any true reconciliation. He would have to bear this until the end.

That is the reward, one sees, of devotion to ideal ends, of altruism, and the rest. Tom used to sigh when he thought of it all, — used to sigh, and lounge at his club. His wife had taken all his ambitions out of him. He no longer hoped for any career. Whatever charitable things friends might say of him, the fact was that he daily grew not better, but worse. Erelong, at this rate, he would become merely a young man about town. And this was the tale of Tom's descent.

When Harold and Tom Eldon had found each other, that morning, at the boat, they amused themselves by pacing back and forth on the broad lower deck, in the rear of the cabins, — not far from where Ellen and her father had once concealed themselves on a certain afternoon. The two talked of the coming election, — of the Sunday law, and of the other things that were at stake in that canvass. They spoke to each other with a certain constraint, all the while, like men who had not quite discovered each other's spiritual whereabouts. Then Harold, approaching directly their immediate business, asked Tom to tell him a little more concerning Alonzo Eldon.

"I have never known your father personally," Harold said, "nor have I known his early career, save by hearsay and in fragments. I 'm to present a case to him to-day. I feel as if I 'd like to have known more of him. Of course I ought to have done so. I 'm ashamed to confess my relative ignorance of one of our first men. But he 's always seemed a matter of course to me, — a great central, social fact that I have n't inquired into. I know, indeed, by the way, that he was born in my own native town in New England. That 's all. I feel, on approaching him, how little an unpractical fellow like myself really understands him."

Then Tom, in answer to this and further questions, rapidly sketched Alonzo's early life: how he was, as Harold knew, a transplanted Yankee; how he was a pioneer of the very early days, having come already in 1844, as an agent of a Boston mercantile house; and how he had settled at Monterey, and then within two years had married Tom's mother. She was the very youthful daughter of one of those first and oldest of the American residents on the California coast. Her own mother was a native Californian, and she herself the only heiress to a vast landed estate. With this marriage Alonzo's good fortune had begun. Tom then told how Alonzo, at that time a man just under thirty, had taken part in the conquest troubles, doing, to be sure, more marching than fighting, though that was the enemy's fault. Then, however, he had changed his place of business to San Francisco, and soon afterwards had taken part in the gold excitement of the summer of 1848. "He saw enough of the mines that year," said Tom, "to keep out of them thenceforth for a long time, to his great advantage." Then followed Alonzo's remarkable career as shipping merchant at San Francisco, his greatest misfortunes, his hardest trials, and some of his finest successes. Then, too, began his influence as a leading citizen. "It was odd," said Tom, "that he would have nothing to do with the Vigilance Committee of 1851. He was in the very singular position of opposing that committee, and yet taking prominent part in the Committee of '56. It showed his independence, I suppose." In the '56 Committee, however, Alonzo was even one of the leaders; being on the executive committee itself. That year was in some ways a turning-point in his career. "Thenceforth," said Tom, "he came to give his attention more and more to the industrial development of the State, and to let the shipping business get into the background. Finally he retired from the latter business altogether." Possibly a good reason for this change, Tom pointed out, was the fact that some of the land titles then began to look as if they might within a lifetime come to be settled, and the further fact that Alonzo had gradually grown to be himself more and more of a great land-owner. "It was in '56," said Tom, "right in the midst of the Vigilance Committee times, that Alf Escott first landed in San Francisco. The impulsive man joined the committee at once, met father, and became quite intimate with him. In 1859, when the Virginia mining excitement began, with the discovery of the Comstock lode, Escott, just after one of his magazine failures, went over early, partly for pure love of adventure, and partly as a newspaper correspondent. It was he who persuaded father to go into silver-mining at all. He advised father early of some of the important discoveries, and induced him to make the journey over the mountains. Escott passed the whole of the starvation winter of '59–'60 in the Virginia mines, and when father went there, in the spring of '60, the two were together for some time. That was the year of their closest intimacy, as I well remember hearing, though I was then but a boy of thirteen. Escott was quite incapable of reaping any personal advantage from a mining excitement of any sort. He came out of the Virginia country as poor as when he went in, and with only an incurable mania thenceforth for buying mining shares on margins whenever he had a little money saved up. It 's been his financial ruin. Escott is a man of very high principles, but he will gamble in mining-stocks at every chance.

"But the thing to remember," Tom went on, "is that they were then close friends, father and Alf Escott; that it was Escott, and nobody else, who gave father good and early warning of the importance of the thing, and induced him to begin investing over there, so that father thus in one sense owes a great share of his fortune to the old professor's advice. I think father 's always been apt to forget that, because the professor himself knows no more about silver mines than he knows about how it would feel to be frightened. What he told father was, of course, only hearsay, warmed up by a glowing professorial imagination. It was father's own brain that made anything out of the information. But still it 's true that, without Escott's urging, father would n't have gone that spring to Washoe, and might never have begun the interest in silver mines which he kept so long and so profitably."

As Tom told this tale, the boat had already reached the new mole, projecting out from the eastern shore. Here, the great railway station, then just finished, was the pride of the California traveler's heart. The two companions passed forward, went out by the end of the boat, walked in the noisy crowd of Sunday pleasure-seekers to the long train under the vast roof of the station, and entered the cars amid a din of bell-ringing that, for the moment, quite suppressed conversation. Erelong the train was plunging with its usual recklessness through a long Oakland street. When it reached the more crowded parts of the city, men jumped on and off it very frequently, and with curiously little concern as to whether it was standing still or not. It made frequent stops at its little stations, but when it rushed swiftly ahead again, it took no notice of the people afoot or of the horses; and they, as they passed to and fro over the quite unprotected tracks, appeared almost as oblivious in their turn of what it was doing. There seemed to be a general faith that any

Oaklander who might chance to get his legs under the wheels would doubtless have by some surgeon, to stop his wounds, lest he should bleed to death. And, in fact, if we may venture upon a little advertising, the distinguished surgeons of Oakland are an ornament and an honor to the place, being, as report says, amongst the most well-practiced of their profession in regard to double amputations, whether above or below the knees.

Tom, meanwhile, continued his account of his father's career. After the war it was that Alonzo, now a vastly wealthy man, had become a leader in many of the greatest industrial enterprises of the State. And this fact yearly required of him more and more personal interest in political affairs. Just there, however, had begun the estrangement between him and the professor. Escott had again and again dabbled in politics, but the one thing for which he had not the faintest shadow of understanding was political management. That a man like Alonzo should venture to influence secretly a party convention, by even the most undoubtedly innocent of means, was, Tom said, a scandal and an abomination to Escott. But to do a similar thing with a legislature, that Escott called simply damnable. The professor, oddly enough, laughed at the proposal of such doings if it came from Boscowitz; but he scorned and condemned without laughing when he heard of such things as coming from a man like Eldon. Some plain speech that Tom's father could not brook had begun the estrangement. Eldon had really tried his best to make the matter good again by securing to Escott the professorship in the Sunset College in 1867. But the breach had only grown wider and deeper, until the great trouble at the time of Escott's dismissal, and since.

"It's the old story of a quarrel between two strong and unyielding men," said Tom, "men who have been close friends, and who have one day said the fatal words." Tom was aware, of course, all this while, that Harold must have heard Escott's account of the later troubles. But when Williamson, last Thursday, had brought Harold and Tom Eldon together for Escott's sake, and at the wish of both of them, enough had been said beforehand to make the two feel, without any explanation, that they were agreed so far as concerned doing their best to right the old wrongs. They both knew that no direct speech about one matter could ever pass between them.

When they reached the station at East Oakland, Tom's carriage was waiting. A short drive along one or two straight streets soon brought them to the beginning of the suburban road, and after passing one little depression they came out close by the shore of Lake Merritt, and then drove along by the plashing little waves of that broad and generally placid pool. Tom's manner was more reflective than ever. He ventured, in answer to further hints, even upon some criticisms of his father's qualities. "I notice," he said, profoundly, "that every strong man 's a heap of contradictions. Perhaps you, as philosopher, can tell why. I can't. But the more there is of a man, the more warfare and dissension there always seems to be in him. People abuse father in every sort of way. I 've heard things said of him that 'd make your hair stand on end. But still," continued Tom, "although I 'm sure I revere my father as the son of such a man should do, I often have to say that some unjust criticisms have a fashion of containing glimpses, as it were, of a true conception of some of his real faults, — one-sided and cruelly distorted glimpses, to be sure, but real ones. The fact is, such a man could n't exist without great faults. He 's a type of the community. He 's grown up in a world of the bitterest contradictions, of the most merciless enmities. How should he fail to show the fact?

"He 's overbearing," Tom went on thoughtfully; "there 's no doubt of that. But yet in some moods he 's as tender-hearted as a woman. He scorns public criticism. I love to see him stand up and defy it. Yet there are people whose lightest word of praise makes him tremble like a leaf, and whose blame simply terrifies him, or, what 's still more a sign of his weakness, enrages him beyond measure. My wife is one of the persons who has such an influence over him, though, to be sure, it 's never his rage that she excites. And yet, do you know, years ago, before we were married, there was almost a feud between them. She has conquered him utterly. But among men, the one whose opinion he most dreaded was, in the old days, Alf Escott himself. That 's why they fought so relentlessly when they did fight.

"The thing," concluded Tom, "that I most revere in him is his grip on life. That 's what I lack. These pioneers who removed so many mountains, — how some of us envy them their clear faith in what they wanted to do! We 're restless like them, but where 's their power and their magic in our lives? What will the State be when they 've gone? Won't it become flat and stale, like so much of the northern Mississippi Valley region, where people and climate and landscape and all seem to me to tend towards nothing but vast production and limitless dull mediocrity?"

Harold was interested at finding Tom so much of a thinker. "What I am always charmed with in the California leader of men," Harold replied, "is his anxiety to leave something of a very impressive sort behind him that shall better future generations. These monumental enterprises — a great observatory or what not — why, if the East produced them as fast, in proportion to its resources, as our leading men seem disposed to make our State produce them, the world would n't contain the things that might result."

"Father's schemes, you know," said Tom, "are as big and as finely conceived as any man's. Perhaps you 'll get him to talk about 'em, if you want to. Of course he has an over-confidence in the power of mere money. But, do you know, it seems sometimes very pathetic to me, who 've had all sorts of educational advantages offered to me, and have used 'em so ill, and rejected altogether so many of 'em, and done so wretchedly with what time I 've spent over books and the like, — I say, it seems to me very pathetic to observe father's suppressed longing for things of that kind. He loves to denounce learning of all the old-fashioned sorts, in the most outspoken way. Education, he says, ought to be entirely reformed. Our American colleges, he declares, even the best of the Eastern ones, are generally nurseries of pedantry and snobbishness. But yet, do you know, he simply adores learning, and of old-fashioned sorts at that. If you want to please him, just tell him very soberly that he was meant by nature to be a professor of moral philosophy, and that he missed his vocation when he came out to California and went into business. You 'll see his face lighten up at once. A man in your position, Mr. Harold, has a great advantage in approaching him, for that very reason. He knows you 've no axe to grind on your own behalf. He doubtless has pooh-hoohed you whenever he 's heard your name of late. He 's called you, I don't doubt (though I have n't heard him), dreamer, bookworm, I won't dare to guess what all. But the solemn fact is that you 'll appear to him to-day as a man from another and brighter sphere than his own. So long as you don't arouse the temporarily slumbering business man in him, he 'll listen to you with a certain reverence. Oppose him concerning a purely business matter, to be sure, and he 'll think nothing whatever of crushing you, or anybody else in the like place, as if you were a fly. Not that I want to frighten you, of course; but, once for all, that's the man, you see. I'm sure I want to be frank about it with you."

"You 're very kind. But, Mr. Eldon, is n't this matter in hand a business matter? What chance have I, then? I suppose I shall not exactly be crushed; but how about my poor plans?"

"Well, you 're to get your instructions pretty soon from one to whom I can't hold a candle. But my opinion is that it's no matter of business at all, with him, this Oakfield Creek affair. I regard it as wholly a sentimental concern. The plain facts are that the settlers have no legal rights whatever, and that they have all the moral rights you please. And father really knows that, and is blinded to it only by his bitterness, which, I assure you, exists mainly towards Alf Escott alone. This bitterness, however, is next door to warm friendship, and has been all the more bitter on that account. Those are the facts. If we fail on this occasion, to be sure, he 'll intrench himself behind impregnable business considerations henceforth, and he 'll defy us forever. But, just now, it 's no more a matter of business than if it were a quarrel between two lovers." Tom spoke these last words with a certain consciousness that checked the flow of his speech.

But Harold, his memory aroused by the sight of roads that had once been so familiar to him, found himself looking northward over the foot-hills, towards his old home, which must be at least three miles distant from their present position. He could see, better than he had yet done since his return to California, the brow of the hill that overlooked the familiar place. The old longing returned, and the recollection of his dream. It seemed a pity to be thus wearing away his time in the company of people who were as puzzling and doubtful in their characters as they were distinguished in their positions. The homely odor of what the Californian calls the tarweed filled the autumn air. It used to seem to Harold, often, as he remembered, the dreariest of the accompaniments of the dry season. But now it made him almost wild with long-forgotten hopes and desires. He burned to be done with all this stupid task, and to be free to wander over the winding roads once more, towards the dear place, in solitary and melancholy delight, looking up at the dark hills, and breathing the familiar air.

While he thought of these things, the team suddenly turned into the winding drive that led to Tom Eldon's house. Harold saw lawn, garden, fountain, and then the high gable ends of the great house. The carriage stopped close by the front steps, and the little journey was done.

BOOK II.—IN THE CONTRA COSTA HILLS.

CHAPTER VIII.

THE ROSE-GARDEN.

MARGARET had been notified by telegram, of course, of the coming of her new guest, and met her husband at the front door with the most gracious of friendly greetings. Harold had so long avoided the company of women that he felt an almost boyish bashfulness as she appeared. He looked a trifle excited; the little flush was on his well-formed face; his eyes were afraid to meet hers. He only saw at a glance that she was radiantly beautiful. He stammered as he was introduced, and felt more like a fool than he had done for years, save in his dreams. He was conscious, moreover, that the journey had made him dusty, and he felt that a drive during the California drought may be displeasing to a man's sense of neatness after he has lived for a while amid cleaner landscapes. It was not until after they had gone up-stairs to their rooms, and had later rejoined Mrs. Eldon in the parlor, that he found himself at ease again. Then he observed with amusement that, after his little flurry of confusion and admiration, all the suspicion and prejudice with which he had come to see her had forthwith vanished; he had already reached a centre of indifference, so to speak, where he regarded her only as a beautiful woman, whom he might or might not come to like. For her part, she was plainly eager to begin the business before them. She was full of some plan that caused her no small delight. But she checked herself to ask about the little journey, and how California scenery impressed Mr. Harold in these days; and then to lament the recent weather, which she had somehow found bad for her roses. Then she inquired of Tom whether he had seen father this morning. He had not. This fact caused her to laugh gently. "So!" she said, "I shall have quite a surprise in store for you." All this time Harold was noticing her low and flowing voice, which seemed very plainly, as he thought, to come from a heart that nature had meant to make full of health and peace, however her fortune might have changed it. At all events, so he observed to himself, the day was sure at this rate to prove amusing. But soon she passed from these first questions to weightier matters.

"I asked you, Tom, about father," she said, with a look of gay and mysterious triumph in her face, "because I wanted to know whether you 'd seen him to-day. I just got the oddest letter from him, written late last night, and sent over by special messenger this morning. It 's very pretty, I think, and it 's about precisely this business of ours. I judge from it that most of our little plots are forestalled already. So the letter 's the very first thing to consider; and yet, as you 'll see, we shall have something important to do when we meet father, after all. So I think, if you 'll let me, Mr. Harold, I 'll read it right now to you both, because it 's so necessary for our undertaking that we should all hear it, and what I shall read of it is n't private, for us at least. I 'm so glad, too, Mr. Harold, that you could come in time to learn of it before seeing father. You 'll be saved much trouble. Shall I read it?"

Both Tom and Harold assented with joyful curiosity. Margaret moved from where she was sitting to get into a little better light; and as Harold rose to help her adjust a chair, he noticed for the first time the graceful outline of her hair and neck as she turned sidewise. There was a magnificent bouquet of roses at the table where she now seated herself, — dark red roses that contrasted finely with her pale face. When she began to read her face lost quite suddenly the lively look that it wore in conversation and assumed a prettily prim and practical seriousness. Surely, Harold said to himself, he would n't be noticing all these things about her if he had n't passed so long a time without seeing any fair woman. It was absurd how he watched her every gesture. There was in her eyes just the faintest reminder of his wife's eyes; and in her expression, also, when she began to read, there was something that made him think of his wife reading to him.

But, of course, all that must have been because no woman save his wife had ever read to him at all. He began at once, and irresistibly, to picture his old library, with the great west window that looked towards the bay, with the red-cushioned window lounge that he used to love so much, and himself, seated this time in his big chair a little back from the window, while his wife, nearer the light, read; not in this voice of Margaret's, exactly, to be sure, — rather in a clearer, fuller tone, without the soft fluency of this voice, but surely with more music and emphasis. But what nonsense! He must listen to Margaret now, and stop dreaming. What was she saying? He had lost the beginning of it, except that of course it was "dear Margaret," and had in it something about expecting to meet company at her house, and wanting in advance to write and confess to her what could n't be said before a miscellaneous group of people. Well, what was coming now? Margaret was reading these words: —

"The fact is, I have just had a strange interview that has brought up a number of old occurrences forgotten years ago. I must tell you about it. I heard the other day of the grave misfortunes that have beset anew our old friend and enemy, the professor, Alf Escott. You and I have sometimes talked about him, of late years. Perhaps you know that upon my side there has never been any malice, though he has forced me to oppose him openly a good deal. I still much admire the old man, as I always did. I should have seen that he never came to harm if he had any way let me. But something, I can't tell what, unless it may have been the malicious intervention of third parties, has years ago turned him against me." . . . Here Margaret seemed to omit something. Her eye wandered a little down the page. She looked the least bit pained, as she did this, and her cheek flushed a trifle. Harold himself, as a quick-feeling man, guessed the probable cause, became conscious of Tom's presence once more, and warmly sympathized in his heart with poor Margaret. Doubtless Alonzo must have made some stupid reference to Ellen. This whole incident was hardly a second in passing, and Margaret's voice was quite clear again when she went on. Harold felt keenly, however, what graves one must tread upon when one entered this seemingly so cheerful household. But, during that second, strange to say, he had already resolved in his mind that Margaret could never have been in the least to blame.

"Well," Margaret's voice went on, reading the letter, "since learning of these calamities of Alf Escott's, the feeling has come over me more and more that it 's a great vexation to have to continually fight a man that 's down. He 's my enemy in the matter of the Oakfield Creek disputes, but those, too, I want to have done with some day, if it 's any way possible. So quite alone, without the suggestion of any body, but just the moving of my, if you please to call it so, conscience, the idea has come into my head: Could n't we, simply in view of this present crisis, find a compromise with the settlers without sacrificing too much of our undoubted rights?" Margaret paused, and looked up smilingly, to watch the effect of her words.

"Wonderful!" said Tom.

"Magic indeed!" Harold exclaimed.

"Answer to prayer, somebody else would no doubt say, as you 'll see in a minute," Margaret added. "But," said she, "what 's so wonderful in all this? We have n't a monopoly of insight in our house, Tom, and for the rest you know that neither of us came upon this idea. It was Mr. Harold's. But that father should have it too is not so unnatural. It only shows that, like Mr. Harold, only of course still more strongly, he has the facts in mind, and is himself not inhumane. But then again, even with this purpose in his heart, little 's yet done for our good cause. We want him not only to have the idea, but to carry it out in a shape that Mr. Escott will accept and Mr. Harold approve. So, as I said, we 've a good deal to do together yet. But I must go on with the letter."

Her warmth of interest had quite won Harold. She was growing every moment more fascinating to him, just because she had dropped all effort at mere conversation, and was looking serious over a matter of business. She began afresh with her reading: —

"I had this idea in my mind yesterday, all day,

and this morning, at breakfast, there came into my head a curious notion. You see, to deal with Escott, hard enough in itself, would also involve dealing with the settlers, and they, on the whole, are a very cantankerous set of people, if you 'll allow me the expression. I wanted to understand their present spirit before moving in the matter. And hereupon I bethought me of a person whom you must sometimes have seen, Boscowitz's daughter Bertha, who is a member of Mr. Rawley's church. The Oakfield claimants were in a considerable measure a colony of that church, in the first place. She knows some of the families intimately, and she 's a great friend of Alf Escott's. It may seem singular for me to contemplate appealing to this curious individual; but I know her to be honest, and think she has a measure of discretion, though some persons regard her as eccentric to the verge of insanity."

"How confidentially and elaborately he writes to Margaret!" thought Harold. "Plainly she 's become his confessor, so to speak." Harold glanced, meanwhile, sidewise and involuntarily, towards Tom, whose calm face was intently studying his boots. The mention of Bertha as being "eccentric to the verge of insanity:" "that," thought Harold, "must remind him of some things quite vividly." But Harold's manner showed no further trace of his thoughts.

"I wrote a note to her," read Margaret, "without Boscowitz knowing it. And to-night I had a long talk with her. She 's a warm-hearted woman, who almost worships Alf Escott. She thinks him a man of no end of learning, and something of a saint to boot, though she grants he 's irreligious, and prays for his soul day and night. But what I must say is, that she managed to bring back to my memory, in the course of the talk, some matters about Alf Escott that make me feel very much worse than ever in being opposed to him now. And, as she describes the settlers' state of mind, the only insurmountable obstacle in our way would seem to be the irascibility and almost invincible obstinacy of the professor himself. If we could induce him to accept a compromise, she says, she knows the settlers would follow him like sheep. They think him, it seems, something considerable as a statesman, though I don't just perceive why.

"Well, Margaret, you 'll say, why do I write all this to you? I write because I want to talk with you about it at the first opportunity; and if you see the way to make me an opportunity to-morrow, so much the better. It seems to me this is essentially a matter for a woman's wit; and you 're the only woman, except your mother, that I retain any confidence in in these days." Margaret laughed gayly as she read these words. "You see," Mr. Harold, she said, "what I am in father's eyes? Poor man, how dull he must find the world!" — "The thing involves considerations that are mainly of no business nature," she went on, reading again. "I have the undoubted right in this case, yet I 'm getting to the age when responsibilities are multiplying, and my strength, to speak plainly, is n't increasing very fast. I don't want to seem hard. I'm willing to be even a little over fair to the old professor; and what Bertha Boscowitz told me to-night brings up associations that at my time of life don't somehow nerve me to be as unfeeling as I can sometimes be. But yet, if I go near Alf Escott myself, I know well that nothing will come of it but more bitterness. It occurs to me that you, Margaret, are pretty much the only person of my acquaintance who is apt to throw light on a question of diplomacy like this." Once more Margaret laughed. "To think," she said, "of all this talk of father's, when you, Mr. Harold, are the sole possessor of the ideas and the means for accomplishing this particular bit of 'diplomacy!' Well, that 's practically all of the letter that I need read, though there 's a page or two more. Father, I may say, Mr. Harold, every now and then overflows in some such long letter to me, about some matter of conscience or other. It 's as if we kept his soul over here on the hillside. I 'm very proud of his confidence, I can tell you. In the rest of the letter there are, if I may dare to say it, Tom, some very sentimental speeches. Father was quite stirred up, I think, when he wrote it. The upshot of it all is that he, quite unconscious of my plots, was coming over expecting to find himself mixed up all the afternoon and evening with a gay crowd of some sort, and to have no time to confess to me before he went back. So he writes this partial account of himself, and of the interview with the odd Miss Bertha, to let me know his feelings before he gets here, and to get me to arrange for a little interview with him. So there, you see, I 've read you the letter, because for us three there 's nothing at all private in it. We 've already been thinking out our little plots, and father 's forestalled us. That 's the plain truth of it. But now, Mr. Harold, your chance is come. If the work 's begun, it is n't ended. You can do everything, if you know how."

"If you will teach me," Harold responded. "I wonder what were the memories that Miss Bertha aroused."

"Oh, she 's with Escott very often, I believe," Margaret answered. "At any rate, she knows his family well enough, and, as father says, she adores the old professor himself. I 've no doubt she 's full of old stories about early days, when the two men were on the Vigilance Committee together, or what not. When father began talking with her, she proceeded to remind him of such matters, which, despite all the quarrels since, would be sure to go a great way with an old pioneer. Then I don't doubt she stated the settlers' present case most ardently. Is she a good talker, Tom?"

"I don't know whether you 'd call it exactly good. She 's impressive, when she wants to be. Then, since her conversion, her prayer-meeting experiences have made her conquer her old shyness a good deal. She can talk like a whole prayer-meeting at once, I believe, if she chooses."

Tom spoke without the least show of painful consciousness; but there was, Harold felt, a certain suggestion of terrible veracity about his words. It appeared to Harold inconceivable, however, that Margaret could have any conception of the particular memories which she was bringing to her husband's mind. Her face, at any rate, showed no trace of any such malice.

"The prayer-meeting seems to be quite an educator, does n't it? Were you ever inside the Rawley church over in the city, Mr. Harold?"

"No, it's of Mrs. Rawley that I've mostly heard, so far, from Escott himself."

"Mrs. Rawley?" replied Margaret. "Ah, she's a character indeed! She's done a vast deal of work in her time. She once even edited a religious newspaper. But speaking of that, Mr. Harold, brings me back at once to my plots about your friend. I'm all full of them. I could hardly sleep last night for thinking of them. And father's letter, while it makes them easier, has n't altered them a bit. But you won't see, Mr. Harold, why thinking of Mrs. Rawley's editorship of a religious journal has anything to do with Mr. Escott. I'm afraid I must explain."

"It's because Escott is a newspaper man himself, I suppose." Harold was wise enough, as he spoke, to perceive that this was not the right answer; and a wild hope at once flared up in his mind that Mrs. Eldon might be thinking of a certain plan that he had lately had in mind. Could she, too, have formed this design? Harold's wild guess was at least partly wrong, however, for she went on: —

"No, not exactly that. I was thinking only of my own brief acquaintance with Mrs. Rawley during the time of her editorial activity. And that reminded me of what she used to tell me about Mr. Escott. I was just then on the so-called executive board, Mr. Harold, of a ladies' society for the elevation of the homeless, or for something of that sort. I won't pretend, of course, to tell you the name rightly, for I was never of any use on that board, or on any other woman's enterprise; and this particular society had an eternally long name. But somebody forced me into the business, and so I was for a while an executive officer, with a face as long as the society's name itself. I was a very grave person in those days. And so Mrs. Rawley and I often met on semi-official business. I'm sure I always stood in the greatest awe of her. She used to look clear through me with her righteous eyes; she has a glance that's as solemn as the last trump. But, in the course of our acquaintance, she used to talk a little of Alf Escott. She attributes most of his troubles, I believe, to the use of tobacco and to the evil of the human heart, — two misfortunes that, in combination, she regards as pretty fatal, of course. But her opinion was that, these sources of evil being as they were, the only way to save him was to get him out of what she called his desultory mode of life. Regular employment, fitted, of course, to his declining strength, but capable of exercising his talents in a steady and useful way, — that, she said, might save him to his family for many years. If, she said, there were only some good chance of his being part editor of a successful monthly magazine! His strength would n't be equal to the whole task, of course; but his talents would be so serviceable. However, of that she saw no chance, and I saw none either. But her old suggestion aroused in me a foolish hope, last night, when I happened to think of it, — a hope of a different sort, to be sure. Shall I tell you of it, Mr. Harold?"

"Certainly. I'm very anxious to hear of it."

"Well, first, you must know, father is dying to found something great and literary here on the coast. His chief plan involves, if I'm right, some sort of an improved British Museum, to be endowed and set up in San Francisco. Oh, you don't know, Mr. Harold, what things we hope for out here. Please don't laugh, now! I know it's funny. But father seriously believes that twenty or thirty millions of dollars, rightly invested, might do off-hand I can't say what for the cause of all the sciences at once on this coast. No matter; perhaps I can't understand his plans, but I know they're beautiful ones. So last night I lay dreaming and dreaming — wide-awake dreams, of course, — about what I could do to reconcile father and the professor again. And then this notion came: Could n't Escott's advice be of great service to father about some of the matters connected with the great scheme? It involves many sorts of scholarly enterprises; and Escott, despite all that has happened to depress his enthusiasm, used to be a very scholarly man, and still has some acquaintance with what goes on in the world of learning. Now, of course, it would be useless to propose directly any such coöperation as this, either to father or to Mr. Escott. But could n't you, Mr. Harold, manage yourself to get into some relation to father about the magnificent plan? He would soon readily confide in you, I don't doubt, and I 'm sure you 're in a position to be highly useful to him as an adviser. And then, you see — this was my notion — you could slowly manage to introduce Escott's name and ideas into the talks concerning the matter. In turn you could slowly interest Escott in father's conceptions. Thus we might bring about in time a common interest once more, and then a feeling of mutual respect, and then — who knows? — we might reconcile them. And so, at last, Escott might even come to find his regular employment in connection with father's new work. It 's a foolish plan of mine, perhaps; it sounds very womanish and sentimental. But, with a man for the instrument of its execution, it might be kept from becoming sentimental. It might even be made a practicable plan. That 's the only foundation I could think of for really bringing the two old friends together. I suppose, to be sure, that the professor, after all his wanderings, has in these days more talent than learning. But I do believe that he could help father immensely about the building of this air castle, not to say about the actual accomplishment of the thing. And then, in any case, Mr. Harold, if they once somehow met, as it were, on this neutral ground of the great design, and if Escott suggested any sort of idea, through you, or in his own person, and father accepted it, the result would be that father, having gone so far, simply could n't keep up the Oakfield Creek matter. Besides, Mr. Harold," — Margaret was speaking very warmly and rapidly now, — "what I want is that those two should frankly join hands again some day. Between those two, so far as I know, there 's nothing happened that makes that impossible."

Margaret's enthusiasm had plainly carried her too far, in these last words, and on to the more dangerous ground. She colored — very beautifully — as she finished; and Harold, delighted with her sincerity, hastened to come to her relief.

"Why, that 's much to be longed for, indeed," he said. "But see, here we have another coincidence. Mrs. Rawley suggested to you, you say, Mrs. Eldon, a possible magazine editorship. Well, do you know, again and again I have dreamed that I might start a magazine myself, and give Escott permanent employment as its editor. And the idea has so fascinated me that I have more than once dwelt on it for hours, though I have n't yet dared to mention it to Escott. Commercially considered, I suppose, the idea is n't exactly promising; for the earth sounds hollow already over the tombs of such undertakings in California. But granting that I did n't care for the money, — and where Escott 's concerned I hardly do, though I 'm a man of comparatively moderate means, — granting, then, that I 'm ready to sink plenty of hard cash, the idea 's not at all absurd. What do you think of it, Mrs. Eldon? Or could n't it, perhaps, be made somehow to coöperate with your own plan?"

"Why, of course, Mr. Harold! You are, indeed, a man of many resources, I must say. What a beautiful notion! Make it coöperate with mine? Why, I should say so! It simply absorbs mine at once. For don't you see, what could be a better means for introducing the conception of the new British Museum to the public than to have a literary monthly as the first outcome and representative of what 's already planned, as well as of what 's yet to result? It would popularize the idea at once, and the public at large would believe in it. Think of it — the 'New British Museum Monthly,' how magnificent the title! And so, don't you see, what we must do is to develop your scheme at once, to get father interested in it, to make him join in it, and to have him take part of the risk. You, however, must be left, as is natural, — you being the literary man, — with the chief management of the magazine in your hands. Father will invest enough money to float it. He will do that, without doubt, if he 's once enough interested in the scheme. Then you 'll quietly employ Mr. Escott as the editor; and the desired mutual approach of our two heroes on some common ground is secured."

"I don't think, by the way," interposed Tom Eldon just here, "that you 'd find any trouble in getting five or ten thousand dollars subscribed to your venture from this house alone, so long as the thing is meant in any part of it for Escott's benefit."

Margaret glanced a very mild approval, as if Tom had picked up a dropped handkerchief for her. "Thank you, Tom," she said. "I 'm very glad you are pleased with our notion. Again, as you see, it 's Mr. Harold who suggests everything. But how benevolent we all are this morning! It 's more religious than going to church, I do declare, — this sitting here and planning the good of our neighbors. I have n't felt so pious since I was on the executive board, in the days when Mrs. Rawley used to visit me."

Harold was by this time fairly swimming in enthusiasm. He began, a little blushingly, to admit his youthful longing to have part in the management of a magazine. For himself alone, he said, he would never have had the energy, let alone the ability, to do more than dream about the matter. But now that Mrs. Eldon had suggested to him the notion in this case, and as Alf Escott was evidently just the man to carry it out, he was almost minded to go ahead on his own account.

Meanwhile, as he spoke, Harold perceived how over-sanguine Mrs. Eldon was. An act of justice from Alonzo Eldon was all that Harold himself had hoped for at the outset. However much

Mrs. Eldon's ardor now carried him away with her, however much his own more selfish longing made him favor her schemes, he felt all the time sure that Escott would never willingly enter into such relations with the Eldon family. The old heritage of wrong and of bitterness was too vast to be offset by such feeble offers of reparation as this. "*Never be reconciled to your enemy if he's a man*," Escott had once sternly said, referring to his own mistake in venturing upon a momentary reconciliation with Alonzo Eldon on that one previous occasion. The mistake, Harold believed, would never be repeated. He had not dreamed of more than a recognition of the rights which Alf Escott and the settlers claimed. The two old men would thenceforth, he had hoped, be free from any further cause of direct enmity. They would remain sundered, of course; but they could respect each other's antipathies, as Escott and Peter Dover had formerly done, and thus they could dwell at peace, each, as might be hoped, honoring the other's manhood, and making no further comments on the other's conduct. That was the best that could be expected. But Mrs. Eldon, in her beautiful ardor, was plainly longing for more. To her, this dark shadow of wrong was a very near and terrible thing. As her words had accidentally shown a moment ago, she had, indeed, no hope that there would ever come to pass a reconciliation of Tom and Alf Escott. That was inconceivable. But what she plainly could not bear was to think of these two old friends now hopelessly sundered, not so much by their own fault as by a wrong for which neither of them was to blame, and for which she herself bore a sort of responsibility. She longed to reconcile them before they died.

Surely, Harold said to himself, the idea was worthy of her. There was something very unselfish in her conduct, and the thought of this woman, who perchance, after all, might be loving her wayward husband as dearly as any other woman had ever loved a man, — the thought of her as living day after day, and year after year, bound fast to this great wrong that her husband's vanity and fickleness had wrought, was a terrible notion to Harold. He felt as if he were a knight commissioned to free her from bondage, and to restore her to her happiness again. He was as enthusiastic now for her as for Escott. He must act so as to serve them both at once.

But Margaret hereupon led the conversation towards the more immediate question of what should be done when Eldon appeared, and so, erelong, their little programme for the afternoon was arranged, and without serious difficulty.

By lunch-time Harold found that he had grown very fond indeed of his new acquaintance. Her low, pleasantly monotonous voice, that still, some how, managed to be so expressive, her delicate face, her sympathetic eyes, had altogether won him. She semed full of conviction, and yet managed to have the air of being extremely deferential. There was, now and then, a passing expression that hinted of a proud self-will behind everything, and that made one feel how hard those timid brown eyes would be to meet, in case she should choose to put the least little bit of scorn into them; and meanwhile, about her whole bearing there was something that told the story of her straightforward, healthy, and many-sided life here in this country home. She was plainly, with all her love of new faces and of new plans, a conservative still, so far as a California lady could be one. She lived on this estate with as much regularity and precision of life as if she had generations of tradition behind her. Plainly she had kept her surroundings unchanged for years. The house bore, throughout, the comforting evidence that everything knew its place; a fact which Harold, much vexed by the air of new-born and uneasy magnificence that pervaded so many California houses which he had recently seen, noticed to-day with great delight. Peter Dover, save in case of his one exploit of the great fountain, had loved and sought unassuming comfort in his home. He had left his house a little too bare; but he had made few positive mistakes. And Margaret, when she came, had gradually added what suited her own taste, and changed what she disliked, without sacrificing the original unpretentiousness. It was a country house, after all, she had said; why should it be too elaborate? The parlor, to be sure, where they had first sat, seemed, with its dark panels, its heavy carved wooden mantel, its brown leather-covered sofas, and its sober chairs, just a little ponderous and gloomy. But the simple brightness of the dining-room, with its stained and polished redwood mantel and panels, and with its large, sunny, western windows, was all the more pleasing by the contrast.

After lunch, Margaret took Harold, at his own request, to see the rose-garden, Tom remaining behind. It was the simple fact that Tom himself had never entered Margaret's garden since Ellen's body had been found there. Harold, of course, had not thought where the garden might lie, and it was not until he was among the roses that, chancing to glance up at the windows of the house, he remembered Escott's story, and found himself shuddering. There was a chill of death in this spot! But the next instant he looked towards Margaret, who was not watching him, and had not observed his expression of face. How full of busy and peaceful life she seemed! Yet how could she have learned to endure this spot after what had happened! Once more Harold looked away, at the heavy shade of the acacias yonder, at the plain and sober foliage of the little oak grove beyond and below the grounds, at the fine vista towards the front, where lay the lawn, the great shade-trees, the distant town, the peaceful bay; and then again his eyes wandered back to her face. Perhaps she began now to notice his abstraction. At all events, she fell to talking very eagerly about the flowers, and Harold's quick-moving mind was soon full of other ideas. The garden interested him as an expert; and besides, while he discussed it with her, his mind was full once more of the old associations that clustered about his own home. These garden odors, how irresistibly suggestive they were! He talked, of course, very well about the flowers. He was now evidently impressing Mrs. Eldon by his practical knowledge much more than he had done by his in-doors conversation. He told her a little about his own gardening at his old house, and then, fearing to appear even the least sentimental, escaped from the personal associations that were too dear to him by describing to her some European gardens. She, too, remembered something about these very ones, and they were comparing notes, when, suddenly, the little boy appeared, just in advance of his nurse. Margaret, as usual, had no great disposition to introduce her child to company. But Harold was delighted. He had not seen a child of that age for so long, he said. In a moment more he and the little Alonzo were taking the first steps towards friendship. Margaret was really pleased to watch them together, and they all three sat down on a garden bench, and remained some time in the place. Harold was now full of another sort of talk for the boy's amusement, and little Alonzo, who was never a shy child, and who yet saw playmates so seldom, took only a little while before beginning to reveal his most cherished confidences. Down where the moss grew, he declared, he had one day seen a snake, and he was going to look for it every day until it came again. He wanted it to take to bed with him at night. Nurse did n't like it, but he did. He had, moreover, broken the heart of his mother's watch, so that it did n't beat any more, and his mother had said that unless he became better he might break her own heart, too, by being so naughty. But he had n't broken it yet, for he had listened to hear that very morning, and her heart was still going, tick, tick. He would listen for it again right now. And so he sprang into her lap. Harold, fearing lest the vigor of the boy's caresses might be a little unwelcome to the mother just at this moment, offered to tell him a short story ; and little Alonzo, sitting in her lap, listened with a wise seriousness that reminded Harold afresh of her own face as it had looked while she read the letter.

"If my own little boy had lived," Harold at last said to Margaret, very simply and quietly, "he would now have been six years old. He died, however, just before I left California. He was fifteen months old then. He outlived my wife only two months." Harold had not meant to talk of his own affairs, for his reserve was usually great about them in the presence of strangers ; but the garden and the child were together irresistible.

Margaret's eyes were full of sympathy. "What a blow it must have been!" she said. "I used to know your wife very slightly, Mr. Harold, when she was only a girl. We met once for a short time at school. I hardly think she could have remembered me. But what a beautiful place that was where you lived! A perfect bower of shade-trees and roses and vines you made of it, did n't you? Have you seen it lately?"

"No," he answered. "I have n't dared to see it since I returned." He looked down into the little boy's eyes, as he spoke, and somehow felt as if he were growing very confidential in this conversation. The nurse was out of hearing. The boy looked very thoughtful and reverent, for he had taken it into his head to study the band of Harold's hat. "The fact is," Harold continued, feeling as if he spoke of deeply sacred matters, "I have a very great hesitation" — But here he perceived that he was about to become sentimental outright, with his stupid personal confidences concerning this matter. That was absurd! He had been trying all along to avoid just such things. She must be, as was plain, a matter-of-fact woman, who looked out for her roses and her baby and the rest of her establishment, and who was thoroughly business-like. Why should he air his little fancies and emotions in her presence? He checked himself, though this, of course, only made him appear the more sentimental. What should he say? Perhaps, in any case, it was useless to try to finish the sentence. He was ashamed of himself once more! What was the use of trying? He could never talk to women in a social way, without this stupid personal feeling coming in afresh! He blushed like a school-boy, raised his eyes, and met hers. They had still the tenderly sympathetic look, he saw, of course! What else was to be expected from her? But that was surely mere politeness. And she, meanwhile, plainly thought him overwhelmed with emotion at the mention of his old home; while in fact his real feeling, for the instant, was merely one of babyish bashfulness! It was all, he felt, a very silly confusion of ideas. He thought himself a fool.

These quickly changing and idle fancies crowded through his head all at once, as it were. The whole thing occupied but an instant, and just then wheels were heard. "That 's father, surely," said Margaret, springing up. Harold followed her, feeling that she somehow doubtless despised him for his stupidity and his awkwardness, and that she was right if she did. Little Alonzo, too, followed eagerly; but his nurse drew him back, and Harold recovered his own even temper by taking a hurried and cheerfully comforting leave of the child. Then he went to the front of the house.

CHAPTER IX.

ALONZO ELDON, AND HIS TALE OF THE INDIAN FIGHT.

HAROLD went by the porch, and reached the front door just after Margaret. A tall, broad-shouldered, every way towering man, with a heavily-bearded, stern, and much-worn face, but with tender and even almost timid dark eyes, had the moment before left the carriage, and come up the front steps. Tom was greeting him on the piazza. As the two stood together one saw a living example of the quick physical degeneration that has marred so many California pioneer families. This fine rugged form of the father, still so full of manly vigor in its every movement, was in the sharpest contrast to the son's weak and almost serpentine body, with its indolence and its indecision of bearing. Tom was of a little less than medium height, and hardly reached his father's shoulder. His voice sounded boyish after the strong tones of the elder man. His delicate, half-Spanish features lacked the full beauty of the pure-blooded Spaniard, and accordingly they looked fairly effeminate in the presence of this impressive face; they were just American enough to ruin them, and of far too Southern a type to pass for Anglo-Saxon at this moment, beside the father's countenance.

Alonzo turned joyfully to receive Margaret's cordial greeting. Then he looked down at Harold, who was about Tom's height, and who felt a little overawed by this great incarnation of business-intelligence and energy. When Harold was presented, however, Alonzo's eyes shone a little eagerly; he smiled, and that, too, in a fashion that made his face look much less intelligent, and greeted the new acquaintance quite warmly.

"I know of you, sir, by reputation," he said. "I'm happy to meet you in person. I confess

I 've long meant to get an opportunity. I knew your father very well, Mr. Harold."

"Did you, father?" said Margaret. "How delightful!"

"Yes; Mr. Harold's father was an Englishman, who came to America in early life, and who, in my youth, used to be pastor in my town of W——. He was the first and the only Episcopalian clergyman in those parts for I don't know how long. I knew him well. He gave me his blessing, Mr. Harold, a little less than forty years ago, when I was just starting for California. I doubt if you were born then. Yet I had then already been for some years in business in Boston."

"You 're right, Mr. Eldon. I was n't born until two or three years after that. But how strange! I knew that you were from my own old town; that, as it chances, was almost the first fact I ever learned about you. But I did n't know that my father had been your pastor."

"He was a worthy man, Mr. Harold; but he did me little good, I fear. I was but a wild youngster! He 's dead this quarter of a century, is n't he?"

"He died when I was a boy of nine."

"Well, well," said Alonzo, sadly, "how time flies! It seems only yesterday since I came here, Mr. Harold, and all this scene" — Alonzo turned and waved his great hand in front of the smoky landscape — "was then, save for a few insignificant ranches and settlements, one Vast Solitude."

Alonzo's voice had grown more deep and solemn than ever with these last words.

Margaret was delighted with this beginning; she smiled approvingly on Harold, — who wondered what he had done to please her, — and then she proposed that, as the afternoon had unexpectedly turned out to be warm, they should all sit on the piazza, in sight of the late Vast Solitude. Only Tom must first take father to his room. These dusty roads must vex any guest terribly.

"It must seem odd to you, Mr. Harold," said Alonzo, as he turned to go, "after you 've been away so long, to notice how everybody brushes down and washes his guests whenever they 've been far enough on a road to turn a corner. Well, there were days when people in California did n't think so much of dust as they do now." And so Tom and Alonzo vanished together.

"Why did n't you tell me this before?" said Margaret, confidentially and eagerly. "Why, you and father are fellow-townsmen, as it were!"

"*As it were*, Mrs. Eldon, cannot be made to count for much in this case, I fear. He left the town some two years before I was born, and I left it some ten years after I was born. That 's not exactly a ground for the much-desired intimacy, I must confess, though I wish it were. But I 'm glad to think he knew my father."

"Yes; whenever his interest in your proposals flags, we 'll fall back on your father's blessing. And surely your father had a good faculty for blessing, Mr. Harold. Look at the result! I hope you 've inherited your father's powers. If you have, I 'll ask you myself for your blessing some day, and then straightway I 'll turn my attention very casually to any vast solitude I happen to hear of, and at once transform it into rose-gardens. That would be my sort of pioneering, you see."

"As if you needed my blessing for that!" said Harold. "I fancy, if you want nothing but roses, you 'll never lack them. But what a mighty man of valor Mr. Eldon is! I 've seen him before, though never so near by."

"He 's as docile as a child, Mr. Harold, not to say as fierce as a lion. Have you ever read any of the published biographical sketches of him?"

"No, I don't read such things often. I 'm shamefully ignorant of all our public men."

"I shall show you one of the sketches some day. It is very amusing. I really am very fond of father, though I believe he used to regard me as a very flippant young person. Since I 've grown aged and sedate, he 's warmed towards me a great deal. But do you know, Mr. Harold, I perceive at once that victory is ours. Those first words of his were enough to show it. When he waves his hand in that mournful way at the great bay, and talks about vast solitudes, he 's in the pioneer-mood. You could ask him for anything then, even unto the half of his kingdom, and he 'd give it gladly."

A few moments later the two Eldons reappeared.

Then the whole family seated themselves in the shade of the piazza, and the conversation began afresh. But erelong, upon some slight pretext, Tom Eldon quietly withdrew, and remained away more than an hour.

Margaret had been so much emboldened by the obvious signs of the pioneer-mood in Alonzo that she now made short work of approaching the mention of Alf Escott's name. Mr. Harold, she said, was a friend of Tom, and also of Alf Escott, and had that very morning been speaking of the old professor's misfortunes. She had been moved, she said, to tell him about Alonzo's wish that all the old troubles in which the professor was concerned could be gotten rid of. Harold himself, she assured Alonzo, had, as a man just returned to California, known for a long time nothing of the professor, and was so much the more saddened now to find an old friend in such distress. Father would therefore discern in Harold a sympathizing person to approach about the matter.

"I 'm very glad, indeed," said Alonzo, speaking without the least surprise, and merely as if Harold were but one of the ideas in his own train of thought, an idea just a trifle novel and quite welcome, but merely an idea, after all, — "I 'm very glad, indeed, to know you take an interest in him. Somehow it comes over me just to-day how much I used to admire — yes, at one time even almost revere — Alf Escott. He had a streak of the most intolerable bitterness in his make-up. I quarreled with him a dozen times before the end came between us. There are few men whom I 've ever so unsparingly condemned, on certain occasions, as the old professor. Yet his knowledge and his hearty good-fellowship, when he was n't angry, and the services he once or twice rendered me, — I can't think of 'em now without a certain mournful sense. It 's melancholy, sir, to a degree." Alonzo sighed deeply.

"He 's one of the pluckiest of men," said Harold. "You 'd be delighted to see how he stands up now and faces his troubles. He won't let a word of mere complaint escape him. But for all that, what a tender-hearted man he is! He 's a splendid lover, when he does love. That 's plain."

"I could tell you some things about that last trait in him," answered Alonzo, "that you 'd find very surprising. His affection extends always so far beyond what one would anticipate. I remember what a feeling of personal devotion he had, during the war-time, to old Abe Lincoln. He and I were for the last time together over in the Nevada region, when the news of the assassination came. At the little place where we were then staying, they made Escott deliver a funeral oration in memory of Lincoln. He said beforehand he was no orator, but I can tell you, Mr. Harold, that was a very great speech! It was all off-hand; Escott had n't a note to read from, and he had n't any stump-speaker's airs, but, my God! he simply wrung tears out of the sage-brush, if I may say so. The camp where we were was about half full of Southerners, who 'd been feeling pretty blue about the ending of the war; and when the news of the assassination came, I thought myself there 'd be trouble. Northern men gathered, looked ugly, talked about cleaning out some of the saloons where the Southerners in previous days most did congregate and speechify, and, on the whole, there was a night or two there that made a man want to sleep with his pistol even a little nearer than usual. But Alf Escott, sir, just because he was the fiercest Northerner in the whole place, saved the peace of that town. When people knew he was to talk, they came together, men of all sorts, Southern and Northern, armed and unarmed, roughs and decent men, all in a jumble. I thought I 'd seen pretty mixed crowds in my life; but that one beat 'em all. 'Boys,' I said to some of the fellows near me, 'there 's *bound* to be trouble. The Northern men here,' I said, 'want blood, some of 'em, — I don't, — and Alf Escott 's the man to make nobody feel less like a fight. He 's simply boiling, himself,' I said. Well, for my part, I was as patriotic as any man, but I had some vested interests in that town just then, and it seemed to me tolerable plain that the war was over, and that we who had n't fought before, out on this coast, would be ill-advised to begin the fight for the first time then and there. I feared Alf Escott's high temper. I was sorry he 'd been called on to speak. Well, that oration was the greatest surprise I ever had. It did n't make any patriot feel less wrathful, less stern, less *intolerant* towards treason, nor less manly in any way, even though it *did* make many a man shed tears. But it did make those fire-eaters there hang their heads for very shame of some of their speeches of recent times. But all that was n't the important thing about it. The important thing was that it made every man so oppressed with the bigness of the issues of that hour, with the awful dangers of the future for the country, and with the great work good citizens would have to do to keep the country's peace, now we had conquered, that, I tell you, we simply *buried* all our petty squabbling in something very much deeper. We went away from that place sober men, — all of us, Northern or Southern. We felt as if we all alike had a country to look out for, now the war was done. There was n't a pistol fired in town that night, — a very exceptional thing, sir, in just that camp at that moment."

Towards the end of this description, Alonzo had become very earnest in manner. He leaned forward and gestured emphatically, while his great face grew sternly excited. He now leaned back and sighed again, and then once more straightening himself, went on: "I 've often wondered just how Alf Escott made that speech. Sam Paddington, whom I was afterwards telling about the matter, assured me that we fellows must have got hungry in the sage-brush for some good talking, and so our appetite was the making of Alf Escott's speech. But I know better. I had n't been in the mines that time more than six weeks. That visit of 1865 was my last and my only thoroughly unlucky visit to the wilder regions of Nevada. I left for Virginia City, and so for home, two weeks later. So there was no illusion in my mind. I simply *never heard* a better talk of a plain man to plain men than that one. Alf Escott himself could n't account for it afterwards. He was always a good speaker; but that time he clean outdid himself. He could only say, in explanation, that when Abe Lincoln was dead he felt as if his own father was gone, so that he was full of wonder that day, as it were, how the country could live without its father. Escott said, later, he hardly thought of the boys as he spoke, or whether they had pistols or not. He was just feeling desolate, so to speak, and his heart was full, and he wanted every man to be a good citizen, and pull all together, and get the country out of the accursed mire of those days somehow. And that, he said, was all he knew about the speech." Alonzo's manner was more quiet now, and he stopped, with a very melancholy sigh. "Well," he added, "that 's long, *long* ago." His great body sank back again in the chair, his eyes looked far off and sad, and his big hands and arms, which always followed his conversation with usually vague but often vigorous gestures, rested now close at his sides.

"Oh, father," interposed Margaret at once, "now you 've begun on those days in Nevada, you must surely tell Mr. Harold that story, — I never heard it from your own lips, or got it at all straight, — that story about some Indian fight you were in with Alf Escott. That happened long before the Lincoln speech, — away back before the war."

Alonzo laughed, a great, hearty laugh, that had a ring of splendid strength and courage in it. "Well, well, our Indian fight, — as if I had n't been thinking of that all night, so to speak. It was an inglorious affair, Mr. Harold, to express myself without any circumlocution and in the plainest language, — an inglorious affair for all but Alf Escott and one or two others. I 'm rather ashamed to speak of it. We met the enemy, and we were most decisively and artistically wiped out, if you 'll allow the expression. I never felt so well whipped in all my days. But the professor, — well, he had to run, too, or at least his mule had to run, and he stayed aboard, sir, with his usual tenacity, — or pertinacity; I don't know which is the right word. But it was no disgrace to him personally that he had to run. I never was in such a stampede before or since. And Alf Escott kept that mule's nose to the foe so long as any power, under Divine Providence, could have done it. He was the hero of the occasion, — not the mule, I mean, but Escott. Yet surely, Mr. Harold, you know about the story of the great battle near Pyramid Lake, don't you, in the spring of '60?"

"I 'm as unhistorical there, Mr. Eldon, I regret to say, as in any other respect. I know there was some such affair, but I have n't any notion what really happened, or how. I was only a boy then, you know, and had but just arrived here in California with my widowed mother. I very much wish I could hear about the incident from you."

"Well, well, I think I must tell you, then, something about that battle of Pyramid Lake, as some of us called it. Some called it the battle of Big Meadows. But you, Margaret, did n't you ever hear about it from me?"

"No; Tom once tried to tell me, long ago. But he was always poor at a story, and I think he was only trying to excite my curiosity about this one. Yes, father, you must surely describe the battle."

"I laugh very easily over it now, you see, Margaret. I did n't laugh then, I can tell you; and in fact it was a very tragic affair, if I may be allowed the expression. Many a good man bit the dust that day, and many a wife mourned somewhere in California, or in the East, for the husband that never came back. I should n't be here now myself, I suppose, if Alf Escott had been less cool."

"What, father!" said Margaret, her eyes looking large and her face very eager, "did he actually save your life that day?"

"He never would admit himself, Margaret, that he did so," replied Alonzo, plainly on the defensive. "It was n't exactly a clear, out-and-out, single-handed saving of my life, as you 'll see when I tell of it. Alf Escott was engaged at the moment in saving the life of another man, and in that he only partly succeeded. But his cool stand was what enabled me to save my own. Perhaps"

— Alonzo grew more and more uneasy as he went on — "you 'll say that 's drawing it rather fine, but wait till you hear the facts. You must remember that at such a moment a man's life 's rather a mixed-up affair, anyhow; and it is n't always easy to say just who did this or that. But no matter, — there is n't the least doubt but Alf Escott was behaving very creditably on that occasion. And the deed was worthy of him. But to begin my tale with what led me over to Washoe. For that was Alf Escott's doing, too.

"I did n't hear much about the great new discoveries in Virginia, Mr. Harold, until near Christmas of 1859. I had n't paid much attention to the reports. Then, however, Alf Escott wrote me a very warm letter. We 'd always been, barring a few tiffs, splendid friends up to that date. He had vanished, in his odd way, some time during the autumn, and I had n't known where he was. Now he wrote me to say that he was the author of certain letters about the new mines which were just then appearing in one of the city papers. He assured me that the whole thing meant business, and that I 'd better go. I laughed at first at the notion of Alf Escott setting up as a judge of silver mines, — he who 'd have been capable of discovering silver ore up in your little cañon among the hills yonder, Margaret, if he 'd been told beforehand that there was any there. No matter, however; his letters grew only warmer as the winter over beyond the mountains grew colder, so that at last I became convinced that there must be something in it all. I resolved to go and see, as there chanced to be a little lull in my affairs just then. Accordingly, at the first fair chance, I set out in the early spring of '60. I formed one of a little party of adventurers, who fought their way on mules through from Placerville to Genoa, against much snow and some pretty bad roads. I 'd then already been faring sumptuously so long that this rough life, full though it was of reminders of the early days before '50, was rather hard on me. Sam Paddington, who was in the party, Mr. Harold, was the tamest-looking cuss, if you 'll allow the expression, that I 've ever seen, the night we reached Strawberry Valley. I think I bore it better than Sam did; but that evening, when he looked up towards the summit ahead of us, and back again into the place where we were to pass the night, Sam had a sense, I guess, that he had n't lost any silver mines. How we did make fun of Sam Paddington that night, — we who could bear our salt pork and flapjacks at Berry's only the weest trifle better than Sam himself! Sam was wishing that we 'd depended on the stage, though that, I take it, would n't have done us much good just at that season."

As Alonzo wandered further on in his reminiscences, Harold observed that he dropped for the most part a certain formality of tone and accent that he had at first assumed. He spoke energetically and rapidly. There was, however, still the same contrast, which had at first so attracted Harold's attention, between Eldon's other strong and expressive features and his weak and almost timid eyes. Even in the moments of his greatest emphasis they looked, by comparison with the rest of his face, gentle and weary.

"The day after leaving Strawberry," Alonzo went on, addressing himself now mainly to Harold, as if the story could interest only a man, "was trying enough, I can tell you. The summit was some eight or nine miles from Berry's, and it was a hard pull. The road was abominable in the afternoon, because then the winter snow, which was still deep, would soften. Even breathing the fine mountain air could n't atone for it all, and when we reached the summit itself, and looked back over those endless stretches of forest to the westward, and then northwards down into the magnificent valley of Lake Tahoe (or Bigler, as we called it then), we were still quite comfortless. 'Sam,' I said to Paddington, 'I'm with you in heart now. Sixteen years have I fought to help to make the wilderness and the solitary place to rejoice and to blossom like the rose, down there by the great bay; and now here I 've come out like a fool into these heaps of granite and pine-trees and slush, to hunt for more wildernesses. I 'm sick of wildernesses.'

"But we went on, though, down into the great valleys again, into the mud and misery, our eyes sore with the white snow, the skin burned off our faces by the reflection of the sun-rays, our mules exhausted by the roads. I well remember the horrors we had passed through by the time we had reached the head of Carson Cañon, a place bad enough in itself. No matter; we reached Genoa, and I was a sick man for at least two hours there, — a thing which had n't happened to me since the summer of '48, when I took the Sacramento Valley fever. My ill turn at Genoa frightened me, of course, much worse than it hurt me. I remember how delighted I was, when, all of a sudden, Alf Escott walked in. He had come over from Virginia City especially to meet me. A man is a little gushing, you know, when he 's sick. I was simply overjoyed. We shook hands as if we were brothers." Alonzo's voice trembled a little, but he looked again towards the bay, and, recovering his courage, went on.

"I had been puzzled, before I started, by the conflicting reports about the country. I was soon a hundred fold more perplexed. In fact, nobody knew anything as yet concerning that region. Everybody spoke as his mood prompted him. Numbers of poor devils had come over, expecting fortunes for nothing. But Washoe was the worst of places for a poor man. Before long, however, for my own part, I began to find my wits, in the midst of all these conflicting rumors, and I set about examining into the evidences, on business principles. Alf Escott, of course, was leader on the favorable side of the discussion. Nothing frightened him; he knew of everything that was good. But there were discouragements enough. The Indians of the region were as mad as hornets, and very hungry. Their pine-trees, whose nuts they ate, were being cut down. They were losing their stock, somehow, also. They stole what they could from the miners, and occasionally murdered. Meanwhile, there were disputes among the miners in all directions about the ownership of claims; and there was much talk of blood among the disputants. This was at the end of April. But just at the beginning of May, all of a sudden, one day, the wildest news came in from the Carson. A man named Williams had appeared at Bucklands, down near the Bend, and had said that his two brothers and five other men had been killed by Piutes at the so-called Williams Station. The poor fellow himself had fled as he could. I remember the date when the news came to Virginia, Tuesday, May 8th, because that was the very day when the first despatch got across the continent, by Pony Express, to tell us of the result of the great Heenan-Sayers prize-fight in England, about which we all talked so much in those days. We 'd been betting on the Benicia Boy like mad. However, with the news about the Williams Station massacre came also the wildest rumors as to what would happen next; and every good citizen who had a rifle was called upon to volunteer for the defense of the settlements. Rangers were to be organized to warn prospectors and others throughout the Carson Valley; a detachment was to be sent at once to defend Bucklands, which was said to be in immediate danger of an attack; and a large force was to be sent to pursue the Indians.

"How unfounded nearly all the rumors were I

hardly need say. The 'massacre,' as they called it, at Williams Station had simply been the outcome of a private quarrel with the Indians about the use of stock-pastures; the party of Indians who committed the murders had fled northwards to Pyramid Lake, offering no sort of violence to anybody else by the way, though they had opportunities in plenty; and in fact the whole country, save for our flurry, was at that moment in perfect peace.

"But it's easy to be wise now. Just then we believed what we heard, and the cost of rifles went up. We even forgot the fate of our bets on Heenan, and said nothing about the international match. We only said, 'This thing's got to be stopped, and we're the men to stop it.' We had public meetings, organized rifle companies in short order, and prepared our blankets and our mules for an outing in the sage-brush. So at least some of us did. There was, to be sure, a greater dearth of able-bodied men in Virginia City that night than one would have suspected beforehand. The bad water of that region, and what not, seemed to claim an extraordinary number of victims, all of a sudden. Those of us, though, who remained in good health and could find arms were busy enough. I remember how Sam Paddington became all of a sudden very philosophical. 'What's the use, Eldon?' he insisted. 'There are plenty of men here to defend the settlements. I've no concern in the Virginia mines, after all. What *is* a good citizen's duty, anyhow? It's to mind his business, is n't it? Now, my business is in San Francisco, where my heart is, too. For there are my wife and my innocent babes! I'm not the man to sacrifice my life on a mere, so to say, pleasure-tour, where no business is concerned.' That was Sam Paddington's view. And I remember the particular fits that Alf Escott thereupon gave him. Alf's blood was up; and Lord!" (Alonzo's voice assumed a tone of reproachful awe,) "how that professor can swear, Mr. Harold, when he 's, if I may say so, incensed, sir!

"Next day we set out. Sam Paddington had to go along, too. And what followed until the fight of Saturday needs no long story. We found the bodies of some of the murdered men, and even once held an impromptu coroner's inquest in the sage-brush, electing our coroner on the spot. It was a grim and desolate scene there in the desert, Margaret. The chief trouble with the inquest was the entire and absolute lack of witnesses to the murder. But that did n't much affect us. We could at least argue over the remains; and we did, and looked at the tracks of horses and men — and coyotes — thereabouts. The verdict, I remember, was that those deceased had come to their death by the act of God and certain Piutes, all to the jury unknown, but which we hoped to find out more about, pretty soon, so help us God. Amen.

"Thereupon we struck the trail of those Indians, and followed it over from the banks of the Carson to the Truckee. I remember well the wind o' nights, and how it chilled and plagued us. The dust blew till it hid the stars. In the morning the whole camp would look as seedy as that uncanny ruined old Nevada landscape itself. As for Sam Paddington, the first night out he got to making speeches to the boys, and that gave his philosophy another turn. He was as courageous now as any man in the crowd. And as he got plenty of whiskey, he seemed to like roughing it pretty well.

"Well, at our best, we seemed on the whole to be no very martial crowd, and I said to Escott that if the Indians happened to stand still and fire on us, when we met them, they 'd doubtless thin our ranks in more ways than one. I waited with some curiosity, I confess, to see what Escott would do in a pinch. He had had even less soldierly experience than myself. But he did n't boast any about this topic, so I had confidence in him.

"About four o'clock in the afternoon of Saturday we came up with the Indians. It was a wild place, and I doubt if many of us knew much, just then, about the country near Pyramid Lake. It was n't so very far from where Wadsworth's now is, on the railroad. The Indians seemed to have posted themselves on a side-hill by the entrance to a cañon, and as we went along through the Truckee meadows we spied them on our right. It was now Indians on one side and the Truckee on the other. There was some brush and timber close by the river, but the barren hills beyond the meadows looked like the curse of God, sir. I noticed a certain unsteadiness about the command, — we were somewhere near one hundred strong, and had all along been riding in a rather irregular order, — and as we watched the movements of such Piutes as were to be seen I said to Alf and to the others of our own immediate party, 'Look here, boys, there are about a hundred great heroes on our side just now, not including the mules and mustangs, but to my mind just about three fourths of us are going to have special business in Virginia City before long. So we of this party must stand close together, boys, and go into the fight side by side, so 's not to lose one another if there 's a stampede.' You can see from what I say that the organization of this whole command was a little uncertain. We had an elected major and other officers; but we had n't had much time to drill, and it was a toss-up whether the major's commands would be obeyed or not.

"Well, the first idea was that we should dismount, leave our animals by the river, in the little belt of timber there, under a guard, form a line, and march up the hill, after the Piutes. But the men in general objected to that. The Indians were mounted, they said, and it would be a long stretch up the hill on foot. Why leave our beasts? We 'd better charge mounted. So, mounted as we were, we began to make the best line we could preparatory to going up. Sam Paddington, by dint of much persuasion, sir, rode just to the right of me, and Escott was beyond him. On my left was a man of our party named Molesworth, and then a young fellow called Bolton. These two were old acquaintances of ours. The rest of my own party were to the right of Escott. A good many of the hundred heroes saw fit to get into a second, or into a third, or fourth, or some other rank behind us; and some had already dismounted, I believe, and were eagerly examining the thickness of the Truckee River trees. I suppose they were planning in their minds to cut down the timber thereabouts some day.

"The front line was some time in forming. 'Now, boys,' said the major, at length, 'the foe is up there. Remember the murdered men, and don't let 's flinch. We 've got a sure thing, unless they run too fast for us to catch 'em. Wait till I give the word.' We waited a little, while the major was trying to get some sort of arrangement established amongst the heroes in the rear ranks. He found, however, that back there there were soon about as many ranks as heroes; so he gave it up. 'Damn you, then!' said he to the rear guard, 'charge in any order you like, but see to it you don't miss the way, and ride back to the Carson.' Everybody laughed. 'Sam,' said I to Paddington, 'what 's the matter with Virginia City whiskey? It don't seem to give your face as fine a color as usual. Cheer up, my man, we 'll all stand by and see you decently buried; never you fear.' I was a little vainglorious, I've no doubt, because of my martial experiences with Frémont. Escott sat on his mule, as grim as a judge; but Sam spoke up of a sudden with joyous excitement: 'See there!' said he; 'they 're waving a white flag!' And, to be sure, one Indian, high up on the hill, was waving something or other lightish looking. 'Hang their white flags!' said one of the boys; 'they did n't wave any white flags to the fellows they murdered.' And as the major turned to look very carefully at the Indian, a general murmur ran through the front rank. The rear rank probably felt about the matter more like Sam Paddington himself.

"Just then, though, one man spoke up that had a telescope rifle. He 'd been looking through it, and he said that the thing was n't any white flag at all, but a polished battle-axe. The Indian was giving signals to the others, he said. So the telescope-rifle was passed round a little, and the major looked through, and said nothing; and I looked through, and said battle-axe; and yet another man called it an odd sort of a spear. But Sam Paddington, for his life, could n't make out anything but white flag. He believes to this day that it was one.

"But now, of a sudden, as we talked, Molesworth, beside me, could n't stand the thing any longer, and he called out, '*Damn* it!' (rather ill-humoredly, as appeared to me, Mr. Harold,) and he raised his rifle and fired point-blank at the Indian in question. It was too long a range, of course, but the shot did the business for us. For thereupon there was shouting, and there came more shots and a general outcry; and some of the mules began to get unruly, and two or three of the mustangs near me reared and plunged; and somebody — I don't know if it was the major or not — gave the word, or what sounded like it; and there was dust, and the crushing of sage-brush under foot, and I saw some horses stumbling, — and so there we of the front rank were, all charging together, in an irregular sort of line, across the level and up the barren hillside.

"The Indians fired, but then gave way. I don't think we lost a man as we first charged up the hill. The little cañon was on our left. We had got well up in our pursuit, when, of a sudden, crack! crack! it went from our left. The major called a halt. We turned to look, and we saw two most *remarkable* facts. The first was that there were only about thirty of us there together, some seventy or eighty of the command being engaged in the care of their animals, sir, down in the timber by the river. That was n't *wholly* unexpected, but it was a little cooling to our ardor to sit there now on our panting beasts and see it. The other fact, however, was an offset, and warmed up our enthusiasm again a little; for, on the left of our line of attack, just coming over the brow of the barren hill to the northwards, beyond the narrow little cañon, were some two or three hundred Indians, sir, mostly on foot. The Indians were n't so well mounted in that fight as they 'd have liked to be, I suppose. But these fellows, who had been quietly hidden there when we first charged, had now come over the hill, and were pouring in a rattling fire, pretty well directed. They had some very good rifles among them, those Piutes, though they also used bows and arrows later, when they got within range for that. If they 'd had more rifles and ammunition, not a man of us who charged would have got out alive.

"Well, we all found out now how it feels to be under fire. And I think we stood it pretty well. Who would n't, when there was but one thing to do, namely, to keep together, and to retreat to the timber before these fellows, falling on our flank and rear, should cut us off altogether? The major ordered the retreat at once, and we went, firing as we could, and looking over our shoulders now and then at those same yelling wretches whom we had first chased, and who had now rallied like coyotes. The situation became momentarily more and more embarrassing, but we reached the timber at last.

"And now the major ordered us all to dismount, and to stand firm in the wood there, and to fire away as steadily as possible on the advancing foe. That was, in fact, plainly our only chance to keep the defeat from degenerating into the most miserable of routs. For all that could yet be seen, we had some chance, if we all held our ground, to turn the tables and to beat them yet; for when we had once got to the timber we had them at a disadvantage. They were the attacking party now, and as so many of them came on foot we had our fair chance to give them back some of their bullets. By this time we may have lost eight or ten men. I 'm not sure of the number, though. I don't think it could have been more than that, so far, anyhow. And you 'd have supposed that the reserves, if I may call 'em so, whom we 'd left behind, would have aided by their fire to cover our retreat to the timber, and, after this moment, would have stood by us to help hold our position. But that was *not* to be, sir.

" For under those trees, when we came in, there was the most hellish confusion reigning. Saddle-horses and mules, pack-mules, rolls of blankets, cans, guns, ropes, and brave men, all in a horrible mess. The heroes of the reserves, if I may use the expression again, — these heroes who 'd mostly dismounted to watch us, — were struggling, fighting with one another for the animals, climbing on to the mules, getting knocked off again by their neighbors or by the tree-branches, and getting kicked freely by the beasts themselves ; they were falling down pell-mell among their broken packs, among the camp-kettles, the powder-horns, the bacon, the biscuits, and the frying-pans. It was a sight to make one proud of being an American citizen ! But we had n't any time for fooling or for expostulating. Amid the yells, groans, curses, prayers, commands, kicks, and so forth, sir, we who had any trifle of our wits left us tried to take turns holding our beasts and banging away at the enemy.

" They, fortunately, did n't charge home upon us as soon as they might have done. They did n't really appreciate our helplessness until, after a little, they saw the heroes, one by one, emerging from the timber on our right, and dashing off wildly southwards. Then, indeed, the Indians saw our game was up, and came down on us like a Washoe zephyr. I suppose there were, now that they had brought up all their forces, between three and five hundred of them; though, if you ever find out there were less, I take it you'll say I was badly scared. At any rate, they did look pretty numerous, I must admit. So far, we of the first charge had acted fairly well together; even Sam Paddington had shown up much better than I had expected, — at all events, if you compare him with the reserves. But now the major himself saw there was no more hope. With this devilish panic in the rear, and the reserves scattering as fast as they could, and only some fifteen or twenty men capable of pulling a trigger, and the real charge at last coming on, he saw that the old goose was cooked, if I may use the expression. 'Mount,' he said, 'all of you, again, and we'll retreat together. We must get back to the pass in the road before they get there and cut us off. But keep fast together, boys, and use the pistols when it comes to close quarters.' The major himself was as cool as an iceberg, though his left hand was bleeding from an ugly bullet-wound, and his face was all over dust and blood. Poor fellow! he was shot down and killed somewhere in the dark, about an hour later.

"But then came the last and hardest tug of the fight. Our animals had been growing all the time worse and worse frightened. Several of them were now hurt or killed. It was not so clear whether we could all get mounted again. A number of the actual fighters, however, were soon on their beasts, and called upon us other fellows to hurry up. The reserves had by this time mostly vanished. Sam Paddington's mule had been shot dead. My own big animal — it needed to be big, of course — had just escaped, and had run a little way towards the Indians in its fright. Molesworth's had started to do the same thing, when Molesworth himself rushed out a little way in front of the timber line to catch it. Alf Escott had been coolly standing and firing away all the while. His own beast was tied to a branch behind him, and was remarkably quiet, like himself. I did n't know exactly what to do about my beast; so, for the time, I simply stood by Alf's side, and loaded up. The Indians were now coming on foot, with what I thought an awful noise. Of course, all this last stage of the thing takes much more time to describe than it took to happen. Well, when Alf saw Molesworth go out in front, he called to young Bolton, who was still near, and who was just trying to get on to his own beast. 'Let 's make a charge for the lost animals,' he said ; and in an instant they were both in their saddles, dashing out in front of the timber line after Molesworth and the beast.

"They closed on Molesworth's mule, and turned it back to the timber ; but then they seemed to hesitate a moment themselves. I, meanwhile, had got in a shot from my own rifle for their benefit, and seized upon Sam Paddington's rifle for a second shot. He was now crouching behind a tree, and trying to remember his prayers. 'Now I lay me,' he was saying, or words to that effect. But Bolton and Escott had hesitated because the Indians had by this time frightened back my mule, too, which was dashing at full speed towards the timber on our left. But just here, I can't see exactly how, about half a dozen Indians, who were in advance of the main body, came yelling up from the left, along the front of the tree-line, driving my mule just in advance of them. The next moment was the decisive one.

"As Molesworth's animal came up, Sam Paddington saw in it an answer to prayer, sprang out like a flash, seized it, and tried to jump on its back. He'd stood things as long as he could, poor Sam! Molesworth was close after the mule, too, and, without seeing Sam, had begun to get on from the other side. He had one foot in the stirrup when Sam, frantic with terror, put up his both arms over the mule's back, and tried to push Molesworth off. At that instant Escott was upon Sam, and, from the back of his own beast, knocked Sam almost down with a blow between the eyes. Molesworth had lost his hold on the saddle, and was struggling with the mule once more. 'You dog!' said Escott to Paddington, 'take this mule and be off with you;' and, with that, Escott flung himself off his own animal and threw the bridle to

Paddington, who lost no time in vanishing. Sam reached Virginia City somewhat in advance of us, I may say.

"Escott snatched up his own rifle again from the ground; but there was now no time to load. Bolton, Escott, and I, all three, thereupon had out our pistols, and were cracking away at the half dozen Indians just mentioned, who were, of course, much the nearest. Meanwhile, however, what saved us all had happened, namely, that our main body, now just about to start off at full speed, had given one good last volley to the bulk of the charging Indians out in front there, and had checked them. Escott's stand, along with that of Bolton, — they were both excellent pistol-shots, — had knocked over two of these nearest Indians, and scared the others of the half dozen, who scattered back into the brush. Meanwhile, I, after firing three or four rather useless pistol-shots, had seen my own beast near by again, had seized the bridle as the animal passed, and had managed somehow to stop the creature. It is odd how spry a man is at such a time. So now Molesworth, Bolton, and I had our animals, but Escott's was gone. We all offered him a ride behind; but he refused us all for fear of weighing us down. There was a little lull now, you see, before the main body of the charging Indians, who were once more joined by mounted ones from behind, got up courage to continue their advance.

"But we four were in a bad way. Our own main body had left. Our trouble with our beasts had made us the last of the crowd. I don't blame the others for going. There was no time to lose; and, doubtless, these others had n't seen our fix, any way. But, of course, we three could n't conscientiously leave Escott. Luckily, though, we had n't to wait any longer to think how to save him, for as we retreated into the timber we found by chance and without serious delay a poor beast tied to a tree, and frantically rearing and plunging. That was Escott's chance. He got on after no little trouble, and we all escaped; Escott just a trifle the last of all, I admit, but that was n't our fault. He would have it so. Just as we were getting out of the timber, however, in retreat, there came a volley from the Indians, and poor Molesworth fell, all riddled with bullets. I got a scratch on my forehead as I turned to look; you can see the scar now, just under the edge of the hair here, and a little out on the brow. Escott himself was rather badly wounded in the arm, and Bolton, too, was grazed. We stopped yet an instant, enough to see that poor Molesworth was twice shot through the head, as well as in the body, and was not even moving. Then we dashed on.

"That was an awful evening. The coming on of darkness soon saved us from further pursuit. Bolton and I at the first chance helped Escott to bind up his arm. He was pretty faint with loss of blood. But he kept up bravely for ten or fifteen miles. Then we overtook a party of our fellow-fighters — not men of the reserves. They had some wounded of their own to look after, and, like ourselves, they did n't want to forsake their friends. It was now about ten o'clock at night. We, of the two parties, had come pretty near firing into each other when we met, before we made out who was who. After a little parleying, we concluded that as we had now about a dozen fighting men altogether, in pretty good condition, besides the wounded ones, we might as well wait until near morning, and give the wounded men a rest. For, as two or three old fellows told us who knew the Piutes pretty well, the Pyramid Lake Indians would be the last to make a vigorous pursuit towards the settlement, hard as they 'd fight whenever they were put into a tight place. Besides, as was plain during the fight, our thieving stock-raisers, who had made all the trouble, had managed to deprive the Indians of most of their horses. So we went aside and camped, without fire, and with very little to eat, and with only two or three swallows of water apiece to soften our whiskey. It was a gloomy time. A little sleep seemed to refresh Alf Escott wonderfully for the moment, for he has a splendid power of recovery. But he could n't be comforted for poor Molesworth's death. He seemed to think it his own fault. I told him that to him and Bolton I owed my life, and that he had done all he could to save Molesworth. But he would n't admit there was anything in what we said. We had been delayed by him, he said; but that notion of Alf Escott's was all fiddlesticks. The whole delay was but a

16

minute, and as to the fatal volley, we should have got that as soon as we came from under cover, if we had been five minutes sooner. The main party were badly treated, as they left cover in the very same way. But Alf Escott never would speak of that day afterwards with anything but shame and remorse. He could n't forgive himself for poor Molesworth.

"In the morning we buried two men who 'd died during the night. Then we went on slowly, quite unpursued. We got back to Virginia by the morning of the 14th. We were surprised to find what a panic the place was in. We knew we 'd been badly whipped, and we thought we had a good notion what a rough job it all was. But when we got to Virginia City we heard that at least a hundred white men had been killed, that the Piutes were three or four thousand strong, that they were coming to wipe out Virginia City and kill all the whites east of the summit, and that the militia had been sent for to come over from California, several thousand strong, to protect us. We cussed all that nonsense, and went to bed. The next night there was a rumor in the town that the Indians were only a mile or so out; and every blessed fool in the place ran about and yelled for mercy. We fellows that had really fought for it would n't even leave our blankets. We knew better than that. That scare, however, was about the last of it for a long time. Then, even the heroes aforesaid began to observe that there were n't any Indians within forty miles, that the Piutes had no wish to come near a settlement, that we 'd all made fools of ourselves by stumbling into an ambush, that the whole thing was the outcome of a stupid stock-raisers' quarrel, and that we 'd simply better wait until a well-organized force came from over the mountains. So we waited, and after a good while there was another raid into the Pyramid Lake Region; one little party of Indians stayed long enough this time to get rather badly hurt, and then the rest of the tribe fled beyond pursuit into the Goose Lake region. I saw nothing of that next fight. Alf Escott did see it. He went, and pulled through it all, — his old wound having healed, — and came back as discontented with warfare as ever. Chasing the Piutes into the Goose Lake mountains had n't done anything for poor Molesworth, whom Escott had n't even been able to find and bury. The coyotes had doubtless saved him the trouble.

"That 's the story of the Pyramid Lake War, sir, so far as I can remember it. I may have got it badly mixed. I hope, Margaret, you 'll forgive my rough style. It is n't just the story for Sunday."

"But, father," said Margaret, after a little pause, "did n't Paddington and Escott have a fearful quarrel when they met again?"

"No, there you 're mistaken, Margaret. Escott only quarrels with a man whom, if I may say, he somehow respects. He simply ignored the topic with Paddington thenceforth; and the two remained as they had been. Once, indeed, Paddington tried to thank Alf for that loan of the mule. But Alf turned on him a little fiercely, and asked him what he thought of the plan of taking to the Pony Express service for a living. Sam looked a little sheepish, and Alf said, 'If you ever mention Pyramid Lake or that accursed mule to me again, Sam, you 'll be sorry, not to add skinned alive, so now let 's talk about Sayers and the Benicia Boy.' That was the last reference to the matter that was ever made in poor Alf's presence by Sam, or by any of us."

"How could you ever have quarreled with Escott, father, after that day?"

"Well, Margaret, he *was* a hero; but I had nothing to reproach myself with. I fought, too, while I could, that day. And as for our subsequent quarrels, they *are* sad things to remember, to be sure. It 's strange, Margaret," — here Eldon's quietly melancholy manner returned, and he seemed once more very abstracted, — "you don't know, you women, how such things come to pass between men." Eldon paused, and then began again very deliberately. "Suppose now you had long cherished designs, Margaret, for benefiting the public on a considerable scale, if you 'll allow me the use of a rather moderate expression; suppose these designs were what you looked forward to as the prop of your declining years, the joy of the time of life when worldly hopes and prospects in general wax a little less conspicuous, as it were — a little less omnipresent in your thoughts, you perceive. Well, Margaret, let 's say you 'd been dreaming over such things, in a quiet way, for a long time. Has n't a hard-worked man a right to his dreams? And my fancies, if I may say so — I won't boast — they were, to say the least, innocent, I think. Here Providence, if you please to call it by that name, has prospered me beyond the custom of men, and made me a sharer in immense responsibilities. I won't say I 've got much joy from them. It 's been often a hard life." (Harold had begun by this time to feel himself almost an intruder; for if Eldon had addressed all the tale of the Indian fight to the young man, he now addressed this rather serious-sounding confession to Margaret exclusively, quite ignoring for the instant the very existence of his former pastor's son.) "It 's been often a hard life; and sometimes the worst of it has been the eternal exposure to misunderstandings, enmities, bickerings, — trifling things in themselves, but there comes a day when one grows weary of them. Well, I don't want to complain of this at all. It 's my share, I suppose, and, as I said, I 've been prospered to pay me for it. But now suppose, Margaret, you stood in this place of mine, and you said, 'Well, the public won't ever understand, or thank me much; but that 's not my lookout. My business is to do good and shame the devil,' if one may so alter an old saying. Suppose, with this in mind, you made your little schemes, and you took your little joy of them, as a father takes in his own baby, you know, and you conscientiously opined, with a reasonable certainty, to the best of your knowledge and belief, Margaret, that these plans meant, not your private glory, but the welfare of this great and growing community, the advancement of human knowledge, the establishment of human liberty, — yes, the extension of the recognition that all men are created free and equal, and endowed with certain inalienable rights. Yes, suppose that you believed that by your plans you were going to further the principles of the Declaration of Independence, and the cause of civilization on this coast, and the betterment of the lives of the youth of the future. Suppose it all meant that to you, — what you planned, I mean." Eldon paused once more, and drew a long breath. His tone, although melancholy, had never been, during this confession, for an instant merely complaining. He had spoken solemnly and resignedly, like a man in the presence of great problems that he must with dignity lament, but cannot solve. Margaret looked endless sympathy from her deep eyes, and Eldon resumed: —

"These, then, we 'll imagine, were your plans. And now, we 'll also say you had an old friend like Escott, to whom you felt somehow driven to confide these plans, as they slowly and gradually unfolded themselves before your own mind. That, Margaret, would be something like my own case in former days, now gone forever.

"But you see" (Eldon's voice grew somewhat sterner), "I confided those plans again and again to Escott, — I don't know why I tried so many times, — and *always* I met the same scornfully unappreciative reception from him." Eldon brought his hands together with a great blow at *always*. "He had *no* practical sense, you see; he scorned means; he had *no* more notion of the fitness of things than when he gave his mule to that blubbering fool of a Sam Paddington during the Indian fight, and then later mourned with such comfortless remorse for the instant's delay which, as he fancied, had destroyed poor Molesworth's life. Escott's moral sense has sometimes such a singular obliquity. He 's so tolerant of the vileness of wretches like Paddington; he 's so inconsiderate to men like me. He laments over every kind of little flaw in a public man's conduct, over every little concession to expediency, every little device of a sort without which, as I assure you upon my sacred honor, political and business and even social life would be impossible. And it was that bitter intolerance that he used to show to me. He wanted me to live like a perfect angel. He would n't have me make any concession to business or political necessity. At one time this idea just a little overawed me. Then I saw my way clearer. I told him that if we were to be friends he must let me choose my own means, even if they involved some such political or business devices as his over-sensitiveness would n't approve. And with that he spoke plainer than ever, and so at last we broke altogether. And then, Margaret, there came troubles, of which I 've nothing now to say, that gradually transferred our private differences to a public sphere; and Escott said to the world what I could n't brook to have said to me alone. So the evil came to assume its present magnitude.

"Perhaps, after all, I have n't made very clear, Margaret, just what Escott used to say and do about my plans and my devices. It 's hard to show you. But he was simply merciless. I'd go to him this way: I 'd say, 'Escott, don't you think that this or this great public endowment would be the thing for a man like me to make, with my extensive means, by and by?' And Escott would say, 'See here, Eldon, can you honestly swear that for no cent of your money some poor widow or orphan, who might have had it but for your merciless use of arbitrary power, is weeping off there in the dark? If there is any such person,' Escott would say, 'for God's sake make the endowment in that widow's or orphan's name, not in your own.' Now, Margaret, I trust I 'm an honest, upright, straightforward man of business. I 've had great power given me, vast and extraordinary power, and I 've loved to use power. And I 've never let my rights be trampled on. But if, in a hard fight, I 've struck a little unkindly, and perhaps, somewhere, — who knows? — have struck unjustly in my heat, I hold it 's not *right* to speak so to me about what an enemy might accuse me of, though a friend should n't always cast up at me such matters. I 've committed great faults in my time; you, Margaret, know and have long since forgiven some of the worst of them. But is that to preclude me from using my means for the public good, even in my own name? Have n't I, after all, worked hard for all the power I have? May n't I make a good rather than a bad use of it?

"But that was n't the worst. Alf was always accusing me, when I went to talk with him about my plans, of having made a great fraction of my fortune by dint of political *management*. About that matter, which he could least of all understand, Margaret, he used to speak most violently. I 'd milked the State, he said, like a cow; and now I proposed to make a gift of a little of the butter and cheese to the public who owned the cow, and so, he said, to get glory for my generosity. That view of Alf Escott's was *utterly* unjust. I think I 've served the State a little, though, to be sure, I 've never held office myself. I 've always resisted corruption, from the days of the Vigilance Committee until now. But, Margaret, to undertake my responsibilities without having to do with political bodies of many sorts is simply impossible. And to deal with political bodies, in this wicked world, in the presence of all the corrupt politicians of this day, without some undertakings that a man like Alf Escott must needs find ground to criticise, or even, if you will allow me the word, to traduce, — that 's once for all something superhuman. I should have been false to my trust if I 'd not run the risk of this sort of remark. Only, coming from a close and warm friend of early days, it was unkind, Margaret, unkind.

"Alf often used to put it this way. 'Devil's spawn like Paddington,' he used to say, 'or like Boscowitz' (he 'd even mention Boscowitz in that way, — Boscowitz, for whom he writes himself, you know) 'may,' said he, 'do what they like for all me. But a man in your place, Eldon,' he 'd say, 'must be clean as the driven snow, especially if he intends to pose before future generations as the benefactor of the State and the enlightener of the youth of the future. You want,' said he, 'to have your name honored as that of one among the first pioneers of California, as the man who won a vast fortune, and then laid it on the altar of his country. Very well,' Escott would say, 'when you come up to that altar, in that illustrious capacity, you ought to be as pure as the high-priest of God himself, or else fire from heaven ought to strike you. Give your gifts in secret,' he 'd say; 'do your good so that no man will know of it; or else, when you set yourself on a pedestal there for all time, be *sure* you 're made of eternal bronze. If you are n't,' he said, 'keep *off* your pedestal. The State does n't *want* you there.' That was Alf Escott's style of talk, Margaret. I tell it to you because, though it sounds well, of course, it 's only a mass of blunders. May not a man do what he likes with his own? My name 's mine, like my fortune. If I want to leave them both to the State, it can do what it wants with them when I 'm gone. I 've done my duty, I take it, whoever I am. And if it gives me just a little natural pride to think that I, who have nothing else to be remembered by, can live a while in this way, who 's to interfere with such cruel speeches as Alf Escott's?

"Well, it was such talk, repeated and insisted upon, that finally ruined our relations. All our public troubles were but the outcome of this private bitterness. If I had n't loved my plans so ardently, Margaret, Escott's talk would n't have been so hard to bear. And if I had n't respected Escott so highly for his own qualities, despite his many failings, I should n't have noticed these words of his. He, who used to feel irresponsible enough to risk his own earnings again and again in mining stocks, who has worked for Boscowitz even while denouncing him, who had no hard words even for a Paddington, persecuted me, because I lived in the world like a man among men, and used human means when I was in a tight place, and sometimes was a little hard on my enemies, and did some political work by the use of various perfectly necessary political means. That, Margaret, is why we quarreled."

CHAPTER X.

A WINNING GAME AND A LONELY HEART.

EVEN Margaret seemed to be a little perplexed as Alonzo concluded his lengthy explanation. There was a pause, and to Harold came the inspiration that ended it.

"I'm not sure, Mr. Eldon," he began, feeling himself very obtrusive as he did so, "whether I ought not to explain to you a little of what I judge to be the feelings of my friend Escott, at the present time. I'm sure I sympathize in great measure with the views that you have just so freely expressed. I think Escott's conscience is frequently inconsistent, and his plainness of speech, not to say his sensitiveness, is often very hard to bear with. Of course, as I'm so young a man myself, and have looked up to him so ardently in many ways, I don't feel, I can't feel, exactly as you must. Yet even I myself know that one has to make many allowances for his failings. But still, Mr. Eldon, I beg you to note this about him: he's now helpless, and he positively refuses to accept my help, though I'm abundantly able to give him help. I've vainly tried to get him to let me. And so there he stands, a weak old man, very much broken in health, and with a poor capacity for work, but as determined as ever to obtain what he thinks to be his rights, and, in any case, to continue earning his own living and his family's so long as he has any strength. In so far, you see, his character is as consistently manly as ever. As I was saying, though, I think I ought to tell you frankly a little of his present views about some matters that may interest you."

Eldon looked narrowly at Harold's clear and open face. This was his old pastor's son, and the youthful-appearing man had impressed him very favorably to-day from the first moment. But Eldon, nevertheless, felt all this to be very dangerous ground for a mere stranger to tread upon. He came to himself a little, as it were; he lost some of the pioneer-mood, with its accompanying abstraction, and now watched Harold's expression rather sternly. "Well, sir," he said, in a far more business-like tone, "I shall be pleased to hear, I 'm sure."

Harold's was the temperament, not uncommon among unpractical men, that easily quails at any time before the business-like tone; but Margaret's eyes gave him courage now, and he continued quite unhesitatingly: "Mr. Escott, as you know, is my guest at present, since his last misfortune. He refuses to stay with me more than a few days; he is, I hardly need say, quite ignorant that I 'm here talking about him now; and he is probably at this minute visiting at the house of Rev. Mr. Rawley, his brother-in-law, where his wife and children are temporarily lodged. But I myself, Mr. Eldon, have taken no little pains, since I met him, to learn from him the whole story of his life since I left the State, more than four years ago. He tells this story, if I may say so, quite unsparingly, of course. His is a rugged nature, at the same time that, in another way, it 's a very tender nature. He has not concealed, Mr. Eldon, as for that matter you could not expect him to conceal, his past attitude towards you. But what really will interest you, of course, is his present attitude. And that, after what I knew of the old conflicts, was, I must say, surprising to me, as it may be, Mr. Eldon, to you."

Alonzo looked eager, while striving to keep his critical expression undisturbed. Margaret still watched Harold very approvingly from under her long eyelashes.

"Several times recently, Mr. Eldon," Harold went on, "he and I have discussed early days; and we have more than once spoken of you, and of the old differences between you both. Escott has seemed much less intolerant in tone than I had supposed him to be. He once said something like this: 'I 've used some severe words to you, Harold, about my old friend Eldon, and I ought to be able to give you the other side. When I abstract,' Escott said, 'from all personal considerations, and forget all private causes of difference between us, I have to admit that, after everything 's said, Eldon is once for all a great fact in the life of this coast, and that he 's destined by his endowments, if he has a chance, to accomplish a large work for the country's future in an intellectual sense. And I,' said Escott, 'ought to be the last man to hinder this result, even in case I yet had any power to do so. Now, however,' Escott continued, 'I do frankly feel that in making as much as I did of the Oakfield Creek matter, in one of the public prints some two or three years ago, I acted more in anger than in wisdom. I really injured the cause of the settlers, and I really did what I could to harass my old friend, to injure him in the public eye, and to hinder his success in his plans for the public good. And so,' concluded he, 'I want you to see, Harold, that if I do remember private troubles, and if, in the first excitement of my new calamities, I laid too much stress upon them in conversation with you, I am capable of a larger view. And that larger view, while it suggests, of course, no line of conduct to me, does lead me to say that I 've often been in a sense unjust to Eldon, that I 'm sorry when I think of the fact, that I want to see his plans for the public good prosper; and that, if it were he that was in my present trouble, instead of myself, I do sincerely think that I could join hands with him again, despite my general opposition to reconciliations of all sorts. Between just us two,' said Escott, 'however things may have gone between some others and myself, such a hand-joining is not inconceivable.' That, Mr. Eldon was the substance of what I drew from Escott. He did n't say it all at once, of course, but in answer to numerous suggestions and questions of mine. And, as I repeat to you, he had n't and has n't the faintest idea of my present meeting with you. He would have forbidden me, of course, to tell you anything about himself, or his moods, or his words, had he imagined it even possible that I should do so. In one sense, Mr. Eldon, I 'm simply betraying his confidence by saying a word of all this. But I 'm moved to do so by hearing you speak so warmly of your former friendship. There are injuries, of course, that Escott could never forgive, but those, sir, have never passed between you two old friends.

"In fact," Harold added, after a little pause, "as the son of your former pastor, Mr. Eldon, I am moved to interpose this very plain word in the faint hope that it may serve a trifle towards effecting a reconciliation, or, if not that, at least a distant understanding, between yourself and this most admirable if wayward Escott. I can't bear to think of such differences as enduring forever. You were once good and faithful comrades, who faced death like brave men, shoulder to shoulder. I never faced sudden death, and I don't know how it would feel; but I admire far too highly the courage of the men who can so coolly face it together, — thinking all the time of one another's safety, and running all their risks together, — I think too highly of them to be willing now to see them failing to understand and love each other."

"You 're *mistaken*, Mr. Harold, if you think I 'm not still at heart friendly towards Escott. It 's *because* I feel so towards him, — I 'm sure of that, sir, — *because* I — sometimes — almost love him — that I" — Eldon stopped, evidently much agitated inwardly, though he sat very still, and gazed once more far off. Another pause, and a slightly painful one, followed.

"Father," interposed Margaret, eagerly, "you simply can't endure to have this thing go on in this way. Something must be done. Your old fellow-traveler and friend, — we won't say now he saved your life that time, but at least he stood beside you, and beside all his friends, like" —

"He *did* save my life," interrupted Alonzo, fiercely; "there 's no use beating round the bush and prevaricating. He *did* save my life. There ran my animal, driven by those half dozen Indians that were charging in on foot by the left flank. I needed that animal to get away on, and Escott at that very instant had none of his own. There he stands, though, as stiff and cool as an iceberg, pistol in hand. 'Steady,' I hear him say to Bolton, — 'steady now till we send these devils off;' and so those two pop away, — Bolton holding his own mule, meanwhile, but Escott quite helpless, save for the pistol that he was using for me. He was forward of Bolton a little, and never thinking of how to get out, but of me. And a dozen arrows flew by him, Margaret, — and one caught in his coat and hung there; and he was saying to me, 'Alonzo,' he was calling, 'get your mule there, you *damned* fool!' — for that was what he called me, Margaret, and he was *right*, I tell you, for, though I think I was pretty cool, I was cussedly awkward in my firing just then, and I was never a marksman anyhow; and he was saying to me, 'Never you mind, Alonzo, I 'll cover you; *get your mule!*' And so I got the beast. *That* was the sort of man Alf Escott was, Margaret; and if I said he did n't save my life, I *lied*." Alonzo brought down his clenched fist on the wooden arm of his chair with relentless energy, as he spoke, though the blow must have been a little painful.

"And yet now, father, there he is in distress, and he thinks he has rights as against you in the Oakfield Creek matter" —

"Drat the Oakfield Creek matter, Margaret! (I *beg* your pardon, I do most sincerely, but I can't help this sort of talk just to-day, somehow.) I'd settle the Oakfield Creek matter to-morrow, Margaret, if it lay with me."

"Does n't it lie with you, father?"

"No, it does n't." Alonzo spoke of a sudden very shortly and sullenly.

"Why, father, how is that possible? Are n't you practically the owner of all the land in dispute?"

"No, I'm not," said Eldon, still sullenly, but very glibly; "it's the Land and Improvement Company that owns the most of the Oakfield Creek region." The explanation struck Harold as one that Eldon must have frequently uttered before; and it seemed to both listeners to have a certain hollow sound.

"Yet what is the Land and Improvement Company but yourself, father?" Margaret continued, gently and persistently.

"There is n't any use trying to explain such things here, Margaret. The matter has a long history. But I take it, at any rate, that it's plain a man is n't a corporation. There are more interests than mine over there; there's more capital invested than mine. When, as its president, I defend the legal rights of the Land and Improvement Company, I'm acting not alone for myself, but for the capital of innocent shareholders, invested in those undertakings. Some of this capital has come into the enterprise since this trouble began, and on the assurance from me that no pains would be spared to uphold all our legal rights. And some of the shareholders have their blood up, with much more reason for it than I myself have. The feeling among them towards Alf Escott is very bitter. They 'd blame me very hard for any concessions to him. They insist on having the suits fought out. They would n't even sell their shares before the end. I can't act alone. I wish I could give Escott out of my own pocket all that he claims for himself. Then it would n't be so hard to get on with the other settlers."

"But I suppose, Mr. Eldon," said Harold, "that you well know his position in that respect. It 's much like the position of you all in the Indian fight. None of your own party then, I take it, save the redoubtable Paddington, were disposed to get out of the affair alone. You wanted to leave that field together. Escott, quite apart from accepting what would look like charity, is not willing to accept privately even what he takes to be justice to himself. He wants, of course, to stand or fall with the settlers."

"Yes," said Eldon, "there 's the trouble. And it 's precisely in his peculiar attitude as leader of the settlers that it would be very hard, sir, to get, I won't say myself — I 'm willing enough, God knows, purely in my private capacity as his old friend, — but the Land and Improvement Company to deal with him. The settlers alone we could have compromised with, somehow. Escott all alone I should just now try to approach on my own responsibility. But Escott *and* the settlers, sir, — Escott, who 's so stirred them up that they won't talk for a moment of compromise, but only of victory, and the settlers themselves, sir, who, by their presence, give the thing all the time a public character, that would make any surrender merely a confession before the world of our lack of confidence in the legality of our own case, — *that* 's the combination that, sir, as president of the Land and Improvement Company I have no right to, nor can't ignore nor yield to." Alonzo's tone was at this point as business-like as his syntax.

"But, father," said Margaret, quite undaunted, "I took the liberty of telling Mr. Harold this morning something about what you said to me in your letter concerning the interview of last night with Bertha Boscowitz. I had judged from it that she told you something which disposed you to take a new view of the matter. Yet now you talk so hopelessly again ! I feel in my mind, father, by the way, that there 's no sort of difference among us three here concerning the main point. We 're all simply enthusiastic for Alf Escott's salvation from his troubles. So I don't see why we should either be pretending to persuade one another, or be keeping anything back from one another. So I trust you 'll forgive me for having taken Mr. Harold into confidence, since he has just so frankly taken us both into confidence. As to Bertha Boscowitz's information, though, — what was that about ?"

"I trust, Margaret, that Mr. Harold will, for his part, consider my difficulties, and will not too harshly judge the exigencies of business life. But now for Bertha Boscowitz. She told me, I may say, three things. First, Mr. Harold, she gave me what now proves to be a most pleasing and convincing confirmation of your impressions about Escott's mood. She said that, since the fire, in conversation with her, he has, at moments, expressed a very conciliatory spirit, while abating none of his eagerness to be true to his friends the settlers; and she adds that he does long, even as I do, sir, to be done with the wrangling between him and me. That was one thing. Second, she not so much told me as reminded me, in her solemn and pious way, as if she were exhorting in prayer-meeting, sir, concerning those long-past days. She did it by telling how, many years since, when Escott was professor in the college, he used on occasion to describe to his students, and especially to herself, some of the scenes of our old friendship, — used to tell of our adventures, even of this Indian fight a little (though, as I said, in my company he would never mention it); and Bertha Boscowitz declares that he did all this in such a way as to make me the hero of all those adventures; and that, even down until our last great quarrel, he hardly ever said to her a bitter word about me. She said, she knew how much he had thought of me, and, well — in general she managed, just because she is solemn and affectionate, and a little daft withal, to arouse old reminiscences in me very considerably. The girl amuses me, in fact; I like to hear her talk. She 's so odd. The third thing that she said had to do with the present prospects. She knew, so she told me, that all the settlers believe in Alf, and will follow him, like sheep, into a compromise, if he will lead them, or into a bloody battle, if he says so. And, in the same connection, she also told me how her father has somehow got wind of the possibility that at this crisis there might be a settlement of the troubles, and she added that old Boscowitz himself is violently opposed to any such settlement. He remembers, she thinks, that if we end these troubles we shall have just one row the less on our hands. And Boscowitz plainly wants me in rows. Such things earn him his living.

"That, Margaret," continued Eldon, "is what this odd Bertha told me. You have seen how, on the whole, it has affected me to-day. These reminiscences, this assurance that Escott is — well, not the bitterest of my foes, after all, this feeling that a compromise might be possible, this sense that it 's interested people who are keeping me in the fight, — all these things, and my mood to-day, they rather unman me. A square fight with a real enemy I believe in, and delight in too. But this trampling on old affections, this hopeless warfare for nothing in particular, and at my time of life, — you see, I don't like it. That Bertha Boscowitz is, as I said, a little weak in the upper story as to some matters, but she naturally has her father's cunning, and she knows the settlers well, I'm convinced, and, for all her cunning, she's true to Alf Escott and is a pious girl, and I don't think she lied to me, not a minute. I'd believe her a thousand times sooner than I would her father; yet even he seldom lies to me. It is n't his interest to. In fact, I'd believe her about this sooner than I'd believe most men of business on the street. *She's* got no money at stake in this matter."

"And yet for all this," said Harold, "you still seem to feel hesitation concerning the possibility of an actual settlement, owing to the connection of the Land and Improvement Company with the case."

"Precisely, sir. A man like me is bound by numerous and extensive considerations and interests." Alonzo spoke glibly again, but this time with a becoming pride.

"Father," interposed Margaret once more, rather mischievously, "why did you say in your letter that this was a matter for a woman's wit, if your hands were so tied in your frightful bondage to the wicked Land and Improvement Company?"

Margaret knew how far she could go. Alonzo dared not become angry. He only began to smile again, and thereupon looked extraordinarily vacant. "What *I don't* see," he said, "is why then you, as woman, don't now suggest something. That *is* what I've come here for."

"Am I to be legal adviser, then, of the Land

and Improvement Company ?" Margaret laughed merrily. "Come, father," she continued, "you know now that the Land and Improvement Company is something about as big as your own thumb. But if you *will* go out of your way to please the old thing, here 's a good sop for the miserable little monster, since I understand that what you chiefly fear is its bitterness of feeling towards Escott. Tell it that you 're going to let the suits come to trial. Then privately tell the settlers not to take much trouble to contest the matter further. Then, when the suits have gone by default in your favor, so that you and the wicked corporation have your rights on paper all clear, the pride and vainglory and bitter feelings, and I don't know what all of those wicked shareholders who seem now to be egging you on, will be pleased. They will then unhesitatingly let you buy back from them the rights which you never, father, — mark my words, *never*, — ought to have sold them. Then all will be in your hands again. You will not be able to ease your conscience with talk about that Land and Improvement Company; and you will be in a position to offer to all the settlers what you know they own."

Margaret had not ventured on such plain speech before; but now her gentle voice gained just enough emphasis to carry home her words with irresistible music. Her face was full of the same sweet seriousness that Harold had already so often admired in her. She spoke not as if it were for the settlers, but for herself, that she was pleading.

Long afterwards, in fact in a moment of terrible excitement, Alonzo recalled her face and her tone as she spoke on this occasion, and said to himself, —and with a very bitter feeling, too, — "Surely she was speaking in her own cause, not in theirs." But just now, as he listened, he quailed before her plainness of speech, as much as he admired her ready ingenuity.

"You 're a woman of business, Margaret," he said, "even if your views aren't always sound. But this time, I may say, I'd almost thought of something like that myself." Then he grew once more silent.

As for Harold, when he afterwards remembered this whole affair, which he had begun in such hesitation and doubt and suspicion, and which had so unexpectedly lightened up before him, through so fine a combination of favorable circumstances, he always found it difficult to recall precisely the sequence of events after this point in the conversation between these two and himself. He easily recollected Margaret's voice, arguing so gently and persuasively with Alonzo concerning the justice and the feasibility of some such arrangement as she had suggested; he could bring to mind his own occasional interference, which was always favorably received; he could see Alonzo's face becoming more and more acquiescent, and at the same time more animated afresh; he knew that amongst them they erelong arranged the preliminaries for their new course of action, and that finally, at some very opportune moment,

Tom Eldon joined them again. But he knew also that, from the instant of those plain words of Margaret's, the cause had been won, and that all the rest had been but a matter of details.

At all events, the outcome of the conversation was certainly an agreement of all three about several important matters. Harold was to offer, in Eldon's name, and privately, a very favorable compromise to Escott and the settlers. The terms of this compromise were not to be settled at once, of course, until Escott had been heard from, but they were to be next door to a promise of a final surrender by Alonzo of those claims that he now regarded with such weariness and remorse. Harold, for his part, promised to get from Escott the best possible recognition of Alonzo's personal good-will in making this advance. But it was in any case to be understood that this arrangement must, for Eldon's protection, be kept for the time as secret as possible, and that the suits must go on, and must remain unopposed from the side of the settlers, and must be decided in favor of the Land and Improvement Company. All this, Alonzo insisted, was necessary for meeting the wishes of those whose capital was invested with his own in the company, as well as for keeping intact the letter of his own agreement with these principal shareholders. They, he said, were but few in number, but they were irascible men, and would insist on this; they would not part with their shares until they should know that the settlers, and above all Escott, had been beaten in the courts; and the value of the shares would turn in part, of course, on a formally successful result for the suits. The suits once decided, Alonzo said he could then himself make a further agreement with the shareholders, whereby their rights should be protected and their opposition removed.

He felt guilty — so, in the course of the conversation, he frankly admitted to Margaret — guilty of having been willing from the start to push the responsibility of this conflict upon the shoulders of others. He had invited in these very shareholders himself to save him responsibility, and now they were much more bitter than he was. He had granted them large interests in the enterprise, he had made them great promises of never yielding to the settlers, and although the money at stake in this one controversy was not exactly an enormous sum from his own point of view, the passions that had been aroused could n't be allayed to-day or to-morrow. The only hope was to let the affair go to an actual judgment in court; and then, his promises being thus fulfilled, and the full advantage in the matter of the value of shares having been gained for the principal owners, Alonzo would be able to use his own judgment, to buy in these interests of the other shareholders, and then to act on his own responsibility, without breaking any engagements. All this would be costly. He knew it. But his designed endowments had recently come to include a vast tract of farming land in the Oakfield Creek region near the disputed territory, to be dedicated to the State for agricultural experiments and other scientific purposes. It would be worth paying a round sum to get this great tract free from discontented neighbors, and from the shadow of a supposed wrong. Alonzo felt, when he put all together, — justice to the settlers, generosity towards an old friend, the interests of his own future endowments, and the rest, — almost more astonishment that he should have let the thing go so far than unwillingness to try now this new plan. But, strange as it was, some such crisis as this one seemed to be needed to freshen the old memories and to bring about the new mood. Alonzo, as he talked to-day, recognized this weakness of his own nature with a frank regret, not unmingled, of course, with the great momentary satisfaction of sunning himself in the approving smile of his conscience and of Margaret. His resolution to make right the old wrongs seemed to his sanguine mind, meanwhile, to be much the same thing, already, as out-and-out success. He grew genial, and more confidential than ever. He once more fell to telling anecdotes about Alf Escott.

Just before Tom returned, however, Alonzo leaned forward, and, looking pathetically into Harold's eyes, said, "There's one thing more, Mr. Harold, that I must mention. The bitterest thing of all, and the one that's often made me the angriest with poor Alf, just because I could n't see how to make the wrong right, and because he seemed to want to visit it all on me, — though I'm as innocent of it as a babe unborn, sir, — is the *very* thing that I hope, through your assistance, we can now do something to make a right feeling about again. And that, sir," — here Alonzo's voice sank to an awful half-whisper, and he leaned yet further forward and glanced sidewise at the window, to see that Tom was not within hearing, — "that, sir, is the wrong that Tom very carelessly, but quite unintentionally, did to the affections of Alf's poor daughter Ellen, — she that died, crazy, sir, stark staring mad, of a stormy night, here, hiding in the garden of this very house, sir, driven here by some singular insane delusion, the result of her mental condition, sir, — I can't tell what it was. But no doubt you know the story. It's awful, sir, *awful*. And *that* is what I most of all want, not to make good, — *what* can make good to a man the loss of his child? Nothing, sir, nothing, — *not* to make good, but to set in a right light before poor Alf, sir, before the man that once saved my life from the Indians." The awful half-whisper continued to the end of this speech, Alonzo's great face coming closer and closer, as he spoke, to Harold's, his eyes having all the while the same pathetic mingling of regret and wild hope, while his voice was full of a terrible emphasis. If Alonzo from the first moment on had been growing more and more confidential to the pastor's son, just this particular confidence seemed as abrupt as it was frightful, and Harold sat like one stunned. There was no reply to make.

But, an instant later, Harold ventured to look

again towards Mrs. Eldon ; and his eyes met hers. Her face was now fearfully pale, yet she did not avoid his glance, though she sat very still and rigid. But her look was an evidence, so he at once felt, of the strangely quick understanding that they two had somehow established between themselves to-day. She knew, he saw, that he was aware of everything; and she plainly felt that he could be trusted neither to misjudge her, nor to triumph over her. She had faith in him, so this mutely appealing glance said, and from this moment, knowing her faith, he revered her. Poor Ellen, at least, he thought to himself, was at peace, but this woman was carrying that horror for her lifetime. How gloriously she bore it all! What a crime that she should be tied here to her husband, and to this well-meaning, blundering, powerful, capricious monster of a father-in-law! Harold knew now that, for his own part, he at least was at her service, to do knightly duty for her henceforth, however and whenever an upright friend might be needful for her welfare.

Yet the glance was but a matter of the most inappreciable instant. Before he knew what had happened, she had recovered herself, was more radiant than ever, showed no consciousness that anything untoward had happened, and devoted herself to sympathizing with her father-in-law's new-born good resolutions, and suggesting whatever might give them support. And so, at the moment when Tom appeared, there were no more doubtful matters to be explained, but all was cheerful and clear. Harold had even forgotten, for the moment, about the magazine.

Margaret had provided for a pleasant evening for her guests. Some of her most agreeable neighbors, old friends of the family, dined at the house, and Harold felt himself in the midst of more gayety than he had known for years. Late in the evening, when the company were together in the parlor, Margaret took care to mention at a happy moment the plan of the magazine as one which Mr. Harold was said to have recently conceived. She begged the little company, of course, to regard the idea as strictly confidential. She connected by no hint Escott's name with the affair; she left all that to Alonzo's freshly kindled enthusiasm. The attempt was perfectly successful. In the presence of all the company, Alonzo forthwith confessed himself an ardent supporter, at least in theory, of the projected magazine, and accepted with eagerness Margaret's ready suggestion that it might be made the organ, in a sense, of what she persisted in gently ridiculing as the New British Museum. Soon afterwards, in a slightly more business-like tone, Alonzo said quite distinctly that he would seek to confer further with Mr. Harold concerning the practicability of some such scheme.

One could n't really say off-hand, he went on to remark, whether there would be anything of practical value in such a project as this of Mr. Harold's or not. Perhaps 'at the first blush, and just to-day, he was disposed to be a trifle too enthusiastic about it. Mr. Harold must n't lay too much stress on his show of interest. In fact, he could n't and would n't promise anything to-night, nor until after ample and careful consideration of every aspect of the matter. But really, at this first suggestion, the whole thing seemed to him very attractive. He would be proud to aid in establishing on the coast a strong, permanent, and useful periodical, and that especially because such a thing would, if properly conducted, have a close relation to his other enterprise, of which Margaret had just been speaking.

That other enterprise, by the way, he thought he should like to represent more completely to Mr. Harold some day. There was no time this evening, of course. It was n't fair, exactly, to call it a New British Museum. That was an old joke of Margaret's, founded, to be sure, on something he had once let drop. His notion had points in common with the British Museum, — points, but that was all. He was n't sure, to speak quite frankly, whether he quite approved of the British Museum itself, let alone trying to imitate it out here in San Francisco. The British Museum, in truth, was n't quite practical enough for the American people, especially in California. He could mention to Mr. Harold, on demand, at least a dozen respects in which the British Museum was an obviously defective institution, not fit to be duplicated in San Francisco, therefore, even if that were possible, which nobody said that it was, as he wanted very emphatically to point out right here.

However, all this was a matter for further talk, Alonzo went on. Whatever his own plan might amount to, there was no doubt but he would like to get suggestions as to the conduct of it. And there was also no doubt but, if a magazine could further it, he himself would be prepared to further the project of a magazine, in case that should prove otherwise practicable. No promises, then, of course, to-night. But during the next week Alonzo would think it all over, and perhaps would like to consult Mr. Harold further, soon, concerning the thing.

But when the company had gone, Alonzo took an opportunity to call Harold aside. With a certain timid familiarity he laid his enormous hand gently on Harold's arm, looked once more with that pathetic earnestness into his eyes, and said, "Do you suppose, Mr. Harold, that it would be any way possible to get Escott into connection, directly or indirectly, with that magazine-design of yours? His talents, you know, his experience, his literary taste, his — well, *don't* you think" (Alonzo's voice sounded very deep and earnest) "that there would be in a sense an opening for him there?"

Harold found his room at the Eldons' large and pleasant. It had an eastern outlook, a great and exquisitely comfortable bed, a few shelves full of books, a little balcony where there were some plants in pots. The moon rose late over the near and rugged hills that night, and, as Harold lay awhile, broad awake, the shadow of the window-sash and of the wide-branching, tall, and shapely plants could be seen on the polished wooden floor, just beside one of the rugs. At last, as Harold dropped off to sleep, he fell forthwith to dreaming that he had been walking in a wild place which he had never seen before. He now lay down to rest, he thought, in the dim light of the waning moon, and wondered if this were not the Oakfield Creek region. But no, for here came one of Margaret's guests, dressed just as she had been this evening. She was a tall young woman, who smiled to herself reflectively. But when she approached him, and saw who he was, her face grew dark and stern. "Why are you sleeping here?" she said. "The summit is ahead, and the roads are very bad. Don't you know you must go and hunt for Margaret Eldon? She needs you. You must comfort her. You must be her friend." "Why does she need me, then?" asked Harold, in his dream, feeling at once delighted and terrified. It seemed to him, meanwhile, that this lady was an Indian just about to kill him. "Because her little boy is dead," said the apparition. "He was born dead. He has never been alive. He was born here one night in a storm. He died, sir" (but now the young girl seemed to assume that terrible half-whisper of Alonzo's), "because she had some singular insane delusion, — the result of her mental condition, sir. You must comfort her. You must be her friend." And with these words the dream vanished, and left Harold once more alone in the moonlight. He thought for a long time after this of the little boy and of Margaret. Then he said to himself that if she did indeed ever prove to be his friend, and as good and true a woman as she seemed, the thought that she was watching and approving his work would give him fresh interest in a busy life. At all events, he went on, she had already determined for him his next occupation. He must labor for Escott, for the projected magazine, for the reconciliation of the two old friends, and, above all, for her own peace of mind, in so far as it was concerned in any of these things Her house, to be sure, it was really not likely that he would very often visit. Her husband was, despite a certain pleasant modesty of bearing and an obvious cleverness, decidedly antipathetic to Harold just now. He doubted, therefore, whether he could have much further concern with the household. Perhaps, moreover, Margaret, after all, disapproved of her new guest. He had been stupidly sentimental that once to-day, and whatever little success he had had with Alonzo was due solely to his being the pastor's son, after all. Why should Margaret give her new acquaintance a second thought? Doubtless, therefore, he must not expect any more interest from her side. But, on his part, he must devote himself quietly to her service. She needed to have all done that could be done towards righting the old wrongs. There, at least, he might prove to be the man for her emergency. If he could be such, she might depend upon him. Full of these resolutions, he at last slept once more: and, when once the rising moon had gone from his windows, he slept dreamlessly.

Margaret, meanwhile, had spent some time alone in her own room, trying to read a certain book. She frequently had just such books on hand, — books that did not interest her, and that she thought ought to interest her. A friend of hers, a very bright woman, was continually forcing them upon her. This lady had really no more interest in them than Margaret; but then the friend in question was one of those vivacious people, so happily constituted that they never observe how little they care for the topics which all intelligent people should understand, and which so few intelligent people, after all, can bear to think of for ten consecutive minutes. Margaret's friend, quite ignorant that she was boring herself, always read through such books as the one in question in a very few hours, frequently eying, even while she did so, the opposite window, or the place where the wall-paper failed to match. What that bright lady remembered afterwards of the contents of the books took the form of a slightly oppressive sensation between the eyebrows, which she always felt while she read the works in question, and which she knew to be characteristic of the moods of all thoughtful persons. Books that had given her this experience she always spoke of afterwards with the most hearty and honest admiration, and she could often even recall the colors of their individual bindings. Such were the volumes, at any rate, which she persistently forced upon Margaret. Now Margaret, in miscellaneous society, was as fond of seeming intelligent as the most ardent advocate of the higher life could have demanded. But when she was alone, or was talking to a few friends, she was, above all, self-critical, though that fact she usually concealed from other people. She really did not like, at such times, to produce any false impressions about her own mental powers. And so she frequently wondered whether she was seriously intelligent at all. True, she certainly admired the ideal man of learning, and she loved, as aforesaid, to fascinate any fair specimen of the real man of learning. But these books,— alas! that feeling between the eyebrows often came to her; she knew it excellently well; but it seemed to her somehow an insufficient experience of the joys of spiritual insight. She wanted, she confessed to herself, to know each book as she knew her roses, or else to let it alone. And the latter alternative, in case of certain of her friend's favorites, often appeared to Margaret both the preferable and the only reasonable one.

But in any case we have no thought of jesting about poor Margaret as she was that night. For whatever usually led her to toil in a desultory and unfruitful fashion over her friend's treasures of learning, Margaret read just now only for the sake of keeping herself from crying. The day had been, after all, one of very great and wearisome trial. Margaret had, for a long time in the past, schooled her mind to an almost perfect calm. Great troubles had come and gone. She could never make the wrong right again; but she was strong and self-possessed and proud, and so she was resolved to conquer the sting of the sorrows. She had thought herself equal to the task. It had been a long and lonesome fight. Only her mother had known anything about it; and her mother, after all, had known but little. There was much that could not be told. Margaret, for a good while at the start, could only look up to the great dumb, rocky hills, that bloomed a little for so short a time in spring, and that lay sombre and barren for so long after the rains were done, — could but watch them and be silent. It was the silence that had ended in making so many of her friends call her hard and cold. For it was such a dumb anguish, — this that she had had to conquer and hold down. And holding down, with Margaret, did not mean merely the sentimental holding down which all the shallower minor poets like to tell about, — when the face smiles, as they say, but the heart is full of woe. Margaret was fully equal to that, indeed, but she bore herself toward these sorrows far more seriously. She meant to take them by the throat and to strangle them, so that when she laughed it would be with the old peace, and when she talked it would be with the old healthy, rejoicing life again. For when she considered these sorrows she knew that, in great measure, they disgraced her. They were only the expression of her shame and of her weakness. As true woman she ought not to feel them. They came from her unworthy affection for a false man; from her unworthy pride in his hollow admiration; from a base, if unwilling, jealousy of the love that he had shown towards the woman whom he had murdered. Had he been an out-and-out seducer, would Margaret not have loathed him? And yet, wherein was he better than an out-and-out seducer? There is a seduction of the soul alone, which kills no less surely, and sometimes with more awful anguish, than the seduction that drives a poor wretch to hide her shame by suicide. Poor Ellen, indeed, had been mercifully spared the worst sorrow of living on in the presence of that fatal betrayal of her heart and hope. She had striven courageously against the first shock, and insanity and death had saved her in time from the inevitable reaction that would have left her for life a broken and hopeless woman. But Margaret, if she knew that Ellen was now safe from all this anguish, must needs think of Tom as no better than a common betrayer. Could she ever forgive him, then? No, that must not be. But not to forgive him and yet to go on lamenting him, — that was shameful! Margaret believed herself too strong and proud for that. So she went back into her little world so soon as her child had come; she took part in all her old amusements, — save that she could no longer share them with Tom, — she worked, she forced herself to enjoy; in a word, she triumphed.

Had she, then (so she often asked herself after this victory had been won), had she ever really loved Tom at all? Was it not simply an admiration for his gracefulness, for the brightness that he used to show so much more than he showed it now, for the high and ideal purposes that he used so often and with such a beautiful counterfeit of earnestness to profess? Was it not mere acquiescence in his worship? Was it not simply a yielding to his flatteries? So she now often thought. As her pride forbade the least confession to the world of her feelings, she still saw him a great deal. And she still had, too, something of the old admiration for his outward bearing, deeply as she loathed his soul. She even cultivated this external admiration. It was a harmless amusement; it did not disturb her laboriously attained peace of mind; she was perfectly safe in it; and, meanwhile, it helped her to keep control of him, and preserved the peace of the household. She spoke gently to him, and hated him; and he, accordingly, was fascinated with her, and kept more or less of his foolish hope that she might some day be won back. Meanwhile, as she knew, he was as proud as herself. He would reveal nothing to others; he would respect her own feelings; he would simply go on trying, by returning flattery with flattery, to atone for his crimes. Life at that rate might, some day, become very dull; but for a proud woman, rejoicing in her beauty and in her power, it was, meanwhile, tolerable, because she had simply made up her mind that it should be tolerable! As to whether he was still sentimentally faithful, — she never gave that a thought. He might go on now breaking whatever hearts he chose. The world was warned of him; it might do what it would with him. And yet, after all, if this was her present feeling, had she, nevertheless, ever really loved him at the outset?

One thing, of course, which made that question so hard to answer was the character of her whole life since her girlhood. She had been made an early sacrifice to her mother's ambition. Something, perhaps her cold and unemotional training at home (but yet more probably the warm, even passionate, love and admiration for her mother which she had been driven to conceal all through her childhood, but which had been the one great experience of her early life), had made her willing to acquiesce in this sacrifice. The act itself, however, had helped to render her proud and self-reliant, had made her mistress of her emotions, and had prevented her from cultivating any merely sentimental fancies about love. That year of marriage with Dover she always looked back upon as the wildest of perplexing dreams. He had been affectionate, even reverent, lavish of gifts, thoughtful of her comfort, but still often petulant with an old man's petulance. His piety, his whimsical precision of life, his pedantic airs towards the world at large, and a certain overbearing will, that with her he usually kept in the background, had all added to her problems. His death was a great horror and a great relief. It had left her a full-grown woman in heart and mind, the mistress of a fortune, self-reliant, full of courage and of energy, but without any experience of a true and womanly love. Only her mother had remained to her then, and her mother and herself somehow never quite found each other again, warmly as the old childish affection still burned in Margaret's heart.

The fact, then, was that, until Margaret came to know Tom well, she had had little opportunity and less desire to consider what it might be to be devoted to any man. Had Tom ever taught her this, even in the most golden days?

Well, at all events, so much was, to-night, quite clear. She felt a great longing for her baby, — so great a longing that at first she dared not go to his little crib, lest she should be all overcome with lonesome weeping. The old sorrows had been cruelly torn from their graves to-day. And she had been sitting there, meanwhile, and smiling on the people in the most contemptible way! What could they be thinking of her, these people from without the family? Had they come to gloat over her woes? But no; she was unjust. She herself had invited it all. She herself would have forced Tom to do this, so soon as she should have learned the need, even if he had been himself unwilling. It was duty; she could bear it. They were very kind to come and help her. Did not the whole world, once for all, know about her? What was one scene more or less in the comedy of her disgrace, after all? And yet, on further thoughts, how vile this daily life in the company of this man, whom the world called her husband, really was! What a false pride to keep up this show! An honest, thoughtful, warm-hearted man, such as this Harold, who had once loved his wife so dearly (as she read in his eyes to-day, there in the garden, when they talked of his old home), what must he think of her conduct? Did he take her to be a timid, helplessly faithful wife, who acquiesced in her husband's vileness and loved him still, as in duty bound? The thought was maddening, although, somehow, she did not find the same thought in the least maddening when it occurred to her with reference to other people. The world at large might think what it chose. That was even part of her game, — to mystify the world at large; she took the most hidden and sacredly secret glory in that very fact. But Harold, — somehow there was, for the first time, a difference in her mind about this matter, between one person's views and another's. Very well, then, perhaps he guessed the truth, — that she loathed Tom and kept him at her feet. And yet, in that case, what did Harold still think of her, — this clear-eyed, faithful man, who served his old friend so openly and loyally, and who appreciated the finest shadings of life and of conversation so sensitively? Plainly he must, then, think that she bound herself to Tom from mere worldly pride, and that she had simply feared to step out and say before the world, concerning this wretch, "I have no part nor lot with him." Harold, in such a case, must think her a mere coward. And was she not one? This pride, as she had called it, was it not mere cringing terror at the world's sneers? Why had she not taken the plain way of separating herself utterly and openly from Tom so soon as she had found him out? Women are such vile imbeciles about their unfaithful husbands! And this of Tom's was no common unfaithfulness. It was rank treason to two persons at once, and it had ended in murder. Oh, why was she so weak and worthless, after all?

All these things Margaret thought out with a nervous and painful exactitude to-night, her heart meanwhile beating loud and wearisomely, her head aching in a dull way, her mind intensely awake. She thought of them before she read, while she read, or pretended to read, and afterwards. The light hurt her eyes, and so she laid the book aside, and set the lamp in another part of the room. But when she had done so her part of the room seemed too dark. She was getting momentarily more nervous and lonesome. She thought of poor Ellen, and remembered the most awful experience of all her own life, — something that she had managed to avoid confessing, long ago, at the coroner's inquest, and that, in consequence, no soul but herself knew. On that stormy night of Ellen's death, namely, Margaret, being just then full of fancies about her hoped-for child, and sad because Tom was away, and nervous because the wind blew, had not fallen asleep until very late, — in this same room, of course, the rain beating against the window-pane, the wind rattling the near tree-branches against the house. She had wakened in the dark before very long, and with a fearful start. There was a lull in the storm. It seemed to her that she had distinctly heard, very far off, a girl's voice calling the dead Peter Dover's name. Something about the voice had made her almost shriek with horror. It had been somehow mixed up in her dreams with wild fancies concerning her coming child; she knew no longer what they were, — only they were unspeakably horrible. She had lain shuddering; then she had thought the voice must be itself only part of her dream; and after a long time had fallen asleep again, only to be wakened afresh from the same awful and inexpressible dream of darkness and of her coming child, by that voice calling for Peter Dover, only now more pleadingly than ever. She had aroused herself; she had forced herself to be calm; she had even gone to the window, looked out, and listened. But the wind had freshened, the rain had beaten full in her face, and she had heard no more of the voice. Only she had not slept again until dawn, and had then wakened to learn whose the voice had been. Something about this voice, coming as it did, had seemed to her so heart-rending that she had felt it even impossible to tell of the thing to any one afterwards. In no case could the fact have thrown any light on the questions about Ellen. No inquiry during her own brief appearance at the inquest had called upon her to reveal the occurrence. She remembered it now with the old shudder; and then quickly rising, she went out of her room, and across the hall, to where her child was sleeping. She lowered the side of his crib, and knelt down beside him.

His breath came soft and light; when she touched him he hardly moved in response, and it was only when, in an agony of nervous weeping, she had pressed her head close against him, and had taken him into her arms as he lay, that he was aroused enough to lay one hand gently against her face, and to nestle comfortably and happily close to her. Long she knelt there, blessed and wretched, proud and lonesome, exhausted and sleepless. He was her only treasure, this darling boy, and he had in a sense no father, or worse than no father. This one precious tie, — to what loathsome bondage did it not unite her! She longed to run off with the child into the darkness somewhere, and find the way to die happily in his little arms, while he breathed gently against her cheek. All day long, to-day, he had been seeking her, crying for her, talking about her, planning his little surprises for her, making up his little stories about her. Did she not know his darling ways? Well, now at least they should not be separated. She lifted him up very softly, and carried him with a joyous and stealthy triumph back to her own room, without disturbing the nurse. And all night they slept close together; for when the moon reached Margaret's side of the house, it brought with it no dreams, but only shone upon the face of the mother, fast asleep, with the little baby-hand on her cheek.

In the morning, nevertheless, Margaret shamed herself before the startled and somewhat anxious nurse, when the latter first sought for her charge. He had been restless, Margaret glibly explained, with a certain lying dignity. She had thought it best to have him with her to quiet him. But the boy, radiantly laughing on his mother, and wild with the novel delight of waking to find her so near him, showed no evil consequences from this restlessness. This morning he loved his bath, his nurse, his breakfast, his playthings; everything; and Margaret was as happy as a queen, and fairly cried with delight.

Harold and the elder Alonzo appeared that morning to be the warmest friends. After breakfast they took hearty leave of their hostess, and, together with Tom, set out for the smoky city beyond the gray and chilly water. And with this day began Harold's new life.

BOOK III. — MARGARET ELDON.

CHAPTER XI.

BERTHA BOSCOWITZ.

When Bertha Boscowitz had finally broken with her father, she sat for a long time alone in their house, glaring at the wall. The blow had fallen at last, she hardly knew why. All her wishes to be good, to save his soul, to convert him from his sinful ways, had ended in this. She must be a wicked woman; Mrs. Rawley would say so. Boscowitz had always been harsh, sarcastic, at times almost ferocious. But he was her father still; and until this very morning she had never quite lost hold upon him. But now he had told her that she could leave the house as soon as she chose. He would give her a little allowance henceforth, he said; but he never wanted to see her face again. She had always been cruel and ungrateful to him, he declared; but he would not quite let her starve. He would always hate her; but he would support her while she lived.

That was the end! Bertha's whole life had been homely and simple enough, save for a very few fiercely passionate experiences, and for her many secret struggles with the wickedness of her own heart. One of her earliest emotional excitements had been caused by the discovery that she was a very bad girl; that she had much low cunning in her nature; that it was mean to listen at keyholes, and to pry into others' affairs in all sorts of ways; and that she naturally loved to do just such mean things. For a long time all this had troubled her. She had lived in a dull terror of being hated by good people, and of going to hell at last. This terror had made her quarrelsome. Her mother was in those early days already dead; her father was a wanderer from city to city,— now a ward politician, now a socialist agitator, now a fawning political servant of some rich man, now a book-seller, and always a fugitive from his creditors. He used to pretend to have ideas; he read strange foreign books about politics and the coming social revolution; he preached to her violently concerning the wrongs of poor men; and for himself, he wronged everybody, rich and poor, whom he could lay a hand upon. But he was a progressive man. His wanderings taught him, as time went on, an immense store of worldly wisdom. He studied his fellows; he grew more of an American; he imitated the manners of more conservative people; and gradually he discovered his art of managing men by a show of insolent coolness, and by a professed devotion to all their vested interests. He ceased to talk socialism; he neglected foreign companionships; he no longer read foreign books; he even settled occasionally with his creditors. And thus, after a while, the successful part of his career began. It was all a triumph of genius over numberless inner and outer foes ; and Boscowitz was as proud of his progress towards wisdom as he was of his power to carry vast numbers of drinks without losing his head.

As the years went on, however, Bertha, whom her father regarded with affection, jealousy, and disappointment, formed companionships, at the public schools and elsewhere, which made her more and more ambitious, remorseful, and timid. These companionships never amounted to friendships ; Bertha was too shy for that. She steadfastly believed that everybody hated her. But every scornful word that she heard sank in deep and stung hard. She wanted to be good and ladylike. She had, however, only a very dim sense of goodness, and no sense at all, save what she gained from bad novels, of what a lady might be. When the girls at the public schools laughed at her awkward walk, and at her staring eyes, and at the pins that she sometimes too manifestly used as fastenings for her dress, she would cry about it for hours, and would devote days of dull meditation to finding out the reason. It was a great day in her life when she discovered that those pins were one cause of her hideousness. She felt like stout Cortez and the rest on the peak in Darien, and gazed with a wild surmise on the ocean of social possibilities that would be open before a girl who should always sew the buttons on to her gown. After that she made in succession some equally grand discoveries about her shoes, her hair, her hands. She took all these things to heart very deeply. She wondered why nobody would ever help her. Everybody could laugh at her awkwardness; but when so much of it was a purely external matter, like the pins, why would nobody explain to her the reason, and teach her to improve? She was sure that she was teachable. She was always thankful for kindly advice. Meanwhile, she was very studious. At home her father addressed her as "Stupid," just as if that were her proper name. She quarreled with him bitterly. But the teachers at school used to think well of her industry, and to praise her.

Then, at last, there gradually dawned upon her the notion that a great world of learning exists, a refuge for every one, a world where the pins in your clothes and the ugliness of your hands have somehow nothing to do with your joys and sorrows, — a world measureless, romantic, sublime, and even cheap; for you could buy learned books with the money that you stole from your father; or, better still, could steal the books yourself from his shop. People thenceforth called Bertha, in their cruel way, "daft," just because she took to this world of learning with such frantic and untrained eagerness, and wandered in some of its more easily accessible mazes so wildly, helplessly, and earnestly. She now tormented her teachers at school with questions about books, and about how long it would take her to acquire what a really wise man, like Socrates, or Shakespeare, or

Darwin, must know, and about how many languages one ought to learn. This eagerness lasted for years, until Bertha herself had had time to become too honest to steal from her father, and time also to make a failure of teaching school, and until she had been for a while the terror of the leisure hours of the professors over at the Sunset College, in the "Dell of the Muses." And the abiding effect of the great craze itself had taken form in her mind in two most noteworthy objects: she had come to know and to revere Alf Escott, and, at the college, she had fallen desperately in love with Tom Eldon. Escott, during his professorship and later, she looked up to as a father. Tom she had hardly ever spoken to; but she had worshiped the very ground young Eldon trod upon.

When she loved people, all her old childish cunning came back to her. She spied upon them; she intrigued, and sometimes even eavesdropped to get news about them. She tried to know all that they did, and was the whole while in an agony of terror lest they should find out the fact. She thought of them the livelong day. And such thoughts never made her eyes less wild. For all her intercourse with people and all her great passions, she, however, could not learn to talk successfully to strangers, nor to behave like her fellows.

At the Sunset College, where she was so long a special and unmatriculated student, the faculty had a great dread of her. Nobody, save Alf Escott, could endure her. For a long time nobody could get the heart, however, to send her off. And not even Alf Escott could teach her more than a mass of mechanically united or else crazily disconnected truths. At last, when the trouble about Escott came, Bertha took his side with a most savage loyalty, quarreled with nearly all the girls in college about him, and capped the climax, one rainy day, by throwing all the books of a tall and dignified young lady student, a senior in the college, out of the window of the ladies' study, which was in the third story of one of the college buildings. The provocation for this act was an unkind remark of this dignified senior concerning the now departed professor. The first consequence of the act, however, was that the books, descending in a scattered shower, fell, part of them, upon the umbrella of the passing president of the college, himself. He was a portly and red-faced man, who thought much of his dignity. The umbrella was shattered, the president's tall hat was crushed, and his glasses were broken. A sophomore, who was casually following the president, very softly, just then, and who was imitating that officer's strut, received a bad blow on the head from another of the books,—a blow that, of course, caused such a youth more surprise than injury. All the books fell into the mud, which, during a rain, lay all about the Sunset College, deep as first love. Finally, however, an express wagon, which was just then standing in front of the college, engaged in delivering some fraudulent Indian relics for the

Sunset Museum, took fright at the mishap, and ran the whole length of the Dell of the Muses, scattering the fraudulent relics, together with many shopping-parcels, beer-bottles, homeward-bound rejected manuscripts, and other valuable property of the inhabitants of the Dell, promiscuously along those fathomless roads where the feet of the Muses were piously believed to wander. In consequence of this incident, Bertha left the college.

Not long afterwards it was that Mr. and Mrs. Rawley found her. The girl was now especially lonesome, weary, and hateful. She felt her latest disgrace keenly, and she knew not where to turn for the right friend. Escott himself made known her existence and her needs to Mrs. Rawley; and the latter proved the one person for the occasion. Bertha soon found that in Mrs. Rawley she had a critic as kindly and as patient as she was unsparing. Mrs. Rawley had just the one quality which Bertha had always missed in her acquaintances. They had assumed that the poor girl must see why they laughed at her; while Mrs. Rawley never laughed at Bertha, and never assumed that the girl knew anything. Mrs. Rawley was, therefore, never surprised at Bertha's ignorance upon topics even quite as elementary as that of the pins had been; and Bertha's degeneracy, however she might show it, Mrs. Rawley explained on general principles, as due to the sinful nature of fallen man. What Escott called Mrs. Rawley's cheerlessness was accordingly sweetness and light itself to this poor lonesome girl; and the result was that Bertha became first Mrs. Rawley's worshiper, and then her convert. The good pastor himself coöperated, here as elsewhere, with his wife; and the result was that the church had erelong few more loyal members than Bertha Boscowitz.

The poor woman herself never grew happy. She remained brooding, suspicious, a natural spy, a stranger to her kind at large. But she made many friends in the church; the weekly prayer-meetings became the great experiences of her life; her fellow-members admired her zeal; and some of the very young people began to think that, just because she was so odd, she must be much more pious than themselves. So she gained at last a position and a work in her little world.

Her father remained her great cross. She became far more faithful to him; she even learned for the first time what fidelity really meant. She for a long time ceased to quarrel with him. But he never came to understand her. He loved her, too, in his own way; but his love only made him show hatred of her worldly failures, disappointment at her lack of mental strength and of practical skill, and no understanding of her new religious feelings. He found only pain in contemplating her uncouth mind and her awkward and feeble body. For her health, both first and last, through all the troubles of her childhood and through all the toils of her youth, had been persistently wretched. Those curious fainting-fits, associated as they were with continual dyspepsia and general weakness, neither of the two ignorant members of this household could ever understand or learn to control. Bertha's conversion to the faith did not mean her instruction in the art of healthy living, and Mrs. Rawley, who had assisted at the new birth of her soul, acquired no influence over her views about medicine.

The new quarrel between Bertha and her father began shortly after her interview with Alonzo Eldon. This was now nearly four months since. Boscowitz had soon found out all about it. But the editor, meanwhile, had been bitterly opposed to Harold's whole plan, since this plan both tended to withdraw Escott from the "Warrior's" staff, and to remove one trouble from the load of responsibilities with which Boscowitz desired to see Eldon weighted down. "It pays him to have me in trouble," Eldon had said of the editor. In any case, Bertha had thwarted her father, and the matter had passed beyond his power to control. He blamed her far more than at worst she could possibly have deserved, for all that had happened to displease him. There was now no apparent chance of defeating the great reconciliation between Eldon and the settlers. It was progressing as well as possible. Boscowitz was still forbidden to make it public, although he well knew of its various stages. He was not in a position just now to disobey Alonzo. Eldon seemed, in fact, to be acting very cautiously and sincerely. He had quieted the suspicions of his fellow-shareholders in the Land and Improvement Company by assuring them that the test cases should be pressed to a judgment before any final arrangement should be made. He had avoided the need of a formal explanation with the settlers by pressing, meanwhile, as these test cases, only the suits in which Escott was personally concerned. With Escott, however, he had a private understanding that was largely verbal. Their communications had been conducted at first through the medium of Harold. Later they had met. The consequence of the whole negotiation so far had been that a quiet feeling prevailed among the wiser people at Oakfield Creek, an assurance that Escott had some good reason for expecting a favorable settlement out of court. And meanwhile, Escott, without in the least relaxing his old pride, had been forced to yield to the charm of the ancient friendship. The two enemies had once more shaken hands. Escott had expressed his perfect willingness to accept for his own part a fair settlement, and, when the time should come, to urge it upon the settlers. This was the easier for him to say, because the settlement promised amounted to a complete surrender on Eldon's part of all that he had claimed. The time for announcing the "compromise" still remained uncertain. Harold was partly responsible for this delay. He believed that the longer they waited, the better would grow the feeling between these two men. Meanwhile, of course, the time of the decisive trial was approaching, and Escott was preparing, upon Eldon's personal assurance, to abandon the defense of his case altogether, and to trust to the expected private settlement. For, unbusiness-like though this course might be, Escott still had perfect faith in the word of his old friend when given under such conditions.

Now all this, though it as yet took no bread from Boscowitz's mouth, deeply offended him. He hated Harold, who had proved most disappointingly practical, and who had even openly made fun of Boscowitz himself on several occasions. Boscowitz hated, again, the magazine-project, because it rivaled his own undertakings, and deprived him of Escott. But the project had ceased to be a dream, and was fast becoming a significant fact. The first number of the new magazine had appeared about the first of January, and now February was almost here, so that the second number had just seen the light. Boscowitz, however, had got another ground for his hatred of the magazine, since he felt that it promised in time to become one more link which would bind Alonzo Eldon to those great endowments. For Eldon was a silent partner in the magazine, and plainly intended, in time, to make it the organ of the great Museum itself. Moreover, Boscowitz had at last quarreled openly with Escott, so far as Escott would permit such a thing. They had parted with no kindly feelings. And thus, on the whole, Boscowitz was in these days very sour-tempered. Bertha being nearest, he had visited the whole upon her.

But why, after all, had they quarreled so

fiercely just to-day? Well, this morning Boscowitz had appeared at breakfast very red-eyed and unhappy-looking, because of late he had once or twice gone so far as to drink, not too much for his wits, but a good deal too much for his comfort. This was one sign that he was in general very ill at ease. During breakfast he had begun to question Bertha, very unkindly, about last night's prayer-meeting. What he said, of course, was disparaging to religion and to Mrs. Rawley, but so much Bertha had long since learned to bear. Then he asked her bitterly whether she had called upon Alonzo last night before she went to the meeting, and what plots against her father she had there carried out. To this, also, she had had nothing to say. When, however, he began a particularly atrocious sort of teasing (which, until lately, he had always been man enough to spare her), and asked whether she was accustomed to meet Tom in his father's company when she called at the house, Bertha (whose long-buried love had a painful fashion of rising from the dead for an instant, if anybody called its name in that cruel tone) could no longer bear his words. Then she burst out in the bitterest of replies. She upbraided him for his unkindness to Escott, for his unwillingness to see justice done to the Oakfield Creek settlers, for his disposition to make a tool of everybody, for the deceit that he had practiced upon herself. She spoke as he had not heard her speak for many years. And he, of course, retorted in kind, declared her his born foe, recalled all the cases, even far back into her unhappy childhood, where she had thwarted him, tried to injure him, disobeyed his commands, disappointed his ambitions for her own success, cheated him outright; yes, in days very long ago, even stolen from him. The longer they spoke, the more heated they both grew; and Boscowitz, especially, showed his excitement by remaining away from his business that morning to continue the quarrel. He must have loved her very much, after all, or this interest in her would have been impossible for one of his temperament. At length he began to try to extort promises from her for the future. She must have no more to do with the Eldons, with Escott, or with Escott's family, without his express knowledge and consent. When she refused all this, matters grew worse still. And at last, between her refusals and her retorts, he grew fairly frantic: so that after a brief interval of gloomy silence, he burst out with the fatal words. Bertha could not remember, just now, more than this of the provocation which she had given him. She must have have said some very bitter things. That was plain. She saw also that what had passed was but the culmination of a long series of disagreements. And the one obvious fact to her was that she must not accept from him a cent of the offered allowance, but must leave his house, and go out into the world to earn her living. She had once tried to earn her living for a time. She must begin afresh. She rose at last from her long reverie, and went out to seek advice.

When she appealed to Mrs. Rawley for help at this crisis, that lady was ready with a plan. There was a pressing need, Mrs. Rawley had learned, for some new influence to be brought to bear upon the settlers at the Creek. Mrs. Rawley, of course, as pastor's wife, took the deepest interest in these people, who were many of them former members of her husband's church. From the first she had been in the secret of Harold's purposes, and had assisted in giving to influential men among the settlers some hint of what was to be expected from Eldon. But she had grown weary of the long delay. It was hard to explain to those concerned why no open engagements could yet be made about the matter, and why the cases must first go by default against the settlers before their rights could be secured to them. All Mrs. Rawley's patience and influence had been needed. And even now misunderstandings had not been prevented.

For meanwhile, of late, some malign influence had been at work among the settlers. The younger and less conservative men at the Creek had been listening much to the talk of a certain McAlpin, long notorious elsewhere as an agitator, but a new-comer in those parts. McAlpin had pointed out, in public and in private, how Foster and Buzzard, two known "jumpers," had bought from the Land and Improvement Company, some half year since, titles to portions of the disputed land. They both lived, meanwhile, on land of their own, not far from Oakfield Creek. So long as these men, and others of their sort, were near, ready at the first chance to pounce on the prey, it was useless, McAlpin said, to try to persuade honest men that Eldon meant to do the square thing. Eldon, McAlpin added, was trying with all this mysterious talk, whose real nature nobody could make out, to lull to sleep suspicion, and to get the settlers at his mercy. McAlpin even hinted that Eldon might be making a tool of Alf Escott himself. They used to be friends, in old days, McAlpin observed. If report was right, they were now very thick again, and Eldon was supporting the new venture of the magazine. Could even Alf Escott be trusted under such circumstances?

McAlpin went further, and organized a secret society among the younger settlers. In the end he even persuaded some of the more conservative men, men in whom Mrs. Rawley had especially confided, to join his society. Such were Collins and Peterson, rough but upright men, peaceable and God-fearing. That they should now be hand in glove with McAlpin deeply pained Mrs. Rawley. Yet what was more natural? The settlers must suspect Eldon. Had he not given them good reason? Was it not their duty to organize for self-defense? Must they not be ready for any emergency? And this McAlpin was so bright, so plausible, and so energetic. He called his secret society the "Brotherhood of Noble Rangers." It had grips, pass-words, drill, and officers. It purposed, if ever these troubles passed by, to turn itself into a Benevolent Association, for the benefit of the settlers. And, meanwhile, it promised to keep the law, but in any case to make the Oakfield Creek country too hot to hold any jumpers, whatever decisions the wicked lawyers might manage to get from the unfeeling courts.

The existence of the Brotherhood, secret at first, became, erelong, known to Alonzo, and much increased the difficulties of his delicate task. To keep the peace with the settlers, and meanwhile to quiet the complaints of his irate fellow-shareholders, who were naturally puzzled by his mysterious conduct, — these were no easy tasks for Alonzo. Mrs. Rawley feared for the outcome of all this.

One clear ray of light, however, she saw in the gloom. Behind McAlpin, she felt sure, was, in secret, Boscowitz. The editor, as she justly believed, was steadfastly determined to thwart Alonzo's purposes. The "Warrior" was long ago publicly committed to a violent opposition to the settlers. Now that Alonzo had changed his mind, Boscowitz was still of his old opinion. The course of events had recently tended even to increase his hatred. His advantage lay in Alonzo's perplexities, which always furnished him employment. He wanted to postpone as long as possible Alonzo's retirement from business life, and to prevent, if might be, the great man's intended devotion of his later years to the care of those projected endowments. And in this special case Boscowitz's personal pride was concerned in defeating this romantic scheme of Harold's. McAlpin was then simply the editor's tool, and he was employed for the sole purpose of bringing about a breach of the peace.

Mrs. Rawley felt sure that Bertha knew of all this. Bertha would not tell tales of her father; but Mrs. Rawley believed that she would this time be willing, in such a cause, to use all her personal power to thwart his schemes. And so, when Mrs. Rawley heard of the quarrel between father and daughter, she caught eagerly at the chance.

"I know nothing of your private family cares, my dear," she said, "beyond what you tell me. You may be aware of many things in your father's plans that I know nothing of. But of this I feel sure, that you are devoted to the cause of the settlers. Can you not go to Oakfield Creek, for a while, and live with your old friends the Collinses, and use your discretion to further the cause of peace? I don't believe in anything underhanded. But we must use worldly means, my dear, against worldly men. You have information, I think, about the true purposes of this McAlpin, which you might use to strip the mask off him. You have influence. The settlers know you well of old, as a pious woman. They know, meanwhile, that you are your father's daughter, and that until to-day you have lived in his house. They know that your father hates their cause, and they will know that he has quarreled with you on their account. Is not all that enough to give you power on their behalf? Use it, my dear, discreetly and wisely, and we will pray for a happy result."

The consequence of all this was that Bertha went to live temporarily at Oakfield Creek, while Mrs. Rawley, having sent for Harold, besought him to use his best influence with the Eldons to prevent this new calamity of McAlpin's agitation from destroying the possibility of a lasting peace. "Do beg Mr. Eldon to be patient," she said. "And can you not appeal once more," she added, "to the young Mrs. Eldon, who did so well for our cause before?"

When Harold heard this, he was sorely troubled and perplexed.

CHAPTER XII.

THE ANNALS OF A FRIENDSHIP.

THE little spot in the hillside garden where Ellen's body had been found was always, in Margaret's eyes, sacred to the memory of the unhappiest of women. Nobody, save one person and on one occasion, had ever heard from Margaret any expression of her feelings about the place. She knew it when she passed it, or sat near it. She knew what she had planted there in melancholy commemoration of poor Ellen. But she had nothing to say of her fancies. Only, whenever she was feeling very downcast or desolate, she used to wander to the little seat near those acacias (the seat where she and Harold had gone on that first Sunday), and to stay there quite alone until the mood had passed. Unreasoning jealousy, suspicion, hatred of poor Ellen, she must, indeed, have felt for a short time during those early days of the great sorrow, when all the world seemed her enemy, and every word that any one had ever uttered seemed false and malicious. But those diseased feelings had long since vanished. Poor Ellen remained to Margaret the unhappy friend, whom she had never seen in life, but had learned to love and to honor in death; the friend whose wrongs must somehow be atoned for, though they could never really be made good. And with a certain deeper joy, Margaret also felt, at such moments of loneliness and desolation, that she, too, bore her share of the burden of Ellen's wrongs, and that in this way she was daily doing something towards accomplishing the work of atonement.

On a gloomy and threatening January day, only two or three hours after the conversation at Mrs. Rawley's between that lady and Harold, Margaret had gone to the little garden-seat in the well-known place, and was now sitting there in the wind. She was wrapped in a dark red shawl; she sat almost motionless, and quite heedless of the unpleasant coolness of the air. She, too, like Bertha Boscowitz, had many things to think of to-day. She, too, was watching in mind the culmination of a long and fateful series of events. Very quickly the facts passed before her memory, much more quickly than we can describe them;

but volumes would have seemed to her insufficient for explaining their causes or their meaning. They made up the history of a friendship such as six months ago would have seemed to her an incredible experience. But it had come to her, this friendship, and now she was bound up in it with all her soul; and while she forbade herself to enjoy its comforts, she would not have escaped its power if she could. Yet she lamented it bitterly, even while she accepted its sovereignty willingly. It was something very dear and very terrible. Was it — so she now asked herself — part of the atonement for Ellen's wrongs?

It had begun, of course, with the Sunday of Harold's first visit. She had awaited his coming that day with an almost girlish excitement. She had heard so much of him beforehand, and had found such an amusement in the project of adding him to her list of friends! All this, to be sure, was no more than she had often felt about many strangers before. And when Harold actually came, on this occasion, he proved to be at first a little disappointing. He was too acquiescent; he did not respond well enough; he was not original enough in his talk or in his manners. Moreover, he seemed, after all, to be a very simple-minded man, and not in the least mystical or profound. In all ways, then, there was at the outset something incomplete about him. The first really satisfactory moment had come when she was alone with him in the garden, after lunch. Then his gardening-skill and his other practical knowledge, as they showed themselves, almost unconsciously, in his conversation, had appealed to her good sense at once; and, a trifle later, his behavior to the little boy had, at a stroke, made them all three good friends. Next, moreover, that momentary and quite accidental confidence, about his old home and about the memory of his wife, had given her an insight, she thought, into his very heart. She never forgot his timidly appealing glance, his hesitation, that plainly meant such suddenly aroused and quite unaffected feeling, and his manly and tender tone of voice. Could he have premeditated this show of emotion, she would have suspected him. But it all came without premeditation, and so, as she felt sure, without hypocrisy. From that time on, as she now saw, they two had had a mutual understanding, which had helped them both all through the long and trying undertakings of that afternoon, and which had comforted her, whenever she thought of him, during those hours of exhaustion and of melancholy, after the great struggle was over. And thus their friendship had begun.

Who could follow its growth during the next few weeks? It was not with Margaret herself, but with Tom and with Alonzo, that Harold had at first been most in company at that time. Margaret he had seen but little until late in October. Then, when the magazine-project was in a somewhat advanced stage, Margaret had come to be consulted about it more and more. She knew little concerning magazines, but then Harold soon began to treat her as if she knew everything; and that amounted to much the same thing. He would come over to the house in Tom's company, and then, after lunch or dinner, Harold would tell her all the latest news of his plans. He soon found that she loved to hear about odd people, whereupon he used to describe to her the characters whom he met with in his search for contributors to the coming monthly. The two had many laughs together over these people and their sayings.

Among them, for instance, was the distinguished young graduate of an Eastern college, who never met you without looking mournfully into your eyes, and begging you to tell all your Eastern correspondents, whenever you wrote, that they must not lose their high hopes in him, even if he did seem a little slow about producing the great poems that they were so anxiously awaiting from his pen. The world was too much with him, he admitted, and just now he was serving Mammon for very poor wages. But the great poems were just below the horizon, so to speak. They would soon lighten up his soul. Meanwhile, he heartily sympathized with his expectant and critical Eastern friends, — the ones, namely, who had sworn on Class Day or on Commencement Day that all his unfledged geese were swans. He lamented the high hopes deferred fully as much as the friends did. But they, he kindly insisted, must not lose heart, nor even lie awake o' nights thinking about him. You must write them to that effect, he said, just as he frequently did himself.

Then there were other poets, not college graduates, men who, perchance, had once gone East with good introductions, and had dined at some celebrated poet's table. All that such youth now knew of English literature they had learned from celebrated poet's lips on those hallowed occasions; and they had since never tired of retailing their knowledge. They had thus picked up the genuine, though somewhat threadbare, mantles of certain among the late prophets. From young poets of this rank Harold's editorial acquaintanceship descended by gradual stages until it reached youth who took themselves for reincarnations of Milton, or Shakespeare, or Homer, and whose desks and arms were full of tragedies and epics accordingly. "If the fire at all corresponded with the smoke," Harold used to say, "we should have no trouble about contributions, nor yet about giving the magazine a strongly local flavor and excellence. But alas," he would go on, speaking of the poets aforesaid, "the smoke is enough to blind one's eyes before one ever sees the fire."

As Harold became more and more free with these editorial confessions in Margaret's presence, she grew fonder of his ready skill in describing the people, and of his willingness to admit his own weaknesses. She saw, indeed, that he was a man who had lived too long in a world of lonesome illusions, of noble aspirations, and of indolence; but she also saw that he was hating his illusions, and trying to get out of them. So she respected him; and she soon learned to help him, by frankly making sport of all his faults and blunders, whenever she detected them. If she enjoyed his stories, she was none the more apt to adopt his opinions on that account. Her taste was very often not his, and she ridiculed his false notions charmingly, but unsparingly. Their conversations came to be full of light banter, of skillful fencing, and of mercilessly gay mutual criticism.

Margaret had trouble to-day in discovering when or how any more serious feeling had come to tinge the friendship. Such transitions are always unintelligible. She, no doubt, in her unnatural loneliness, had needed a warmer sympathy; Harold, in the enthusiasm of his new life, had longed for some object more animate than that long-cherished ideal image of his dead wife. But if all this had been true of both of them, neither had even remotely guessed it at the outset. They had been absolutely innocent and straightforward with each other. Margaret, long ago, in her youth (in her early acquaintance with Tom, for instance), might possibly have been, on occasion, something of a coquette. But never, in all her life, had anything been more remote from her thoughts than the notion of undertaking to charm Harold. The better she knew him, the more he seemed to her during these early days simply an honest and friendly man, who had good purposes, but many faulty opinions about matters of taste. She loved to discuss with him, and to set him right. She was, meanwhile, more fascinated with him than she herself at the time knew. But that the friendship was more serious than this never for a long time occurred to her.

The first slight approach to a closer intimacy must, therefore, have been occasioned by Harold's controversy with Boscowitz. Some time during the latter half of November, Boscowitz had ventured so far as to print in the "Warrior" a column and a half of personal assault upon Harold. Boscowitz's relations with Eldon were such that Alonzo would, of course, have prevented the publication of this attack if he could have known of it beforehand. But he was not accustomed to predetermine Boscowitz's course in more than a very few and important respects, and he learned of the attack precisely when the other readers of the "Warrior" first discovered it. And, for the rest, it was nothing more than any regenerate man ought to be willing to bear in a good cause, however much the natural man in Harold might be vexed when he first saw it.

This personal sketch was *à propos* of the new undertaking that Harold was already known to be planning, and *à propos* also of some very early literary efforts of Harold's, which a kindly public had, of course, very easily and thoroughly forgotten. Boscowitz now dragged these early efforts out of their graves, made short work of their remains, and asked, very plausibly, in the name of good sense, what business such a fellow as this could have with undertaking to edit a new magazine on this coast. But herewith, of course, Boscowitz, or the young rogue who wrote all this for him, had only begun the real attack. There followed a witty personal sketch of Harold's manners, past career, supposed sentimentality, indolence of life, and eccentric opinions. There were even a few personal references that were in themselves not slanderous, but that were as hard for Harold to bear as if they had been. They mentioned, in a flippant tone and in parenthesis, Harold's antecedents, and some of his past friendships, and even the name of his dead wife. The article closed, however, with a few jocular and vague accusations, of a very disagreeable sort, against Harold's private character.

In short, the whole thing was of the kind that stings the sensitive man like a whip-lash the first time (but only the first time) that he experiences it. A half dozen such experiences make the tenderest soul utterly callous. Now Harold, however much he had mixed with the world, had never seen himself in print in just this way. The column and a half gave him, accordingly, much more than a bad quarter of an hour. All day long he felt unwilling to see Escott, just because he knew that Escott would laugh in his face and call him a fool for minding the article. Had he not had a strict appointment to meet a new friend at the Eldons' house that night, he would not for the world have gone there. And, as a fact, the appointment in question was canceled, during the afternoon, by a message intended to tell him that the new friend would fail to appear, owing to some mishap. But Harold added one more to the miscarriages of the day by being already absent when the message came to his house. And thus he found himself the only guest, on just this evening, at the Eldon house. Tom, on the failure of the projected dinner-party, had gone back to the city. Harold, coming just in time for dinner, found Margaret alone.

Margaret well remembered, on this gloomy January day, as she sat and thought over the past, the Saturday evening alone in Harold's company. She had done her best to make him at home when she learned of his mistake, she had exerted herself to the utmost to recompense him for his disappointment, and had, of course, made him stay all the evening. At first she had noticed that he was depressed and abstracted. She could not guess the cause; for she had not looked at to-day's "Warrior." After some time he confessed, very shamefacedly, the true source of his vexation. Then, at his request, she found the paper, and looked over the article in his presence. Hereupon he had admitted that he ought to be ashamed to think twice of an attack from such a quarter; but then, he was unused to attacks. Besides, he was not feeling very well lately, having somehow overworked a little. Margaret was all sympathy, of course; and this fact led him a step further. He pointed out to her the careless mention of his wife's name. That was the worst part of it all, he said. To see that was a terrible shock to him. All the rest was but a grain of dust in the scale as against this, the real weight. Hereupon, as her sympathy continued, he grew more confidential, and finally began to talk about his wife and his old home, and about the long-past days of his happiness.

That he had usually tried to keep his loneliness to himself only made his present confession more voluble. He told her of his baby that had died so soon after his wife; and then Margaret and he discussed young babies at great length. Afterwards Harold grew, as usual, afraid of having been wearisome with his confessions, and tried to pass, in the conversation, to her own interests. She prevented him. She was ashamed of herself, she said, when she compared her own light and flippant life with his serious purposes, joys, and sorrows. Then Harold replied, of course, that she seemed to him one of the most earnest of women, who had borne great sorrows with most heroic patience. At this, however, he feared lest he had said too much, and was surprised when she showed no sign of embarrassment. She felt, in fact, only gratitude that he should understand her, and when he took his leave, rather early in the evening, they both knew that they were far closer friends than ever before.

In her memory to-day Margaret found that this one evening stood out as the beginning of their true intimacy. Yet what had happened? Nothing, of course. It was not what they said, but the fact that they had now somehow broken down the barriers. Neither had any longer a separate world of sorrows and perplexities. Each had looked into the other's world, and with the owner's consent. Yet thenceforth, when they met, they still assumed on nearly all occasions the old mutually critical tone; they fenced as lightly as ever, and laughed together over the follies of the world. With Tom, meanwhile, Harold became almost intimate. The two hunted and rode together, or joined in various other entertainments, and seemed to agree excellently, though Harold, it was certain, never at heart forgave Tom for the old sins.

Once, towards the middle of December, Tom invited Harold to stay at the house alone with him, at the very time when, as it chanced, Margaret had arranged to spend a few days with her mother. Harold needed a short rest, and gladly forsook the city, much as he regretted, of course, Margaret's absence from the place. But in this very way, as it turned out, the friendship gained a new tie, stronger than any previous one.

The boy Alonzo, namely, had been left in charge of his nurse, who herself had proved much more faithful than most of her predecessors, and who had now been in the house a full six months. The strictest orders had been left as to the care of Alonzo. He was to eat this only, and to avoid that most carefully, and to remain in the house after a particular hour in the afternoon, and to be put to bed promptly at a certain minute. The first night of his mother's absence all went well.

The next day Tom and Harold took a long ride together far into the hills, beyond the summit, to see a new bit of land that Tom had been buying for a summer camping-ground. They returned late in the afternoon. Little Alonzo had been playing usurper and tyrant all day long. He had left uneaten whatever he ought to have eaten, and had stolen several things that he should not have eaten. All this, however, made little difference, because he was a boy of excellent digestion, and even, as boys go, of very moderate appetite. More serious it was that he had spent much of the afternoon hidden in the oak-grove. For during the morning, in his character as tyrant, he had broken several valuable things, and, having quarreled furiously with his nurse, had taken the first chance to escape his lunch and herself by stuffing his pockets with lumps of sugar, and betaking himself to the woods. The sufferings of the nurse and the sentiments of the gardener, as they both hunted for him, need, for knowing readers, no description, and cannot be described to others. When found at last, Alonzo had fallen asleep in a damp place among the rocks.

Tom heard of all this, on his return, with a natural and manly vexation. You paid these people, he said, to look out for your boy; and so they, apparently, went fishing. If they did n't, they might as well have done so, for all the good they accomplished. For the rest, little Alonzo would be sure not to suffer any further. California dampness, even in December, is, of course, very different from dampness anywhere else in the world, and never hurts children. Alonzo, moreover, despite his mother's nervous fears, was a very tough child. Women had fretted and fumed over him from the first day of his existence; dozens of nurses had done their worst by him; processions of doctors had been sent about their business for failing to prevent him from being naughty. And yet, with all that, he had never been very ill, and had usually been in glorious health. He was sometimes a little pale and nervous; but the great test, said Tom, was whether a boy could make a noise or not. A sickly child makes no noise. A healthy boy makes your house like a boiler factory, and your head like a spinning-top. These conditions Alonzo had always fulfilled. He was therefore healthy. And if the nurse had been worried on this occasion, that served her right. The nurse, however, reported meanwhile that she was quite sure that the boy would be ill.

Margaret had heard the very next day of Tom's sentiments at this crisis, and she had not failed to remember them thenceforth. She knew, moreover, the other events of that evening. First, Tom had received a telegram asking for his immediate presence in the city to attend to a matter of business. The business, she felt, was doubtless something that he might easily have postponed. There could not have been any necessity about it. Yet he had actually gone so far as to forsake Harold and the boy, and to go over at once. Harold, Tom had said, was a good enough friend to know how to make himself at home until morning, when Tom would return. As for the boy, he was perfectly sound, and the nurse would have no manner of trouble with him. She might, perhaps, need to put an extra blanket over him to-night. That would be all. Tom, therefore, asked for Harold's indulgence in this case, and so left the guest alone with a sick child.

For despite all Tom's confidence, little Alonzo was very ill. At about nine o'clock, Harold, who had been enjoying the somewhat lonesome hospitalities of the great house by reading before the open fire in the parlor, began to hear a little disturbance among the servants, a running to and fro, and much talking. Erelong the frightened nurse appeared in person, confessed that the child had the croup, and asked if he knew what to do. Now, Harold, ever since his own somewhat croupy childhood, had retained a fair knowledge of how one treats such attacks, but he was of course indisposed to take unnecessary responsibilities as to other people's children. He asked about the symptoms, learned that so far they were serious chiefly in the prospect, and then very naturally recommended sending at once for a doctor. Meanwhile, he said, he would be glad to do all he could until the doctor came.

But herewith his perplexities only began. For the nurse, in her ignorance of this side of the bay, knew of but one doctor in Oakland, and with him she had long ago had a furious quarrel. And after months of struggle she had just brought Margaret to take sides with her. So now, as the nurse assured Harold, this one doctor had lately been detected in fairly murdering one or two of the neighbors' children by his fearful blundering, and accordingly, Mrs. Eldon had given up the thought of calling him again. Mr. Eldon would have known what doctor they had chosen instead; but Mr. Eldon was away.

The poor girl wept and wrung her foolish hands as she confessed all this, and Harold went at once to the nursery. The chambermaid was there, holding little Alonzo close by the fire. He was in his night-dress, which the girls in their fright had just managed to tear, so that one of his little white shoulders was quite bare, as were also his small, wriggling feet. A draught from the open door blew across his shoulders. His feet were, however, painfully near the flames, which made him squirm with their heat, and which seriously threatened the girl's dress as she sat. Alonzo was very sleepy, was fretting, breathing hard, and occasionally coughing in the well-known and indescribable fashion.

The scene was not exactly a model for nurseries, but it meant trouble to come, as Harold plainly perceived. The two girls now regarded him with trembling reverence, and began asking him confidential questions. Would the boy die? Would the weather be warm to-morrow? Did you rub a boy all over, in such a case, with cayenne pepper, or give him a big dose of whiskey, or put him into a tub of ice-cold water, or pat him steadily on the back to prevent his choking to death, or keep him awake for fear he would die in his sleep, or put him to sleep forthwith by means of a double allowance of paregoric? All these conflicting theories as to the best treatment had, as it seemed, already been advanced. And, next to the boy's immediate death, the girls plainly feared that which nothing, from cayenne pepper to paregoric, could avert, namely, Mrs. Eldon's wrath. As they were good modern servants, they would not have feared that, however, very much, had their consciences been easy. As it was, they were decidedly the worse for fright.

That Harold did the best possible thing under these circumstances he never afterwards pretended. But the one-eyed man is king among the blind, and Harold had at least more sense than the poor girls. Alonzo was soon more warmly wrapped, and Harold demanded hot flannels, and one or two of the more familiar medicines suitable to the occasion. He gave no doses however, just yet, for the boy was in no great present distress; and he overruled the whiskey, the cayenne pepper, the paregoric, and the tub of cold water. He held the boy for a while himself; and Alonzo, feeling a quiet arm and an even temperature, ceased fretting, nestled close to Harold, and half fell asleep for a few minutes, until another coughing fit aroused him. Harold, wisely expecting worse things soon to come, asked, meanwhile, in a very low voice, about Oakland doctors, of whom, in former years, he had known much, though recently he had never thought of them.

The nurse was ignorant who there was, or where to find any of the tribe, save that murderous one; and Harold had at last to send at a venture for any one of several whose names he mentioned. The coachman was dispatched on this errand.

He, however, was in very ill-humor, having already made a late trip to town with Tom. He had rheumatic twinges himself that night, and believed the boy's illness to be all humbug. He set out, indeed, but finding that the first doctor on his list was absent for the evening he went no further, and contented himself with leaving a message for this one to get on his return. The doctor, in fact, returned to his home at about eleven o'clock, and, finding the message, started on the quest. But the night was dark, the doctor had never before gone so far into the hills as the Eldon estate, and accordingly he first missed his way, and then ran into a deep rut on one of the bad roads, and so broke down. There was no joy in heaven over what that belated doctor hereupon said, nor was Tom Eldon's house brightened that night by the face of a doctor.

And so the consequence of these accidents was that Harold, after a very solid night's work, and after a reasonable degree of worry, gained, thenceforth, in the eyes of Margaret, of the two servants, and of all who heard the tale, save Tom himself, and the doctor, the reputation of having saved, single-handed, the precious life of little Alonzo! How unfounded this reputation may have been nobody knows. As Margaret thought the thing over now, she, at least, had no doubts. The chances are, of course, that Alonzo, being very little tormented with medicines that night, by his cautious guardian, and being kept steadily warm, managed to do the whole saving of his life himself. But to the average layman it always seems a miracle that any child lives through anything; and when the welcome dawn came, and Harold no longer had to listen to that horrible breathing, but could seek sleep in his room, even he was disposed to take to himself much credit; and while he lay drowsily watching the gray light that drearily lit up his eastern chamber, he was already enjoying, by anticipation, Margaret's smile. And in Margaret's memory he was indeed to be thenceforth little Alonzo's savior.

Orders had been given, of course, to have both Tom and Margaret telegraphed for at the earliest moment. Harold's sleep was short, and, after his breakfast, he went again to the nursery. The room was miserably close, and the nurse as sleepy, cross, and remorseful as could be expected. The boy, however, with just a little flush on his pale cheeks, wandered gayly about, too nervous for any of his usual games, but very happy and proud withal. One would have supposed him the nurse and the poor girl his patient, to judge by his gently authoritative airs and her dejection. A convalescent child is the vainest, and, in its way, one of the blessedest of God's creatures; just as a baffled nurse is one of the most debased and miserable. Harold passed the morning amusing the boy. The doctor came as early as possible, but soon went away, promising to return in the afternoon.

Tom arrived by noon, anxious and crest-fallen. When he had seen the boy and heard the tale, he secretly resolved, however, that there could have been no real cause for alarm. But he feared Margaret's frown, and returned to the city, ostensibly to meet her at the San Rafael boat, but, in fact, with the intention of not seeing her until dinner-time. He felt much vexation with himself, of course, and not exactly the full degree of gratitude that he should have experienced towards Harold. Tom had never seen a child with the croup, and his impression, so far, was that that disorder, though doubtless an invention of some imp, was designed solely for the purpose of frightening women, and was always worse for the mothers than for the babies.

Margaret reached home early in the afternoon. All the way from the train she tormented her coachman with endless and indignant questions, and came to the house in a nearly frantic condition. Fortunately the doctor was already there for his second visit. He was able to quiet her somewhat, although he was a stranger to her. The boy, he said, would have a return of the trouble to-night, of course. But it need not be serious. The treatment would, he added, be this, and then that, — and thereupon the wise man described the approved methods very carefully. The case he refused to call exactly a terrible one, and he said that he had come twice to-day only because of his failure of the previous night. He wanted to show, he said, that he had done his best, although he had been quite misdirected last night by a bungling messenger, sent during his absence, and although he had suffered in consequence a bad break-down on a fearful road in the dark. All this, he remarked, for a case of mere croup, was somewhat unusual, to say the least. He would not complain, but he regretted the incident. As he was a plain-spoken man, and not exactly a young man, he took the liberty of adding that this season of the year, with its chilly afternoons and nights, and generally uncertain weather, was a very bad time to leave children alone in the care of ignorant and incompetent nurses. Mr. Harold, he admitted, had acted with great discretion, and perhaps had alone prevented the case from becoming somewhat alarming. The doctor would be glad to come, he said, if the thing should grow really serious again. Only he ventured to beg that they would send somebody who knew the roads to drive him out, if they wanted him at night. At his age, he concluded, the eyes were not quite as keen as they used to be.

Margaret listened to all this with saintly meekness and motherly terror, while she thankfully clasped her little boy in her arms, and looked sometimes at the doctor, sometimes with appealing and grateful glances towards Harold, but mostly down at little Alonzo himself. The boy, perceiving that he was the hero of the occasion, and that his mother held him more warmly than usual, seemed swimming in an ocean of languid delight. He did not move, save that his eyes wandered from one to another, and his face smiled happily. Harold was looking abashed in the doctor's presence, and was trying to apologize for his share in the misdirection and the other mishaps. The nurse peeped from behind the half-open door of the next room, and the chambermaid was trying to hide beyond the nurse. The nursery, meanwhile, was a model of melancholy disorder, and the air of it was like the morning air of a sleeping-car.

But thenceforth the friendship with Harold had bloomed like Margaret's roses in June. Margaret could hardly remember all the times they had met during the seven weeks since that night. There was the little Christmas party, when Harold had been invited to celebrate with the family the feast of rejoicing for the boy whose life he had saved. There were, again, the long talks in private, when Margaret began to make confessions to him about her past neglect of a mother's duties. Leaving the child just when she did leave him was, she had insisted, simply a crime, the culmination of years of indifference to her office. Unjustly, of course, she thus accused herself, but mothers always feel self-condemned at the thought of any mishap that their children have suffered, and Margaret again and again assured Harold that he alone had first taught her true fidelity to her boy. In saving the boy's life, she said, Harold had brought first clearly to her mind that if a mother wants her child, she must care for him. In vain Harold pointed out that this mishap was the merest accident. No, Margaret said; if the boy had died, she would have felt herself no better than a murderer. And then, in the long talks about this matter, she had gone on to confide to Harold all her plans about little Alonzo's future, how he should be trained and educated, and what kind of man she wanted to make him.

How many of these and other confidential talks had taken place Margaret could not recall. Never before had Margaret known what it was to find anybody, near her own age, whom she could trust, and who trusted her. She felt herself the guide of all Harold's work, and he grew daily more truly her own supreme adviser. It was strange, perhaps, and yet again, rightly viewed, not so strange, that neither Tom, nor any one else, had seemed to notice anything questionably warm about this intimacy. It had come to pass so naturally, it was apparently so frank, so simple, and so closely associated with Tom's own friendship for Harold, that there had been no real ground for doubt. Besides, Tom was not a jealous man. And finally, and above all, neither Margaret nor Harold had known, she now felt sure, what it had meant, until just a short time since.

She remembered with a terrible vividness that evening when they were last alone together. This was now just a week since. They had been riding out on a little horseback excursion that afternoon, in company with Tom and one or two other friends. As they returned, they two rode together, a little ahead of the others, and became somehow very earnest and thoughtful as they talked. Margaret had been telling Harold about her mother, and about her own early life before she knew Dover. She had been confessing the strange relations between her mother and herself in those childish days, — how she had always longed for a warm and demonstrative love from her mother, and had somehow been put off with a coldly affectionate care, and with much good advice, and with melancholy airs of foreboding; as if the mother expected so light-hearted a daughter to find a very unhappy life awaiting her in a world where only cold wisdom succeeds. Margaret had hinted, as she went on (for how could she nowadays try to hide anything from Harold?), that the marriage with Dover had been made by her mother's ambition, rather than by her own choice. Her young life had been rendered too submissive to her mother's will for her to be able to make any resistance. And then Margaret had somehow suggested, without meaning to do so, that her later life, since childhood, had been almost as friendless as in childhood it already was. Harold had listened to her quietly, feeling perhaps a little afraid, because she let him see so freely into her very heart. That evening, by one of the chances of which this intimate friendship had become so full, they were again alone together. Tom was absent from the house until after ten o'clock.

A certain feeling of vague excitement, as if they stood on the edge of a great precipice, had taken possession of both Harold and Margaret, as they sat talking in the parlor. They sought vainly for indifferent topics, they tried hopelessly to assume the old tone of light banter; discussion would not prosper between them to-night. Either they agreed about everything, or their disagreements sought for no expression. They grew at length less and less talkative. Then, after a while, they were even alarmed to find that both, for what suddenly appeared to have been an age, had been sitting quite silent, now gazing at the fire, now glancing towards each other. Margaret became hereupon afraid that she alone was noticing this fact. She did not want to be conscious of it; still less to have Harold guess that she was conscious of it. She began to talk gayly of the ride to-day. Then she passed, with almost feverish haste, to telling about friends of hers. She criticised them, she made sport of them, she was merciless concerning their failings, she tried anxiously to seem heartless; and she continued till she saw that Harold was looking a little pained and gloomy.

"I know what you are thinking of," she said to him at length: "you are fancying that this is my way of talking about everybody, — about you, too, for instance." She was feeling perfectly reckless as she spoke.

"I am very far from imagining such a thing," he answered, but with a perplexed manner, as if he feared that he was somehow offending her to-night.

"What *do* you imagine, then? You know I have no heart. The heart was crushed out of me when I was a baby."

"I know you for one of the most devoted of mothers, at least. That means heart."

"Nonsense! I tell you, when I look back on my wretched career, I feel that I have always lived as a mere critic of people, making sport and being made sport of. You 've no idea of true deadness of soul. I know it as I know nothing else."

"How about your toils in the service of Escott? Were they sport?"

"I had a reason for that. It was a simple duty. Had I not been the destroyer of his daughter?" Margaret spoke very shortly, and almost fiercely.

"You! What *can* you mean?" Harold's tone was even reverential, and he appeared meanwhile as if her cruelty to herself gave this reverence a very painful shock.

"Yes, I! Did I not entice away from her her own betrothed lover? Do you know, Mr. Harold," Margaret's voice became all at once very solemn, "the place where she was found in my garden is for me a sacred spot. Were it not for others, I should mark that place with a cross, as in some countries they mark the scene of a murder."

"If it was a murder, surely your soul is guiltless."

"And if my soul were," answered Margaret, bitterly, "if it were guiltless, as it is not, am I not bound fast, for this life and for the life to come (if there be a life to come), bound fast to a soul that surely is guilty? Are husband and wife, then, not one? Can I sunder his guilt from mine? No; I tell you plainly that there is no way out for me. I am in the dungeon, the traitor's dungeon, where I deserve to be. The gates are locked — for eternity. The sin is done. There is no atonement. I ask for none. Do I not, after all, enjoy the prize of this sin?"

The union of pride and despair in her tone (of pride that still forbade her to tell all the hatred she bore towards her husband, and despair that was forcing from her, word by word, this fatal confession) quite overcame Harold's self-control. He rose excitedly, and stood by the mantel, facing her. Then he looked anxiously about the room, as if seeking what to say. At last he burst out:

"Surely, nobody, Mrs. Eldon, could bear to hear you say this. But if you will feel in this way, then remember, at least, I beg and implore you, that I am here as your servant, your slave, to help by my friendship and my intercession to make you happy again. You are innocent, innocent as the wild flowers, of any offense in this matter. I pray you to think so. I must persuade you that you are innocent. There was a wrong done, God knows. But it was not your doing. And if any work, any atonement, any devotion, can restore you to your own life and your true self once more, am I not at your hand to help you in that work? And then, too" (Harold's voice was very pleading now), "you must n't think your marriage a bondage to a lost man. *He* can atone, too. He is trying to atone. He loves you, and you must not give up your hope in this way. I am sure you will find the way to love him again, whenever he has had time to show you how he feels about this." Margaret dared not look up at Harold. His pleading voice only made her despair more unendurable. "Never!" she said at length, with a scornful bitterness, — "never will that be! I don't know," she went on, feeling at every word more helpless, "I don't know what I should say. Everything I say about this is a new treason, a fresh crime. Our — our hatred — in such cases — is something sacred — the hatred, I mean, of a wife whose husband has betrayed — but *no*, Mr. Harold" (Margaret made one last fierce effort to recover herself), "I *must n't* speak of this. You are my friend. I thank you for your kind words. You don't know how they cheer me. But no, I must not let escape me another syllable of all this. It is a wrong, a disgrace, that I have spoken so at all. I am a base and cowardly wretch. Nobody can be worse than I am." She rose now herself, and turned, as if trying to flee. Then she glanced once more towards him. Their eyes met, and again she looked down on to the table. She seized a book, and began nervously to turn the leaves. What was she doing there? Was she trying to go away? How foolish! He was her guest, and her only friend beside. Why could he not say something now to end all this? But what was there to say? She had brought about all the trouble herself. She had used the word *hatred.*

He knew everything now. She had no longer a single secret from him — save one. And *that* one, until this very moment, had been a secret from herself, too. She trembled all over, and strove to be calm. All this lasted but an instant. It seemed an age. What? Was he saying some word about going? How miserably she had acted! She turned towards him eagerly. What mattered it now, after all, whether she said this or that? Surely life had in it nothing more that she could fear.

"You have n't understood me," she cried, observing with terror that she was standing somehow very close to him, "you have n't understood me to-night, nor ever before. I must seem to you so worthless! I shall never seem to you anything better! But hear me out, at least. There can't be anything kept back from you henceforth. You speak as if I had been a devoted wife, whom *he* offended, whose love *he* betrayed. I 've spoken so, too, myself. But it 's all a lie. My crimes don't end with enticing him away from the woman who loved him. I have never loved him myself. I thought I did. But I never knew what love was — not in my miserably sacrificed youth — nor when I first knew him — nor when I enticed him away from her — nor when I lost him — nor ever until" — Her voice seemed to choke, she clasped her hands despairingly, her eyes were full of tears.

She never knew how it happened, but the next moment her hand was in his, and he was looking into her eyes, which now no longer avoided him.

"Margaret," he was saying, in a trembling voice, and with the same deep reverence in his tone, "I have never lived until now. Forgive me for causing you all this pain. I know now — that everything must end with this evening. And yet — how can I ever be anything but your slave?" He stopped. They stood motionless and silent.

The next moment a glorious sense of freedom came over her. Everything that she had heretofore dreaded in talking with him was past. He knew all, and his eyes said that for this one moment, at least, despite all her former life, her heartlessness, her treason, and all her crimes, he somehow loved her. The thought was full of wealth and of happiness. She felt perfectly safe in his presence. He would be her guide, her conscience, and somehow, she knew not how, her deliverer. There could be nothing wrong about such thoughts at this moment. Never, of course, would they stand thus side by side again, unless indeed that glorious, remote deliverance somehow really took place. But just at this instant there were no barriers to this perfect union of hearts. The whole world was far off and worthless. He was everything.

"It is so long," she said, in a broken voice, — "it is so long that I have been wanting to have you understand. I don't care for anything else if you only understand. We shall have to part. We can't ever see each other again. We both have our lives. We must be true to them. It may be hard. I must n't ask you to do more for me than just to know how I have — sometimes — tried — not to be — so worthless as I am." The tears were flowing freely at last. She was very happy and very wretched.

"You are a saint, Margaret. Don't speak so sadly, I beg you. You shall be served forever. I will do all you desire, whatever it is! I would wander over all the world to help you. You shall be happy. But oh, Margaret, how can I now ever leave you! Yet it must be. You are right. We must not meet any more. This moment is the first and the last of our joy. But tell me, Margaret" (he dwelt on the name), "what must I do to help you now? Oh, there must be more than I have ever heard of, or thought of."

"There is nothing more," she said, sadly, "except to think of me sometimes. You must go now. I have more to say, — so much more! But I am afraid. This is so new, and yet somehow so old. We have been this way at heart towards each other for so long a time! Weeks is it? It must be years. I shall have to write to you very soon, to tell you something very important that I have in mind, or that I just had in mind. I can't think now what it was. Only I know that you must go, and that we must n't meet again, — not alone, that is, nor in company either. For then, you see, if we met in company, we should have to use disguises, and that would be worst of all. Oh, this seems so frank and plain and simple to-night, — just as if we had always known each other, or as if there had never been any barriers. I wonder if it will ever seem so again. I had no idea that I could feel so happy and innocent when I am so wicked and guilty. But you are so good. All the wrong is my doing. But I said you must go. Yet no, again, there is one thing more. Wait — yes — come with me — follow!"

Margaret led Harold quickly out of the parlor, across the hall, through the now darkened reception room on the other side, and then, by way of a glass door, out on to the piazza. The night was clear and cold, and the bright winter stars were shining. Harold had followed closely her silent step, seeming to himself all the while like a man in a dream. When they were once out-of-doors together, she turned and whispered: —

"I want you to go with me out to the little seat where first we had our talk in the garden. Ellen's little garden-plot — I always call it that — is just beyond. There are no roses now, or I would give you one. But I want you to sit down with me there again — once again — just one moment before you go. You must forgive me for the fancy. There 's also one thing more that I want to tell you. I can't tell it there in the light. Please come. Then we shall part forever. All will be over, but I want you to remember it always."

She spoke with girlish eagerness. Harold followed her softly down the steps, across the bit of lawn, in the starlight, and then they soon found the little bench where they had sat together, with the little boy, that Sunday, and once again they were side by side, but now in the darkness. Her hands were clasped. She seemed afraid, and anxious to avoid his touch, but he remained motionless and speechless.

"Do you know," she said very softly, "now it has come to this, I feel all at once how from the moment we sat here that day you have been my guide and my savior from my dead and wicked self. I must tell you, because it 's the last thing I shall ever tell you on earth. For you must know that you have not only saved to my boy his life, but you have taught me the true worth of loving him. Before you came he seemed to me too often only his father's child. I was in despair about the father. I tried to care for my little boy, but I used to be impatient with him and weary of him. I used to see him as little as I could. I sometimes called him my disturbing genius, who made me cross and ruined my days. I did n't know that I was losing myself, too, in losing him. I don't know even now how it was, but from the first day of my friendship with you I began to love him more closely. And when you saved his life, it was as if — oh, forgive me! — I must say everything to you just this once — just to-night — I never knew before that this was so — but I see it now — when you saved him, I say, it was as if that man, who forsook him that night, who cared so little for him — had now — no longer — any fair right to be called — his father. I have hated Tom worse than ever, since that night; and I have loved my boy so fondly, I have lived with him so happily, ever since. Oh, you 'll not understand, I fear; but it is so hard to love the child truly and ardently enough — as a mother should — when you have all the time to be reminded that he is the child of such a man! Somehow I 'm not so much reminded of that since *you* have loved the boy, and have saved his life. Can you understand me now? And then, your devotion to your own family in the old days, — that has been my daily thought and idea! I am a cold, hard, cruel woman, who was born without heart or soul! But I 've tried, since I knew you, to love my boy as your wife would have loved yours, had they lived. I don't know, I can't tell, how your esteem and your goodness have so grown into my life. But they have. And what I wanted to say, for this one last time, here in the dark, was how much your presence has taught me of my duty and of my joy as the mother of my child. That, at least, is left me. Wherever you go, I shall think of you as my hero, my conscience; yes, as the only one who has taught me to love. Good-by, now. We are so near where Ellen died. Can you promise to me, by her memory, not to forget me?"

Harold sought to answer all this, though his voice was broken and half choked. Margaret well remembered his low tones even yet, and how he tried to tell her what she had been to him also. But at this she had felt the tears coming fast, and had grown very much afraid. She checked him; he must indeed go, she said. She would soon write to him. But he must never write to her unless she asked it. And now, since he had sworn to remember her, she felt strong, she said. This lonely world had in it one friend for her, and she had not deserved such blessedness. "You must let me go back to the house first, dearest," she said, finally. "No one must see us. Then you may get ready to go." Then she left him, and vanished into the house, knowing only that, as they parted, he had once more taken her hand, and had kissed it. That was the end!

Harold, in those days, had become accustomed, after he had dined at the house, to ride down to an evening train on his own horse, leaving it in Oakland, and then returning to the city. Margaret listened to-night until she heard the horse's footsteps on the bridge on the road below the house. Then she knew that Harold had gone. She was locked in her own room long before Tom returned; but she had no moment's sleep until dawn.

From that time on they had not met. But they had corresponded. This latest stage of their friendship was now of but the shortest duration; and their letters had been confined so far to consultations about the Oakfield Creek matter. Of the fatal evening they had hinted in these letters nothing. Margaret herself had invited this further correspondence. She had called it to herself a duty. She had excused it to herself as a necessity. And yet, as she sat to-day, guilty and desolate in the wind, she knew that without just this coldly conducted correspondence, with its brief notes of business to cheer her, life would now be worthless.

Was she right, after all, to feel guilty? she sometimes asked herself. That she could never love Tom had long been an established fact in her mind. That, however, was his fault, not hers. But as for this new love, this only real passion of her life, had it not been a surprise to her, as to Harold, — something irresistible and inevitable? And when they had found it all out, what had they done but part, as they must? Save for those few words, wrung from them both by the passion of the moment, — save for those, and that one instant at their parting, what had happened for them to regret? He had called her Margaret? But whose concern was that? They had sworn eternal truth to each other, but that meant truth in the very fact of utter separation. She had, just once, called him by one tender name. But could she have helped it? Was it not the truth? They corresponded; but that signified only that they had common duties, which could not be shirked because of this strange discovery of theirs. They were both strong, faithful, and honorable. Such loyalty as Margaret still believed herself to owe to Tom should always, she insisted, be his. More she had not to give, and he, who had wronged her so deeply, had no right, she told herself, to ask more. There was, then, she said to herself over and over, no sin, no treachery, no real unfaithfulness, in her position. On the contrary, she was now, for the first and only time in her life, a true woman, who loved, and suffered for her love, as a woman ought to be glad to do.

And yet all the while, as Margaret waited to-day for some change, she knew not what, the load of guilt and of weary anxiety weighed her down. And this time the mood would not pass.

She rose at last, from the little garden seat, with a new plan in mind. The day seemed, indeed, threatening; but she had somehow no belief that there would be rain. In any case she felt quite reckless, and longed to escape from herself and her house for a while. Come what might, she would risk an outing to-day. And in fact, as she prepared for her ride, her plan seemed to be more and more favored by the weather. The clouds parted now and then, the sun shone fitfully through, between the drifting masses, the hills beyond the bay were almost free from haze. When Margaret at length started, the little mare was in the liveliest of moods, and insisted at first upon cantering joyously over the road. Margaret chose a northerly direction, and gradually persuaded her mare to be content with a quick trot. The ride was not to be a very long one, for, when about three miles out, Margaret chose a side road, that led up towards the hills; and she did not follow it any further than Harold's old home.

She rode past the house, and then paused a long time, looking into the grounds. Since she had resolved not to see him any more, to make this little pilgrimage had more than once given her consolation. The road was lonesome and the house vacant, so that nobody ever noticed her. But this time, after she had finished looking at the house, and was turning back, she had only reached the place where the side road joined the main road, just at the edge of the grove of trees, when, on turning the curve into the main road itself, she met Harold.

He must have been but just now riding rapidly. His horse was very warm; yet it was now walking. Harold's face, as she caught a momentary glimpse of it before he saw her, was excited and anxious. He was looking down on to the ground, as if he were afraid to see this familiar spot. The thought came to her at once: "This, then, must be his first visit, after all." As he saw her, he started as if he had been shot, and drew rein at once, just before he had reached the corner of the roads. The two paused as they met. She had no time to reflect. Her only thought was, What could it be that was so troubling him?

"You here, Margaret!" he exclaimed, in a low and even awe-struck voice. "Oh, I have been trying hard to decide whether I dared ask you to see me. I wrote you a little note, before I left San Francisco, telling you that I had much on my mind, and must see Alonzo Eldon at once about the business between us. Then I thought, so soon as I had sent the note, that you alone could rightly advise me, and that I ought to see you first, before I saw him. Then I grew more and more troubled. I resolved, at any hazard of offending you, to come to you. Who but you knows any ground why I should not? Then, again, when I had come to Oakland, I was afraid of disobeying you. I set out, I hesitated, and then I rode here, — I hardly know why, only I was very lonely and perplexed, and I wanted time to reflect. And this was a place I had long meant to see. But now, by this chance, I find you here. May I ride back with you, Margaret?"

Harold spoke with the greatest rapidity. He seemed afraid that she would interrupt him, or leave him. But she was perfectly calm now, and, looking very kindly into his troubled face, she at once bade him come with her. They rode southwards together, and at her suggestion they went on rapidly until they could turn into a less frequented road which leads through the foot-hills above Lake Merritt, and by which one might in a somewhat roundabout way reach her house. Then they let their horses walk side by side, and he began to tell her the cause of his present anxiety. He first narrated the meeting with Mrs. Rawley and the news about McAlpin; he explained Bertha Boscowitz's present position, and her proffered assistance in the character of a messenger to the settlers; and he described the feeling of the seriousness of the crisis which had prevailed at Mrs. Rawley's house during the conversation to-day. Then he went on to say that this was not all. The worst was what had been made known to him on his way to the boat in San Francisco.

"I met Boscowitz," he said. "I tried to pass him without speaking. But he stopped me, and held out his hand. For once in my life I was a little of a man. I refused his hand plainly, and tried to walk on again. 'Why,' said he, 'what 's up, Harold? You have n't anything against me, have you?' His eyes fairly glittered. I knew that after his quarrel with his daughter, whom he really loves above all things, he was simply furious with passion. Yet there he stood, looking as cool, and grinning at me as calmly, as if he had never known any chagrin. Only his gleaming little eyes showed his temper. 'I have no use for the hand of a man that 's insulted my family,' said I. 'What?' he answered. 'Do you mean that article in the "Warrior"? Come, come, man; an article is an article, and let by-gones be by-gones. I only wanted just now to tell you something for your own good.' 'Well, sir,' I said, 'speak quickly, then. I 'm on the way to my boat. Don't make any long roads over this ground. I want nothing but business from you.' 'Harold,' said he, not so blandly now, 'our day of reckoning may come yet, if you 're so much in want of a reckoning. But just now, I say, as a friend, don't dabble in Oakfield Creek stock. You might get your fingers burned.' 'What concern of yours is Oakfield Creek?' I replied; 'I 've heard enough from you about that matter before.' And again I tried to pass on, but he stopped me. 'What I have now to tell you,' said he, 'is that the settlers are in revolt, so to speak, under one McAlpin. And they mean, these rascals, to turn on some of the friends of their would-be benefactor, Eldon, and to lynch those same persons. And Alonzo Eldon knows this. I 've taken care that he should know it. Alonzo Eldon 's my friend, sir, and a gentleman, too, mark my words. And what 's more,' Boscowitz went on, 'I 've taken pains already today to let him see that this conduct is what he has to expect from Alf Escott, and from Alf Escott's friends, associates, followers, worshipers, — poetical numskulls of worshipers, I mean, sir. So good-by, Mr. Harold. Only know well that Oakfield Creek stock has dropped, sir, in Alonzo's market since morning. Good-by.' And with this, Margaret, Boscowitz left me. You see that he changes his tone about Mr. Eldon frequently. I 've heard him revile your father-in-law freely, when he happened to be in the reviling mood. But, as you also see, Boscowitz is furious, and is fully awake, and has seen your father first. The loss of his daughter Bertha makes Boscowitz a far worse enemy of our designs than ever. He will not rest until all possible mischief has been done. When he learns, as he must learn, that she has gone to Oakfield Creek in the way that I mentioned, he will grow still more dangerous. And, in his fashion, too, he has a power with your father. Boscowitz himself is a man very greatly influenced, I know, by the fact that he finds himself once for all in a contest. Whichever side fortune puts him on, he fights furiously for that side, and crushes mercilessly, until he sees some sufficient reason for ending the thing. Save money and malice and family affection, he knows, however, no sufficient reasons for conduct. In this case all these reasons interest him against us. He hates me, he now hates Escott, he hates the settlers, he hopes for money from your father, he finds in this quarrel with Bertha a fresh wound for his one great affection. He is the most savage enemy conceivable.

"This, then, is my new perplexity, Margaret. Do you wonder that I come to you? I need your help. We all do. Only you have the influence with Alonzo Eldon that can serve us now."

Margaret was very thoughtful. She seemed to have utterly forgotten that they two had anything of a private nature between them. She was absorbed in the new question of the moment. But Harold, amid all his perplexities, was most conscious, as soon as he had finished his long speech, of a feeling of rapture at the thought that he was riding here on this lonesome road by her side. The clouds had altogether broken now; and the low sun was shining in long white rays through some of the smaller drifts, and in great floods through the larger spaces, lighting up the rugged hills with the splendor of such winter afternoons in California. The meadow-larks sang out their delight in the brightening skies, though since the early morning hardly a bird's note had been heard in the hills. Harold felt that life has a few good moments, and that this was one of them. They might, indeed, never meet again; but now, this glorious instant! — was it not worth the care? And that old, sweet seriousness, too, on her face, as she rode silently along, thinking of what he had said to her.

But when she yet waited for some time without speaking, a cloud passed over the sun, and Harold, with a little shiver, found returning to him yet another train of fancies, that, namely, which had mingled with his present perplexities as he rode towards the old home a short time ago. The old and the new, could one bind them together? And the old had just come up so strongly again. Was this the sacred pilgrimage? Harold found himself even laughing at his old dreams. "After all," he said to himself, "I did not visit the old home. And the larks do not remain silent. Yet I met her just at the edge of the grove."

Margaret spoke at last. She, at least, must have been just now a stranger to these confused passions that were struggling so irrationally in him. For she was perfectly calm and straightforward in speech, just as she had been in manner.

"Why," she said, "did Boscowitz talk in this way to you? What I fail to understand is his reason for this odd sort of frankness. If, as you think, he is inciting the settlers himself, in secret, through this McAlpin, why should he tell the news to you so soon? If, as he says, he is anxious to excite father's anger, why does he let you know his plan, in time for you to counteract it?"

"Boscowitz felt over-confident," replied Harold. "I have noticed before that in over-confidence is his weak point as an intriguer, and, for that matter, as a politician. The 'Warrior' has led a forlorn hope, you know, in two or three political canvasses already. This time, then, Boscowitz felt as he has so often before, and, meeting me, he could not forego the temptation to boast. Moreover, he does n't know the real secret of my power over Eldon. He does n't know, namely, how I stand towards you, Margaret."

Margaret shuddered. "May he never know!" she said fervently. She seemed a little indignant. It was not kind for Harold to have disturbed her with such thoughts just now. But he hastened to make amends.

"It 's my only comfort now," he said, "to think that you can help us. Without you, everything would fail; the settlers' cause would be lost, and our two old friends would be more bitter foes than ever. You must see your father-in-law. You must set before him his real danger. You must pledge the honor of us both that all is honestly and faithfully carried on upon our side, so far as this whole defense of Escott is concerned. You must show him that in all probability Boscowitz himself is the one who has stirred up this trouble among the settlers. Yes, and you must somehow reassure him about my own character; for I have no doubt that Boscowitz has done what he could to give me a bad name with Mr. Eldon."

"The plain fact is," replied Margaret, still

very thoughtfully, "that you and I must not now continue apart from each other. We must meet and consult over this often, and we must see father together."

Her words gave him great happiness; but they also terrified him. How could he dare to renew their friendship on the old terms? Yet, surely, she was right.

"I thank you," he answered her reverently, "that you grant this. I am sure you may trust me to understand what you mean, and when this affair is over, then, indeed" — He paused in an anxious way.

"Then, indeed, all the rest is over," she said very quietly; and hereupon they rode along for a while in silence together.

Tom found Harold at the house when he came home that night. Tom greeted his friend very warmly. "What a stranger you have been, of late!" he said. And after Harold had pleaded business as an excuse for his truancy, they all sat down to dinner. During the evening they consulted freely about the whole situation, and before Harold returned to the city they had adopted together a plan for further operations.

So this afternoon was the time when Harold came nearest of all to making his pilgrimage. He never went near his old home again.

CHAPTER XIII.

THE VISIT OF AN ENEMY.

ALONZO ELDON found his life, during that winter and the following spring, uncommonly tóilsome and sorely perplexing. We who have fewer responsibilities can hardly realize the extent and the complication of the business to which the great man was always a slave. Considered merely as business, the Oakfield Creek affair was one of the least of his concerns. It was only because this affair had so much personal and private interest that it occupied his thoughts so often. Other undertakings, vastly more important to the State at large, he occasionally neglected in those days, to deal with this matter. Yet such neglect had less dangerous consequences in Alonzo's case than it might have had in the case of other men. For Alonzo, at his worst, was still a born manager, and he had learned his trade as a business man in the hardest of schools.

His daily life was now, as always, prosaic, systematic, and tremendously industrious. He owned, of course, a vast mansion on the great hill in San Francisco; he had filled it with rare and curious things, and he had so well known how to choose advisers that his rare and curious things were much finer than the architecture of his house would have led you to suppose. But this prodigious house itself was usually a solitude;

not as vast, indeed, as the one that Alonzo loved to tell about when the pioneer mood was upon him, but nearly as lonesome. Alonzo had a great deal of respect for that mansion. He was very proud of it; but he lived in one corner of it.

He had always longed to have his son come into the dwelling and live with him. One of his dreams of late years had been to see Margaret the mistress of it. But though she treated with the most respectful kindness his remarks on that subject, he somehow knew that, whenever he was not by, she shrugged her shoulders at the notion, and despised his house. He had guessed as much long since, and it had deeply pained the warm and tender love he bore towards her. His old age was sure to be very lonely, save for her and for his grandson. Why could she not admire what he admired, and be ready with Tom to share his home?

To be sure, he had not built the house for her. He had built it eight or ten years ago, principally because other millionaires were heaping up great houses on the hill, and partly because he hoped, some day, to take more comfort in his own son, and to see Tom occupying the new home. When the betrothal of Tom and Ellen came about, Alonzo had felt, indeed, a certain obvious incongruity between the house on the one hand and his old friend's daughter on the other; and yet he had been so happy in the thought of healing the old wounds by uniting the families that he had even planned out the whole scene that would take place when, by way of surprise, he should make the house one of his wedding-presents to the young pair. The quarrel between Tom and the Escotts, whatever it was (for of course it had puzzled Alonzo sorely), had, therefore, deeply disappointed him. He had felt forced, however, to take his son's side in the controversy. He had signified to Escott his grave displeasure, and the later conduct of the old professor, even before the beginning of the Oakfield Creek troubles, had made the breach worse than ever. Yet always, as Alonzo saw, he was fated to be put in the wrong in his quarrels with Escott. Ellen's death had made him feel as if his son had somehow been her slayer. Yet still he had hoped that in new ways his plans might be so rearranged that Tom should yet come to enjoy the home prepared for the son of one among California's first citizens.

The fatherly love of Alonzo for Margaret had been the last and the crowning passion of his life. She never made him any concessions as to matters of taste and principle; but in every other way she showed him all a daughter's fondness. She was quite sincere in this. She saw his strong and rugged faults; but she pitied his declining life, his loneliness, and his affectionate heart, and she honored those qualities that made him truly a great man in the community. He always quite rightly saw, from the very outset, that she had no need and no desire for anything which he had to give her, save his affection. Her life in the country had now become so conservative, so independent, so complete in all outward respects, that she would have felt more wealth a burden, and another house a mere nuisance. That he was one of the richest of California millionaires meant to her little more than that he was one of the most burdened and responsible of men, who needed sympathy in his toils, and could not be expected to devote much time to her in return. But what she did wish from him, and got in full measure, was confidence and love. He appealed to her so often for advice, when matters of conscience were at stake, that she daily felt more and more strongly the importance of the particular kind of influence over him which had fallen to her lot. Her love of controlling others was hereby constantly appealed to and gratified. She found in Alonzo a strength of soul of which she thought Tom incapable. She lost all her youthful prejudices, too, against Alonzo. He could easily bear from her what Escott had vainly tried, in the old days, to give him without offense, namely, grave condemnation for his failings; her blame was to him like the judgment of some superior being, — severe, dignified, and charming.

This winter Alonzo's old responsibilities only grew upon him instead of lightening, even while he determined to think more of the future undertakings which were to crown his life. It would be vain to describe the range and the significance of Alonzo's daily work. His fortune was too great and too well managed to be in much danger of very serious injury at any time; but he had bound himself by ties of honor and of interest to so many enterprises, industrial and commercial, that every political change of any importance, as well as every great movement in the financial world of San Francisco, needed afresh his attention and his judgment. His decisions affected, directly or indirectly, the fortunes of thousands. He knew this, and, while he enjoyed the sense of power which the fact gave him, he often felt restive under the bondage of these present public cares. What he really wanted was to continue this activity after death, and in far nobler spheres, by means of the much-talked-of "Museum," as well as by means of many lesser endowments. To these things he was more and more determined to devote himself; yet the whole world, as it were, fought against his resolve. The last struggle, he felt, was approaching. The world must give way. Of that he felt sure. The ideal must, for him, take the first place. His present worldly work must become subordinate to the future, in which he was to join the choir, not exactly "invisible," whose music has crystallized into public bequests.

The Eldon Museum (it was the name that had first given any obvious ground for Margaret's humorous comparison) was still in many respects an incomplete ideal. Eldon, who had several times visited Europe with the matter in mind, would have been glad to spend years there in perfecting his schemes. But, so far as formed, they included some such conceptions as these: —

In the city of San Francisco one still lacks sufficiently elaborate and extensive libraries; one is in want of art-collections and of resources for the study of antiquity; and one desires museums of natural history, and several similar aids to scholarship. Whatever institutions of learning may rise there in future, there will always be a use for permanent treasuries of that sort. Why, by devoting, say, twenty-five millions of dollars to the undertaking, might not one found a group of collections, which should be under the care of great scholars and investigators, and which should also be devoted, so far as possible, to the education and enlightenment of the people of California? Popular education is founded on scholarship, while, on the other hand, scholarship is of no use save as it makes itself directly helpful to the people.

So thought Alonzo. Equality, he said, and all the other principles of the Declaration of Independence, are furthered by offering to the people educational advantages on a vast scale. His group of collections, to be united, of course, under the one great name of Eldon, was to hold in time, after sufficient growth, some place a little corresponding (yet, of course, not wholly corresponding) to the place that certain very famous European institutions hold in the Old World. It would remain thenceforth, he hoped, an example of public spirit, and a memorial to the devotion of the California pioneers. The libraries and other collections were to be used for the researches of scholars. They were also to be thrown open to the public as much as possible. And popular instruction was, meanwhile, to be given in the form of public lectures.

So far, Eldon's feet were on solid ground. The Eldon Museum was an ideal, but it was, in some respects, at least, a promising ideal. The twenty-five millions could actually be left to the Museum without making Tom a pauper, even if Tom were to lose all his own present independent fortune. In fact, Tom might, doubtless, pick up, of the fragments of Alonzo's wealth that would still remain, some seven millions. But Alonzo went further, in his fancy, and left this solid ground. He indulged wild hopes as to the number of great European scholars and the quantity of European antiquities that one can purchase, or bring over the ocean, for money. He had extravagant plans as to the laying out of the Museum. And, above all, he had formed singular and elaborate theories as to the policy to be pursued by the governing board of his institute. All these things gave his scheme a very romantic air.

The Museum was to be founded somewhere in the region where Valencia Street now meets the barren hills. It was to take advantage of the hill contours, of the sunny slopes, of the magnificent outlooks. The grounds were to be vast, well walled in, adorned with magnificent gardens (such as should serve both ornamental and scientific purposes); and these grounds were to have in their midst such a building as the world has never yet seen. Kubla Khan's dreamland home little surpassed in magnificence, and that long unfinished, dismal ruin, called on earth the San Francisco City Hall, rivals not now in wandering immensity, the Eldon Museum as it was planned in Alonzo's glowing fancy. But those matters, if they should be realized, would be, after all, things of brick and mortar, and concern us not here. Other thoughts of Alonzo are more important.

The Eldon Museum was, as we have seen, to support lectures for the people, and was to engage, in its capacity as a lecturing institution, in a propaganda for certain political and social theories that Eldon felt to be now in the air, and that, so far as he understood them, he supposed himself to share. Equality is an old notion; but in modern times we have found, he believed, that equality has been misinterpreted. Probably, for instance, the true equality is to be gained by something akin to what are now often called socialistic methods. Very probably, too, private property in land is an evil, if not a public crime. So, at least, Eldon, by dint of much hard reading at leisure moments, had brought himself to think. He was more than half a follower of Mr. George's theories about land ownership. He knew, indeed, that for him, at just this time, these theories were out of the question, save as mere ideals. He could not give up all his lands to the State without doing more harm than good, nor could he in any other way properly refrain, during this present imperfect life, from appropriating to himself that rent which his modern teachers suppose to be the just property of the public. But Alonzo ardently believed that Mr. George's theories belong to the future, and not to the present. He kept his adherence to them, as he kept many others of his views, profoundly secret. Even Margaret heard nothing from him about land ownership. Yet Eldon had sincerely planned that, when all his wars were done, and when the brand Excalibur, whose value was between twenty and thirty millions, was quite ready to be thrown away, he would confess to the public that he had been a socialist all along, and had only accumulated his vast fortune because the public, to whom it belonged, knew not just yet how to use it, save by giving it to him, temporarily, as trustee. He meant to give it all back, or at least so much of it as Tom would not need. And then, while giving it back to the public, in the form of this vast and impressive gift, he would openly proclaim, as the last confession of his life, that he was not only an orderly socialist himself, but was anxious to found an institution that, by lectures and by learned publications, should labor to investigate, to systematize, to rationalize, and to propagate the doctrines of the higher socialism. Of course, the intelligent reader knows that Alonzo's ideal socialism was not to be of the baser sort, but of the nobler, the modern, the learned, the philosophical, the lawful sort, which is founded on elaborate political theories, and which proposes, by orderly, righteous, and sober methods first to convert the public, and then gradually to reform the present social order. From the Eldon Museum, as a great public institution, Alonzo hoped that this new and lofty notion of equality might be preached to a still ignorant world.

In short, this man of business, who, as Tom had hinted in a conversation with Harold, was at heart a glowing lover of the theoretic life, was longing to make his own career a splendid paradox. He had spent his strength in accumulating a vast fortune. He meant now to devote the bulk of this fortune to the public (not forgetting, indeed, his own glory). But in doing so he desired to have taught thereby, to the public, the doctrine that vast private fortunes are social evils, and that the social order must erelong be so reformed as to make such fortunes impossible. Such was the romance of the Eldon Museum.

Yet this man had for years gone about to destroy the settlers at Oakfield Creek. And even to-day he felt perplexed to see how he should escape from his own undertakings against them. For, amongst the many Alonzo Eldons, there were two most prominent selves that went to make up this man's character. One was the Alonzo Eldon, who, at leisure moments, gazed off into the blue distance from the library of his house on the hill, or found a chance to commune with Margaret at her home beyond the bay. The other was Alonzo the leader of men, whom the very dogs on the streets knew a great way off, and revered as a man of might, but not of mercy.

It was Alonzo Eldon the business man, who was at the office on California Street, one morning in the following May, awaiting an appointed visit from Boscowitz.

The test cases in the Oakfield Creek affair had recently been decided, and against the settlers. A brief stay of proceedings had been granted. The gravest excitement had since prevailed at Oakfield Creek, for Alonzo had not yet seen his way clear to make public his designs. These test cases had been suits against Escott, who had, of course, been depended upon by the settlers to defend their rights to the utmost. A fund for legal defense had, in fact, been raised long ago, and placed at his disposal. Yet he had let the main points be decided against him almost by default. His lawyers seemed to have been instructed to make the least trouble possible for Eldon.

Since the decision, there were now two parties at Oakfield Creek. The first consisted of a few of Escott's most steadfast friends. They had been given to understand all along that there had been some private arrangement between Escott and Eldon, and that the arrangement was favorable to the settlers' interests. They were, indeed, at a loss to explain the long delay in the announcement of this arrangement. They found it hard to defend Escott against his enemies. But they still trusted, although it now often seemed to them that they were trusting against hope. They wondered if the suspense would ever end. Escott, meanwhile, true to his engagement with

Eldon, remained stubbornly and even fiercely uncommunicative. People must have faith in him, he said. That was all he could tell them at present. They would learn more by and by. He would only assure them that, if they would wait, all would be well.

The other party at Oakfield Creek, however, consisted of the Noble Rangers. McAlpin had led them captive. He used to gather them together in the bar-room of Spofford's Hotel, the central building of their little town, and instruct them in the principles of free government. By way of giving them practice in the same, he once made them march down to Buzzard's house, during a very dark night, and drag that gentleman from his bed. Buzzard was carted some ten miles on the road towards Martinez, and was then ordered to march. If he ever came back, the Rangers said, they would give him a coat of tar and feathers. He was a jumper, they assured him, adding fitting adjectives. The air of the Mount Diablo region was bad for jumpers. As for the rest of the deeds of McAlpin, and the speeches that he made, are they not written in the files of a weekly paper, "The Herald of Justice," which he edited during his stay at the Creek? It stands to reason that the Noble Rangers, after the adverse decision, had little confidence left in Escott. What they said of him was at best very impolite. It generally included a threat to shoot him at sight. Even Escott's best friends were now almost ready to join the Rangers, and they would surely fight at the first overt act that indicated any real treachery behind the supposed private arrangement with the Eldon party.

Such was the situation at the Creek. Escott had remained quietly in San Francisco, writing occasionally to his friends at Oakfield Creek, but busy for the most part over the magazine. His health was better. He himself was very weary of Eldon's delay, but he kept his feelings proudly to himself. With Harold he was still very intimate. Yet he guessed nothing of the relation of Harold to Margaret.

Boscowitz, too, for whom Eldon was waiting this morning, had found this spring a very melancholy time. For him, indeed, the trouble was of a special sort, both as to occasion and outcome. It was caused by his daughter's absence. Since she had left him, Boscowitz felt himself yet far more to be what throughout his life he had been, namely, with all his successes, a terribly lonesome man. Multitudes feared him nowadays; but he had no friends. Bertha's vacant place at his table made his heart ache. For Boscowitz, of course, had as real a heart as his neighbors, though his happened to be a bad heart. Then, too, Bertha, in her solemn and dutiful way, had been used to do little things for his comfort that he could not bear to forego, nor to have anybody else do; and when he tried to do them for himself, his heart choked him. The consequence whereof was that he first wrote to her, and next secretly visited her at Oakfield Creek (where he failed not to use his visit for the sake of dropping one or two private hints to McAlpin), and even once persuaded her to return with him to the home in San Francisco. Yet she stayed only a day or two. The sources of difference between them were now too serious to be gotten rid of. She asked that he should abandon his hostility to the settlers; he demanded that she should wholly return to her allegiance to himself. Nothing came for them out of the interview save a new quarrel, more bitter enmity than ever on the part of Boscowitz towards the settlers, and the suggestion of a new thought to the editor's own mind.

For, in the course of this conversation with Boscowitz, Bertha was induced to go over the whole ground of her opinions concerning the actors in this controversy. Her long absence, her real love for her father, and her anxiety to get a clear understanding with him made her too communicative. She did what she never afterwards forgave herself for doing. She revealed to him certain suspicions of hers about Harold and Margaret. What she gave was the barest suggestion, yet Boscowitz acted upon it thereafter with the greatest vigor. Here was a hint of a possible means of avenging himself upon his worst foes. He had never before thought of this combination. Bertha had no real evidence to give, but then Boscowitz did not need evidence.

One immediate effect of Bertha's visit to her father, which took place early in April, had been to increase considerably Alonzo's natural perplexities about the whole affair of the settlers. He did not understand what seemed to him her change of side. That she returned again to Oakfield Creek made things even more puzzling. Alonzo had trusted her, as he had trusted several of the more conservative settlers. Was she betraying him? If she thus returned to her father, who had been so much opposed to her friends, she was surely betraying those friends. And if she was betraying them, might she not all along have been betraying Alonzo also? And if she could not be trusted, why should one trust the others? These personal and family relationships grew thus very complex. Alonzo hardly cared to try to unravel them. His general sense of insecurity was, at all events, much heightened.

When Boscowitz entered the office that morning, Alonzo himself was sitting smoking, and very much harassed. Alonzo was subject to a particular variation of the pioneer mood which Margaret had never witnessed. For Alonzo's wrath seldom dared to give itself full vent. In the presence of those whom he took to be cultivated men, he was always embarrassed at such moments, and tried to disguise his passion under a show of dignity. Another sort of dignity, moreover, controlled him, usually, when he dealt with his business equals. And to ordinary inferiors he was far above showing his passions. His true rage he had to reserve, accordingly, for very rare occasions. Only such men as Boscowitz seemed to him suitable persons to witness it. He cared not what Boscowitz thought of him, and dignity counted for nothing in the editor's presence. So this morning Alonzo, full of fury at the perplexities that were troubling him in these last stages of the Oakfield Creek controversy, was even longing to see Boscowitz. Just then, however, Boscowitz entered. Eldon now gruffly invited him to be seated, and looked at him rather sternly.

"Well?" he said.

"I 've called, Mr. Eldon, to speak to you, just as I always have spoken to you, and that means very honestly."

"Damn your honesty, Boscowitz, not to use a stronger expression. What do you want to say now, sir?"

"It 's about your proposed settlement with Escott."

"Hum! I knew you 'd hear of that just about now, if not sooner. And let me say, by thunder, that I don't care this accursed cigar what you think of my settlement with Escott. It 's my affair. I 'm honorable in it. I 've betrayed nobody. Some say that I ought n't to have met him privately awhile ago, nor to have entered into any personal undertaking with him before the suit was over. Some call it unbusiness-like. I 've just got a letter from that miserable old Patrick Fleet, saying so. Hang Patrick Fleet! Have n't I offered Fleet the full present value of his shares in the L. & I. Company, now when the test suits are won, and the whole thing decided in our favor? I know that my late acts about this Oakfield Creek affair are unbusiness-like. But who suffers for them but me? Don't I stand ready to pay the piper? It's my tune. If I like it, who in thunder need call it bad music? I'll have some men know, Boscowitz, and you among the rest, hang you, that my own private affairs are mine. If any man feels wronged, — any shareholder, I mean, — in all this business-like, sanctimonious, blood-sucking monster of a Land and Improvement Company, let him come down to my office and settle with me. That's what I say. I'll give him a check for whatever he's lost. I'll enter into all the private undertakings I choose, and pay for 'em too, and don't you forget it. So there, now. As for you, I know beforehand what a miserable little skinny fragment of a man like you, with your invisible animalcule of a God-forsaken lost soul, thinks of my settlement with Escott. I know you disapprove it. You need n't tell me. Any fool would disapprove it! The man that has the sense to understand me and my motives has n't written me a letter this morning, nor opened my door to come in here and talk with me, — not yet."

Boscowitz bore his punishment very meekly, sitting with crossed knees, his eyes fixed on the floor, his face very placid, his hand busy stroking his chin. When Alonzo had ended, the editor began, as if nothing singular had happened. The harshness of his voice was in sharp contrast to his quiet demeanor.

"About the general policy of your settlement,

Mr. Eldon, you 're the only judge. I have n't come to speak of that. There 's another aspect of the case that possibly is not so clear to you. I 'm a person who sometimes can get extraordinary private and important information. I 'm in duty bound to give you the advantage of it, in case it concerns you. Just now I know a fact about this matter which I think you don't know, and which I must mention, if you 'll let me."

"So far as I 've observed, Boscowitz, there are a good many facts nowadays that are no better than infernal lies. But keep on. I 'll not believe a word you say, this morning. I 'm wrought up, if I may say so."

"I hope you 'll be no more wrought up at a quite new evidence that Escott's friends, at least, are betraying you, and that he likely has a hand in their doings."

"I 'm sick of Escott betraying me. I suppose you and the Piutes at Pyramid Lake would agree that Escott has always betrayed me for his living ever since he could toddle. Some day, Boscowitz, if you 'll pardon my frankness, I 'll go *out* of this office, do you understand, and I 'll hunt round till I find a little fellow somewhere, crouching down behind a packing-box, or under a bar-room counter, — some miserable, puny little burlesque of God's handiwork, — who 'll have been saying, as he sneaked and prowled about, that honest old Alf Escott has been betraying me. And then, do you know, Boscowitz, I 'll catch that same diminutive, unhealthy, yellow-hided sinner, and I 'll pick him up between my thumb and finger, this way, and I'll drop him into the middle of eternity, — do you understand me now?" Alonzo roared out this last with a fury that was not wholly untouched with a certain kind of humor. Boscowitz only laughed a little, and Alonzo rose, and strode fiercely to his high desk across the room.

"See here," he said, picking up a letter that lay there. "This, I received yesterday, and from Alf Escott. You'll forgive me if I remark that, although I yesterday got a note from you, this letter of Alf Escott's was (in a very large correspondence, you understand), it was the *only* letter received here yesterday bearing the signature of a perfectly honest man. And now, if you're wise, you'll drop that controversy, and pass on to any serious business that you may have here to-day with me. — By the way, Boscowitz, will you have a cigar? They're wretched stuff, these. But I want a fresh one myself, and you must keep me company." Alonzo took his seat, lit his fresh cigar, and began to smoke more quietly. He had partly talked out his mood. Boscowitz thanked him, very pleasantly, for the cigar, and began his attack after a moment's silence, and with the greatest composure.

"What do you think, Mr. Eldon, of Alf Escott's friend, Mr. Harold?"

"Think of him? What should I think of Alf Escott's friend, thinking as I now do of Alf Escott?"

"I'm not saying anything against Harold as

Alf Escott's friend, mind you. Only what do you think of him in himself?"

"I don't see, Boscowitz, why time has to be wasted now over my opinions of Harold."

"But I've reason, Mr. Eldon, to attract your attention to-day to this Harold. He's not been treating you fairly."

"What's he done?"

"He's tried to make a tool of you, Mr. Eldon."

Alonzo laughed, heartily this time, instead of bursting out as he had done before, when the suspicions about Escott were mentioned. "I guess I can stand the wear and tear of being *his* tool," Alonzo said, "better than he can stand the wear and tear of swinging me. Don't you think so?" And Alonzo, for some moments, went on chuckling. But, Boscowitz, now that the pioneer's wrath had passed by, was all the surer of his man.

"Yet consider, Mr. Eldon. I hate to see you made use of by designing sneaks like Harold; for he *is* a designing sneak. Just because you're powerful, and have so much to think of, a man of his sort can get a great deal from you without your knowing it. Now, just think. First, he's managed to get your backing for his wretched magazine" —

"Hold right there; his magazine is n't wretched. It has its faults, like himself. It's unpractical, and sometimes it's pretty heavy reading. But it's clever, and the best thing of its sort on the coast."

"That's a matter of taste, Mr. Eldon. And

about literary taste I don't yield to no man living, I don't. I tell you, from the point of view of an experienced literary critic, that magazine beats hell. But no matter. That's only one thing. Secondly, Mr. Eldon, he's taken advantage of your leniency, and of your confidence in him, and of the late troubles, to make a good spec over in the Oakfield region, by secretly buying in claims at low figures. I think, myself, he's used this so-called McAlpin to stir up the settlers, so's to create a feeling of insecurity and cheapen claims. At any rate, he's known how to put his money where it'll do the most good. When you give up land to the settlers, you'll *not* be giving it to 'em. The claims 'll still stand in their names, but Harold 'll be the owner of many of those same. Your gifts 'll go into that miserable literary poet's infernal pockets, Mr. Eldon." Boscowitz, of course, knew that he was lying, so far, in the most baseless fashion. Such lies, however, he always regarded as a necessary preliminary to the truth. And he felt that it was the truth which he was soon to tell, however much even that might have to be mixed with error. One must prepare Alonzo's mind a trifle.

"How should you know this, Boscowitz?"

"I have a daughter, Mr. Eldon, who"—

"Boscowitz, if it were polite, I should say something about your daughter that, as it is, I prefer to say about yourself. What I do say is that you and your gossip may be hanged. Unless you can show me documentary evidence, sir, *doc-u-men-ta-ry* evidence of the truth of your accusations, I 'll not believe your daughter, who everlastingly changes sides for her living; nor you, sir, whose business it is to blackguard every gentleman that you chance to be opposed to. Harold has his faults. He 's unpractical; he 's dreamy; he 's whimsical. But he 's a gentleman, sir, and that 's more than can be said of *every*body hereabouts."

"Mr. Eldon, I 'm sorry that you have to speak thus about my poor daughter, — that I am. You must remember, sir, that, in fact, to my very deep regret and pain, my daughter has not changed sides in this controversy. Anything that comes from her comes from a staunch friend of the settlers, however I may feel bound to use it."

"This is all none of my business, — I mean about your daughter, Boscowitz; but she passed some time recently with you, I notice, though she was supposed to have left you for the sake of the settlers. Why did she do this?"

"Solely, sir, in the hope of converting me to her views. She failed, sir. I take a certain honest pride, I may say, in our common obstinacy and tenacity of purpose. It pains me, therefore, to hear her accused thus by you at a time when, to my deepest pain, I myself am compelled to so serious a difference with her about a matter of my duty to you and to the public." Boscowitz spoke with great feeling, and Alonzo was not untouched.

"Well, Boscowitz," he answered, in a much changed tone, "I 'll take back all you please of what I 've suggested, so far as it concerns your daughter. The topic in hand, however, is really Harold. If, as I say, you can show me good evidence of anything wrong in that man, I shall not be obliged to you, but I shall yield to reason. I 've frequently been deceived in men, sir, but seldom has a man's character seemed to me clearer than does this of Harold's. And now, to speak to the point, will you state to me categorically what reasons you have for believing Harold guilty of any false play in this matter of the Oakfield Creek controversy?"

"If you 'll let me say so, sir, it was n't mainly on account of that matter, in itself alone considered, that I came here this morning; and as time is short, if you 'll permit me, I 'll pass on to"—

"Hang you, what won't you pass on to? You 've already said that you came here to enlighten my mind about Escott and his friends. Then you mention Harold, and you begin an indictment against him. Just as I think I 've surely got you, off you dance on to something else. What *is* your business, then? I 'm sick of fooling, Boscowitz. I 'm a straightforward man, and I 've much else to do."

Boscowitz sighed. "I 'm sure I can't help it," he said, "if this business is so mixed that there is no fair chance of covering it all in a short interview? I came here, as an honest man, to tell you what I can't help knowing, and what, so to speak, the whole world will soon know if you don't beware. And that is something which puts Harold in a very bad light. But I wanted you to appreciate from the start the enormity of Harold's offenses, so I reminded you of what you know to be a fact, namely, that he 's got your backing for his magazine; and also I told you what I have n't time to prove to-day, to wit, that he 's taken an unfair advantage of your kindness by secretly buying in claims from the settlers. Both those matters are only preliminaries. When I pass on from them, I pass, Mr. Eldon, to the real matter before us. But if you have n't time, sir, to think of something that concerns your son far more even than it concerns yourself, why then, I suppose, I must be going." And Boscowitz took up his hat, and rose from his chair.

"My son?" queried Alonzo, a little anxiously. "Why my son? He now owns no claims at Oakfield Creek. He has sold all he had to me, three months since. He has no interests there."

"He has interests elsewhere," said Boscowitz, solemnly, — "interests in the peace of his own household, for instance."

"What do you mean, sir?" thundered Alonzo.

Boscowitz knew what a tender spot he had touched, but he paid no attention to Alonzo's new outburst, save to say: "I beg your pardon, indeed. I had just resolved to tell you no more this morning. I don't think you 're in the mood, Mr. Eldon, to receive the truth in the right spirit to-day. Facts are facts. That 's my view. I did n't make these facts. I 'm not to blame for them. I was only going, as a friend, to give you warning before the world stepped in, in an unfriendly spirit, to do it, instead. As it is, I'm going to take my leave. Good-day."

"By all the devils, come back here, Boscowitz!" cried Alonzo, springing up. Boscowitz turned and faced the great man very calmly.

"You 're irascible to-day, Mr. Eldon," he said, as quietly as his harsh voice would permit.

"And have n't I a right to be, man? Is, then, my son's family nothing, sir? You talk mysteriously about being interested in the peace of it, and about the world stepping in to disturb us with news that you now kindly and privately offer to us in advance. I'm a blunt man, sir. When you mention my son's household, you mention what I simply won't hear named lightly. There can be no trifling as to that. I don't like your manner, Boscowitz. Sit down and be plain. *If* you have any facts of importance to bring here, nobody is going to kill you for bringing them. If you have n't any facts, and have come here merely to trifle, you 've dared more than I think you 'll ever dare again. So lay down your hat, and talk straight."

Boscowitz slowly obeyed, and both again took seats. The editor's face was stern, his manner was that of one who has to do a disagreeable duty. "You 'll bear me witness," he began, awkwardly fumbling, meanwhile, in his coat pocket for something, — "you 'll bear me witness that, from the first, I have suspected this man Harold, and, so far as in me lay, I 've tried to counteract his influence. Now that I have reason to think him guilty of serious indiscretions, to use a mild expression, you 'll also soon bear me witness that I have acted promptly and considerately. Editors, sir, have exceptional advantages for getting information, and, accordingly, exceptional temptations to misuse it. But I—ah! here I have my paper." Boscowitz had drawn from his pocket a mass of letters, bills, and the like, and had been looking slowly through the handful, enjoying, meanwhile, Alonzo's impatience. What he at last produced was a bit of printer's proof, evidently taken from a printing-office file, for there was a hole at the top of the proof-slip. Boscowitz looked at the paper a moment, restored the other papers to his pocket, then leaned back and gazed once more into Alonzo's eyes, holding the proof between his fingers as he did so.

"This piece of paper, sir," he said, "has a history, which I must tell you before I show you the contents. I had a call but yesterday, at my office, from my rival and enemy, Chatterly, the editor of the 'Little Bird of the Air.' This bit of proof comes from the office of the 'Little Bird.' Chatterly himself brought it to me. You may see, sir, from this one fact, that there must be something decidedly noteworthy about such a proof. Chatterly, Mr. Eldon, bringing his own proofs to my office? Why, sir, you 'd as soon expect the devil to go and ask Gabriel's advice about his own infernal journal. But, in fact,

Chatterly *did* bring this proof to my office." Boscowitz paused once more, very solemnly.

The "Little Bird of the Air" was a weekly journal, fairly well known in certain circles in San Francisco. It was a paper far worse than Boscowitz's. It appealed both to sporting men and to lovers of scandal pure and simple, while Boscowitz's, as we know, appealed to the wealthy classes and to families. Both papers did little to improve and something to debase their patrons; and therein they were alike. The proprietor of the "Little Bird" boasted of some twelve or fifteen generally bloodless shooting affrays, the result of a score of years passed in amusing fools, in harassing the families of citizens. The "Little Bird," meanwhile, had done, by the way, some decidedly good work as public scavenger, and as furnisher of occasions whereby rogues might be made to fall out. One hardly need add that the "Little Bird" and the "Warrior" were violent opponents, and abused each other most vigorously on all occasions. In public their proprietors were, accordingly, deadly enemies. In private they had considerable respect for each other, and met for business reasons whenever they saw fit. It was to Chatterly that Boscowitz had appealed for aid in carrying out his new scheme against Eldon's peace. What aid he had got this bit of proof expressed.

"Chatterly," continued Boscowitz, "addressed me very much as follows. 'A young writer of mine,' said Chatterly, 'has prepared this article, which came near appearing in the last number of the "Little Bird,"' so Chatterly began. But, Mr. Eldon, I cared nothing beforehand for what should or should not appear in the 'Little Bird,' noways. And so I asked Chatterly what business this was of mine. He said that he had kept the article back because it affected you, and he thought that a man in your position ought to have a chance" —

"See here, Boscowitz," interrupted Eldon fiercely, his face fairly pale with wrath, "this is the worst yet. Why should I have to sit here and listen to stories about how Chatterly wants to blackmail me? If he 'd come to *my* office, sir, and had got as far as you 've got now, I should have kicked him down-stairs, and made an end of him. Is there anything more to come in your story?"

"There 's not a trace of blackmail in this whole business, Mr. Eldon, as you 'll see in a minute. Chatterly is quite capable of blackmailing, I 've no doubt; but usually he finds something else more profitable than blackmail, and that 's the published scandal itself. The public will usually pay more than the victim for a good domestic narrative, Mr. Eldon; of so much I can assure you unhesitatingly. But Chatterly's purpose this time was, as you will see, neither blackmail nor the publication of scandal. The fact is, Mr. Eldon, that, despite our business rivalry and our public enmity, Chatterly and I must needs have certain concerns in common. We 're not without some limits to our mutual scorn and contempt. When Chatterly had before him this item, prepared for the press by an obscure, irresponsible, and unprincipled young writer of his (I can't tell you who, Mr. Eldon, — such secrets are sacred), — when he saw, sir, that this item affected deeply personal interests which I myself would, so to speak, die to defend, namely, your own family interests, Mr. Eldon, Chatterly paused — and trembled. He feared, I 've no doubt, your wrath. I venture to add — not immodestly, I hope — that he also feared mine. He resolved to bring me the item, as a personal favor to myself. Its publication, he remarked, must be permanently prevented by prompt action on your part. I *don't* mean, sir, anything like hush-money; I mean simply that prompt action which a man takes when the honor of those near him is endangered. As Chatterly said, he simply did n't want to publish the thing. He trusted me, of course, to let nobody but you know of it. I hope, Mr. Eldon, that you 'll be able to prevent this and all equally disagreeable publications altogether." Boscowitz took breath, and then went on, Eldon now gloomily and somewhat helplessly watching him in silence. These long speeches of Boscowitz's could never be prevented, unless one could make up one's mind to throttle the editor off-hand. Eldon saw no way but to submit. He kept down his rage, however, with great difficulty.

"So much for the history of this item. Now

for its meaning. Items affecting the peace of a family, sir, are never concocted, even by the most foolish reporter, without some real cause. The cause must be either really scandalous goings-on (which God forbid that any one should imagine, sir, in this case), or else some foolish and boastful and slanderous talk on the part of one who has been admitted into the family. That last, sir, is the undoubted and sole ground, to my mind, for this particular half column of scandal. Somebody, in a gossiping way, has been boastfully, and with incredible baseness, using names that every honest man should regard as sacred. Who is that person? Nobody, as you 'll soon see, can be credited with that baseness, in this case, but Harold. Ah! Mr. Eldon, when I look it all over (your friendship with Harold, I mean), I 'm constrained to say, 'Whom the gods would destroy dies early.' No, that 's not it; 'goes crazy,' I guess. In fact, it 's a great drawback for one who, like myself, has enjoyed an impartially cosmopolitan bringing up, that he in vain seeks to express his feelings by means of the proverbs of any nation or tongue. He gets 'em all mixed up, Mr. Eldon."

"Boscowitz," said Alonzo, more calmly now, but with a dangerous glitter in his eye, "stop this infernal nonsense of yours at once, and hand me that proof." Boscowitz knew this glitter in Eldon's eye of old. When that came, no further trifling was possible. Boscowitz lost no time in handing over the paper, and then leaned back to watch its effect.

It was, indeed, a very carefully poisoned dart. Boscowitz, after carefully considering all that Bertha had told him, and all that he could gather from his discreet inquiries as to Harold's position in the family at East Oakland, had asked himself what interpretation must be put upon this intimacy. He had managed to hear of some interviews that even Tom, he thought, might not have known of, such as that meeting of the two friends, by appointment, as it seemed, close by Harold's old home, and that long, slow ride together over lonesome roads, in close and confidential conversation. These things, of course, meant to Boscowitz whatever he wanted them to mean. Other gossip joined itself with this.

But even if it all were as innocent a friendship as Tom plainly thought it to be, Boscowitz knew that a properly chosen word might embitter it at once. Say that the world suspects such a thing, and you have said what forthwith makes it suspicious. Yet even this would be only the beginning of Boscowitz's little plot. The really fatal sting would lie in making Harold himself appear to be the real slanderer. Boscowitz intended to set forth to Eldon that the world would never have heard of an innocent friendship at the hillside house, in case Harold himself had not been boasting of a conquest in the family. That he had been boasting, however, the item was to imply, by its wording and its statements; and it did so.

The little article into which these ideas formed

themselves contained, of course, many innuendoes, but no names, and there were many quite unmistakable references to persons and places, and as unmistakable though indistinctly worded charges. The sketch declared that some things needed looking into; it threatened more disclosures in future; it warned careless husbands to beware of trusted family friends. In style it resembled the sort of items that Chatterly had often admitted into the "Little Bird." Yet it went much further than Chatterly would have dared to go, in an article intended for actual publication, at least, in a case where such important persons were concerned, and where the real evidence was, after all, so very poor. Boscowitz's plan, however, involved and rendered safe such boldness. As the item was not to be printed, and as it was to be shown, in proof, in a friendly way to Alonzo and to Tom, a good deal could be risked for the sake of starting the quarrel with Harold. And if all should fail, there would be the abominable audacity of that shameless and nameless young writer of Chatterly's to fall back upon as the cause of all the mischief. Chatterly had lent himself to Boscowitz's little scheme very cheerfully, and for much the same reasons as those which Boscowitz had actually given. Chatterly, from time to time, had business relations with Boscowitz. And in this case Chatterly saw no risk and much possible advantage in thus playing into Boscowitz's hands, and in meanwhile appearing as Alonzo's considerate friend at an unpleasant crisis.

When Alonzo, however, had read the item, he threw it contemptuously on the floor. "What is this, after all, on its face, Boscowitz, but just the most accursed piece of blackmailing imaginable?" Eldon spoke with a certain forced self-control; but his passion was now more violent than ever. Boscowitz was not in the least put out. He replied, very firmly, picking up the article as he did so: —

"I, sir, am as well able as my neighbors, I guess, to tell blackmailing when I see it. Therefore I call your attention to these facts: A blackmailer asks for money, or uses threats. Chatterly wanted nothing, but came and freely gave this to me, one of his worst enemies. He does n't intend to publish it in any case. It got into type without his knowledge. Not for an instant, of course, do I imagine the thing to have any other foundation than Harold's boasting. But what is plain, at all events, is, first, that a warm friendship of Harold at your son's house exists, — that you know. Such friendships, in the next place, are sacred, and should never be commented upon out-of-doors, so long as they are what they pretend to be, — that, also, is admitted. Now, however, this friendship *is* being commented upon very freely. That, Mr. Eldon (I speak as a personal friend), is a thing which I can verify myself. Of late, sir, I have heard a number of comments, such as I deeply regretted to hear; and if you 'll take the trouble to inquire, you 'll find out as much yourself. But not only are comments current. They 're beginning to boil down into things of this sort, articles so unpleasant that Chatterly himself suppresses them, and gets me to inform you of them. Now, who, sir, *who* can be to blame for this? Is not your son's household above reproach? Who gossips in such cases, and in this way, in advance of genuine information? But suppose now, *suppose*, Mr. Eldon, that Harold has been boasting? Does n't that seem plausible? I have another evidence.

"Just look here, now. Have you seen this poem of Harold's in the last number of the 'Monthly'? Look at it, sir" (and Boscowitz promptly produced the number in question from where it had been lying, under his hat). There 's something, if you 'll allow me to say so, darned love-sick and complimentary about those verses, sir. Plain matter-of-fact men, like you and me, can't understand why every modest, blushing poet in God's creation is privileged to come out insolently and call *some* lady (name, of course, not mentioned) by tender titles, to talk to her about sorrowful separations, and about the woes of trying to live decently, and all this without anybody asking him plainly how he reconciles that sort of talk with common respectability. Suppose he published in prose love-letters of doubtful sense and of more doubtful morality. What 'd you and I think of him, sir? I ask you as a practical man, judging him on plain business principles, what 'd we think of him?"

"Bosh, man!" interrupted Alonzo, sternly, but

with a certain tone of relief at this little prospect of a diversion. "This is no evidence. I 've read in my day bushels of poems as full of damned nonsense as this one. That 's just literature, you see. A fellow reels off that sort of thing by the mile, when he has the hang of it, just to show what he can do. He does n't mean a word of it. Everybody knows that any great poet gets famous for telling lies in a sort of way that makes you like to take note of 'em, as it were. It 's how he earns his living, you perceive, namely, by pretending to be pious, or drunk, or in love with another man's wife, or excited any way, and then raising an infernal row over it all. I 've known poets before, sir, in my life, men that have visited with me from the East, or that have gone hunting with me, or once or twice that have been in business near me, and been my friends for years. They 're, like enough, rather no account men, if you choose, but they 're all as mild as skim-milk, — except, to be sure, Alf Escott. Mostly they don't know enough to be bad, sir. They 're too childish-minded, as it were. As for what they say, I tell you, that 's just literature, — nothing more in God's world! You can't place *any* dependence on it, Boscowitz! As editor, you ought to know that. As for this poem before us, I 've read it. Such poems have n't any more to do with real life than novels have, sir. It 's a poet's business to take on in that way whenever he 's supposed to be wrought up, if I may use the expression." Alonzo's voice was quite philosophical by this time.

"Now *is* this all sham?" queried Boscowitz, taking every advantage of the momentary change in Alonzo's attitude. "This whole inquiry is only parenthetical, as it were, but I think it important. In matters of this kind everything is important. This here poem is *primâ facie*, sir, if I may say so, addressed to some female woman that the poet thinks he has n't got *no* sort of business, sir, to be in love with. He insinuates as much, Mr. Eldon, in the plainest language that you can anyhow get to rhyme with itself, though that, to my thinking, is n't usually the plainest of all language, even if it *is* sometimes rather darned pretty language. But, I repeat, he insinuates his love of that same woman in the plainest accessible language. You may say that that 's all. He does n't give her name, sir, nor her post-office address. He does n't describe her exactly, except that he does remark that she beats the general run as to good looks. But what would you expect? The poet, may be, could n't get her post-office address to rhyme with anything. And if he could, and did, he could n't any ways expect to keep a whole skin here in this city of San Francisco thereafter, nor forevermore. But look once again, to take this in a sensible fashion, *what*, in plain English, and for present purposes, does this poem here say? It says, 'I, Harold, editor of this God-forsaken, sickly, half-baked monthly magazine in San Francisco, am in love with some woman that I have n't any mortal business to be in love with. And, accordingly, I ought to be kicked by some honest citizen. Done under my hand and seal in this year of grace,' and so forth. *That's* what it says, Mr. Eldon, neither more nor less."

Alonzo's strained mood loved this relief just now, and it was quite to Boscowitz's purpose to grant so much for the instant. Alonzo replied very promptly, and as if contemplating the general problem with great care: —

"But look here, Boscowitz, it 's something like a fiddler, is n't it? You go to a concert, and one of these cussedly clever foreign fellows gets up with his monkey-shines, and paws and saws till he quite affects you, if I may use the expression. I don't know anything about music, and I 'll be hanged if, until I heard by chance some really good fiddling, I had any great respect for a man that 'd pass his life as a fiddler. I 've always honored science, and thought, and learning, and architecture, and painting, and wisdom generally. Modern thought, sir, is my ideal. I want science to become pretty much universal. I want that every intelligent young man should read and understand Herbert Spencer, and Darwin, and Huxley, and all the leaders of modern science. And I believe, too, in literature; that is, if literature means books like Macaulay's Essays (Lord, how I 've loved Macaulay's Essays!) and the Dialogues of Socrates (I read some of 'em once in a good translation, and it made my heart glow!), and Shakespeare's plays, and Daniel Webster's speeches, and Drake's address to the American Flag, and Poe's

Raven. Such things, not to mention others that I admire in private, and won't tell about now, I believe in, from my heart. But, as I was saying, I never thought well of fiddling until I heard some of these darned foreigners fiddle. And then, I grant you, I was pretty much captivated, as it were. But to return. This thing before us, I maintain, and I stick to it, Boscowitz, is like fiddling. A fiddler comes out, and makes his monkey-shines as aforesaid, and you listen, sir, with what I may call the most unfeigned and unadulterated depth of emotion. He makes you, not exactly laugh or cry, — you 're too old for that; but he makes you feel that *if* you were a boy again, — like my grandson, for instance, that fine little rascal! — you 'd be sure to do something of the sort, if you felt as strongly as you do now. But, see here, this fiddler, what does he feel of all that rigmarole that he 's stringing off? He does n't want to laugh; no, nor to cry either, — not a bit of it all; on the contrary, the darned cuss just wants to fiddle, because he *likes* to, and there 's the end of it. Now I say, it 's so, too, with a man who 's getting up one of these blarsted novels that you keep seeing round all the time; and *just* so, too, and above all, with a fellow that grinds out poetry like this poem before us. You know nothing about a man when you see his poems, sir, any more than you know about a politician by reading the platform that he proposes to stand on. A political platform is a pack of darned lies. So, also, I take it, is a poem. And that 's the end of it."

Alonzo drew a long breath. This digression had been a desperate effort to forget the real problem before him, and Boscowitz watched with delight this sign that the venom was at work. He continued, for the instant, in the same strain:—

"But yet, Mr. Eldon, in war-time, if a man wrote a poem to give Jeff Davis a general God-blessing, you did n't only cuss the alleged sentiments of that poem; you wanted, sir, as a good 'n loyal Northern citizen, to hunt round till you got a chance to kick that same man that wrote it. And if, a while ago, a man was to 've written a poem on the case of Guiteau, making him out a blessed martyr, I take it you 'd a seen with a certain holy joy that cantankerous poet with a coat of tar 'n feathers on him. Now is there so much difference here after all? To be sure, I 'll allow this Harold says rather little that you could so definitely catch on to in this poem. He does n't directly say that this here lady of his, the poet's, heart, is another man's wife, any more than he says she lives near East Oakland, on a well-known spot. But he does, sir, to use my former and strictly accurate expression, with a slight improvement, he does, sir, categorically insinuate of himself that he has no sort of business to be in love with this same female. Now in this free and enlightened age, when all men, Mr. Eldon, are equal in the sight of God and man, when the bonds of unholy and mediæval superstition are, if I may use the term, quenched, upon what, sir, can you yet predicate the assertion of a given man that he, as a free-born American citizen, has no business to fall in love to a given adult female, who is of sound and disposing mind? Upon what, sir, but one of two considerations: first, that the citizen afôresaid is the husband of another woman; or, secondly, that the female aforesaid is the wife of another man. Now Harold has no wife. There remains, therefore, but *one* alternative." Boscowitz paused triumphantly. Alonzo had listened to much of this with skeptical curiosity and a show of theoretical interest. Towards the close of it, however, the former expression of painfully suppressed wrath and of worry had returned.

"I don't see," he answered weakly, at length, "what 's the good of all this wretched talk about poetry, anyhow. Hang poetry!"

"The good is, sir, that we get a piece of what I should call concomitant evidence. If Harold has thus risked his affections by exposing them for sale in the monthly at three bits a copy, shall we wonder if we find good proof that he 's been boasting in private of a conquest that he 's never made?"

"Never made!" said Alonzo, bitterly. "I should say he had n't." There was another pause.

"Well," Boscowitz went on, "I confess to you that, had I wanted to make out a case upon coming to you to-day, I should have taken time to collect much more evidence. But you see, Mr. Eldon, not to make out a case, but to give you the first hurried, ill-prepared, friendly warning, have I visited you. I may be mistaken. It 's human to err. But consider the probabilities, and then investigate, sir, investigate. The more this is looked into, the more, I'm convinced, will you find it damning to Harold. Everything points that way. But now, Mr. Eldon, as to the method of investigating. Where's your son? Is he in town?"

"He has just gone to Los Angeles on business for me. He started this very morning."

"I did n't know that, Mr. Eldon. Strange that I had n't heard." Boscowitz had heard, days before, of Tom's expected departure, and had chosen this time accordingly. "So much the more reason why you should act promptly, and for your son's honor. Is n't it plain, at all events, that, if this gossip is current, Harold must be kept away from your son's house until all is explained and made good? Even if he were innocent, as he is n't, he must n't call there any more now, above all in your son's absence. I'm sure your daughter-in-law will grant that, if you lay the thing before her?"

"I think, Boscowitz, that I'll first, if you please, confront Harold with this proof of yours, and hear what he has to say for himself."

"And what should he say, Mr. Eldon? Declare at once that he knows no ground for such an item, of course. And how much will you be forwarder of your business? You put the sneak on his guard. You gain nothing. No, be prompt, investigate rigidly, — that's what I say. Only don't begin with Harold."

"With whom, then?"

"Mr. Eldon, if you honor me by asking for a

word of my advice further, I should say this: Don't lay this thing before Harold, nor yet before Escott, who pets Harold, and whom Harold in turn feeds. Don't lay it before anybody until you 've used your right as father and as venerable friend, and have given fair warning to Mrs. Eldon herself." Boscowitz was playing a bold game, but he thought it worth while to do so, and boldness was always his favorite fault.

Alonzo looked a little startled, and a good deal displeased. "No," he said. "She shall hear nothing of it. *There* 's something, Boscowitz, that you can't understand. It 's not for you, sir, to presume so far. She shall hear nothing of all this until it 's passed, if she does then. It 's the first and deepest duty of a man to protect a woman absolutely from this form of insult. If anybody you please has misused her name, her name, sir, is sacred, as sacred as God's word. And she shall never know that it 's been profaned, if I can keep her from it."

"But you can't keep her from it. The thing has plainly gone too far. She 'll soon hear of it. Why not from you?"

"I 'm not so sure the thing 's gone that far yet," answered Alonzo, grimly. "At all events, I 'm thinking you 'd better do your own level best to keep it from going any further." He looked at Boscowitz darkly, and again a little suspiciously.

"Mr. Eldon," began Boscowitz once more, "I 've tried to serve you faithfully. I 've kept everything as quiet as I could. I 've aided in suppressing this item, I 've quieted Chatterly, I 've come directly to you. If you don't believe me, ask Chatterly himself. As for the gossip that 's now going, I can't help that" (Boscowitz, of course, had privately set it going). "You may hear of it soon, in any way you chance to. I can't prevent its spreading. I only ask you to meet the thing squarely. What can you do? Mere sitting here and talking of sacred names is lovely, but it is n't war. You want to crush this gossip, at once. How can you do so? Only by finding who 's to blame for it, and crushing him. I 've no doubt myself that Harold 's to blame. But you can't expect him to say so himself. Your son 's absent. Escott can't help you. What remains? Go to Mrs. Eldon, and lay the thing before her. I know it 's hard. I 'd give my eyes, sir, to prevent the necessity. But then, what 's kindest to people? To let trouble gather round 'em without warning, to treat 'em as if they were children? Or to say plainly, 'You 're in danger: face it, explain the cause of it, fight your way out of it.' If I were n't quite straightforward, sir, in my goings-on with you, an appeal to Mrs. Eldon would be my last thought. It 's for her own good that I ask it. She 's no mere girl, sir. She 's an extraordinarily able, thoughtful, business-like, cool-headed woman. She understands the business details of her own estate as few men know their personal enterprises. She 'll comprehend and deal with this present complication as if it were a new money matter. Go to her, sir. Don't fear. Don't hesitate. Ask her a plain question, that paper being meanwhile in your hand. Begin the investigation with her. I have perfect confidence in her, sir. I *know* she 's all right. I ask this for her own sake."

Boscowitz's air of honesty was, indeed, irresistible. And in fact the editor had an honest element in his desire for this appeal to Mrs. Eldon. As he was fully convinced that the intimacy was really a dangerous thing, he had confidence enough in Margaret's strength of feeling to be sure that, if surprised by this bit of printer's proof, she could not fail to show much agitation. And this would tend to give the whole matter a new seriousness in Eldon's eyes. But even if Margaret were quite innocent, then surely she would show indignation against Harold. In any case, Alonzo Eldon's own anxiety, in his son's absence, to do the best possible thing for the family honor would surely force the old man to some hasty course of conduct. Thereby he must be expected to anger Escott, and to bring about serious trouble with Harold. What further might have to be attempted Boscowitz could find out as time went on. The result, at all events, of these last remarks of Boscowitz's was that Alonzo reluctantly yielded, and, by the close of the interview, he had promised to mention the matter to his daughter-in-law first of all.

How wearily Alonzo passed through the business of the rest of that troubled morning it would be hard to say. He spent more than an hour with his private secretary, giving orders about a mass of correspondence. Then it was needful to deal with a long procession of minor business callers. Alonzo disposed of them very rapidly and peremptorily. None of them had made previous appointments with him. None of them, to-day, as it chanced, were even interesting people. They had complaints, proposals, suggestions, queries, begging missions, and the like. He dealt with them all not ungenerously, and yet very shortly. To them, no doubt, their various purposes were worth a great deal. In many cases they had pondered for days about this meeting with the omnipotent Eldon. To him, on this occasion, however, they seemed like so many ugly painted pictures. They all belonged to various well-known classes, and he treated them accordingly. What he dealt out to them was usually justice, but he was hardly conscious of the fact to-day, nor of anything, save his new and weary load of care. When these necessary cases were disposed of, and Eldon had refused or postponed, in addition, twice as many more applications for a chance to see him, he gave some further directions to his secretary, and announced that he should not return in the afternoon. Then he left his office.

It was his custom to lunch at home, but why should he now go to the great house on the hill? He wanted no lunch, and he did need to see Margaret. Moreover, through the time that he had lost in Boscowitz's company, he had let his lunch-hour long pass by before leaving his office. There was nothing to do but to set out for East Oakland forthwith. Meanwhile, Alonzo felt very much exhausted, very ill at ease, very anxious. He had a dull sense that he must have forgotten something, he knew not what. His mind was full of forebodings. He was also afraid lest he might meet some one on the boat, and be approached concerning matters of importance. He felt sure that in that case he would make great mistakes. Only one thing was quite clear to him, namely, that Margaret must be perfect, and that, whoever might be to blame for this new calamity, she, at least, was innocent. But to think that her name should become the sport of worthless gossip! The notion was horrible to him. Ever since he had first surrendered himself to her charm, she had been his highest ideal of womanhood. Why must some wretch try to cast a shadow on this perfect being?

As for the blame, he had only an imperfect assurance, as yet, where that could lie. Boscowitz, of course, was a man of no principle. That Eldon knew. But then, surely, Boscowitz had no reason to assault Margaret's fair fame. Boscowitz would not dare! Then, also, Boscowitz had given every token of honesty. The proof-sheet was certainly in the well-known and peculiar typography of Chatterly's paper. The most natural explanation was that, at all events, such gossip was current. Was Harold, then, to blame? Apparently. For it must be either Harold alone, or both the friends together. And both it could not be. The natural inference is that if the friendship of an undoubtedly innocent woman with a given man is unfavorably commented upon by malicious strangers, the man must be to blame. But to blame for what this time? For vile boasting, as Boscowitz had said? If so, a pistol ought to make short work of the boaster. Or for giving any other occasion, through his conduct or through his foolish speeches, whereby others might frame absurd and malicious slanders? Then, in any case, one must forevermore avoid him, as a dangerous companion. But Eldon had been trusting him, and becoming intimate with him. And, again, that poem, was it not, after all, a really indiscreet sort of publication? Boscowitz's ideas were, no doubt, absurd. Boscowitz was no true judge of poetry! But how much less disagreeable it would be, at this crisis, if Harold had been printing no foolish verses of late! These verses had no real personal bearing, — of that Alonzo was sure. They were too fanciful. People do not write poetry, he thought, about live women, but only about made-up women. Yet malice could misconstrue such things. If Harold had only avoided every faintest appearance of evil! Apparently, however, he had done quite the reverse.

The more Alonzo thought of the matter, the less he liked Harold's share in it. After all, why need this man be forcing his presence upon this family, in any case? If he had not come, nobody could be accusing him of too much friendship with Margaret. Innocent or guilty, he was at best the actual cause of this thing. And what was this thing? Margaret's dear name, suggested, in the vilest connection, to the readers of the worst weekly in San Francisco! Nay, but the article had not actually been published! What matter? Save for Boscowitz it would have been published. Such were Alonzo's thoughts as he prepared for his journey to Margaret's house.

CHAPTER XIV.

THE TRAGEDY OF THE HOUSE OF ELDON.

SINCE the day of the ride, there had been, between Harold and Margaret, no talk of keeping wholly apart. They had soon begun to wonder why they had ever thought of such a thing. To break off all intercourse, without any visible reason, would it not have been merely to excite suspicion? Would it not have been a wanton sacrifice of their true duty? They had a manifold work to accomplish; and they could only accomplish it together. It was a work for themselves, for Margaret's child, for Escott, for the magazine, for the settlers. Heaven had ordained for them this work. Dared they slight it merely because Heaven had also sent them this mutual love? They were guiltless as touching this love; so much they both felt. They had not foreseen it, nor chosen it. It had simply come to them, because they were meant for each other from the beginning, and because they had been separated only by the evil fortune of their lives. When they had once met, what could they have done but submit to fate and to this love? Meanwhile, the very harmony of nature that had thus bound them to each other now made them capable of working together in those manifold tasks. Could they bury their common talent, and prove false to their appointed trusts, merely because their love was as dangerous as it was precious? No, so they felt; they must risk the danger and enjoy the pain of this dear and agonizing friendship; they must do so for the sake of their duty, if for no other reason. Meanwhile, were they not both strong? Was there, after all, any true danger? They were their own rulers; they were safe in their pride, in their sense of duty, in their very loyalty to each other. Nothing should ever pass between them henceforth, they had resolved, save what all the world might, if it chose, know without a shadow of disapproval. They might meet almost daily, but they would be quite careless whether they met alone or in the company of others. Their secret was safe, their mutual understanding perfect. Their task might grow very hard, as time went on. But that would not be their fault. It would be only their destiny. And in coming often to the house Harold had felt himself no violator of hospitality. Had not the peace of this household already been wrecked when he first entered it? What had he done save to try to be a true friend to the family? And if thereupon the discovery of this love had been granted to him, yet surely Margaret needed him now as much as before. And his going away could not help Tom. As for Harold's relations to Margaret from this time forth, the young man had often said to himself, in these days, that Tom might, if he chose, be present all through every one of their conversations, might hear every tone and study every glance, without detecting the smallest thing that could give just offense to the most jealous heart. Their confessions had now, once for all, been made; the fatal words could not be unsaid, nor yet repeated, nor ever forgotten. Their hearts might ache; but never more should their eyes or their lips give a sign of the truth, though the truth would always be filling their minds whenever they were together. Why, then, should Harold doubt his right to remain Tom's friend, and to visit the house as often as Tom and Margaret desired?

So things had in fact gone on until this very day. Margaret was alone, and, not far from the hour of Boscowitz's interview with Eldon, Harold came to see her, very weary and much harassed. He had, in fact, just been misled into publishing in his magazine, through some strange oversight, a stolen article, which a certain ambitious young man of promise had copied, and sent in. The thing, of course, looked plain enough when once the magazine was out, and Harold was as much pained by the discovery as Boscowitz had been rejoiced. Margaret, however, seemed that day to be in the best of humors; and her cheerfulness soon partially restored Harold to himself. Her laugh he had always found one of the most charming things about her, and when she fell to-day into her old gay fashion of making fun of all the world, she became perfectly irresistible. He could have knelt at her feet and worshiped her. He began before long to feel, in the transformation of his mood, very young and careless, and even boyish, and to find all the fresh charm of a first love coloring this present intercourse. His manner grew as gay as hers. He told old stories, confided to her childish fancies of many years ago, and gloried in the sense that all his ancient illusions were nothing to him now in the presence of this, the master passion of his life. Suddenly he became aware that a long time had passed since he had arrived. He had carelessly endangered an afternoon engagement in the city. He rose to go, feeling the anxious shock that comes to a man when he recalls such an accident. He turned towards the window, and with the sight of the outer world all the chagrin, the depression, the self-contempt, with which he had come to-day swept back over him like a flood. He looked again very gloomy and weary.

"This has been indeed a poor May," said Margaret, in rising to bid him farewell. "Somehow I always feel rebellious at the quick flight of our little spring, as the drought comes on."

Harold looked up at her despairingly. "Life seems very like the long drought whenever I am not here," he answered, simply.

"No, no, Mr. Harold," she said, still smiling

(it was by this name that she had required herself still to address him). "I thought you had just determined not to be cast down. You 'd grown courageous since you came to-day. I can't allow this long face as you go away. I shall feel, after all, as if you 'd been attending a funeral here, instead of joking with me."

"Oh, Margaret," he burst out, feeling suddenly very lonesome in the presence of all the gayety of her face and manner, "if I might only, once in a long while, — when I am with you, — speak out my real mind! It is so hard to be confined to mere business and to joking. I have been feeling so anxious and desolate lately. And yet you will not let me tell you anything. I may not confide in you any more. You have forbidden me."

"Confide in me, Mr. Harold?" she queried, a little coldly, becoming at once very sober. "You speak as if I took no care for your comfort or your cheer. I had thought" (she stood looking down now, and seemed offended), "I had thought I was trying my best to please you. I am sorry if my little arts are of no worth in your eyes. They are all I have." She became, of a sudden, much agitated. Harold repented instantly of his words.

"Margaret, forgive me if I speak so, and forgive me, too, for breaking now our little treaty. It is hard, — somehow I cannot always be true to myself, or to you. I am unkind and peevish. But if you knew" —

"If I knew, Mr. Harold." Margaret seemed to struggle with herself. Then she went on: "I can forgive you anything. But you surely do know, — neither of us has these things to bear alone. I thought you had made up your mind. But if *you* lose courage, Mr. Harold, how shall I" — She stopped short, and looked down again, joining her hands in a nervous, uneasy clasp.

"Margaret, how long must we — how long can we — endure this life of lies in which we have called it our duty to exist, we who love each other? Oh, how long?"

"Always, Mr. Harold. Please do not call me Margaret. It is not right. That was not to be any more. It was on that understanding that we said we could dare to meet again." Margaret's voice was very quiet and despairing. Harold knew not what to say, and she went on, after a little, turning away as she did so, and looking out of the window, towards the hills: —

"I cannot see why you speak so, after all. There is something impatient in your voice. I don't know, — you seem somehow angry with me. Am I to blame? You said once, when we made our 'little treaty,' as you call it, that it was comfort enough to see each other in an ordinary way every few days. We could live so, you said, for years, without any word of — without any word like these that we are now speaking. I knew nothing about it. I thought you must know what it means to be strong. I trusted you. So long as you are strong I can be. But — when I hear that tone in your voice, and you seem to complain of me, and feel bitter towards me, and" — Margaret's voice faltered. She seemed near crying.

"No! no!" cried Harold, "I beg you not to speak so. I was feeling stupid to-day, and was unmanly enough to say what I did. But I meant — oh, you must surely *know* that I meant no kind of bitterness towards you. It is this terrible life that I can't bear." He had come once more nearer to her, but she kept her face turned towards the window and her hands tightly clasped. She even drew back a little, as if afraid of him.

"It 's I that am the weaker, no doubt," she went on. "I complain and accuse you, and am peevish beyond endurance. But if you could only know! You call this a life of lies; what is it for me, who see him day after day, and eat at his table, and am supposed to be his wife? I thought I was strong. I'm not. I only speak so because when *you* seem weak all the ground melts from under me, and I 'm lost. But oh, at the best, even when I 've most faith in you, I pass long, sleepless nights, full of terror and — and of crying. The loneliness is unbearable. Sometimes I think I shall go mad. I have fancies that I dare n't tell you, — fancies about Ellen Escott. Sometimes I wonder if it is n't her spirit that is avenging her wrongs upon me. The idea is so childish! I 've struggled with it — oh, so hard! There was something that happened the night she died, — but I can't tell you that; I 've sworn an oath to myself never to tell anybody." Harold was terrified at her voice now. She had turned, and was looking at him. He had not fancied that she could have just that expression of face. He was afraid that she would faint. He started, as if to support her; but she drew back again, half unconsciously, and went on: —

"But when that fear I just spoke of comes over me, I lie trembling in bed for hours. It is as it was when I was a child, and feared the dark. Once — oh, don't be afraid, I'm not really in danger of going mad. I know myself. I know all my fancies. They will never be too strong for me. But once, after that day of our last ride, I dreamed of poor Ellen all night, the most fearful dreams. And then when I started up from one of them I saw her — oh, so long it seemed after I was awake that I could n't drive away the sight — I saw her all white and dead, and so beautiful, standing beside my bed. No, dearest, don't be afraid. I know what it was, well enough. Have n't I had nightmares all my life, and dream-sights that lasted a little after I was awake? I'm not superstitious; but if I know it was only fancy, it came all the same. And I, dearest, I was all alone in the dark. But when such things come to me, then, as soon as I can get over my agonizing fright and tremble, I get up and steal away to my baby, or bring him to me. And then I can bear it and sleep. For when he comes, dearest, I can some way — find my tears — and then I feel more peaceful, and can rest. That, you must know, is how I have to live. It is n't anything, I grant, except what I ought to bear.

It 's not your fault; please don't look so unhappy about it. I never meant to tell you. It 's not your fault, only don't, oh don't think that I live without feeling every day — yes, every day — how lonesome, how bitter, how cruel, this life of ours is.

"And yet, no, again — please don't misunderstand me, love," she went on. "It 's such a happy life now, when I think how dull and cold and heartless and dead I was before you came. I was a lifeless being; and that Sunday, — it is as if your voice and your goodness raised me that day from the dead. I never knew life till I knew you. I had no youth. I was always old. I have lived like a child born and brought up in the wilderness. You, dearest, have been my one spring of water. You have taught me to be something like a true mother. You 've taught me all, yes, all I know of life. I used to wonder about love, — what it was. And sometimes I thought it would be very bright and peaceful and joyous, just like the life of little children. *I* thought this — *I* did. I, who 'd been twice married, and who knew my world as a guide knows a picture-gallery. I never saw anything in life till I saw your eyes, dearest; yes, until I heard your voice. And now I do know what love is, — something very terrible, and full of anguish and struggle, and as bitter as death, darling, and as sweet as the light.

"Forgive me for all this. It was just what I must never speak of; just what you were never to hear. It 's death to say such words. I feel it.

I 'm a guilty wife, who should be killed, if justice were done her. I 'm not worthy to be the mother of my child. But now, somehow, I 've told you all this. I had to, though I 'd sworn not to. So I must tell you yet one thing more." Margaret turned from the window towards him, and suddenly seized one of his hands, and then held it tightly and very still. He was as if in a trance. She seemed to him like one come from some other world.

"Oh, dearest," she said, "I have for my one greatest joy these times when you come to see me. When you know that, you will forgive me for being so bitter to-day. If anything happens to mar the joy, I feel as if the world were all so dark! It makes me cold and cruel again. When I know that you are coming, the house seems so cheerful. Everything is light. I plan what we shall do, where you shall sit. Yes, — it is so foolish, — but I plan what you shall say, and how you shall look. Then, if you are going to dine with us, I think so much about everything that is to be ready for you. My mind is so full! I can hardly rest for thinking of you. I walk to and fro all over the house. I sing. I am so joyous. And yet this is so simple, so childish, I hardly dare say it, you will laugh at me; but when you come, if it seems that I don't please you, that all I do for you only leaves you grieved and even angry with me, why, then, what is left me? What is left me but to wish, oh, so fiercely, that I were dead, and that this, which you call a life of lies, were all over? It is, yes, it *is* a life of lies; but, my only love, you must know that this life is all I have, or ever shall have. It is my last possession. When that is lost, when you get weary of me and go away, as you ought to do and will do, I shall have nothing left, — nothing!" She dropped his hand only at these last words.

Margaret had been near weeping now for some moments. When she finished, she, who so seldom showed strong emotion, flung herself once more into her chair, and cried as if her heart would break. But Harold fell at her feet, and seized her hand and covered it with kisses. A moment later he had left the house. They never met but once again.

On his way over to Oakland that day, Alonzo Eldon, while on the boat, sat in a remote corner, and buried himself in his copy of the first edition of an evening paper, defying the approach of acquaintances. At the railway station he found awaiting him the hired carriage for which he had telegraphed, and he was driven at once to the house on the hillside. He was not expected, that he knew; yet no doubt Margaret was at home. Suppose he should meet Harold there! The thought was unpleasant, yet it was ungrounded. In fact, when he came he found that, besides Margaret, only a lady caller, a near neighbor of Margaret's, was at the house. The two ladies joyously greeted Alonzo, who, as usual, entered without ringing. He was a great stranger! He was so welcome! Surely he must stay until evening. Margaret, who was very pale, was meanwhile trying to tell him that her mother was coming to dine to-night, together with this very neighbor, and that Alonzo would be such a welcome addition to the little company. They had in vain tried, she was going to say, to get any man, and had supposed Alonzo of late far too busy to be invited on a week-day. Mother, Margaret meant to add, was expected on the very next train. All this she was trying to get a chance to say, but she could not yet more than begin it, for her vivacious neighbor was so full of conversation. This lady had a flood of little things to tell for Alonzo's amusement, a torrent of questions to ask him. It was so long since she had seen him! They were always such good friends when they met! She had for ages been meaning to tell him this and that! Poor Alonzo sat, meanwhile, uncommonly awkward and half dazed. He replied as he could to the visitor's talk; but Margaret, as she watched him, grew anxious about him. Could he have been over-exerting himself recently? He plainly needed cheering and comforting. Before the neighbor had finished Margaret had almost forgotten about the little dinner. As her first business, she had determined to find out, at the earliest chance, what was the matter with Alonzo.

But erelong the caller rose. She must go home now, and return for the dinner. She had a little business of her own to look out for, she said to Margaret, laughing. Alonzo wondered why she laughed. It was no doubt some trifling womanish affair, but women, he thought, look so deep and full of intrigue when they smile mysteriously at each other over their little plots. Could it have anything to do with Harold? How suspicious he was growing! He had been half unconsciously watching Margaret's face while the visitor talked. There was something, he fancied, a little hard and cold about it. Was Margaret beginning to grow old? She looked too worldly; yes, he had never thought of it before, she looked *too* self-possessed. The dark brown eyes were deep, to be sure, but could they not be deep for intrigue, as well as for thoughtfulness-? God forbid! And yet, in those clear-cut features there were already appearing, were there not, the first traces of the lines of age. There was a certain too firm look about the mouth, a lack of the old incomparable sweetness and gentleness when she was sitting silently watching those near her. Alas! could it be that Margaret was becoming less perfect? Alonzo had loved too few things in the world to be used to any decay of his idols. Change seemed to him now, even, as it seems to sentimental young people, a horrible fault to detect in what one loves. He felt rebellious at the least suggestion of such a thing.

Well, the lady was taking leave at last! Alonzo rose mechanically to say farewell. She was to return soon, she said. That was odd, so he thought, in his present confused way. If she was to return soon, why did she go? He could not make it clear to himself. He must be very weary. He remembered now: he had not felt well, even at breakfast, and had eaten hardly anything. And he had also gone without lunch. He was faint. Yet he was not hungry. And, besides, should a great strong man like himself be put out in this way by the loss of a meal or two? In the old campaign with Frémont's battalion he had once gone for two whole days with only — But, nonsense! How was he replying to the visitor? No matter, he had got through it somehow, and she was gone. Thank God!

But just as she left, Margaret seemed also to be called away by something. She returned in a moment, looking troubled as well as weary.

"I'm so sorry," she began. "Here is a telegram from mother, who was to have been here this evening. She cannot come. I wanted her to be here ever so much. But surely, father, you will stay — Oh, there! I forgot. You don't know what it was. I must tell you."

He was standing, watching her curiously, but attending with the greatest difficulty to her words. "No, Margaret, I can't stay," he said. "My carriage is waiting for me. I must go back to town, almost at once. I had come" — He was speaking very slowly, and Margaret interrupted him with anxiety.

"What is it, then, father?" she queried. "You are not looking well; something worries you."

"No, no," he answered hastily, controlling himself with yet more difficulty. "What was that you were saying? Was it company this evening?"

"Oh, no, only mother and my neighbor. If mother had not failed, they were going to dine with me, and then we were going to talk literature afterwards. By the way, I wish you had been here the other evening before Tom left. There was a little gathering of friends at the house, and Mr. Harold read to us. He is, you know, something of a reader, and I should have been so glad to have you hear" —

Alonzo cared nothing for the rest of this speech. He listened to it word by word, as it came, but it meant nothing to him. It was rather a long speech, and during the course of it Margaret made him sit down. Plainly she was trying to interest him, in her usual way, by telling him about her plans and her friends. Only why should Harold be so prominent on the list? Alonzo observed, meanwhile, about himself, that he had a dull headache, which must have been going on for some hours without his thinking to name it before. Meanwhile, he felt sure that for the moment he was hating Harold out and out. His temper was very bad this afternoon.

He interrupted Margaret at length. He could not himself say whether or no he did it too abruptly: —

"I could n't have come that evening, Margaret, in any case. I thank you, but I 'll not meet Harold, if you please, at all, for the present."

"Why, father!" Margaret turned pale.

Alonzo began afresh, after a moment, feeling that, now he had come to the topic, it was impossible, spite of all his determination, to go on freely. He felt calm enough, to be sure. He was only sluggish, and his thoughts came stupidly. But he urged them a trifle. "In all frankness, Margaret, I regard some of Harold's recent conduct as deserving a degree of — if I may say so — suspicion. Until some matters are cleared up, I 'll not feel precisely justified (to use a mild form of language) in sitting at meat with him."

He had committed himself now, assuming all the old-fashioned dignity that he could summon to his aid. Yet he was aware that she was very much excited, and that his own eyes must look at this instant very cowardly. She did not even make a reply. She must be furious. She sat calmly awaiting his defense of himself. For plainly it was now no matter of onslaught from his side. He felt that he was already hiding behind his own intrenchments. Yet she had not uttered a syllable since he last spoke! He must continue as he could.

"In the first place, Margaret, I have a certain amount of what I regard as considerable evidence, which leads me to suspect that Mr. Harold has been taking advantage, in a certain sense, of me personally, not to mention those whom I lead and represent, in the course of this extremely wearisome and harassing and complicated Oakfield Creek affair. He ought to be aiding me in every way. On the contrary, Margaret, if the information of which I have just come into possession is correct, Mr. Harold has been not only hindering me, but taking a serious advantage of my embarrassments." All this, Alonzo felt, was, as had frequently happened in his more serious talks with Margaret, very ill-expressed. He had been much more brief and direct when he disposed so swiftly of that long procession of business callers to-day. But if he ever felt opposed to Margaret in any way, it was hard to be direct with her. He must needs be diffuse. Moreover, as he also observed, he was just now not only diffuse, but also disingenuous. He had no notion upon what Boscowitz had founded that accusation as to Harold's unfairness in the Oakfield Creek business. Alonzo had not believed it when he heard it. Margaret listened to the accusation calmly and sternly.

"In what way has he done this?" Her voice as she spoke was very cold, but her face showed her suppressed indignation.

"By buying in settlers' claims at low rates, so as to get in his own person the profit of my sacrifices for them."

"It is false!" said Margaret, fiercely. "Who has told you this, father? I *know* it to be false." As she grew warmer, Alonzo felt a certain insane suspicion of her already striving to find expression in his words.

"And what 's more," Alonzo went on, obstinately, "he 's been cheapening those claims by having very secretly a hand in this McAlpin business and in the Brotherhood of Noble Rangers.

By thus creating an unfounded sense of general insecurity, he has been able to get the settlers to part with their claims cheap to him and his confederates."

"Father, you should simply be ashamed of yourself to credit any of this for one instant of Harold. He 's the soul of honor! You know, father, that, on the face of this, it 's wildly absurd."

"It 's my information," responded Alonzo, curtly.

"But come, confess that your information means simply Boscowitz." Margaret had now begun to plead with him. She was, meanwhile, trying to pardon his bearing towards her.

"I must be permitted, Margaret, to judge of the trustworthiness of my sources of information myself. That 's my part. I tell you what I 've felt warranted in holding to be the at least probable facts, disagreeable as they are."

"Yet now *do* confess. It surely *was* just Boscowitz, was n't it?" Margaret's manner was a mixture of anxiety and wrath and expostulation. "How excited she is on his behalf!" thought Alonzo, gloomily! "Not exclusively Boscowitz," he answered, after an instant's pause. This was to all intents and purposes a lie, but Alonzo tried to justify it to himself by the fact that the entire thing hung together, and that not Boscowitz alone, but the whole chain of evidence, in which that bit of proof was the chief link, actually did seem to him to support this among the other conclusions.

Yet it was surely ominous that he had dared to lie to Margaret.

"Father," she went on, her anger rising as she spoke, "I must really remind you that, in speaking thus of Harold, and in giving no reasons for what you say, you are not alone maltreating your friend Harold himself, but you are doing a personal injury to me."

"Why, Margaret?"

"Mr. Harold, father, is my most trusted and honored friend outside of my own family. To insult his honor is to insult mine."

"Margaret" (Alonzo spoke now very coldly, and with a sort of a shudder at the sight of her earnestness), "these are, if you 'll allow me, very warm words to use about a person whom you have come to know so recently. He is an acquaintance of yours, whom we all have found an amusing talker, and an apparently" —

"He is my dearest friend, and I will not hear him maligned. I may be a very wicked woman, father, in other respects, but in this, at least, I am decently honorable, namely, that I am loyal to my friends. And Harold is no common friend. He is a great deal to me, — indeed he is."

"Margaret," Alonzo replied, feeling for the moment, in his worry and exhaustion, simply helpless before his own emotions, "would you say this as plainly to your husband?"

"Father!" Margaret rose to her feet in wrath. He had never seen her look so lovely or so terrible; he felt at once as if he had sinned away his eternal salvation. How could he have dared to speak so? Yet something about her manner was very shocking to his mood. "I do not forget," she said, bitterly, "who you are. I have honored and loved you all these years. I have nothing to blame myself for in our dealings together. I do not know what is the matter with you now. I will not reproach you. But this is what no woman will listen to or can endure. Tell me what you mean, or let me go." She was actually going as she spoke. Alonzo rose to call her back.

"You must forgive me, Margaret," he cried. "I truly meant nothing. Please do not leave me. You don't know how troubled I am this afternoon." Of course his impulsive question must have been an outrage! In a sane moment he could not have dared it! He must make amends.

She turned, with an expression of wonder at his strange tone, and seemed to be sympathizing with him a little. But he dared not look at her any more. He stood with his eyes cast down. She spoke again, and a little more kindly. Both still remained standing.

"If you are tired, father, or ill, or anything of that sort, please say so. I don t mean to speak unkindly. But what you just said — and your tone — I could not bear it! What do you mean? Have I too offended you? Why do you come to-day, in such a strange fashion, and try to malign my best friends to me? And then, when I defend them, as I must, why do you say intolerable things? This is not yourself. I have never found you so before. Some one has been slandering us. We are not afraid of slanders. Only we ask that *you* should not come to throw such things in our faces."

The *us* and the *our* grated again harshly upon Alonzo. His anger returned. If he must offend her, why not let it go on to the end? He answered rather sharply: —

"Nobody has mentioned any slanders against Tom, Margaret."

"Why do you say this?"

"Because you, Margaret, said, '*We* are not afraid of slanders.' Nobody referred to any slanders against this household as a whole, nor threw anything in what you call '*our faces.*'"

This was an awkward sally, but Alonzo had no time to choose his retort better. Margaret paused a little, as if measuring his words. Then she continued, growing once more cold and stern: —

"Well, I will say, '*I* fear no slanders,' if you like that better. And since you still go on in this way, I want to ask you plainly, father, why at one instant you appeal to my pity, and beg me to stay, and say you are in some unspeakable trouble, and why, then, when I try to have patience with you, you return to this cold tone, and make fresh suggestions of suspicion and slander. If you have any ground for this, tell me at once, or else please spare me altogether."

"Margaret," replied Alonzo, with a great effort to be full and clear, "the fact is simply this: I want to know of you whether, in case I plainly showed you that Harold has betrayed your interests as well as mine, has played false to your good name and to my affection for you as well as to my business confidence in him, — I want to know whether your friendship with him is such that *then*, Margaret, you 'd drop him utterly, despise him, scorn him, hate him. I want to know that. Or again, I want to know whether, against the plainest proof, the clearest evidence, the most damning facts, you 'd hold by him, talk of him as your dearest friend in this unhappy way, and side with him against the world. *That 's* what I want to know. Won't you please tell me?"

This was the point where, as Alonzo thought, Margaret would surely use that good sense of hers. She would meet such an issue fairly. She would show of what stuff her feeling for Harold was made, by answering shortly and simply. As yet, however, she did nothing of the kind. She was moved indeed by his earnestness; her face had even lost its indignant look. But she would not answer him directly.

"Father," she began, changing her manner once more to the pleading one, "I see clearly now that you must have been deceived by some vile enemy. This Boscowitz, surely, has been maligning poor Mr. Harold. How warm and true a friend of yours Mr. Harold is only I myself have had a chance to know. Really, I will tell you, he confides everything of importance about this affair to me. It 's because of this Oakfield Creek affair that we have become — that we have remained — I should say

— so much — of late — in each other's company. So I know well, indeed I do, every feeling of his about this whole matter. He has the most delicate appreciation of your perplexities, the warmest desire, father, to lighten them. How often have we not talked together about this whole thing, and regretted that it was so painful to you! How often have we not planned to set your mind at rest, as to all the perplexities that we knew of! Now, therefore, please do *not* come to me with suspicions of him! If you knew his true character, as I do! *I* have never dreamt of a more loyal nature! I have in vain looked elsewhere for his qualities. And yet you believe slanders of him. They even betray you into saying cruel things to me, things which you cannot possibly mean. I am ready to forget all that. I see how worried you are to-day, how sad, and tired, and gloomy. I do indeed forgive you for all you have said. Only listen to me now. When people say absurd things about Mr. Harold, come to *me*, father, come to *me*. Do not believe such nonsense. I simply *know* to the contrary. I think that there are really few persons in whom he has ever confided as he has been led to confide in me."

A stranger would have seen in her beautiful earnestness only a proof of her innocence. Alonzo watched it with a still growing feeling of gloomy suspicion. He had presented to her the plain issue, and she had avoided it. And how her face was glowing as she defended Harold! Surely she had never looked in this way when she spoke of Tom. This was no common friendship.

"See here, Margaret," he said at last, and grimly interrupting her, "I'm not the man to understand all these profound confidences which you seem to be explaining. My notion is that a man who's admitted as a sort of a chance acquaintance into another man's house ought to confine himself, as it were, pretty strictly to open and above-board business while he's there. But just now, as you've mentioned confidences, I want to ask you a question about one of them. Perhaps I'm foolish. My head, I grant, is in a general mix to-day, and things keep coming to me wrong end foremost. I have n't yet even touched on what I came to tell you first of all. But no matter. There's a foolish question that bothers me, and I must out with it, plain and blunt. Harold tells you everything, does he? He confides in you as he does n't in anybody else? Very well; did he ever tell you, Margaret, who that woman was for whose benefit he wrote that sickly, woebegone, sentimental poem of his, in the last number of his 'Monthly?'" Alonzo's voice had assumed a tone such as he never before could have adopted towards Margaret: it was rough and harsh, and almost fierce. His emotions had again carried him away. He felt that he was desecrating his own idol, but what could he do? How beautiful she was, meanwhile, in all her wrath! And she did not turn now, nor try to run away. They were still both standing, he at the back of a chair, she beyond the table. She, however, looked at him with a sort of indignant pity.

"Have you any more just cause to give than this," she said, calmly, "for this intolerable way in which you dare speak to me?"

"Well, no doubt the poem is nothing. What 's a poem but a lie? But there are other lies in the world, Margaret, too. And I 'm not afraid now to say to you whatever I must. I 'm wrought up at last. I came here not to hurt your feelings, — God forbid! I came here as your father and friend, and as the natural guardian of the peace of my son's home during his absence. I came here to help you. I did n't want to anger you. I wanted to put plain facts before you. I trusted, Margaret, in your good sense to take things in a right spirit. I came to you as I 've so often come before, to consult with you, to advise with you, to reason together, as it were. Oh, how often, Margaret, when I 've come you 've been different to me: you 've enlightened me and helped me, and I 've grown to look up to you so, and reverence you, — yes, reverence you!" Alonzo's voice choked, but he recovered himself at once. "And now, Margaret, I came quite sincerely, and I was going to lay before you extremely kindly and discreetly the facts in this case; but you fly out at me so! Why? Because you 're so fond of this Harold, so it seems. I don't understand that. I 'm only a simple-minded old man, and you 're a very wise woman; but I don't just approve it. I can't. It seems to me you ought n't to speak that warmly of any man, Margaret, that 's not your husband. And this Harold is, comparatively speaking, a stranger, I may say. Yes, *comparatively* speaking, he 's a stranger. No matter! Perhaps I must n't talk of that. I see it excites me, and may be I adopt, as it were, a tone of reproach and animadversion, Margaret, that afterwards I should regret. You 're wiser than I am. I ought n't to be blaming you. But I'll leave that, anyhow. It 's too much for me, in my present mood, to quite justly deal with. The facts, however, which I was going to present were, to-day, just these. I don't doubt but there 's more behind. Only *to-day* these were what the state of my information enabled me to present to you. And so, as I say, I was going, extremely kindly and discreetly, I hope, Margaret, to show you a clear evidence, and of what? Evidence of the fact that Harold 's been *slandering* your fair name, Margaret, — your name, that I and my son would die to save from the least breath of scorn or disrespect, — slandering your name by boastful and impudent speeches about you, in the city of San Francisco, to his young friends, Margaret, to persons who 've access to the most debased representative of the press of that city. This little newspaper article, Margaret, shows him up in his true light. He, as this shows, is" —

Alonzo had begun to take the slip out of his pocket as he spoke; but Margaret interrupted his words so fiercely that he paused.

"These are impudent falsehoods that you repeat to me here, father! I will listen to no single word of them." Her voice fairly hissed defiance and rage as she spoke. Alonzo started as if he had been shot, and his hands dropped by his sides again. He stood helplessly watching her.

"But, Margaret," he began again, at the end of a little pause, and as if trying blindly to recover his position after a fall, "you see I meant for your own sake — quite in a spirit of kindness — I assure you — to warn you against — the machinations" —

"Say no word more of my friends, sir, now or henceforth." The thought that Harold must be himself the object of newspaper slander was, meanwhile, the only clear one in her mind.

"Yet, Margaret, indeed, I appeal to you, for the love of your faithful husband, who is away from you, do not speak so hastily, so frantically. I can assure you I can almost prove to you even now — I can make plain to you that all the evidence points that way — I can, I hope, convince you beyond a reasonable doubt, so that you 'll see — Oh, remember my dear son's honor! I can assure you that he would now agree with me about this Harold. I know you love Tom dearly, and it 's now only a moment of excitement! Don't betray in any way his interests, his affection" —

"I tell you, I *hate* your son, and it 's he who long since betrayed *my* affections!" Her nervous weariness and her alarm for Harold had proved too much for her at last.

Alonzo staggered back a step. "Margaret," he cried, "you *can't* mean that. My son betray your affections?"

"You know how and when. Surely you remember Ellen Escott."

"But that was an unfortunate, a most lamentable misunderstanding, and Tom" —

"I tell you, it was the basest of betrayals, both of her and of me. And as for this Tom, I hate him."

"But this is something new, Margaret, surely. This was never heard of before."

"The hatred is as old as the crime, sir." Her voice was under complete control now. Whenever she once felt herself at a crisis of her fate, she was always as brave as a lion. She knew at this moment that the end had come, and she rejoiced in it. Of any consequences she had not now the faintest expectation or dread. What this supposed new evidence might be she also cared not one whit. She only saw that Harold was in very serious danger, that he was slandered, maligned, hated, and that he was even the object of some miserable assault in what Alonzo had just called the basest of San Francisco papers. She knew that she must stand beside her friend to the last. She thought only of Harold's interests. And she knew that this old man before her had joined Harold's enemies, and was accusing him as even Boscowitz would not have dared to accuse him a short time since. She simply abhorred Alonzo at this moment. He was to her only Tom's father and Harold's slanderer. Yet Harold had been recently toiling so hard in this matter of the settlers, and on Alonzo's behalf, to lighten his task, to disarm his enemies! "The hatred, I tell you, is as old as the crime. Do you understand me?" She stood like a warrior at a pause in the battle, perfectly cool and merciless.

Alonzo shook his head, with a dull feeling of terror and disbelief. Surely all these past months and years could not have been one long lie. Alonzo had been dreaming that his son was so happy, had been enjoying so innocently the quiet peace of this perfect household. That old calamity he had thought of as a sad mistake, nobody's serious fault, but only the result of a little natural carelessness on Tom's part, — a lamentable blunder, that Alonzo himself would have been glad to atone for if he could; but never had he conceived of it as in any true sense a crime. That it had been the destroyer of her love for her husband Alonzo could not believe. This fond delight of his own heart a dream! This happy home, during all these years, a delusion! This fair house a dwelling-place of lies and of hatred! No, it could not have been so! This must be Harold's work. That fellow was to blame for this present mood of Margaret's.

"Margaret," Alonzo said at length, in a tone that was almost a wail, "you can't mean this! Your affections have lately been distorted, somehow. You 've been fearfully deceived and misled. This rascal, this wretch of a Harold" —

"Don't speak so of him again in my house," she interrupted, with the same fearful calm in her voice and manner. "Don't dare to mention his name once more in my presence. I tell you, I love him!" Now, she felt sure, she had ended this horrible talk! The words were out! She might regret them for a lifetime, yet she gloried in them now!

But Alonzo stood a long time, with his eyes on the floor, before he could recover his voice or his thoughts. Then at last he spoke, or rather something else seemed to speak with what faintly resembled his voice, and to use his lips in doing so. This voice sounded very frightful. The world was dark before his eyes. He felt awkward, even bashful.

"Pardon me, Mrs. Eldon," this voice was saying to her; "I had — forgotten somehow — as it were — that this is really — your own house — after all. I was thinking it had been the same thing as Tom's house."

Alonzo found his carriage waiting for him by the front steps. He stepped in, and was driven back to the railway.

CHAPTER XV.

WHEN THE LAMP IS SHATTERED.

VERY early one morning, not long afterwards, two horsemen were riding on a road east of the Contra Costa hills. The dawn-light was growing clear. The air of this inland valley, some miles from Oakfield Creek, was crisp and cool. The last stars were fading. Mount Diablo, rising towards the east and southeast, had just ceased to seem so much like a vast and shapeless monster. Its outlines were sharp against the faintly rosy sky, far above the horizon. The meadow-larks and the grosbeaks had begun to sing. A rabbit was busy in the road; and as the two horsemen rounded the curve, it dashed into the long, green grass. Beyond it, as it fled, the horsemen could not have failed to see, had they looked up, the seemingly endless fields, covered with grain or with wild-flowers, and dotted with oaks. These oaks grew with a singular precision of arrangement, as if somebody had long since laid out this but recently wild region as a great park. For many miles there were almost regular intervals between the separate trees,—intervals of about twenty or thirty yards. One could hear occasionally, this morning, as one rode, the musical sound of some wild dove's wing, as the bird flew from one tree to another. Just here, on the road, there were no houses to be seen. Before very long, however, one would reach the settlement at Oakfield Creek. The spring had dealt kindly, so far, with this region. The road was, indeed, already dusty; the drought was coming; the perfect sky overhead meant, before many hours should pass, a hot sun, a parching air, a dreary and dying look in the grass on the higher hill-slopes. Yet, at this moment, one could imagine one's self in an earthly paradise, so full of life, so placid, so maturely vigorous, all nature appeared in this hour before sunrise.

The two horsemen were Escott and Harold. They had ridden as rapidly, during the earlier part of the journey, as the steep hills, now behind them, and the dimness of the night had permitted. Once they had missed their way, by trying to take a shorter road. They had with difficulty found their path again, full of shame that they had so easily lost themselves in what they had supposed to be familiar country. They had then hurried on once more, faster than was actually necessary for their purpose. They must be in Oakfield Creek shortly after sunrise, but why sooner? And now that they were at last sure of being in season, they had slackened their pace, and were giving their weary horses a little indulgence. For the first time during the long ride they had begun to talk together freely. They looked down at the way just before them, as they went, taking little or no notice of the dawn, the birds, the flowers, the vast natural park, the oaks, the noble mountain. They showed no signs of weariness, indeed. Their minds were wide awake and very busy. But their business had as little to do with these things as had that of the rabbit himself.

"It was a stormy talk, that one with poor Alonzo," Escott was saying. "I really pity him now. It seems that he has been doomed to pass his life in illusions."

"Like all of us," said Harold, as the horses walked along together. "Think of your own illusions about Her. They were gloomy, natural, cruel, bitter illusions. You could not help them. But you see through them now. You yourself could hardly have lamented more sadly that old wrong, nor yet could you have struggled more fiercely to avenge it, than she did."

"After all, Harold, when did I ever show any feeling of vengeance? I was bitter! You 're right. Was not my Ellen my chief treasure? And she was taken from me so suddenly and mercilessly! A dull sort of hatred I felt, — the hatred of one who wants to hide in the dark and be forgotten. But after the first I never talked of revenge. Tom I had once wanted, I remember, to kill. But there was no use in that. I left him to his conscience, if he yet had any. And Alonzo, I hardly blamed him for this new wrong; no, not at any time. He was my old friend and enemy, just as he is now. The thing, indeed, yet more alienated me; it embittered me, and made me feel it impossible to approach him or to look for any reconciliation. But I knew all along that for just this he bore no real added blame. As for her" —

"Well, surely you remember how you spoke of her to me, in the long talk that first day. I went to her with the greatest prejudice. 'These Eldons,' I had said to myself beforehand, including her, of course, with the others, 'these Eldons, will they shut me up in a cave and demand ransom?' I thought of the house on the hillside as a sort of den of brigands. I recall how the first glance and the first word disarmed me. I dared not tell you of it all until long, long afterwards. I knew you hated her. I thought you could never recover from that feeling."

"Alas, my boy, did you take me also for a brigand? Did you think I had no heart? Your tale is enough for me. I only wish I could see her to ask her pardon. But welladay! so it goes. We wrong people in this world only too often. We never get the chance to make it good. I wish you could tell her, Harold, of my too late repentance."

"You forget," said Harold, gloomily, "that I shall never see her again."

"That's the trouble, Harold, is n't it, with our moral American race? I see how it is. It's inevitable. Inevitable, that is, for us, being as we are. You will never see her again, and why? Because this external family tie, this marriage that is the worst of lies, save, to be sure, as it may be useful to her boy, must be kept sacred. Well, you 're both plainly people of pluck and courage. It pleases me, and yet it pains me, Harold. You 've deserved far better of fortune. How bright the dawn's getting to be!"

"How do you know, after all, that I have any courage?" Harold spoke very gloomily. He hated to hear his old friend talking so coolly about this. Yet Escott, at his age, was a privileged person.

"Well, have n't you shown it in your three meetings," continued Escott, — "and one of them, you know, I saw myself, — meetings with Alonzo, with

Tom, and with both; and all, too, since that fatal day?"

"Courage? I call it despair! I with this load of guilt on my soul, I honored with a love of which I'm not for one instant to be deemed worthy, not even if it were but an atom to what it is,—what could I do, when driven to bay, but to say all that I did say? I said very little, after all."

"Yes, I know. You, so you would have it, were alone to blame; it was only her pity for you that had driven her to this fatal avowal; it was only her pride and her loyalty that made her refuse to explain it; you were really nothing to her, you insisted, and as for yourself, you stood always ready to meet all the consequences of this present situation. Boscowitz was a liar, and you could prove it. Meanwhile, you would n't leave the city, nor quail before anything they could do, unless indeed she wished it, or it were for her good. If there was to be public scandal, you would throw the responsibility upon them. You could not and did not conceal, indeed, that, however she felt, you, at least, were ready to die for her. But all the while you were also ready to answer for her absolute innocence with your oath or your life, or whatever else was needed. That was your talk, Harold, made none the easier for you by the fact that, save for me, you had no backing. The whole thing, in this phase of it, was as secret as we four could keep it. No outsider, save old Boscowitz, even now really knows why this trouble at Oakfield Creek has begun afresh. I should not have known myself, if the Eldons, merely for the sake of venting their own passion upon me, had not insisted on telling me. Now, all that talk of yours was, to be sure, simply your duty, when these men came down upon you as they did. Yet, knowing the case as I do, I think that it required some pluck. And for that I honor you!"

"A fig for my courage, Escott. A man is a coward whenever the woman whom he loves is injured by her love for him. I have done her the deepest injury. It is n't duty that keeps me from ever trying to see her again so much as shame. I despise myself for having put her in this hateful and terribly unjust position."

"Whose secret did you betray, Harold? She need not have made that avowal if she had not chosen. I, as I hope, appreciate her feelings. Since you 've told me about her, all my old bitterness is dead. She is to me a most honorable woman, who could not bear to hear her friend maligned. Yet, after all, how much better if she had controlled herself, and kept quiet! Boscowitz could not have hurt her, in simple-minded Alonzo's honest eyes, if she had merely laughed at the slander, and remained silent."

"She is the truth itself, Escott. All her noble soul, all her frank, simple, loyal, heroic, perfect heart, was in that avowal. I should have died before revealing her secret; that would have been indeed a small thing for me to do. But the secret was hers to keep and to sacrifice. To keep it meant her life-long peace and her freedom. She sacrificed it for me, and that only because she fancied, for the moment, that I was in need of her aid, and that the whole world, Alonzo at the head, had turned against me. Beside such unquestioning, unhesitating devotion, all possible deeds of mine are mere sham."

"Did she tell you much about the scene, at your last meeting?"

"I gathered something from her, — more from a lady friend of hers, at whose house we met for that once. That last meeting, however, was a very short and sad one. There was nothing much in it, if you choose, Escott. She — I mean the one whom I dare not name — and myself were very gloomy, and frank, and simple. She insisted, you know, that her friend should be present at that one final interview. And I could only reverence her wish. It was a horrible moment! I shall never live through another such. She was much calmer than I was. She had explained all to this friend of hers, — an old confidant of her girlhood. Just now, she said to me, there was no place for further foolish concealments. She wanted to see me only to confess that, in a moment of rage and of terror (terror on my poor behalf!) she had been guilty of what she called betraying our confidence. It was a sin; she knew that. But I must know, for my part, that she had not spoken as lightly as I might think. She would not excuse herself (as if she could need excuses!). She was not unaware, so she went on, of the consequences of this act. It meant, she said, the ruin of all our plans for you and the rest, and so untold misery to innocent people. She exaggerated the mischief wildly, I am sure, She spoke meanwhile, so gently and calmly that a stranger might have thought her but little moved. But I — well, Escott, I understood her. Our whole friendship has been mostly a matter of very simple and quiet conversation. Seldom, very seldom, have we said words that the coldest stranger might not hear. I am used now to listening between her words, and reading, so to speak, between her glances. It is the nature of these barren and hopeless friendships that they make you preternaturally clear-sighted. You listen so anxiously, as if you were in the desert, for every faintest sound that means life. That time, with all my horror in the presence of what I knew to be an everlasting parting, I lost no slightest accent of her true meaning. She was immeasurably unhappy and remorseful, — she, upon whom no shadow of guilt rests! I tried, as calmly as I could, to cheer her. I felt with every word as if I must break down before her and before them both. No damage had been done, I said (save to her own happiness), by her hasty and heroic word on my behalf. I was not even remotely worthy of it. I despised myself for having been the cause of it. I begged her to forget me, to reconcile herself with — the others — to explain away her words, to deny that they had had any meaning, to speak cruelly of me, to believe all things evil of me, to think of me as a base wretch who had betrayed her, to call me the coward that surely I must be. For I have entered her house, and wrought this sorrow for her who is so pure and so innocent. I said all this as well as I could. It was the least I could say.

"But she listened to me unpersuaded. She did not repent on her own behalf, she said. But she could never forgive herself for having exposed me to my enemies, and for having lost the good cause by so wild a blunder, by so hasty a crime. The words could not be unsaid, she added. And moreover (and then, for this once only in the interview, she smiled a little), those words were true, and forevermore they would remain true. And now that we must surely part, to meet no more on earth, she wanted me to know this fact. This, her old friend, knew it already. There was no harm in saying it once more, in this so quiet way, here and now. But it was not to tell me this that she had come. It was rather to explain to me, fully and frankly, what the other facts were. 'I cannot bear to think,' she said, 'of a life-long and senseless misunderstanding between you and me. If we must not meet any more, I know that you will not feel cold towards me on that account; but it would kill me to believe that people had not rightly told you what I said that time, and why. You will not forgive me,' she went on (oh, Escott, she said that, she, whom I hardly dare name for pure remorse and reverence!), 'you will not forgive me; but you must not despise me.' Then she continued, with her quietest air of gentle and serious reflection, and said that this was not a mere affair of sentiment. It was a practical matter. The consequences of her words would be seen in my acts, and perhaps in the fortunes of many people. I must not be misled. I must act with clear insight.

"She went on, Escott, yet a little farther. The breach between herself and — them was impassable now. She had no heart to try to win back Alonzo; she had no desire for an explanation with Tom. Their suspicions of herself were enough to end all, in any case. Such things she would not even once stoop to answer! She could make no compromise, for her own sake. But for her boy's sake and for the world's sake, she would agree, if they chose, to live as before, in this mockery of household unity, and to keep the secret. Those two villains of the press could be bought off. The public need never hear. Idle gossip would cease with our friendship. That was to be her future. She would not complain. Unless some outburst of theirs changed her life, its course was predetermined.

"This was all, Escott, that passed. Down to the moment of our farewell, she forced her friend to stay. We merely shook hands, at last, and said good-by. And then I hurried away."

There was a long pause. The sun was now very near the eastern horizon. The level way wound among the oaks as they rode. It was still vacant, save for the two early travelers. A hawk wheeled near them. Two or three horses, that had been wandering in a vast pasture-field by the roadside, looked at them wistfully, as they went by, and neighed softly. In the west, behind the travelers, scattered masses of fog partly hid the summits of the Contra Costa hills. Mount Diablo loomed up ahead of them, larger than ever.

"The gray of the morning is, indeed, somehow the time for confessions," said Harold at last. "I had no idea that even to you, my oldest friend, I should be able to tell this story. It is, indeed, due to you, I think. You need to know the facts as much as I do. Some of them you knew already. But I should hardly have thought myself able to tell them. The end of it is, you see, that she is to live henceforth for her boy; and I am to live for — I know not what."

"Live to hold on and fight, my boy! What have I lived for? You know my doctrines as well as I do. The Great Spirit needs brave children. We are all of us poor specimens of what he 's looking for. But, alas! he can make us no better. For if it were he that made us better, we should be worth nothing. We alone can give ourselves the bravery that he wants. And so, bad as we are, our game is his game, if we only stand up to it, and fight for our side. That 's the whole story of life. The man that demands more of life than that is a fool. The man who, by chance, gets more is fortune's spoiled child, who 's like as not all the worse for his good luck. This seems a little dreary, at odd minutes, when a fellow has neuralgia, or feels worn out, but it 's God's truth.

The world is the home of brave men, and the prison of cowards. That 's all I can see in it. Apart from that chance to be a brave fellow, in a good cause, and for one's friends, what is there, after all? Consider my life. Since Ellen's death it has only been more and more full of dreams and delusions. You made a gallant fight for the settlers and for me, and you 'll bear the wounds of that fight to your grave. But we, at Oakfield Creek, are where we were at the outset, only worse off. My family would not be wholly left in want, if I died. I think they 'd be better off without me. I had purposes once that have come to nothing. I know where my mistakes were. Nobody need point 'em out. I wanted freedom, and I got it, and here I am. And I 'm not so much of a wretch as I might be, after all. In any case, I should n't object to going at any time, for good cause. By the way, Harold, whenever I die, I want you to see me buried at Oakfield Creek, among the poor fellows for whom I spent my last little fortune."

Harold was weary of this talk of defeat and of death. The sun was now just coming over a northern spur of Mount Diablo. The shadow of the mountain covered the hills and plains to the southwards of the travelers. The morning had lost its first bloom and its heart-compelling charm. The time for confessions was over. This was a very matter-of-fact place, after all. The fences were worn, and often broken down. A stray cow was wandering along the road. She had a wicked look and a broken horn. The stream-beds, as one passed near them, were hereabouts already dry. The smoke from the chimneys of the hamlet at Oakfield Creek was, at length, plainly visible. The oak-trees clustered more thickly just ahead, as one approached the banks of the creek. Harold gave a new turn to the conversation: —

"You were saying something awhile since, Escott, about your talk with Alonzo Eldon, and about his rage and his illusions. How incredible it seems that a man of so much business skill and sagacity should have become so fast bound in the meshes this time!"

"A great man is doomed to be once in his life blind, as the old stories always have it. The situation is simply absurd, at the Creek. But Alonzo tried to do too many things. First he somehow got into the quarrel with the settlers. Then I heard of the thing, and, being in love with justice and in trouble with Alonzo, I invested my all hereabouts. Then the trouble went on, until Alonzo resolved to be reconciled to the settlers and to save his soul. That thought was desperately unbusiness-like, and the consequences have been fatal to poor Alonzo's peace of mind. He could n't well use his mere fiat, and say, 'Let this trouble end.' It was now the company's affair, not his. Therefore he must buy out the other shareholders, or give up his new plan. He could not at once do the former thing; so he undertook this most unsatisfactory of all compromises. What confusion of interests and of events has since disturbed poor Alonzo's purposes we know. But just now, the position of things is, I declare, almost unprecedented. Alonzo thinks himself and his son wronged by you. I persist, of course, in standing up for you. So then he also thinks himself wronged by me. He even fancies it must be all my deep plot to avenge myself for long past injuries. Therefore he tears up and throws away all his private agreements with me. I 'm a traitor, he says. He owes me nothing! As the court has meanwhile decided against me, he has nothing to do but to call for execution of judgment, and then eject me, or rather my caretakers, from my tracts of land. So far again, to be sure, it 's once more a private fight between Alonzo and me. But there, of course, the poor settlers enter afresh. An ejection of me, after the decision of the test-cases (which were my own cases), means, the settlers are sure, a coming ejection of all of them. Accordingly, they want to fight. Hence the absurdity of this moment. Alonzo, with the United States government behind him, is on one side; the moral law sits there quietly on the other side, and won't budge. The settlers, with their shot-guns, are meanwhile trying to hide behind that moral law, but even they can't. And you and I ride along here at sunrise, intending to see whether we can find some way to keep the peace in the Oakfield Creek region. The whole thing, in one sense, is confoundedly funny. I 'm almost disposed to sit down by the roadside here and laugh at it."

Harold was quite unable to share Escott's disposition in this last respect. "I wish," he said, "that you 'd tell me about that conversation with Alonzo. I had no heart to ask you concerning it when it happened."

"Well, it was moderately clear and pointed, Harold. Much of it, doubtless, might be found in the proper place, in a sufficiently extensive dictionary of the profanity of all nations. Alonzo and I were, if you please, a little incensed, as Alonzo would probably say. Here he comes to hunt me up, trying to look dignified, but, in fact, just boiling. The sight of him in that state always did amuse me. I can't help it. This time I try to hide my amusement as I can; but I fancy that he detects it. He begins about you. His story is tolerably incoherent and slightly ferocious, as it were. As I 've already judged from your face that something is wrong, I am on my guard. You, as you remember, told me that day how you had just received a message from the house on the hillside. I knew that your message had more than an ordinary significance. I asked you whether anybody was suddenly ill, or dead; and you responded in the negative so sadly and anxiously that I perceived that what had happened was almost as bad as my conjecture, or may be worse yet. So, as I say, when Alonzo goes over his story, I 'm already on my guard. I ask him shortly what business all this is of mine. Alonzo bursts out furiously, telling how Boscowitz assured him beforehand that I was, in this as in other respects, your confederate. I, of course, replied, thereupon, that for the first, I was perfectly willing to be your confederate in all your plans, purposes, acts, and sufferings, so far as you ever wanted me; and, secondly, I said, rather imprudently no doubt, that I still could not have been in any conspiracy with you about what Alonzo now had in his silly old head; 'for,' declared I, 'I have not the honor of the lady's acquaintance, and, since certain events of years since, have always regarded her with dread, and even with resentment. How,' I added, 'can I then be aiding my friend in this mythical love affair of his?' For, of course, Harold, even at that moment, though I perceived that you were in some trouble over the bay, I still regarded this tale of Alonzo's as a myth, and believed that he had been imposed upon by some scandal-monger or other.

"My hasty remark was the completion of our ruin. Alonzo was now wholly overcome with his wrath. 'Resentment!' he cried; 'ay, that's just Boscowitz's word. He said you'd always been nursing resentment, and that all this was your long-pondered and deep-laid scheme to be avenged upon her, upon my son Tom, upon me, upon all of us. And you confess this, Escott,' Alonzo shouted, 'you confess this yourself! This is your friendship, then! This is the meaning of your hand-clasps, of your honest airs, of your intercessions for the settlers, of your lofty principles! When one scheme of vengeance failed, you tried another! When the law was turning against you, and you foresaw the loss of your suits, you chose this new way. You incited this Harold to ruin our family peace. This ends all our agreements.'

"Well, I spoke back plainly. 'Your chief obligations just now,' I said, 'are to the settlers, not to me. Whatever you think of me, you must carry out your agreement. Yet it seems that you choose just now to make and believe charges against Harold and me which I won't for an *instant* think of denying. It's beneath me to talk of them. I despise them. But if you will persist in those charges, and if, as you seem to intend, you will break your engagements with the settlers and with me for the sake of mere vengeance, then go to Boscowitz and the devil, and consult with them over your plans for your so-called vengeance, all you please. I'm ready. I can stand another unjust charge as well as not. I pity my friends the settlers; but, Alonzo, I won't use one soft word to you now for their sake, nor for anybody's sake. If you want to make yourself a curse to mankind, go and be one!' That was my talk, my boy.

"It is fearful to think, Harold," Escott continued, "how much poor Alonzo must be excited just now, in order to be so blind to his honor and his duty. He actually thinks that he can separate me from the settlers, and that those private pledges are void, so far as we're concerned. I don't think that even now he intends to eject anybody but me and my men. He still means to be fair to the settlers. But he can't do everything at once. The settlers can't be kept from firing on any officer who comes to execute the court processes hereabouts." Escott paused, and then summed up reflectively: —

"In fact, Harold, I don't think that, in his present excitement, poor Alonzo has much conscience left. Doubtless, as you say, his conscience was bound up in her. Since he 's lost faith in her, he thinks that the good Lord is dead once for all, and that he himself and the universe must somehow manage to get on as they can alone. That 's the matter with Alonzo. One would not have thought how much her words would upset him. Women do play an odd part, Harold, in the mechanism of this world's morals, don't they?"

"Don't you think it strange, Escott," said Harold, at length, "that Alonzo should have come over with the officers?"

"No, it seems to me very natural. It is n't his way to make others run a risk without running any himself. He thinks there 's apt to be trouble, so he comes here and uses the influence of his own personal presence, so as to overawe opposition and to give moral support to the marshal. He 's not the man to shirk such responsibility. He never was. If a man 's to be shot at on his behalf, he wants to be there to see the thing done himself, and to get his share of the bullets."

"But, for my part," answered Harold, "I 'm disposed to dread the effect of his presence, for the very reason that you attribute to him as his ground for coming over here. If he 's feared, he 's also hated. I think that the first shot-gun is apt to go off in his face rather than in the marshal's own. It will give us much more trouble to keep the peace if he comes."

"You may be right, my boy. By the way, Harold, a very odd thing happens to strike me. Is n't this the 12th of May?"

"Yes."

"Hum! Twenty-three years ago to-day — well, I 'd better not mention it. It 's nonsense."

"What is it, Escott?"

"After all, though, I may as well speak of it, as it 's against myself. Twenty-three years ago to-day, Alonzo and I were in a scrimmage with a number of Indians at Pyramid Lake. You 've never heard of the affair, I fancy. It was a miserable scrape. We were all ashamed of it afterwards, and hated to talk of it. It took place just before nightfall, in the hills and meadows of the Truckee, near Pyramid Lake. We all ran, somehow. I believe I got a sore arm in the course of the row; falling down, perhaps. Alonzo acquitted himself pretty well; fought as long as a man could, and then caught a ferocious mule in full flight, and got aboard at the last minute, only just in time to escape the Indians. As for me, I 'm no soldier; I did worse. While I was hunting around for a mule to ride off on (mine had got away, somehow, and never stopped, the darned brute, until it reached Virginia City), while I was thus hunting, I say, the other fellows of my crowd, Alonzo among them, *would* stay to help me, though they were already mounted. They kept offering me rides behind. Think of me riding on a beast behind poor Alonzo! But I wanted a comfortable saddle to myself, and while I was fooling the Indians that were after us came up, somehow, and shot one of my crowd, — a good fellow, named Molesworth. I had delayed them, you see, and his blood is upon my soul, Harold, so that I 've never felt easy about him since. I think all my troubles have been a judgment for his sake."

"Was Sam Paddington there, Escott?"

"What, did you ever hear of that fight, Harold?"

"Oh, a brief and garbled report, once, — very imperfect, I assure you; not equal to yours."

"But I 'm not giving any report, my boy."

"Yes, you are. Was Sam Paddington there?"

"I think he was, Harold. I believe that some time during that fight, when we thought we might hold the place for a while, we dispatched Sam to Virginia City for reinforcements. He was a good rider, and he accomplished his mission very well."

"Did he come back?"

"There was n't any occasion to. We reached Virginia City a little time after him, having concluded to retire without waiting for his return."

"Escott, you 're a true historian!"

"Thank you. Now that we 're coming into the settlement, you 'll also see that I'm a true orator, too, though in a funny way. The settlers for the last day or two have been wholly idle and very excited, because they 've been expecting the marshal at any minute, who will, as we know, actually come about noon to-day. So, instead of minding their regular business, they 've been under arms, holding sessions, making speeches, and otherwise behaving like asses. If this thing only blows over, they 'll go back to work to-morrow like honest men. We shall find them, just at this hour of the day, all cross and sleepy. Besides, they think I 've sold out to Alonzo. If they don't shoot us off hand as traitors, Harold, I want to make 'em a speech. They 'll first treat us with the cussedest impoliteness in any case; but we 've got to keep cool. I 'll do all the talking, my boy; you look out for the horses. My talk, however, won't be precisely of a classical sort; it won't even begin with 'Fellow-citizens,' nor make any references to the bird of liberty. It must be judged, Harold, by no academic standard. In fact, what orator ever tried before to move the multitudes at that sacred hour of the rosy morn when the head feels biggest? Not even Demosthenes, I take it. I 'm proud of the opportunity. How I wish Sam Paddington were here! But the speech, I 'm afraid, would n't bear reporting. It will be an old man's plain words to a pack of amateur loafers, and I 'm afraid it may be profane. The effects, you know, have to be a little startling on such occasions. Well, we shall see."

The reader would in vain hunt upon the defective maps of this generation to find marked the position of this Oakfield Creek. But at all events, after passing a few houses, as you entered the place, you came to Spofford's hotel, where, of course, there was a large bar-room. But this morning there were collected about the tavern door, even at this early hour, a number of the Brotherhood of Noble Rangers. Several had their horses tied to fences close by. Two or three of the men sat and sulked on the low front steps; more leaned back in chairs on the hotel porch; one supported himself against a post of the porch; others, as Escott and Harold rode up, peered through the door and from the windows of the bar-room. Somebody, at the same time, kicked a lazy dog down the steps, between the men there, and almost under the feet of the horses. The chickens about the front of the tavern cackled and fled in dismay; a frightened woman looked out of a second-story window, and then drew back suddenly. Meanwhile a dirty child stared steadily and with fascination from the ground at the corner of the hotel building, admiring all that went on. It had been for the last half hour taking its chance to throw an occasional stone at the legs of some one of the horses tied near by. The building was of a dirty white color, with green blinds and a peaked roof. In front were a pump, a dirty horse-trough, and many empty tin cans.

These Noble Rangers had but few firearms in sight just now. Most of the men must, indeed, have been drinking the whole night; but however they felt, they looked as sober and stern as Mount Diablo itself. This was not a moment when a resolute man very willingly confessed to the effects of his rum. Some of the Rangers, moreover, were, no doubt, temperance men. Save for the act of kicking the dog, nobody seemed disposed to move for our two travelers. To Escott's greeting there was a poor response. Peterson, who was leaning against the post, answered most noticeably, but still very sulkily. Collins, who stood in the doorway, was even less cordial. Nobody seemed willing to look at Harold. The two friends were plainly in disgrace hereabouts. Escott made not the slightest delay in getting off his horse as well as his feebleness permitted, and found his way up the steps, between the curious but almost motionless men there. Harold, springing lightly off his own horse, took the reins of both, and looked about for a place to fasten them. None was near. Nobody helped or directed him; and so he stood still, and awaited Escott's next action. By the time Escott had reached the top of the steps, a young man, holding high over his head a light chair, pushed through the doorway, past the unwilling Collins, and offered the chair to Escott. Escott greeted him cordially, thanked him, and laid his hand on the chair, but did not sit down.

"Johnny," said Escott to the young man. very quietly, "would you mind just taking our horses round and giving them to the man at the stable? There seems to be no great flourishing about here this morning to help a new-comer. I suppose Spofford is n't on hand yet, nor his son either, or else we should have seen them here by this time. I wish, too, you'd wake up Spofford, if you can. I want to talk with him."

"I'm awake enough," said Spofford, making his appearance at the door. "I dunno, Escott, why you need ask Johnny Milliken to do my work, nohow."

"Johnny and I are very old friends, Spofford," said Escott, coolly. "By the way, allow me to introduce my friend, Mr. Harold. Mr. Harold, Mr. Spofford."

"I know Mr. Harold, I think," replied Spofford, gloomily. "He was here before. Johnny, by the way, I think you need n't take Escott's horse to *my* stable. Plenty of other stables in town. Escott, I'm sorry to be rude, as it were, to an old friend, but the fact is, the gentlemen of the Brotherhood of Noble Rangers has taken possession of this here hotel this mornin', 'nd I 'm darned if there 's any room in it for another man. I guess you 'll find house-room down to your old tract."

"If old Alonzo 's right, there 's to be lots of room down there before long, and nobody knows it, Escott, better than you and this friend of yours." It was Collins who spoke these last words.

"It 's to tell you a little about Alonzo that we 've come to-day, if you please," began Escott, calmly drawing a long breath, as if he expected to speak at some length, "and it 's the whole Brotherhood that I want to find, right here and now, so that they may learn what we 've got to tell. And what's more, Spofford, I want first of all to remark that I don't care for any of your blarsted airs, anyhow. If you choose to stand there so glum, you and these other Rangers, you may. I don't mind how you look. Harold, here, and I have ridden all night to come to this very place, and to talk to you like men, before you get misled any more by some ghastly nonsense or other, and so fall into a mess with better people than Alonzo's crowd. As for Alonzo, nobody's in a worse row with him than we are ourselves, think what you will. And you need n't look so sulky, either. You must know that I sha'n't greatly worry, Spofford, whether any body believes my story or not. For the fact is, I've come here to say just whatever I choose, so long as it concerns you fellows to hear it. When you've heard, believe it, or call me a liar, or do any other square and polite thing, and I'll not blame you. But what I do want is, I say, to talk with men, not with sickly-looking, half-awake fellows that roost on door-steps, and hold up posts, and look as sulky as that youngster yonder, that's throwing pebbles at horses' legs for its living. Hang you, man, if you want to sulk, go over to Alonzo's crowd! The sulking there's been this spring in the camp of Boscowitz and of the other boon comrades of that great American land grabber beats all that I see in this crowd even now. And now, Spofford, what do you want to do about it? *If* you choose to be civil, and rouse up such of your Rangers as have a grain or two of decent courtesy about them, fellows who 'll talk squarely to an old man like me, — if you 'll do that, Harold and I won't make any ceremony. We 'll speak our piece, and you can speak yours, and when you 're through we 'll all think it over. After that, if you have any confounded grudges left, and you call it worth while to have 'em out with either of us, why, blaze away, or do whatever else you darn choose. But *if*, Spofford, you are n't man enough for that, and if your crowd is to go on sulking at this rate until the next rain, why, then, we 'll leave the men of this district, Harold and I will, and we 'll call a public meeting of children under five years. They, sir, would be at least honest with us, and they 'd speak their minds. So that 's my little speech for now, Spofford. I take it you and the rest of this darned statuary hereabouts have heard Alf Escott talk before, and perhaps you know how to treat him on this present occasion."

"But see here, Alf," replied Spofford, rather weakly, "I tell you my house is under the control, at present, of a sort of general extra session of the Brotherhood of Noble Rangers. Your approach just now, as I may say, was seen by our patrol about two miles out. A resolution had already been taken last night that, in the now present state of our affairs and controversies, we preferred neither to oppose your coming, if you 'd come, nor to precisely, as I may say, welcome it. We 'd deal with you through a sort of a delygation, Escott. We 'd prefer to send a delygation to kind of interrygate you as to certain dubyous points; and it was meanwhile resolved and accord-din'ly ordered that it was n't right, you bein' a little under a cloud, for us here to, as it were, welcome you to this hospitable roof. Now this is n't my work, Alf, not exactly. It 's the Brotherhood that orders it. I don't say I don't approve it. I only say I don't noways bear the sole and individual responsibility, Alf. So I 'll ask you to pardon me for my seemin' unkindness, and regard this here that I say as, as it were, final." Spofford spoke all this with the air of one who had prepared himself as well as possible beforehand for this scene. Escott, still standing, measured him quietly as he spoke, and then said: —

"Is this all?"

"Yes, Alf, it is."

"How much do you mean to say the Brotherhood here paid you for learning this little oration?"

"I, as the owner of this house, Alf" —

"How much would you own of this house now, Spofford, if it had n't been for me?"

"But, Alf, I don't mean to imply anything personal. It 's the Brother— "

"Personal be hanged! I asked for a man that could talk, not for this kind of stuff. What have I to do here with your resolutions, and the rest? I know them. They begin, 'Whereas Alf Escott,' and they go on with a long rigmarole that not one sinner here and now chewing the cud of bitterness about this doorstep can remember or repeat. As for your orders, and your delegations, and the rest, they can go hang. Try that game on Alonzo. He deserves it, and he 'll think it 's dignified. But as for Alf Escott, you know him well. He 's pulled several of you boys out of the mire in various ways. You, Spofford, he cleared from a disagreeable charge before the Vigilance Committee, twenty-seven years ago; and every man here knows that. And he helped you out of one deucedly bad money scrape; that, too, you know. You, Peterson — but I won't particularize. You all know the facts. Now, why do I come here, where I 'm not wanted? Why do I persist in staying? Why do I say now, this very instant, to the face of all of you, that I *won't* go till you 've heard me out? Why? Because I shall speak for your good, not for mine. What can a miserable delegation do that you can't do now, if you 'll only wake up some man with blood and brains in him to talk to me? To be sure, I 've not ridden all night to hold forth here to a crowd as dull as this one is, so long as your chiefs don't come out. See here! Where 's McAlpin? If there 's anybody in all your Brotherhood that I ought to fear, if I 've any way betrayed you, it 's McAlpin. As for you, Collins, I know you 're a leader, but you always take until to-morrow to hear what 's said to you to-day, and I want a man with quick wits. Bring out McAlpin."

The settlers were evidently staggered by their old leader's vigor. He stood leaning on the chair, as feeble, as clear-voiced, as fiery, as ever. But a short time since, despite some doubtful appearances, they had, nearly all of them, worshiped him. Yet they had just been spending half the night in voting him a traitor, in threatening to slay him, and in preparing an open letter to voice their opinions of him in the public press. They had dreaded his coming, as possibly meaning an effort on his part to win them over afresh, and so to betray them yet again. The notion of a delegation, with set questions, had been hit upon as the best for their purpose. They desired, namely, to get all they could from Escott, in the way of information, and they feared his blunt persuasiveness if used upon a large company. The night ride and this early appearance had surprised them. They were well on the lookout for the expected marshal; but that an old man like Escott should arrive on his weary horse at sunrise, after so long a journey, they had not thought possible. Spofford's effort to carry out the purposes of the Noble Rangers was therefore a little weak, and was certainly doomed to failure. Escott had not even fairly finished his last appeal before Peterson turned about sharply and spoke. He was a tall, intelligent-looking man, with gray eyes and a hooked nose.

"Boys," he said, "I 'm not in favor, now that Escott comes to us in this way, — I 'm not in favor of sending him off till the whole body has seen him right here, and voted on the thing again. If he 's got anything to say, we ought to hear him out. There 's been no alarm this past night. The marshal may get here to-day, and may not; but at any rate, there 'll be no such hurry before he comes that we can't talk things over. I move, Spofford, that we here, now on guard and awaiting news, receive Escott into this house on our own responsibility, until the boys are all awake. That Alf Escott should be sent off when he comes to us at this hour, it is n't noways fair, nor right. And it 's so with Mr. Harold, too. You see, Escott, McAlpin and the others that were looking out for our affairs early in the night are sleeping now in the further wing of the house. We 're looking out for that marshal, to whom we mean to show our teeth when he comes. As for you, I think things have looked black for you lately over here. And it 's odd. You 're in trouble. You 're the one against whom the writs are issued. Yet it looks to us as if you 'd sold us out, for all that, because yours was the test-case, and you defended it ill, and let the story get abroad that you had private dealings with Alonzo Eldon. Now, though, you 've thus let all the main points come to decision in the courts, and they've gone against us; and it seems that your private arrangement is worthless, at least for our interests. We believe you 've been bought out, and that your ejection is only good to show Alonzo's triumph and to bring us to his feet. We mean to have something to say about that ourselves, though; and, all the while, we suspect you very seriously. That 's our meaning this morning, and it 's Spofford's place, of course, to give it vent in this way. But when the boys voted not to receive you here, they did n't know you were coming at this hour. I vote to receive you now, and to put off action about your case until, say, nine o'clock. In the mean while, you and Mr. Harold can rest, and your horses. That 's my notion about Escott, boys. What do ye say?"

Peterson's words met a general assent now, and Spofford rather gladly sacrificed his dignity, and retracted his former speech.

"Well, boys," said Escott, "if you 'll promise us a hearing by and by, I 'm content to have no more talk now. May be I need rest. But there 's one bit of news that you doubtless have n't heard yet. I know for a certainty that the marshal is this side the Contra Costa hills, that he has quite a party with him, and that Alonzo Eldon and his son are of that party. You may say that I know this because I 'm on their side. I 'm not on their side, though; and I prove it to you by coming and telling you this, which they 've done all they could to keep secret. Alonzo thought, boys, that the sudden appearance here of a larger band than you expected, with his big and wonderful self at the head of it, would scare you to death. I 've taken the edge off this surprise, boys, by riding over in the night, and letting you know. But that, as you 'll by and by see, is n't my main purpose in coming here now. I want to develop to you a plan by which you can so take advantage of Alonzo's presence as to secure, boys, all the guarantees from him that you like, as touching your own interests. I myself, as you will see, am to gain nothing by that. You are to get what you demand, and my tract will be lost to me, as, perhaps, I deserve to lose it. Before sundown, boys, if you take the thing rightly, the controversy may be ended in your favor, — not, to be sure, in mine. I shall be the only sufferer. Well — no matter now. I can't develop my plans yet. Wait until nine o'clock. Only I 'm in earnest, as you 'll see."

Escott's manner went far to restore confidence in him, despite all the suspicion and the sullenness of this early morning detachment of the Noble Rangers. Their whole life during the forty-eight hours since their "extra session," as Spofford had called it, had begun, seemed to them already like a troubled dream. They had been waiting for the marshal, disputing what to do next, passing resolutions, discussing Escott's betrayal of their interests, planning publications in the newspapers, swallowing many drinks and many big stories, and breathing out threatenings and slaughter. Escott's coming seemed to them now, after all, like an awakening voice. They began to hope that he would set all right, and become their trusted friend again. They had, at least, no real desire to begin war against the national government. They only knew that, somehow, they were being cruelly wronged, and that they were determined to make life impossible for any "jumper" in this region. They still hoped not to be led into any direct contest with the marshal himself. If he came, they meant to turn out in full force, to threaten violently any jumpers who might be in his company, and to induce these jumpers to retire from the contest. As for the marshal himself, — well, if he grew troublesome, they might have to surround him, and quietly to disarm him! All must be done, however, decently and in order. A moral victory at least, they fancied, must result, such as to make Alonzo feel that there was no room for him and his jumpers hereabouts. Then, perhaps, he might be induced erelong to settle his cases in a way favorable to them.

When Escott made this startling announcement about Alonzo's coming, and also said that he himself had a new plan to propose, the result, as far as it went, was very much what he had desired. Curiosity was aroused, new excitement was created, other Rangers, on awaking, were erelong informed of the new turn of affairs; and, while Escott and Harold were resting from the ride, taking a little breakfast, and even trying to nap for a brief space, the Rangers outside their room were awaiting eagerly the meeting at nine o'clock, when they would assail Escott with reproaches and questions, and would have a chance to find whether there was really, as he had promised, any escape from this fatal down-hill course of threats, of recriminations, and of violence.

Escott, meanwhile, was trying to prepare his energies for what he looked forward to as one of the greatest efforts of his life. He must quiet the suspicions of these angry men; he must divert their minds from their dangerous purposes; he must propose to them an armed negotiation with Eldon; he must be ready to offer himself in every sense as a personal sacrifice to their cause; and, above all and in the midst of all, he must keep the peace. Escott was very sanguine of success. Harold was more doubtful and anxious; but he, too, was fully devoted to the undertaking. If only Alonzo and the marshal did not come too early! Escott had mentioned nine o'clock, because the old man believed, from his present sensations, that, after the toils of the night, he could not venture on his task any sooner. Besides, he felt sure, from his information, that the marshal could not arrive before noon.

But Escott's information was, in this respect, mistaken.

At about half past eight o'clock that morning, a young man who had been acting as patrol came in with the news that the marshal's party were in sight. The young man who brought in this news had ridden far out, had met the party, had seen the marshal, Alonzo Eldon, Tom Eldon, Foster, and Buzzard, had recognized all of them, and had then put spurs to his horse and galloped across fields to the settlement, jumping two or three ditches by the way, and taking advantage of broken fences. The youth himself was very proud of his success so far. He was a truant from the city, who had been for some time trying to avoid letting his father hear of his whereabouts. He was much surprised to learn now that his father was in the hotel. The young patrol's name was Sam Escott.

Sam's honesty was so obvious, his simplicity was so engaging, his frequent quarrels with his father were such familiar facts at the Creek, that when he had come to the settlement, a few days ago, nobody had thought of fastening upon him any of the suspicions to which Alf Escott was subject. His services had been cheerfully accepted. He was a good rider, a dead shot, an enthusiastic and boyish young fellow. For the last two days he had been in the saddle almost all the time, riding about on errands for the Rangers, and acting as a patrol. Of what the people now said about his father Sam had heard little and understood nothing. He loved this exciting moment, with its suggestions of warfare. He hoped that it would not all end in mere talk. He longed for a chance to stand under fire, and to shoot some one. As for the consequences of resisting the law, Sam had no special concern about them. Nor had he any heart-searchings as to the right and wrong of this affair. The Eldons were old enemies. Especially Tom was hateful to Sam, who had never for an instant forgotten Ellen. The thing was a family feud. Sam wished to have a hand in it. Of the immediate causes of the present crisis he had, however, no idea.

What Sam witnessed of the scene that followed was, with a very few additions, something like this.

When Sam had shouted out his news at the top of his voice, he rejoiced to see that he was at once the centre of observation. The windows were full of faces, the steps were crowded, and Collins, Peterson, and the others, men who had usually snubbed Sam of late, and ordered him about harshly, were listening respectfully. Then there arose a general call for McAlpin. McAlpin did not appear. "Who saw him last?" "Where is he?" asked various voices; but there was no satisfactory answer. He had ridden over to Murphy's saloon, at the other end of the town. He was sleeping in the attic at Spofford's. He was here a moment since. He had not been here since midnight. Such were the opposing views. But McAlpin responded to the many calls no more than if he were Baal. Nobody could find him. Then somebody called upon Collins, as nominally the next in command among the Rangers, to take the lead. Collins looked sullen, and said that he had resigned last night, as they all knew, after that quarrel with McAlpin. He would follow anywhere, but Peterson must lead. Peterson was, therefore, really the next in command. And so he was called upon. "Well, boys," he said, "if *I* undertake this affair, I want order. We intend to give old Alonzo an infernal scare, if we find him, but we don't want no powder wasted. I wish somebody else could take charge of this thing, I do, because I 'm no leader, if I *am* Second Grand Chief of the Brotherhood. But I'll do my best, and I won't shirk. Every man to his horse!

And then we 'll ride out to meet Alonzo in good shape."

Hereupon there was more rushing about after the horses, and much confusion, and a good deal of swearing. The women of the house, as Sam saw, were crying. In the midst of all this, however, Escott and Harold appeared, and Sam quailed before his father's eye.

"Well, Sam," said Escott, however, good-humoredly enough, "we have n't met for some days, my boy. How is everything with you? I hope, my dear chicken, you won't get hurt to-day. Look out for yourself, Sam. Keep cool. Obey orders."

Sam had been sure of an angry outburst, after their last quarrel; for that had been quite a serious one. Escott's voice gave Sam a glad sense of reassurance. He looked very sullen and proud, however, and replied that he had for some time been here on business of his own.

"But what's the price of your pony, Sam? You 'll go to the dogs before long, if you indulge in such extravagance as this."

Sam's pony was a sorry mustang, and was now quite hot and worn out. Sam resented the pleasantry a little, and began to tell Escott the news afresh. "Fiddlesticks, my boy, you need n't describe the party. I did n't expect them so early, but I know all about how they look. They meant to scare us by the bare sight of 'em. See here, Peterson," continued Escott, turning to the leader, "I understand you 're the captain now. I 'm no fighter, you know, but we want, my friend

Harold and I, to join on to this army of yours in the character of special war-correspondents, as it were. We shall hide behind the fence posts while the shooting is going on, and write up the campaign afterwards, with eulogies on the heroes, and so forth. Won't you let us? I 've no doubt that Boscowitz is retained to write up the other side. I believe in giving every man a chance. We 're ready to obey orders, if you 'll let us go along. I believe Harold has a pistol. I am unhappily weaponless myself, but if any man has a spare pitchfork about his clothes, I 'd be glad of a chance to carry it, so that I may prod Alonzo a little somewhere about the fifth rib, if he shows any sign of going to sleep while you fellows make your set speeches to him before you begin the war. *I* believe in giving every man a hearing, I do."

Peterson was looking very anxious as he sat there on his horse, amid the confusion of the men preparing their arms and their beasts. Fresh news had just come in that Alonzo's party were pausing in a field outside the town, apparently for the sake of reconnoitring. They numbered only some fifteen, all told, whereas there were now about forty Noble Rangers in sight, and armed. Peterson seemed not to enjoy Escott's fashion of talk; nor could Sam make out his father's purpose in treating the affair as a farce. Sam wanted to hear a few glowing words about courage, and the defense of home, and the cruelty of the oppressors, and all that. But still, if Peterson was offended at Escott's manner, he was probably less disposed to think the old man a false friend than he would have been if Escott had now chosen a more unnatural and eloquent strain. He answered rather sternly: —

"I thought, Alf, that you 'd come here to look at this business like a man. I don't see as this is any time for infernal nonsense, especially from a man in your place."

"Well, Peterson, if I did n't talk nonsense, you 'd doubtless just now believe me lying. There 's no time to hear my speech to the boys, — for I, too, had very carefully prepared a speech. But what I really do want of you, Peterson, is your attention for one instant to a request. It 's a personal favor to me. Let me speak three words to these fellows here before we go. Grant it, man! It may prevent bloodshed!"

Peterson was plainly moved by the sudden change in Alf's manner. His face softened. At the earliest chance he called order, and began in a good but artificially emphatic voice, to address his mounted men: "Boys, — I *should* say Noble Brothers (but, *darn* it! that 's no matter), — news has just come that Alonzo Eldon, with his whole pack, has stopped outside in Carson's field. They 're reconnoitring. Now, we mean to go out and meet 'em square and in full force, and show 'em what stuff we 're made of. I say we 're made of peaceable stuff, and have been all along; I say we are n't going to give up our rights; and I also say that we here are the last men in the

State of California to violate the laws, unless we 're driven to the wall. But if we are, boys, then the law of God is higher than that of man, and even the crushed worm will turn again and rend you." This last doubtless trite allusion met exactly the feelings of the assembled Rangers, who interrupted the stern and honest voice of Peterson by a torrent of approving shouts, such as seriously frightened some of the more nervous and ill-fed of the mustangs. The terrified women at the upper windows gazed tearfully and silently down; a turkey-cock near by loudly expressed his customary feelings in a number of successive outbursts; while the lazy dog rose from his latest resting place, put his tail between his legs, and chased the dirty child once more round the corner of the house. Collins, however, who had been standing on the ground, very busy with his saddle-girth, looked more ill-humored than ever, as he quieted his beast during the applause. At the close of the disturbance, Collins took the first opportunity to remark, in a loud voice, to his next neighbor: "Darn the old thing, it 's busted." This remark referred to the saddle-girth.

"Never mind, Collins," began Peterson, in a conciliatory tone. "Take my horse, and I 'll ride yours barebacked myself." — "But, boys, as I was saying, we here don't want to shed no drop of useless blood" —

"Useless blood is good, of Tom Eldon, for instance," muttered Escott to Harold, by way of comment. Sam thought this a fine joke as he overheard it. He chuckled softly until his face was crimson.

" We want, I say, to shed not one God-forsaken drop. We only want to overawe our foes by the irresistible force of him who is thrice-armed, because his quarrel is just and his powder is dry. We want to send Alonzo peacefully and irrevocably home to his own vine and his own potato-patch."

" I 'm darned if I think he owns any potato-patch, — by rights, that is," said Collins. There was a laugh.

" No," admitted Peterson, more cheerfully. " I think we shall really have to send him home to some other man's potato - patch that Alonzo 's stolen. But no matter. We 're brave. We 're willing to shed the last drop of our blood in defense of our homes, but we don't want no cuss to say in the newspapers that we began the fight." The mention of newspapers attracted attention once more to Escott. " But now," said Peterson, " we have a minute before we go out, and Alf Escott asks to be heard for that minute. I 'm in favor of granting this to him. We *have* believed in him, boys, we all know how much. He 's under a cloud now, but he 's come in among us frankly, with every show of honesty, and I move he be heard. Alf Escott, speak up."

" Well, boys," began Alf, as he sat on his horse near Peterson, " I had a speech ready, but there 's no time for that. I was going to vindicate myself to this crowd, that I have loved a good deal, after all, and that has turned against me for poor reasons. No matter. I don't ask you now to think well of me, nor to believe a word I say. I only want to propose a plan, as a sensible man, talking to sensible men. If you think there 's no good in it, we 'll say no more of it. If you think well of it, I 'm at your service. You 'll ride out here, and meet Alonzo. Well and good! Now, what has Alonzo come for? To eject my care-takers from my land. You think that he 's in collusion with me when he does this. He is n't, mind you; but no matter. Suppose he was, or suppose he was n't, my plan is good all the same. Let me go with you, and let me, first of all, before anything else happens, walk right out in front of you, and then, in plain sight, and where all can hear me, I 'll address Alonzo thus. 'Alonzo!' I 'll say, 'you come here, armed with processes of the courts, to take my land. So far as I now am concerned, Alonzo,' I shall say, 'take it and be damned. But so far as these men here behind me are concerned, men who have trusted in your solemn promises to me, you shall not take my land until here, openly, in the presence of all, you solemnly renew your undertakings on their behalf, and promise that this ejectment business shall end with me.' That 's what I shall say to Alonzo, boys. And I shall say it while I 'm standing in fair line of fire from both sides, and my friend Harold will stand there beside me. And if we play you false, you can shoot us dead right on the spot. And so, if you let us do this, and if you wait till we are done, Alonzo will show you what he means, fast enough. Thus, again, we 'll put the responsibility of the first blood-letting (if there 's to be any) upon him ; for if he 's disposed to keep his word to you, and will enter into fresh agreements right there, you can afford to see me lose my land. But if he is playing you false, then the consequences are his own, to take as he wants to. That, boys, is as square as I can make it. This is no speech, but it 's a fair business proposition, at any rate."

A general murmur of approval greeted Escott's words. Peterson began to consult anxiously with Collins and with one or two others, and after a general hum of conversation had filled the air for a few moments Peterson once again called order. The more Peterson talked as the leader of the assembled Rangers, the more anxiously dignified this man became, who had begun the discussions of the morning with such a quiet and manly simplicity of bearing.

"Noble Brothers," he said this time, "I 've heard with unmixed admiration this proposal of old Alf's. It 's worthy of him, say I, worthy of his old self. As I understand his meaning, he predicates this now imminent row to be a private controversy of him and old Eldon, founded on some difference now in process of going on behind the scenes. And he undertakes to prove this before us all, and to meanwhile serve our cause by this proposition of his. I believe in accepting of his notion. We can't lose anything by it. What do you say? Shall we vote?"

The Rangers were in a hurry. They called for the question at once, allowed no discussion, and accepted the proposition.

"Why," asked Peterson the next moment, privately, of Escott, "do you want Mr. Harold to go beside you, when you ride out in front to talk to Alonzo? One is better than two for such a thing."

"Harold and I want to show, sir, that we two are the really hated ones in this business. Bring us out there alone together, and Alonzo will quickly say whether we are the men he means. If we skulk, when the parties meet, Alonzo will be only the worse, and there 'll be a fight. If he sees us, if we demand a parley, then we can ask him to say squarely that we are the only ones he has a fight with. Thereafter you fellows won't care to sympathize with us very much. You 'll see, from what he says, that it 's a personal and private fight. You 'll be disposed to draw out of it. And if he observes that fact, he 'll be disposed to let you do so. Anyhow, this is our forlorn hope, Peterson, to prevent this trouble. Our plan is n't exactly legal, I know, any more than yours; but neither Harold nor I can skulk just now, if there 's to be a clear understanding of this business all around. And only a clear understanding can possibly prevent bloodshed this day. We may fail, but as you fellows feel, there 's no other plan. If we don't both go out in front, you fellows won't believe in us, and you won't believe Alonzo even if he says that we are the sole men that he 's trying to hurt; and, again, you won't know how to deal with him as I do; and so, altogether, you 'll be sure to blunder into a battle. We may do the same thing, but, as I say, it 's a forlorn hope."

This last decision of Escott's life seems, when judged by the sequel, to have been a blunder.

A few moments later, Sam, who had ridden beside his father and Harold as long as he was allowed to, was watching the scene from the front rank of the irregular line of settlers, while Peterson, Escott, and Harold, a little in advance of the main body, were confronting the marshal's armed men. These were drawn up in a field near the roadside; they were clustered under an oak-tree, and about the wagon in which they had been carrying their arms and equipments. The marshal was calling out in a loud voice to the new-comers: "I want to hear no word from you men. I am doing my duty. I cannot parley with armed bands. I have no quarrel with any of you. I have come to put these here parties in possession of certain tracts. You must not bar my way. Disperse, I tell you, disperse." The marshal was a great heavy man, like Alonzo, but his face was red, smooth, dull, and fat, and his little black eyes looked mean and wicked. Yet he was plainly a brave fellow, who meant to do his official duty. Beside him, just in front of the wagon, were

Alonzo and Tom, both on horseback. Buzzard and Foster, armed with repeating rifles, stood up in the wagon, behind the other men. Sam, who himself had a rifle slung over his shoulder, found himself uneasily fingering it, as he looked at Tom. "That is my sister's murderer," he said to himself. But now Escott was speaking.

"Alonzo Eldon," he said, "it's with you that I want a word here, before all these people; and not on my behalf, but on theirs. You don't want the shedding of innocent blood, man, and so" —

"That's a brave word there, Escott!" shouted out with a harsh and unnatural exertion the usually so soft voice of Tom Eldon. Tom was terribly excited. His black eyes flashed, his body quivered with rage; the horse on which he rode took impatiently a step or two forwards, as Tom spoke. "It's a brave word that, about innocent blood, when you lead here these innocent men armed for a fight in your own cause. Disperse them first, and then there'll be no blood shed here, at least no innocent blood."

"Tom Eldon," said Escott sternly, "with you I've no reckoning now, nor do I come here to talk to any but men who can hear a fair speech to its end. To you, Alonzo Eldon, I have something to say that may end this land trouble at once. Will you hear me, I ask you again? Will you hear me on behalf of these innocent men, whose property you seem to be threatening?"

"Your own bogus property, Escott," answered Alonzo sternly, "is what's now in danger. For to-day I have come here to dispossess traitors. Innocent men and quiet citizens have nothing to do but stay at home."

"I'm glad to hear you say that, Alonzo. I don't come here on my own account. Take my property if you will. Call me traitor if you must. What I ask of you is a word on behalf of these men."

"Not a word, sir, until you and they lay down your arms."

"I myself have not asked them to arm and come here, Eldon. Finding them armed, I have joined them, unarmed myself, to intercede with you, and plead for a prevention of bloodshed."

"Fine interceders you and Harold make, sir!" Tom again broke in.

"If, Mr. Eldon," said Harold now, and in his clearest tone, "*if*, as I well know, you and your son have come here to-day more on my account than on that of any other man living, I may join my voice to ask that you should behave like honest men, and that you should fight out your quarrels elsewhere with me whom you call your enemy. But don't come here to vex the peace of this place merely because you hate me. You know what you are here for. You are here because you believe that *I* have wronged you. If so, meet me as you will and where you will; I am ready for you. But, now that you are here, say plainly to this company that your fight is n't with them, but with Escott on my sole account, and with me for myself. Then, when you have pledged your word not to molest them, take Escott's land as you will, and leave the settlers in peace. He and I can be ready for you elsewhere."

"Our fight," came back Tom's voice, "is with traitors, old and young, and with all who follow them, and bear arms here to help them against the law and the courts of the land."

"I'll not hear my father called traitor!" cried Sam Escott. As he spoke, his horse was becoming very restive. Peterson roughly ordered silence, and Alf Escott's stern voice joined itself to Peterson's. But a certain confused murmur from behind encouraged Sam. The marshal had been, meanwhile, very quietly removing his hat and wiping his forehead, for the sun was hot and the marshal's courage was cool; but at Sam's words the marshal was once more on the alert. His hand seized the bridle, which had fallen on his horse's neck. He laid his other hand by his belt.

"Steady here, all of you!" he shouted to his own men, perceiving that they were excited. The two main bodies were not more than fifteen or twenty paces apart, and the situation was growing momentarily worse. Nearly every one heard all that was said at the front, for the speaking was loud and clear, and an almost perfect silence had prevailed in the main bodies. Sam, however, went on: "You, Tom Eldon, are no man to call Alf Escott traitor,—you, whose whole soul is nothing but an accursed lie." Sam had once heard his father use this expression, and it pleased him now in his rage. Alf and Peterson vainly tried to quiet the young man or to drown his voice. As for Tom Eldon, his Spanish eyes glowed none the less for this word. He drew his pistol —

The next instant firing began. Nobody could ever afterwards be sure whence came the first shot. Most witnesses declared that Buzzard fired first from the wagon, over Tom Eldon's head. There was, however, much conflict of testimony; and Sam, who was indicted later for murder, was never tried on that charge, just because of this conflict of testimony. At all events, he himself was sure that he heard several bullets whiz by him, and at least a dozen shots fired, before he did more than to try to control his terrified horse. But thereafter, as soon as he realized what it all meant, he sprang from the saddle, let the horse go, raised his own rifle deliberately, and shot full at Tom Eldon. By that time more than half of the marshal's party were in flight, the settlers were discharging their guns from all sides, and a number of settlers also had either fallen or fled. Buzzard, a tall, fierce, dark, heavily-bearded man, fired steadily and coolly with his repeating rifle from his standing-place in the wagon. Alonzo Eldon, like Escott, had carried no arms to the battle-field, and at first sat, grim and stiff, on his great black horse, which seemed as cool as himself.

All these things Sam saw, but like a man in a dream. He seemed, after his one shot, to stand for a moment paralyzed, — not with fear, for he was positively amused at the sights before him, but with a numb sense of wonder, and a feeling that something unheard of had happened. What! had he actually shot his man? And Tom Eldon? The ancient wrong avenged! For Tom had fallen. The next moment, however, Sam saw his own father close by his side, felt that he himself was staggering, saw strange colors before his eyes, and then knew no more for a long time —

Harold, five minutes later, found himself at the centre of the excited group. The firing had ceased. Buzzard lay dead where the wagon had left him, when the horses at last grew unmanageable and ran away. Tom Eldon was close beside him, whether dead or alive could not be told as yet. Escott and his son were just being carried off by some settlers. Alf Escott was not senseless, but had received two or three ugly-looking hurts. Alonzo Eldon, uninjured, was kneeling beside Tom. The marshal, also unhurt, was now disarmed, and a prisoner in the hands of the score of Rangers who, with shot-gun, pistol, and rifle, had borne the brunt of the battle. These men also surrounded Alonzo. The firing had been remarkably effective, owing to the very short range. Somewhere between two and three hundred shots had been fired, and, on both sides, as many as sixteen men had been struck. Of these, five were already certainly dead, among them Collins. Peterson was helpless with a bad wound. The most effective work, during the skirmish, had been undoubtedly done by Buzzard's repeating rifle. Six or eight men must have been struck by him. How Alonzo Eldon had escaped unhurt was thenceforth a mystery.

Alf Escott and Harold never spoke to each other again. During the day Harold, at his own serious peril, was first busy in saving Alonzo's life from the fury of the settlers, who had taken the old man prisoner; and, having succeeded in this, was then seeking to get Alonzo and the unconscious Tom to a place of safety. But Escott, his wounds ill-cared for, his mind anxious about his son, his bed hard and uncomfortable, was slowly dying, through loss of blood and through an old man's weakness, at the house of the nearest settler. He lived until about sunset. He was very cheerful, save for his anxiety about Sam. He could not be persuaded, even by Bertha Boscowitz, to spare himself. He much hastened his death by restlessness and by talking. When they told him about Alonzo's peril, and that the settlers were threatening to hang the old man, Escott could hardly be prevented from going out to speak against the atrocity. As it was, he sent Bertha with a message to Harold. When they told Escott how Harold had taken advantage of a lull in the storm of indignation to speak on Eldon's behalf, how Harold had openly and with reckless courage taken the blame of all that day's bloodshed upon his own shoulders, had insisted that he himself, by some unexplained act of treason to Eldon, was the cause of this scene, and was alone the murderer, and had then successfully used the dying Escott's name as a last and highest ground of appeal, Escott applauded the news rapturously. Just then Sam seemed much better, too, and Escott fell thereupon to joking. "I don't want old Alonzo to die before old Chrysostom Hahn," he said, "because it is n't fair to Alonzo that Chrysostom should preach the funeral sermon. Alonzo deserves better of the world than that."

When he later heard that Alonzo had really managed to convey his sorely wounded son out of the town, Escott expressed yet more satisfaction. "Poor Harold," said he, as if to himself. "It 's a lonely life before him, whoever lives or dies. He 'll see but few friends in the world from henceforth." Late in the afternoon, Sam improved so much that the one doctor, who at last, in his slow rounds among the wounded, had come here, assured Alf that the boy was in no danger. "You need n't say anything about whether I am myself or not," said Escott. "I know all about it."

The last hour or two Escott employed, when his voice would let him, in giving messages and directions to Bertha, who bore up wonderfully on this day for one who was in such poor health. He had good advice for Bertha herself; messages for his wife, for Emily, for Harold, and, last of all, one for Alonzo. "Tell Alonzo," he said, "be sure to tell Alonzo — that if he 's satisfied now — on thinking over what Harold has done — to see that this is all an infernal mistake — and that

I 've never betrayed him — well, then, *I* don't, as I die, care for the mistake any more. Tell him I die his friend, Bertha. And tell him, too — as my dying declaration, that there is — as I solemnly believe, no cause — why he should not be reconciled to his daughter-in-law. Tell him that last in secret, Bertha, and from me. Don't neglect it. As for me, Bertha, my last lecture is about done. Class is excused!"

Escott died very quietly, and he now lies buried in the shadow of Mount Diablo, The settlers honor his grave. Nearly every one in San Francisco has by this time forgotten him.

But Sam lived to be tried, with others, for conspiracy to defeat the processes of the courts. The ingenuous fellow was acquitted. And to-day he is his mother's only comfort.

There is little more to tell. All these events are so recent! What can have happened since? Tom Eldon was brought to Martinez, where he soon afterwards died. Margaret was with him at the last. He probably never recognized her as he lay there. She and Alonzo were later, though very imperfectly, reconciled. Harold's bearing that day had put him and the past in a new light before Alonzo's mind. But what would have taken place between them had they ever met afterwards does not appear. Harold waited long enough in the State to find that no prosecution would be begun against him for his share in the affair at Oakfield Creek. Then he vanished. He is now traveling somewhere in Europe. He is too much of a man, one may hope, not somehow to overlive the shock of that murderous day, but from California and his old friends he feels himself banished as if by the curse of Cain. There is blood on his hands, he says. He has no great hold upon life at present. His only comfort is that, though he will never meet Margaret, nor communicate with her again, yet no distance and no horror of blood can separate them in spirit. To be distant in body is for them now and henceforth to be the nearest to each other.

Boscowitz has had a singular fortune since that day. He, of course, was not present. But the thing indirectly proved his ruin also. In the course of his efforts to defend Alonzo for the great man's share in the business, Boscowitz was embarrassed by the fact that he could tell no secrets. In his despair, he began telling very imprudent lies about the other party. For one of them he was shot in his office by an angry relative of a settler. The shot did not kill Boscowitz, who was as tough a little man as we should have expected to find him in such a case; but it indirectly produced a partial paralysis, which incapacitated him for his business. Thenceforward, and in consequence of this misfortune, though Boscowitz himself lived, the "Warrior" languished, and languishing died. In vain would you nowadays ask the newsboys for it. They have forgotten its very existence, and perhaps the disappearance of the "Warrior" is the cause of that beautiful elevation of the tone of journalism which, if you are clever enough, you will doubtless observe in the current literature of San Francisco.

In a year all recent things are forgotten. Nothing, as we all know, is so dead and inaccessible as contemporary history after once the newspaper that contains it is burned; and hence it is absolutely safe for us thus to narrate the recent fortunes of Boscowitz and the others. You could learn nothing in San Francisco, just now, about the poor crippled adventurer. But his daughter has come back to him, nurses him, mourns for her dead by his side, innocently harasses him day and night, and hopes sometime to convert him.

Alonzo, too, is in failing health. He suffered from a slight stroke of apoplexy not long after that day, and has now retired from active life. His loss is seriously felt by many people, but the waves will find no trouble in closing over him as he sinks from public view. The bulk of his great fortune is indeed safe. He has, however, recently abandoned all the old Oakfield Creek claims, and, for that matter, all contentious and ambitious undertakings. Others help him to manage his investments, which grow, year by year, more conservative. As for the endowments, since his son's death and the dethronement of Margaret, everything ideal has come to seem to him vanity. He is peevish in his ill-health; he has the airs of a disappointed man, is easily displeased, and is anxious only to talk of long-past days. The proposed endowments themselves he has forbidden any one ever to mention. He hates and despises them. He has resolved to leave all his property to his grandson.

He visits Margaret occasionally in the house on the hillside, but only in order that he may see the child. In talking with Margaret herself he appears quiet, matter-of-fact, commonplace. The old fierce bitterness is dead. But so is everything else in their relationship. To strangers they often seem to be very cordial towards each other. But it is all cordiality about matters that lie on the surface. Alonzo received Escott's dying message. Perhaps it helped to reconcile him with Margaret. Nothing, however, can restore what she once shattered.

But Margaret, — she is still the faithful mother of her charming boy, and the mistress of the house on the hillside. Her health is poorer now, her face paler, her step not so light. People in general do not know the real cause. The true story of the Oakfield Creek tragedy has never before been told. Many false impressions are abroad. But Margaret cares for none of them. Her child and her absent friend and the shadow of the old wrongs, these are all that she cares to know of life. Perhaps, were it not for the boy, she would not have the strength to live. But he is, indeed, all that a mother could wish. And to him, in her turn, she seems the source of all good, the ideal of ideals, the playfellow, the teacher, the friend. His smiles, even the gentlest and most fleeting of them, make her forget at moments all the desolation that fills the rest of her world. And if he lives, she will some day teach him to understand her heart.